EBURY PRESS

THE MAN WHO AVENGED BHAGAT SINGH

Abhijeet Bhalerao is an author, translator, speaker and visual artist. He has been recognized for his research into Shaheed Bhagat Singh's jail notebook, which he has also translated into Marathi. Alongside serving as an income tax inspector in Mumbai, Abhijeet also shares his insights on Maratha war strategy and tactics as a visiting faculty at Mumbai University. He is passionate about exploring literature, history and art.

T0124135

Celebrating 35 Years of
Penguin Random House India

ADVANCE PRAISE FOR THE BOOK

'Abhijeet Bhalerao's *The Man Who Avenged Bhagat Singh* is a lucidly written account of a very little-known episode in our history of revolutionary struggle. Bhagat Singh was a valiant fighter and an ideologue of the revolutionary cause. We are now aware that he stands tall due to his egalitarian ideas and his impassioned faith in composite nationalism. However, this book goes into the lesser-known details about the revenge that the revolutionaries took on the approver who identified Bhagat Singh and his comrades in the court. A spellbinding account that will keep readers glued to the book till they reach the dramatic end'—S. Irfan Habib, former Maulana Azad Chair, National University of Educational Planning and Administration

'The armed resistance to the British occupation of India has many forgotten stories of extraordinary courage. Abhijeet Bhalerao brings alive a corner of this history—a young man who avenged his heroes'—Sanjeev Sanyal, bestselling writer and economist

'With meticulous detail, Abhijeet Bhalerao throws light upon a revolutionary period of Indian history that is being re-recognized today. His focus brings to life some well-known freedom fighters, but the most heartening are details about lesser-known revolutionaries, who, equally, were ready to sacrifice everything for the cause of freedom. Many of them did not get recognition or acclaim, and therefore, the work of Bhalerao is most welcome and is to be treasured'—Hindol Sengupta, historian

'The assassination of Phanindra Nath Ghosh, the man who betrayed Bhagat Singh and sent him to the gallows, is a story barely known today. Baikunth Sukul was the man who made his life's mission to avenge Bhagat Singh, and Abhijeet Bhalerao brings him alive as never before in a rivetingly engaging novel that is difficult to put down. Told in an immersive and powerful way, and with love, anger and precision, this is a story that will now be difficult to forget again'—Satvinder S. Juss, academic and author of *Bhagat Singh: A Life in Revolution*

'Abhijeet Bhalerao's novel is a dramatic retelling of Baikunth Sukul's life, a schoolteacher from Bihar, who was hurt deeply by the execution of Bhagat Singh. Phanindra Nath Ghosh, a central committee member revolutionary of the HSRA, from Bettiah, Bihar, turned approver and helped the British police destroy the revolutionary organization. Baikunth Sukul, a follower of Yogendra Sukul, a true revolutionary and comrade of Bhagat Singh, decided to avenge the execution of Bhagat Singh. There has been a tradition of creative literature in the form of poetry, plays, short stories, novels, etc., in many Indian languages on revolutionaries, but in English most books were biographies or analytical books on Bhagat Singh's ideas and actions. Now . . . creative books on Bhagat Singh and revolutionaries are being written [in English]. A graphic novel or biography on Bhagat Singh's life and ideas was published recently, and now Abhijeet Bhalerao's novel has come out . . . Though the novel is not based on Bhagat Singh directly, it shows how much Bhagat Singh was loved by the Indian people, and that the betrayers of the revolutionary movement could not enjoy the fruits of British rewards and had to pay the price of betrayal. The real saga of Bhagat Singh is so fascinating that when some related events come out in narrative form, they become even more charming . . . Abhijeet Bhalerao's novel highlights the role of some neglected heroes of the freedom struggle, such as Yogendra and Baikunth Sukul!'—Chaman Lal, editor of *The Bhagat Singh Reader*

'A fantastic story which every Indian must know about! Not to be missed!'—Sameer Anjaan, Guinness World Record holder and lyricist of, among other films, *The Legend of Bhagat Singh*

THE MAN
WHO AVENGED
BHAGAT SINGH

ABHIJEET BHALERAO

EBURY
PRESS

An imprint of Penguin Random House

EBURY PRESS

USA | Canada | UK | Ireland | Australia
New Zealand | India | South Africa | China | Singapore

Ebury Press is part of the Penguin Random House group of companies
whose addresses can be found at global.penguinrandomhouse.com

Published by Penguin Random House India Pvt. Ltd
4th Floor, Capital Tower 1, MG Road,
Gurugram 122 002, Haryana, India

First published in Ebury Press by Penguin Random House India 2023

10 9 8 7 6 5 4 3 2 1

This is a work of historical fiction. With the exception of some
well-known historical figures, institutions and events, all situations, incidents,
dialogue and characters mentioned in this novel are products of the author's
imagination and are not to be construed as real. The author and publisher do not
endorse any of the views or practices mentioned in the book. There is no intent
to hurt any sentiments or be biased in favour of or against any particular person,
community, gender, caste, tribe or religion.

ISBN 9780143461616

Typeset in Goudy Old Style by MAP Systems, Bengaluru, India

www.penguin.co.in

For my parents, Shri Ashok Bhalerao and
Smt. Pratibha Bhalerao,
my lovely wife, Sandhya, and the light of our lives,
our daughter, Mokshada

Contents

Chapter 1

Prologue

November 1932

'One thing remains before we enter the town,' Baikunth stated. They were just outside Bettiah city, standing in knee-deep water.

'What?' Chandrama asked. He was also having a bath.

'It has to draw blood,' Baikunth said. 'If it doesn't, our chances of success will wane.'

Chandrama retorted, 'Your blade already drew my blood. What more do you want?'

Baikunth clarified, 'No, it was an accident. I mean, in a sacrificial manner.'

'Come on, you are a teacher. Do you believe in these old wives' tales?' Shocked, Chandrama asked.

'Well, this is a once-in-a-lifetime opportunity. I don't want to leave anything to chance.'

The water in the lake was at freezing point. The fog gently caressed the surface of the placid body of water. Chandrama agreed, 'All right, but if we have to get some animal like a rabbit, it will delay our plans.'

'Who said anything about having to sacrifice animals? The myth says that to fully realize the strength of the blade, a *khukri* must taste blood.'

'What shall we do now?'

'Go and bring our weapons.'

Chandrama emerged from the water, trembling in the winter chill. There were two bicycles on the shore. One was black, the other sap green. From the luggage on the carriers, he took out two khukris—sharp machetes. He took the knives in hand and went into the water for the second time. The sun had risen. The heavy fog produced an orange glow on the lake's surface. The long, curved blades sparkled.

Baikunth was standing with his eyes closed and his hands joined in a namaskar. His face took on a grave expression. Chandrama called out his name. Baikunth, still motionless, extended his left hand. Chandrama held out the oiled, wooden handle of the weapon, slender and deadly. Baikunth ran his fingers down its cold spine. In the next moment, he raised his right hand and made a little cut on his index finger. The action was so swift that it seemed as if the knife had never met the finger. And yet, a trickle of warm, red blood flowed down. Baikunth held the khukri under the blood. A few drops slid over the blade. The khukri was now alive. Chandrama followed, cutting his finger and letting the blood flow into the water. After drying themselves off, they headed to Bettiah on their bicycles.

Chandrama asked, 'Is it true that a khukri is impervious to damage in battle?'

Baikunth said, 'Yes, it is considered an indestructible extension of the soldier's arm.'

'I wonder how they make it. I've heard that they last a lifetime.'

'I don't know about the others, but these are made from the steel of a railway sleeper's iron. It is one of the hardest substances available. The handle is walnut wood, and the notch at the base bears the OM symbol.'

'Where did you get railway steel?'

'Our comrades borrowed a little bit from His Majesty's Bengal and North Western Railway, then someone took it to a man in Nepal to have it converted into a khukri.'

'Clever way to borrow. Would you trust this khukri over a gun or a bomb?'

'Come on, don't start that again.'

'Baikunth, it still does not make sense to me why you are so adamant about using a khukri for the task. I mean, you and Ranendra have taught me how to use it, but I would prefer a gun or a bomb any day.'

'I agree with your concerns, but the pistol comes with its own problems. I believe this blade will have a special place in history.'

'I wonder who taught you to play with a khukri.'

Baikunth was riding fast and Chandrama was falling behind. The cold air entering his mouth, as he spoke, caused him to catch a breath. Chandrama saw a smile in his eyes.

Baikunth asked, 'Do you know who taught Bhagwan Parshuram to fight?'

'No.'

'Mahadev.'

'Okay, who is your Mahadev?'

'The same man who trained with Bhagat Singh and Batukeshwar Dutt.'

'Really? Yogendra Baba?'

'Jai Yogendra Sukul!' Baikunth shouted and went ahead.

Chandrama cheered, 'Jai Yogendra Baba', and followed.

They arrived in Bettiah at approximately 8 a.m. It was the start of the day, and the town was stirring. The streets were wet with the early morning dew. The shops had opened for business. Chhath Puja had ended just the day before. With the festival spirit still lingering in the air, the mood was cheerful.

They travelled to the Kali Bagh, a Bengali neighbourhood. While on the pavement, they stopped near one of the houses, newly painted white. A constable, positioned outside, sat on a metal chair with a firearm on his lap. He appeared to be tired after night duty. Baikunth signalled Chandrama, saying, 'This is the house.'

'Let's get to work,' exclaimed Chandrama, putting his hand on the brakes.

'No, wait, let us stroll along this road and observe.'

They rode back and forth on the street and observed the house. On their second round, they saw a little girl coming out of the house, a doll in hand. Behind her came three other children from the neighbourhood, jumping around. Someone called out to them from inside. Another constable came over and took the seat vacated by the night constable. On their tenth round, they saw a man stepping out. He was short and dark-skinned. The thick gold chain around his neck was shining against his skin. He was wearing only a dhoti. His centrally parted oiled black hair, flowed sleekly to shoulders. He was coming out after performing puja. Facing the rising sun, he offered the water, contained in the holy copper vessel in his hands. A woman stood behind him, holding a teacup.

'Now, what shall we do?' Chandrama asked.

Baikunth said, 'Let's go. I was always against doing it at home. This is not the right place to deliver justice.'

They rode to Meena Bazaar. It had been the town's attraction for decades. Over a hundred shops were full of a thousand useful items. The pleasant odours of grains, spices, new garments and shoes mingled about in a complex maze of small alleys. Meena Bazaar was where one could find anything. While shopping, they investigated all the entries and exits of the market on foot. After leaving the southern entrance, they stopped at a mess where low-wage workers were eating. Chandrama caught sight of something and his expression turned sombre. He said, 'Our mission may be in jeopardy.'

'Why do you say that?'

'Look,' and he pointed towards a massive stone building. The King Edward VII Memorial Hospital was standing in all its might not far from the bazaar. Baikunth's face became creased.

Chandrama asked, 'Do you understand the meaning of this? No matter what we do, people will bring him to this hospital in just two minutes, and he will survive.'

Baikunth said firmly, 'No, he cannot survive. We only get one chance.'

'How? Trust me, let's switch weapons. Only a gun can do this job. Let us go back and return with a firearm.'

'No, I will make sure he dies. You do not understand. These British dogs can smell a gun from a hundred kilometres away. Last month, Rambinod Singh gave me a revolver just for this job. The next day, the CID came to my home. By sheer luck, I escaped with my life. There is no going back from here. I trust my weapon.'

'Understand this, Baikunth; we must be extremely sure.'

'Indeed, I understand.'

The placement of electric lamps in the market by the government had encouraged business in the area. Tiny shops were lit up by gas lamps and the bazaar sparkled in the glow of electric lamps. People milled about, shopping or just roaming about during the festive season. As the sun went down, fog engulfed the town again. Just outside the western entrance of Meena Bazaar, Baikunth and Chandrama waited anxiously. They had leaned their bicycles against an electric lamp post. It was shortly after 7 p.m. The market was flooded with people trying to get their hands on their desired goods. Both grown-ups and children were happy, having a great time. After some discussion, Chandrama ordered tea from a street vendor. Baikunth's eyes were fixed on the road.

Suddenly, a harsh whistle pierced the air and the mob made way for someone coming up the street. A lumbering constable, with a sharp, twisted moustache, emerged. A loaded Lee Enfield .303 rifle hung on his shoulder. He stared at the gaping crowd for a long time, then walked away. Two men accompanied him. One of them was the man for whom Baikunth and Chandrama had ridden around 175 kilometres on their bicycles. He looked even shorter at close range.

In contrast to the clean white kurta and red embroidered cream-coloured dhoti that he wore, his dark face was scarred with pockmarks. A semi-automatic Mauser pistol was strategically positioned around his waist, intended to be noticed by observers. The second man talked to him in an ingratiating tone. They entered through the western gate. The bazaar was just as crowded. Suddenly an enthusiastic look sparked in Baikunth's eyes. His fist tightened into a ball.

The stall owner came forward to hand him the tea. 'Do you know who he is?' he enquired.

Chandrama, bored of waiting, said, 'Enlighten me.'

'His name is Phanindra Nath Ghosh, the infamous traitor responsible for the death of Bhagat Singh, Sukhdev and Rajguru.'

Chandrama said, 'Really? I thought Phani Babu went to London. The English king must have promised his daughter to him; otherwise who would think of betraying Bhagat Singh?'

The stall owner laughed and said, 'I don't know about the daughter, but the king gave him fifty acres of land and a shop to sell liquor.'

'Fifty acres! For the life of Bhagat Singh, what a deal!' Chandrama said in a sarcastic tone.

Baikunth spat scornfully on the ground and mumbled, 'Swine.'

For a moment Phanindra and the constable seemed to disappear in crowd.

After closely observing, Baikunth found Phanindra sitting on a bench in front of a shop. His friend, who was joking about something, had joined him. The constable approached Phanindra and said something in his ear, before proceeding in the direction of the northern gate. Either his duty was over, or he was taking a break. Baikunth took a deep breath. Chandrama took out a printed leaflet from his pocket and held it in front of the stall owner. The latter studied it in the dim glow of the gas lamp. It was a photograph.

The image depicted an older Sikh man and two elderly women holding the decapitated heads of three young men in their hands. He recognized the dead men immediately because they were prominent freedom fighters—Bhagat Singh, Shivram Rajguru and Sukhdev Thapar. The reverse carried a sketch, showing a head in a noose. It was Phanindra's head. The message printed on the leaflet read: 'Will you carry the traitor's blot, or will you dare to wash it away?'

The stall owner gulped nervously. A single bead of sweat appeared on his brow. He asked, 'What is this? What brings you here?'

Chandrama placed a hand on his shoulder and said, 'My friend, this is a message from Lahore. And about us, you will know soon.'

Baikunth said, 'Chandrama, let's go; it is time.' In an instant, both slid their hands into the bags and took out two leather scabbards.

They covered their heads with shawls as they entered the western gate. The stall owner glanced at them with admiration and fear. Even in the gloom, he could make out sheaths of khukri knives that were as long as his forearm. They pushed their way through the crowd, heading towards Phanindra's bench.

Baikunth emerged from the shadows, his face hardened with determination. He stopped a few steps away from Phanindra, his silhouette casting a long shadow. His voice echoed, 'Namaste, Phani Babu.'

Phanindra barely acknowledged Baikunth's presence; he continued to talk with his friend.

Baikunth persisted. His voice resolute and stronger this time, as if demanding acknowledgment, he repeated, 'Phani Babu, namaste.' The echo of his voice reverberated through the surrounding air.

Phanindra's face creased into an irritated expression, eyebrows knitting together in a clear display of annoyance. But still, his gaze remained transfixed on the void, not once falling on Baikunth. 'Yes,' he replied gruffly, his voice bearing the slightest trace of annoyance. Baikunth said, 'I have a message for you.'

'What is it? From whom?'

'From Bhagat Singh.'

'What?'

Phanindra stared at Baikunth wide-eyed. The shawl flew off Baikunth's face as he roared. A long, sharp khukri rose in the air. In the wide-open eyes of Phanindra, Baikunth saw the reflection of shiny, vicious steel coming down like a lightning bolt.

Chapter 2

August 1928

Dr Gaya Prasad rented a two-storey house in Mohalla Shah Ganj, Ferozepur. It was the revolutionary party's original headquarters. Dr Prasad had established a clinic on the ground floor while the upper floor was earmarked for the party. Professor Jai Chand Vidyalankar did not have any trouble finding the house. He was proud of his students, even though they had dropped out of college in the middle of their studies. His pupils had called him to a crucial meeting.

He was invited inside after a predetermined knock on the door. About ten or twelve young men were seated around the room, some on chairs, and others on the bed and the floor. The meeting had already started. All stood up as a sign of respect for their beloved teacher. He told them to take a seat and continue the meeting. A young man stood up and offered his chair to the professor. He was unusually tall.

He was dressed in a white, full-sleeved shirt and khaki pants. His long hair was tied on his head in the traditional Sikh way. A few hairs, having escaped, lay curled on his neck. He smiled cordially at the professor and his political guru. The teacher tapped his shoulder and said, 'Bhagat, continue.' Bhagat Singh nodded.

A large man stood to the right of the professor. He greeted the professor with a smile and a namaste. He was short, but he had a wrestler's build. A white, half-sleeved shirt showed his toned biceps and muscular chest. The professor returned the greeting to Chandrashekhar Azad with utmost respect. Meanwhile, Sukhdev handed the professor a glass of water and sat down on the floor. Now, Bhagat had everyone's attention.

He began to talk. 'Before we proceed with our debate, let me give our beloved professor a quick overview of the meeting. Sir, as you know, we have left our studies and our families behind for a glorious purpose. We are ready to take the next step to free this country from British rule. The objective is to draw up a plan to establish a national revolutionary party. Some of us attended the Cawnpore meeting last month. This meeting is organized to complete all aspects of our programme. As you are aware, all senior revolutionaries of the HRA, the Hindustan Republican Association, were arrested in 1925. Many factions of the party now operate at a regional level. To achieve our common goal, we propose to join them all under one banner, one ideology and one programme.'

Sukhdev rose to his feet and declared, 'Bhagat, I, and many others present here, will be the representatives from

Punjab. The United Provinces will be represented by Shiv Verma and Bijoy Kumar Sinha. We have Panditji and Bhagwan Das Mahore for the Central Provinces. We have Kundan Lal for Rajputana.'

'This has been decided so far,' Bhagat said.

'What about Bengal?' Prof. Vidyalankar enquired.

Sukhdev remarked, 'Sir, Anushilan Samiti and Yugantar's contribution to the armed struggle is legendary since the beginning of this century. The secret organizations now lack leadership like Aurobindo Ghosh, Barindra Kumar Ghosh and Bagha Jatin. Most of the current leadership is in prison. We tried to contact those who were out, but they refused to join.'

'Why?' The professor asked.

Bhagat said, 'The core principles of the party will include socialism and democratic structure with voting powers. The Bengalis refused to reconcile these two concerns.'

'Okay,' the professor said, 'but what about Bihar?'

Sukhdev responded, 'We're a little confused about Bihar. The majority of the revolutionaries in Bihar are aligned with the groups in Bengal. We don't know anyone personally from there, either.'

Azad said, 'I know someone. Yogendra Sukul. He used to work for the revolutionary party of Bundelkhand under Dewan Shatrughan Singh. The great Dewan later turned to the Gandhian way. Yogendra joined HRA, but the Kakori train robbery had occurred by then. After the train robbery by the HRA revolutionaries, everyone went underground. Within months, the CID had arrested almost everyone. Only Kundan Lal and I escaped. The CID found proof of conspiracy against the empire and they hanged Ramprasad Bismil, Ashfaqullah Khan, Rajendranath Lahiri and Roshan Singh. The HRA dream was over before it could bloom. Yogendra did not get a chance to prove his mettle. However, I know him. Acharya Kriplani has worked with him for years. This is a man of weapons, a hardcore soldier. I trust him!'

Bhagat said, 'Then it is done. If Panditji trusts him, I trust him.'

Bijoy Kumar Sinha said, 'There is someone else. Phanindra Nath Ghosh. He is the senior-most of the Bihari revolutionaries. In the late 1910s, he was a member of Anushilan. The party had commissioned him to create a shelter for revolutionaries. His address was also a rebel post office box. In 1918, he was arrested in connection with Anushilan under the Defence of India Act and imprisoned for one year.

'In 1925, he started his own organization called Hindustan Seva Dal to gather Bihari rebels. But I didn't hear of any activity from them until now. I thought of his name because he is an expert on guns, revolvers and pistols.'

Shiv Verma said, 'I know him from a specific mission. My dear friend Mani Bannerji considered Rajendra Lahiri as his guru. In the Kakori case, the great Rajendra Lahiri went to the gallows. A deputy superintendent of the CID gave a deliberate statement before the judge, which led to the hanging of our beloved Rajendra Lahiri. Mani Bannerji knew this CID officer named Jitendra Bannerji. So, he decided to kill him.'

Bijoy added, 'I knew Sanyal Babu had some useless guns. For this mission, I asked him to give two rusted and useless revolvers to Phanindra for cleaning and repair. I wanted to test his craft. I sent Shiv after a while to Bettiah to get the revolvers.'

Shiv said, 'I travelled to Bettiah. I discovered the address of Phanindra with the help of a relative who lived nearby. I met him at the Meena Bazaar shop. When I asked him about the revolvers, he asked me who had sent me. I told him Sanyal's name first, and then Bijoy's. But he did not relent. He sent me back without the revolvers, as he did not know who Bijoy was.'

Bijoy said, 'He travelled himself to Benaras and personally gave Mani Bannerji the two working revolvers and bullets.'

Shiv said, 'It was determined that Phani Babu would accompany Mani in action against the CID officer in Benares, but unfortunately, he changed his mind. Perhaps he was not familiar with the terrain, or he was frightened.'

Bijoy said, 'On his birthday, 13 January, Mani attacked the deputy superintendent of CID, Jitendra Bannerji, and put three bullets in him. It was the same revolver that Phani Babu had repaired.'

Azad said, 'I did not know it was Mani's birthday. Long live Mani.'

All the others echoed the words.

Bhagat said, 'So Phani Babu can be valuable to us as a gun expert, and maybe he can provide us with revolvers from his old contacts. What else?'

The professor responded, 'I also know him. When Gandhiji came to Champaran to fight for the peasants, he was among the first volunteers. I met him in Patna a year ago, where he urged me to ask my brother Inder to teach him how to make a bomb. But at that time, my brother was in prison for the Deogarh Conspiracy Case. I know that Phanindra had trafficked guns from Bengal into the United Provinces for a long period. In Bengal, he has many contacts. I'm disappointed that no Bengalis have joined your venture. But mark my words, you will need bombs to bring Inquilab, and no one in this country makes better bombs than Bengali revolutionaries.'

Azad said, 'It is decided. We will invite Phani Babu to represent Bihar. Bijoy, you'll travel to Bihar tomorrow and explain everything to him.'

'Yes, Panditji.' Bijoy stood up.

Shiv remarked, 'Change your appearance, Bijoy. Try to appear to be a Bihari. I believe that Phani is being monitored by the CID.'

Bijoy took a train to Delhi the next day. There he changed trains twice to reach Bettiah in Champaran. He changed his garb. He donned a long, white kurta, pyjamas reaching a few inches above the ankles and a classic Iranian topee. He looked like a traditional Bihari Muslim. He waited at the office of the Congress. After sunset, he called a boy working in the office and gave him an anna.

Bijoy said, 'Go to Meena Bazaar, find Phanindra Nath Ghosh and tell him that someone is waiting for him at the party office. Tell him to come here after closing the shop.'

The boy accomplished his job quickly. Around nine in the evening, Bijoy was sitting on the porch. It was pretty dark. The office was outside the city. A crimson light gleamed in the dark, then some thick smoke appeared. Emerging from the background, a man of modest height appeared; he was delicate but had a determined air. He was no more than five feet tall. His frame was slender—his shoulders narrow, the bones subtly pronounced beneath his cream-white kurta, making him appear even more fragile. His clothes, a touch too large, hung on his frame, giving him an air of slight vulnerability. He was smoking a beedi. He watched Bijoy, while squinting his eyes, and muttered, 'As-Salam-Alaikum.'

'Wa-Alaikum-Salaam,' answered Bijoy.

'I'm sorry, but I haven't recognized you.'

'Yes, we are meeting for the first time. My name is Bijoy Kumar Sinha. Jitendranath Sanyal Babu sent me here.'

'Oh, Sanyal Babu sent you. I don't know whether your name has ever been mentioned. How can I help you?'

'I bring you a proposal from my comrades. From United Provinces's (UP's) Revolutionary Party.'

The words, Revolutionary Party, clearly made Phanindra nervous. He glanced around consciously.

Bijoy added, 'Look, you know, all the senior revolutionaries are in jail or hanged after Kakori. The days of Anushilan and Yugantar are over, too. Young blood is essential for the country. We are building a unified revolutionary party throughout the country, and we want you to join it for Bihar.'

'How?'

'A covert meeting will take place in Delhi next month. We are going to form a party there.'

'Who is organizing it?'

'Mostly, the surviving HRA leaders. The plan was created by Punjab's Bhagat Singh.'

'Ah, Bhagat Singh! Is this the same boy who formed a new organization? What is its name? I cannot recall. Yes! Naujawan Bharat Sabha.'

'Yes, it's more like HRA's public face. You should be aware that in Punjab, the Sabha has more members than the Congress.'

'That's great! Though I've heard of him, he isn't someone I personally know. He's too young to trust. Who else is going to attend?'

'Do you know Chandrashekhar Azad of UP?'

The name made Phanindra look up. The light of the beedi was reflected in his moist eyes. He said, 'What? Azad is joining this venture?'

'No, he's leading this company. We also have Kundan Lal from the old HRA.'

'From Bengal?'

'Yugantar and Anushilan rejected our proposal.'

'Do you aspire to create a revolutionary party without Bengali members?'

'We plan to form a party with socialism and democracy as the ideological backbone. Anushilan and Yugantar, however, don't like these principles. We appreciate and admire the contributions of the Bengalis to the revolution, but we have no option.'

'Do you know that I am a member of Anushilan?'

'Yes, and also a Bengali. It will be like getting Bihar and Bengal together if you join us.'

'How do you call a party national if only north India is participating?'

'You're right. We also have representatives from Bombay, but not any further south. I expect that we will be able to spread our network further south as we enhance our methodical work.'

'Why did you come to me? Why not other people?'

'Phani Babu, we know your expertise and your birthday gift to Mani Bannerji.'

Phanindra stepped forward and placed a hand on Bijoy's mouth. He whispered, 'Shut up. Don't utter any names. I cannot give you my answer now. I am meeting you for the first time. First of all, I'll need to consult Sanyal Babu and my friend, Manmohan Bannerji.'

'We respect Sanyal Babu, but his working technique is too slow and archaic. Even if he refuses to join the event, I urge you to come.'

'All right. Tomorrow morning, we will meet Manmohan and make a decision.'

Both slept on the Congress office veranda. In the morning, they walked to Manmohan's home in Bettiah. Phanindra introduced Bijoy and explained everything. Manmohan agreed.

Phanindra questioned, 'How shall we go to Delhi?'

Bijoy offered directions to Feroze Shah Tughlaq Fort in Delhi. 'Travel by third class to avoid suspicion from CID,' he suggested.

Phanindra enquired, 'What about the railway fare?'

Bijoy was puzzled by the question. The man, a senior revolutionary and a wealthy shopkeeper, was asking for money for train fares for the third class.

Bijoy said, 'You will have to manage it yourself. The party will pay you back at the meeting.'

Phanindra and Manmohan agreed. Bijoy departed from Bettiah by train at 8 p.m. He was glad he had persuaded Phanindra, yet something did not feel right. He brushed off the thought as he had completed the task given by Panditji.

Phanindra and Manmohan boarded a train to Muzaffarpur on 4 September 1928 and subsequently to Allahabad in a third-class bogey. As Allahabad approached, they got off the train at Izzat Bridge Station, one stop ahead of the town, to avoid CID scrutiny. From there, they travelled in a *tonga* to Sanyal Babu's house at Colonelganj Mohalla. Sanyal welcomed them both and sat down to talk after lunch. After asking about Bijoy, Sanyal said, 'Bijoy is a great revolutionary. You may trust him and cooperate with him freely.'

'What about Punjab's Bhagat Singh?'

'I don't know him, but everyone loves him. My brother, Sachin Dada, cannot stop praising him.'

'What? Does Sachin Dada know him?'

'Yes, Bhagat considers Dada as a mentor. Have you heard about the Ghadar watch?'

'No,' Phanindra answered.

'Rash Behari Bose bought a watch with a silver chain when the Ghadar plan was on in 1915. He used to call it the Ghadar watch, stating that a time of difficulties had begun for the British. Later, because of the traitors and other reasons, which you know well, the Ghadar movement failed. For obvious reasons, Rash Behari Bose had to leave the country. Sachin Dada was quite interested in Ghadar, and he was also pretty young at that time. So, the last time Bose met him, he handed the Ghadar watch to Dada. He declared that Dada's time had just started.'

'What happened next?' Manmohan asked.

'Bhagat Singh met Sachin Dada and evidently impressed him excessively with his speeches. When the Kakori arrests began, and Dada was about to leave, he called Bhagat, handed him the Ghadar watch, and said that he was the future of the Indian revolution.'

Phanindra sceptically asked, 'Is the story true?'

'I don't know. You can ask Bhagat, but I can say this, if Dada trusted him, I do too.'

Phanindra and Manmohan caught a train to Delhi the next day. Sanyal Babu told them to stop by on their way back to apprise him of whatever transpired in Delhi.

Phanindra reached Delhi station on the morning of 8 September. They took a tonga to Jama Masjid, then walked from Jama on foot to the Feroze Shah Tughlaq Fort via the Delhi Gate. Near the door, Bijoy approached them with a wide smile. It was hot in Delhi, and both were sweating profusely. Bijoy took them to a giant mango tree, and they sat in its shade.

Bijoy said, 'Some members have not yet arrived, so the meeting will happen tomorrow.'

'No problem,' Phanindra added.

Meanwhile, a young man approached them and sat on the grass nearby. He was slim and fair, and his eyes were small.

Bijoy said, 'This is Kundan Lal. I think you must have heard of him.'

Phanindra stated, 'Who hasn't? The Kakori hero. It's a joy to meet you.'

Kundan Lal smiled shyly.

A crisp wind carrying a hint of the approaching winter rustled through the corridors of the fort. A meeting was being held on the ruins of a staircase. Seven persons were talking there. Bijoy got up and joined them. A Sardar was arguing aggressively. Even while being seated, he seemed taller than the rest. The Sardar was fair, with a sharp nose and expressive eyes. He wore a modest cream *pagdi*, one end dangling down his back, and moved as he spoke. He wore a white kurta, sleeves rolled up to the elbow, with a black jacket. It was hard not to notice him.

After some time, around 11 a.m., Kundan Lal said, 'Let us go. Our presence is needed here tomorrow. Today, we may relax.'

Kundan Lal took them to his friend, who owned the Maharathi press near the fort. The owner gave them two iron cots to rest on. The noise of the printers and the workers bustling about made it hard to rest. In the evening, when the press stopped and the workers left, Phanindra and Manmohan were able to rest. At around 8 a.m. the next day, they arrived at the fort. Others had apparently arrived earlier. Everyone sat around informally. Bijoy stepped up and introduced everyone at the meeting briefly.

Bhagat Singh rose and said, 'Thank you for joining us. I propose to establish a central revolutionary party. The name of the party will be Hindustan Socialist Republican Association (HSRA). We have decided to add 'Socialist' as our aim is to establish a socialist democratic system in free India.' Everyone nodded.

'After much deliberation, I propose a central committee of seven people. Each person will be a representative and leader of the respective province. Sukhdev will represent Punjab; Shiv Verma for UP; Phanindra Nath Ghosh for Bihar; Kundan Lal will be responsible for Rajputana and the central office, which will be set up in Jhansi. Bijoy and I will act as connecting links between the provinces.'

'Why do we need a central office in Jhansi? Why not in Delhi?' Phanindra asked.

'As none of us belongs to Delhi, having an office there doesn't make sense. Numerous princely estates surround Jhansi from all sides, and we have their support. There have been fewer revolutionary activities; thus, the CID monitoring is minimal,' Bhagat replied.

Phanindra asked, 'Who is the seventh member of the central committee? You've only talked about six.'

With a smile, Bhagat said, 'I'm coming to that. The seventh member will be our commander-in-chief, the leader of the army wing, and the sword of the HSRA. I suggest the name of none other than Chandrashekhar Azad.'

Phanindra looked around. All nodded and replied, 'Aye.'

Phanindra questioned, 'Is he here?'

Bhagat replied, 'No, Panditji is suffering from an eye infection; so, he stayed away, but he has sent a message saying that he will accept anything discussed here.'

Bijoy commented, 'Who could be a better commander than Azad? It will be an honour to work under his command.'

Manmohan whispered in Phanindra's ear, 'I thought Bhagat would call himself the commander. The boy seems different.'

Phanindra did not say anything. He nodded in agreement with everyone.

Bhagat continued. 'Each provincial leader has absolute power over his state. But they will have to get permission from the central committee for any action, such as dacoity or murder. The central committee will keep all the arms and ammunition.

The provincial head can procure it at the time of action. The weapons should be returned to the centre after the action.'

'Agreed, but what about money?' Phanindra asked. 'How will we create funding for the work?'

Sukhdev rose and spoke, 'We will establish a fund with the central committee. We cannot depend now on anonymous donations from politicians, landlords or princely states. We must generate our own income. I suggest that we resort to dacoity at the beginning.'

All of them nodded in agreement.

Bijoy said, 'HRA had committed too many robberies in UP. On top of that, they initiated Kakori. UP is, therefore, out of the question. There have also been dacoities in Punjab for quite a while. I think Bihar's going to be a fantastic starting point.'

Manmohan added, 'Yes, there has been no incidence of plunder in Bihar. We also know a lot of rich landlords who will be suitable for our purposes.'

Phanindra pinched him on the arm to keep him quiet.

Bhagat asked, 'What do you think about this, Phani Babu? Can we begin with Bihar?'

For a moment, Phanindra was stunned. 'There has been no revolutionary activity in Bihar since 1918, since the time of Anushilan Samiti.' He remarked, 'I will have to think about it and look for suitable venues and persons.'

'How many days will it take?'

'Give me ten or twelve days.'

'Once you mark the targets, how will you contact us?' Bhagat enquired.

'Do one thing, Bhagat. In ten days, you come to Bettiah. But you can't arrive like this; you will have to alter your appearance.'

'How?'

'Trim your hair and shave off your beard, keep the moustache and wear Bengali attire like me. Come as a Bengali to Bettiah, and I'll see what we can do.'

'It's decided then. I will do as you say.'

Phanindra's mouth stayed open in shock for a minute. He had not anticipated that Bhagat would be ready to get rid of his hair and beard. No Sikh was prepared to do that.

Bhagat smiled and said, 'Don't be startled, Dada. I am an atheist. What is the worth of long hair and a beard when we are ready to give up our heads for the country?'

Phanindra grinned slightly and nodded.

Sukhdev intervened, 'Phani Babu, we need some help in the matter of bombs. A revolutionary party without bombs is a dead entity. I know that in Bengal you have many contacts. We need you to find a bomb-maker for us.'

Bhagat added, 'It would help us to work a hundred times faster if you could go to Calcutta to find a bomb-maker.'

'Look, I can't travel to Calcutta immediately. Under the Bengal ordinance, all my associates are in prison. If the British do not extend the deadline, they will be out in December. In addition, there is a Congress session in Calcutta around the same time. I will go there at that time so as not to raise suspicions and will try to find someone.'

Bhagat responded, 'It is decided then. I shall come with you too in December.'

Phanindra nodded again.

'Let us come to resolutions,' Sukhdev stated.

Bijoy said, 'I propose that we should strive first to rescue Jogesh Chander Chatterji from Agra jail. I received a letter from him. Police are torturing him inhumanely because he is a Kakori criminal. The cops are going to transfer him to another jail. We should attack the wagon and rescue him.

Bijoy added, 'Sachindranath Sanyal should also be retrieved from Lucknow Jail. If he comes out, our power and resources will multiply by a thousand.'

Everyone agreed. Sukhdev said, 'Bijoy, you go to Agra and keep a watch for an appropriate time.'

'Phani Babu, you'll be meeting Jitendra Sanyal on your return, right?' Bijoy asked.

'Yes,' answered Phanindra.

'Tell him to transmit the message in coded language when he writes a letter to his brother, Sachin Dada.'

Phanindra nodded.

Bhagat said, 'We need to do something which will capture the imagination of the nation's youth. Britain has imposed the Simon Commission on us. They are here to draft the Indian constitution; there is not even one Indian representative amongst them, and yet they are here to decide our nation's destiny. I propose to take action against the Simon Commission.'

Sukhdev said, 'If we attack the Commission, it will help us reach out to the masses. Let's figure out the bomb-making first and then we shall test it on the special train carrying the members of the Simon Commission. It will send shock waves through London.'

Everyone agreed. Shiv Verma said, 'The most significant loss to HRA was caused by traitors in the Kakori case. We need to undertake a mission to execute all the traitors.' Once again, everyone agreed.

Bhagat Singh adjourned the meeting and left Delhi as the Delhi police were on the lookout for him. The rest ventured to New Delhi to see the newly constructed Assembly House and the Secretariat. Bijoy paid the tonga fare. Sukhdev paid for lunch, and Shiv Verma paid for dinner at the end of the day. Before leaving, Sukhdev invited Phanindra to Punjab. When Bijoy arrived at the Maharathi press, Phanindra and Manmohan were ready to go. Bijoy had promised them reimbursement for their travel fare from Bettiah to Delhi. However, ever since they had reached, Bijoy had not said anything about the money.

Phanindra asked, 'I suppose you have our return tickets.'

Bijoy apologetically replied, 'Yes, I had bought your return tickets, but due to a shortage of funds, I had to sell them at the station.'

After some hesitation, Phanindra asked, 'What about the train fare?'

Bijoy felt a rude shock again.

He said, in an apologetic voice, 'I am sorry, but you will have to manage by yourself. The party will reimburse you later.' Phanindra made a face as if he had smelled a dead, rotting animal.

Bijoy went away. Phanindra and Manmohan went to Meerut for work and then returned to Delhi. Phanindra sent the latter away in the evening and went to see a film called *Maya Machhindra* by V. Shantaram.

The following day, Phanindra took a train to Amritsar, heeding Sukhdev's invitation. There, he visited the party office at Mughal Bazaar. Sukhdev had rented a room above an aluminium ware shop. He welcomed Phanindra and showed him two books named 'Manufacture and Use of Explosives' and 'Small Arms Training'. Then, he took an empty bombshell out of his pocket, and said, 'I want to make this a live bomb. In short, I need a striker and a safety switch for the bombshell. Can you help me?'

The question was straightforward. Sukhdev was a man of few words. A drop of sweat appeared on Phanindra's head. He said, 'I can repair faulty pistols and revolvers; I can also make crude bombs. But I am not an expert at this. I do not know how to fix the detonator on the bomb. However, once I reach Bettiah, I will try to find an expert and learn about what to fill inside the bombshell.'

Sukhdev's face turned sour. He said, 'If I can make this work, I will produce a thousand bombs here in Amritsar.' He gave the books to Phanindra and put the bombshell back in his pocket. He said, 'You can leave for Bettiah.'

'Bijoy was going to reimburse our train fare, but he couldn't.' Phanindra enquired hesitantly.

Sukhdev stared at Phanindra for a time, then looked away. 'Wait until tomorrow, 'he said.

The next day, Sukhdev gave Phanindra twenty rupees and said, 'As arranged, Bhagat will come to you. I hope you'll find an appropriate place for the action we propose to take.'

'Yes-yes, I'm going to try,' Phanindra replied, putting the money in the inner pocket of his kurta. Then he returned to Bettiah.

Around 25 September, Phanindra went to the local board office for some work in the afternoon. As he smoked a beedi, he saw a single-horse carriage nearing the town.

Inside the carriage, he saw a Bengali man with sharp features, resembling Bhagat Singh. Phanindra tapped Manmohan's shoulder and said, 'Follow the carriage and, if it is him, ask him to stay at Sant Ghat Garden. I'll meet him in the evening. Ask him not to come to Meena Bazaar.'

In the evening, Phanindra walked to the garden after finishing his work. Two men were waiting for him. Bhagat Singh stood up and Phanindra greeted him. The other man was muscular and short and had a few pockmarks on his face. He stared at Phanindra.

Bhagat Singh introduced him, 'Meet our commander-in-chief.'

Phanindra bowed slightly and greeted him. Azad smiled but did not stop staring.

Phanindra exclaimed, 'Bhagat, you look exactly like a Bengali. You actually got rid of your hair and beard.'

Nodding, Bhagat asked, 'Have you identified any places? We are ready for action. I've got an associate in Muzaffarpur, if needed.'

Phanindra stuttered, 'No, sorry, I mean, I am still looking. I have not found a suitable option.'

Azad stood up in a rage, looked at Bhagat and scolded him. 'Bhagat, this is not acceptable. Is this how a national revolutionary party works? I came here for no reason. You wasted my time.'

Bhagat seemed embarrassed, staring at the ground, motionless. Phanindra was terrified at the sight of Azad's rage. He said, 'Panditji, forgive me. It is my fault. Your visit is not wasted. Let us do one thing. Manmohan will take Bhagat to Muzaffarpur, where Yogendra Sukul is active. I hope you know him.'

Azad answered, 'Yes, I have confidence in Yogendra.'

'So, Yogendra and Bhagat will look for a place in Muzaffarpur where we can mount a dacoity. You will stay here with me; we will look for sites in Bettiah.'

Azad thought momentarily and then ordered, 'Bhagat, go with Manmohan and tell Yogendra that he is responsible for the fund collection.'

'Yes, Panditji,' Bhagat replied.

The next day, Bhagat Singh visited the Jalalpur village of Yogendra Sukul.

Yogendra had a lean boxer's build. His eyes were brimming with fire. He had an infectious smile. As soon as Manmohan introduced Bhagat Singh, Yogendra came forward and embraced Bhagat.

Yogendra spoke with fondness, 'How long have I heard your name! Finally, you came to see me yourself. Tell me, how can I help?'

'Panditji has sent us to you with a message.'

Yogendra straightened up like a soldier and asked, 'What? Is Panditji in Bihar? What is the message?'

'You will identify the places near Muzaffarpur where we can commit armed robbery. He stated that you are now in charge of collecting the funds.'

Tears appeared in Yogendra's eyes. With a heavy voice, he said, 'Do not worry. I will fulfil my duty. Can I meet him?'

Bhagat replied, 'Why not? You can come to Bettiah with us.'

Meanwhile, in Bettiah, Phanindra took Azad to Meena Bazaar. Roaming around the market, he pointed at a row of shops and whispered, 'These shops belong to the Marwaris, Panditji. I've heard they keep a lot of cash.'

Panditji, disgusted by the selection, remarked, 'Phani Babu, we're talking about dacoity, not petty theft. This is not how we work. You are indifferent to our work.'

Azad left Phanindra and walked alone to Sant Garden. Bhagat returned with Yogendra in the evening. Azad embraced Yogendra, who, speechless and with teary eyes, kept looking at Azad for a few minutes. Azad invited Yogendra to sit beside him.

Yogendra said, 'Panditji, I will arrange everything as you ordered. Do not worry about the funds anymore.'

'If you are taking the responsibility, I will consider it done.'

Yogendra remarked, 'Panditji, I have handed two revolvers and a few cartridges to Bhagat. They are the only asset I have for now.'

'Thank you. The visit is not totally pointless, at least.' Panditji looked at Bhagat and said, 'Tomorrow morning, go to Phanindra and ask him to find landlords nearby. I cannot stand his face. Either he doesn't know how to work, or he does not want to work.'

Bhagat went away the following day and came back quickly. Panditji was just completing his daily practice of 500 press-ups. Looking at Bhagat, he raised an eyebrow.

Bhagat said, 'Panditji, Phanindra left for Calcutta early this morning for some personal work.'

Panditji's face reddened, and he exclaimed, 'People like him only talk about revolution. I told you, Bhagat, I trusted Bihar to Yogendra. Something is troubling me about this Phanindra.'

Bhagat said, 'Bijoy and Sukhdev said the same thing about him, but we need him for a while. Let him prove his worth.'

Panditji said, 'If you say so. Just don't bring him in front of me again with his petty excuses.'

Panditji travelled to Jhansi with Bhagat Singh. On the way, they met Rajguru, who was waiting for Bhagat's message to assist in a dacoity at Muzaffarpur. Bhagat gave the revolvers to him and asked him to take them to Bijoy in Agra. Meanwhile, Yogendra started preparing a list of wealthy landlords whom they could target.

The Simon Commission was supposed to reach Lahore on 30 October. Since the commission's arrival in the country, it had faced protests wherever it had gone. In Lahore, every political party organized a massive protest against the commission. The country's senior-most and most respected leader, Lala Lajpat Rai, was going to lead the procession. The law and order system prepared itself to contain the protests.

Bhagat Singh and Sukhdev decided to participate in the protest through the Naujawan Bharat Sabha. Bhagat Singh was the general secretary of the Sabha. He got a tip-off that the police would try to isolate Lalaji and attack him directly. Hence, Bhagat Singh instructed the core members of the Sabha to form a human chain around Lalaji to protect him from any untoward incident.

On 30 October, when the commission arrived in Lahore, it was greeted by unprecedented protests, black flags and slogans of 'Simon, go back'. The police unleashed the terror of batons on the peaceful protesters. When the demonstrations got out of hand, the superintendent of police, J.P. Scott, decided to attack the leaders. He instructed his deputy, assistant superintendent of police John P. Saunders, to attack Lalaji. Saunders, along with his platoon, singled out the senior leader.

Lala Lajpat Rai was assaulted with an iron-capped lathi by Saunders. Lalaji's umbrella broke the first blow, and the umbrella wires scratched the aged leader viciously. He fell down after a few blows, but Saunders and the constables continued hitting him with their leather shoes and batons. Sukhdev, Bhagwati Charan Vohra and other associates tried their best to stop the attack but failed miserably. Lalaji was hurt grievously, but it was the psychological shock that affected the aged leader. He said that every blow on his body would put the last nail in the coffin of the British Empire. On 17 November, Lalaji succumbed to his injuries.

Bhagat and Sukhdev wondered how a lowly official could attack one of the country's most respected leaders and get away with it. They thought of it as a national insult. The whole nation mourned for Lalaji. Nevertheless, there was no action taken against Scott or Saunders.

Bhagat Singh called a meeting at Mozang House—a two-story building located near the famous Anarkali Bazaar. The revolutionaries had rented a room on the first floor as a hideout. There he proposed avenging the insult to the nation by killing superintendent Scott. Panditji agreed. Sukhdev was assigned with the task of making a foolproof assassination and escape plan.

Yogendra arrived in Lahore on the same day. He reached Mozang House. The meeting was almost over. Azad welcomed Yogendra and gave him a seat beside him. Yogendra looked at everyone and announced, 'I understand what pain is brooding in your hearts. But I am here with a small piece of good news.'

Azad replied, 'Speak up.'

'As per your instructions, Panditji, I have accomplished the given task. I have brought some money.'

Azad replied, 'Good. How did you get it?'

'After meticulous planning, my team committed a dacoity at Bazidpur. It went smoothly without anyone getting hurt. I was able to get around twenty-five thousand rupees. This is the money.' Yogendra placed a bag in front of Azad.

Without changing his expression, Azad said, 'Good job, Yogendra. You have satisfied our monetary need for the near future.'

Jai Gopal's eyes widened at the mention of the amount. He excitedly said, 'Panditji, this amount is almost three times the loot of Kakori.'

Azad did not like the comparison but chose not to speak.

Yogendra replied, 'My young friend, every rupee taken at Kakori has the mark of Bismil and Ashfaq's sacrifice. The Kohinoor cannot be compared to a paisa of Kakori.'

Jai Gopal apologetically said, 'Sorry, I didn't mean it that way.'

Azad ordered, 'Yogendra, you will leave Lahore by tomorrow morning and continue your work. Remember, every penny you get us is fuelling the revolution. It goes without saying but do not shed unnecessary blood during your exploits.'

'Understood, Panditji.' Yogendra went back to Bihar.

After meticulous planning, the fateful day arrived on 17 December.

Long shadows were formed over Lahore's streets as the sun started to set. The four young revolutionaries readied themselves to strike. Panditji kept the Mauser; the revolver was given to Rajguru and the automatic pistol to Bhagat Singh. Two bicycles were placed close to the lavatory of D.A.V. College. Jai Gopal, who was in charge of one of the bicycles, took a stand close to the police station while exuding a calm assurance. His job was to identify Scott and signal the others for confirmation.

Panditji waited behind the walls of the D.A.V. College campus, ready with the escape plan. Rajguru and Bhagat Singh moved swiftly down the street, their faces displaying a mixture of resolution and anxiety. They effortlessly mixed in with the nearby students and passers-by.

A clean-shaven, young uniformed British officer walked out of the police station. A tall, uniformed Sikh constable followed the sahib and delivered a packet. The officer sat on his motorcycle and kick-started it.

Jai Gopal, out of excitement, mistook the sahib for Scott and immediately, without thinking, waved the confirmation signal to Rajguru and Bhagat.

But as the motorcycle drew nearer, Bhagat Singh's keen eye detected a discrepancy. This was not Mr Scott. A surge of doubt and uncertainty washed over him. Rajguru, unaware of the truth, fired a shot at the cop riding the motorcycle, without any hesitation. The bullet went straight to his heart. The cop instinctively lifted his hand from the handlebars as the gunshot rang out. As he fell, his leg was stuck under the weight of the motorcycle. Despite the commotion, the engine kept on purring, creating a mechanical symphony.

The unexpected change of events caught Bhagat Singh off guard, but he quickly adjusted his course of action. He ran towards the officer, clutching his Browning automatic rifle hard, his blood pumping with adrenaline, and unleashed a volley of shots. Each shot resounded with a deafening echo in answer to every blow that had fallen on Lala Lajpat Rai. Lalaji's death was avenged.

Bhagat and Rajguru escaped to Calcutta and then to Agra. At the Agra centre, bomb-making had started, and ideological debates ensued for future action. Around March 1929, Bhagat Singh came up with a brilliant idea. To catch the attention of the nation's working class, he decided to oppose the passing of two unjust laws. The method he chose to protest would change the track of history forever.

Chapter 3

April 1929

The safety clip of the hand grenade fell on the polished wooden floor with a clank. The grenade flew with a firm trajectory from the right hand of Bhagat Singh right towards the centre of the assembly floor. A blinding flash and a deafening explosion followed. Blue smoke rose in the grand circular hall, and chaos ensued. While everyone was trying to absorb the shock, another bomb flew from the hands of Batukeshwar Dutt and fell near the first one, rocking the hall once more.

There was no one sitting near the site of the explosion. The finance minister of the Council of India, Sir George Schuster, was the nearest to the blast. Splinters from the wooden floor and the furniture flew in all directions, injuring the dignitaries around. A ruckus followed as the assembly members tried to run out of the hall. In the stampede that followed, a few hurt themselves. Amidst the hysterical cries and shouts, Bhagat Singh took out a pistol and started firing shots up in the air. As they ran, members of the assembly heard the roar of the slogans 'Samrajyawad Murdabad' (Down with Imperialism) and 'Inquilab Zindabad' (Long Live the Revolution). A few Indians understood who the perpetrators were, but they still ran for their lives.

Sergeant Terry was on duty on that fateful, sweltering afternoon. He was sitting in the Ladies Gallery of the Central Assembly, Delhi. The controversial 'Public Safety Bill' and the 'Trade Dispute Bill' were the subject of a hot debate on the floor. The former enabled the government to deport or arrest extremists without trial, and the latter empowered them to penalize and punish trade unions for protesting. The viceroy and the government completely ignored the opposition of the Indian leaders and chose to promulgate the acts by the special powers of the viceroy. As the debates went on, there was a sudden deafening explosion.

Sergeant Terry's legs were shaking. After the second explosion, he ran towards the central door. The sight was a British police officer's nightmare. A young man was firing pistols in the air. Another was hurling pamphlets on to the chamber floor. Terry had not forgotten the fate of deputy superintendent Saunders in Lahore. Armed with only a baton, he saw Death standing before him. When the assembly below had thoroughly dispersed, Bhagat looked back and saw the sergeant.

He came forward with his pistol facing the floor. His face was flushed and red with excitement. He was almost smiling. Terry stepped backwards. Bhagat's height and posture were intimidating. From the central door, a horde of constables entered the gallery. Terry gathered some courage. Bhagat turned the gun around, took out the magazine and offered it to Terry.

Sergeant Terry was dumbfounded. He had not expected them to surrender. Was this some sort of a plan? But there was no time to think. He immediately took the weapon and restrained the hands of both revolutionaries. The constables got hold of them and pushed them out of the gallery. They started shouting slogans again. The police hurried. The police vehicle was ready. Terry went up to Batukeshwar first. Then he signalled to Bhagat Singh without touching him. Bhagat nodded and stepped inside. While taking his seat, he heard a child's cry, 'Lambu Chacha!'

Durga Devi Vohra, the wife of Bhagwati Charan Vohra, fondly known to revolutionaries as Durga Bhabhi, was standing on the side of the street, holding her three-year-old son, Shachi, along with Sushila Didi, another revolutionary. Durga Bhabhi had placed a hand on the kid's mouth. The vehicle started and began moving in the opposite direction. Bhagat could not wave at Shachi for one last time. His vision blurred as tears clouded his eyes. Batukeshwar placed his hands on Bhagat's to reassure him.

As the vehicle left, Terry thought of something and ran back into the assembly. This time he went to the floor and saw the damage done by the bombs. It was not much. A few medics were treating the injured members. But the injuries were very superficial. Then he saw a few pamphlets scattered on the benches. He picked one up. The header was bold; it said, Hindustan Socialist Republican Army, and the first line was, 'It takes a loud voice to make the deaf hear.' It was signed by Balraj, the commander-in-chief.

He had seen such a pamphlet by the same organization in Lahore after Saunders's murder. Terry was glad that there was no casualty under his watch. But he was baffled by their behaviour. Why did they throw the bomb into an open space? Why did they not use shrapnel in the explosive? And if the revolutionary had a pistol, why had he surrendered?

A constable came up to Terry and reported, 'Sahib, you are needed at Civil Lines police station.'

'Okay,' said Terry, and followed the constable.

At the station, the sub-inspector was preparing a First Information Report (FIR). Terry gave him the required details.

After the FIR, the officer entered the prison and asked Bhagat Singh, 'Do you want to make a statement?'

Bhagat responded, 'No, we will only make a statement before the court.'

Bhagat and Batukeshwar were kept in separate cells far from each other. They knew this would happen. After a while, lunch was served to them in the cell. It was barely afternoon, but the day felt like it had gone on forever.

Bhagat recalled the cold, humid morning. Bhagwati Charan and Sukhdev had taken him to Qudsia Park at around 8 a.m. Bhagat had worn a grey shirt with a pointy collar, a dove-coloured coat with two pockets and khaki shorts coming down to the knee. A pair of worn-out leather shoes and woollen socks completed the look.

On top of that, he had a pigeon-coloured felt hat he had bought from Lahore. Batukeshwar Dutt was wearing a similar grey coat and khaki shorts, except for the hat.

Sushila Didi and Durga Bhabhi were waiting for them. Little Shachi jumped from his mother's lap and rushed towards Bhagat. He picked Shachi up and played with him on the grass for a while. The ladies did not know about the plan. Bhagwati only said, 'Bhagat and Batukeshwar are going for action.'

They had brought aloo parathas for him. All of them ate silently, sitting around in a circle. Sukhdev and Bhagwati kept looking at Bhagat and Batukeshwar. They knew it was their last meeting under the clear sky. Batukeshwar Dutt took a small envelope and handed it to Bhagwati. It contained passport-sized photos of Bhagat and Batukeshwar in the same attire. They had had their photographs clicked at a photo studio near Kashmere Gate a week ago.

Shachi peeked as Bhagwati was looking at the photos. Bhagat's portrait in a felt hat looked so stylish.

Shachi pleaded, 'Baba, can I have a photograph of Lambu Chacha?'

Bhagwati smiled, put the photo in his pocket, and said, 'Yes, I will give it to you later.'

Shachi then turned to Bhagat and demanded, 'Chachu, I want a hat like yours.'

Bhagat picked up his hat and put it on Shachi's head. It was too big for him, and covered his forehead and eyes. The child ran around, fell and giggled. Everyone laughed. Bhagat took the hat and said, 'I'm going to get you one just like this in your size.' The child seemed convinced.

As they turned to leave, Bhagwati and Sukhdev embraced both of them. It was probably the first time anyone had seen tears in Sukhdev's eyes. Everyone used to call him Aurangzeb because of his strict, disciplined nature.

Batukeshwar pinched Sukhdev and said, 'Bhagat, look, our Aurangzeb is crying.'

Trying to hide his face, Sukhdev clarified, 'No, no, there is something in my eyes.'

Bhagat Singh consoled him. 'Do not worry. Everything will happen as per the plan. Tell Panditji this is just another way to fight. We will fight from the inside. You all must continue the work outside.'

Sushila Didi took out a safety pin from her purse; she punctured her index finger and made a *tilak* on the foreheads of Bhagat and Batukeshwar.

Finally, Bhagat sat down on his knees to say goodbye to little Shachi.

Shachi looked down; the shoes of Bhagat Singh were torn, and his sock-clad toe was peeping out. Shachi exclaimed, 'Chachu, buy yourself nice shoes first, then get me a hat.'

Bhagat smiled, and Shachi gave him a peck on his cheek.

After the bombing, the HSRA machinery came into full force. They made sure the event received detailed news coverage in every newspaper. The government had limited the use of telephones for official use only. However, the journalists had some tricks up their sleeves. The passport-sized photos and the intention behind the bombing were sent to each newspaper. The *Statesman* created a special edition with photographs of Bhagat and Batukeshwar on the cover page. They also published the pamphlet as it was.

In the evening, Jaidev and Shiv Verma were quietly sitting in their room. Jaidev had actually accompanied Bhagat and Batukeshwar to the assembly. It had been his task to get a room in Delhi and get acquainted with a member of the assembly, posing as a political science student. It was Jaidev who had managed to get the visitor's gallery passes for Bhagat and Batukeshwar. When Bhagat was leaving, he noticed Jaidev's shoes were in tatters while his own boots were brand new. Bhagat had bought the boots in Lahore to pose as a British officer to escape after Saunders's murder. He was done with putting on one shoe, and then he stopped. He removed the shoe and picked up Jaidev's shoes.

Jaidev asked, 'What are you doing?'

'Whatever I wear is going into the police repository. I am not planning to come out very soon, so it would be better if you wear my shoes.' Bhagat wore the weathered shoes. 'These fit me well.'

Jaidev did not know what to say. Then Bhagat took out a round, shiny watch with a silver chain. Handing over the watch to Shiv, he asked, 'Do you know what this is?'

Jaidev and Shiv replied together, 'Is this the Ghadar watch?'

Bhagat smiled and said, 'Yes, brother, this piece is a companion to the Indian revolution. Sachin Dada entrusted me with this. I hope to live up to his expectations. Keep it safe.'

Jaidev had made up his mind not to cry, but his heart became as heavy as a boat's anchor. He went on to the roof and wept in solace. Shiv came up and joined him.

The following day, every newspaper had front-page coverage of the bombing and HSRA. Someone in Jhansi bought a newspaper and went to the party head office. Around ten revolutionaries, including Azad, were present.

When they saw the photographs and the news, everyone got emotional. Watching them, Azad sat like a stone with a grave face, observing everyone.

Later, someone spotted Azad sitting on the roof, tears flowing from his eyes. When asked, he said, 'I am not sad because Bhagat and Dutt have parted. It was bound to happen. All of us will be arrested, hanged or shot some day. I was affected by seeing how affectionate you all have become towards Bhagat, while I cannot feel anything. I have become just a machine for the revolution.'

On 13 April, Lahore Police got a tip-off from a confidential source that an ironsmith was making bombshells for the revolutionaries. When the CID kept watch and followed the trail, they confirmed a hideout in the Kashmiri Building, located on MacLeod Road. On 14 April, a special squad of armed forces raided the shelter, encircled the building from all sides and entered with loaded guns. Sukhdev, Kishorilal and Jai Gopal were there, busy making bombs. Sukhdev had a loaded gun, but the police apprehended him before he could move. Then a magistrate arrived, and the police took an inventory of the weapons they had found.

When the inspector was poking around with his baton, Sukhdev calmly said, 'Do not touch that box. It contains a live bomb. Handle it with carelessness, and it will be the last thing you will ever do.' The inspector almost ran away and called the explosive expert.

The CID recovered many letters from the Kashmiri Building. The HSRA had closed its Agra office by 1 April 1929 and moved its headquarters to Saharanpur, United Provinces, and the letters revealed the address of the Saharanpur hideout. On the night of 13 May 1929, the

CID raided the office and found Jaidev and Shiv Verma busy making bombs. After taking them away, the CID did not break any news about the Saharanpur raid. Two days later, Dr Gaya Prasad returned to the office with bombs and materials. He tapped the door in a rhythmic code, only to find it being opened by CID officials. He was arrested too. The Jhansi office was also raided, but Azad had already sent everyone to safe places with instructions on how to communicate and stay underground.

A few days later, Bhagat and Dutt were moved from Civil Lines Station to Delhi Jail, and then they were presented at the court of Additional Magistrate F.B. Pool. When the judge asked him to make a statement, Bhagat said, 'Your Honour, we will make our statement only in the Sessions Court.' The Magistrate's face flushed. He had not thought that these young lads would know so much about legal procedures. He adjourned the proceedings.

On 4 June, the trial started before the judge, Leonard Middletown, in Delhi Sessions Court. Bhagat Singh had prepared a detailed statement and smuggled a copy out of prison before presenting it to the court. Irrespective of the statement and witness, on 12 June, the judge pronounced punishment of transportation for life for Bhagat and Dutt. The same day, a constable came to their cell and said, 'Tonight, you and your friend are being moved to Lahore. Pack your things. There is another case waiting for you there. Also, your friend, Phanindra Nath Ghosh, has been arrested in Calcutta on 8 June.'

Bhagat told Dutt, 'I hope Phani Babu does not break under police pressure.'

Dutt replied, 'Bhagat, do you remember what Panditji said?'

Bhagat remembered the words of Azad, 'You are playing a dangerous game. Except for yourself, nothing and no one can be trusted. Your worst nightmare can come true. Your friends and brothers will become approvers, and they will sabotage everything sacred to you. I have gone through this pain in Kakori. Most of my friends died because of the traitors. What is the guarantee that it won't happen again? This is the country of Mir Jafar and Jaichand. This is why I prefer to fight as long as I am free. I think you should not risk your life. After you throw the bombs, I will personally rescue you and Dutt from the Assembly, like I rescued you after Saunders's murder. What is the logic in getting arrested? This is suicide.'

'Yes, I remember every word of Panditji. I was and am ready to take the risk. I trust my comrades, but I am prepared for the worst. If this country is of Jafar and Jaichand, then this country has also bred Guru Gobind Singh, Shivaji Maharaj and Rana Pratap. I understand the difficulties, and there is no turning back. Panditji will continue the fight outside while I fight from behind bars.'

Meanwhile Jai Gopal and Hans Raj Vohra had been tortured by the police for information and they had spilled all the names and addresses of important party members. CID immediately alerted all regional offices to look out for the HSRA leaders. On 8 June, the CID arrested Phanindra Nath Ghosh in Bhawanipur, Calcutta. He was hiding at the home of a relative. He had been walking home at around 9.30 p.m. when the CID grabbed him. He was taken to

Lal Bazaar station. A heavy garrison was put on the station overnight. He was frightened to death. Phanindra wasn't able to sleep all night. The following day, he was presented before the magistrate. The magistrate asked, 'Are you related to HSRA?'

Phanindra said, 'Yes.'

'Would you like to make a statement regarding your association?'

'No, I will not.'

Immediately, a convoy of police officers took him and boarded the Punjab Mail. On 11 June, the Mail reached Lahore. The CID kept Phanindra in Fort Jail, separate from the others.

The next day, a constable walked Phanindra into a room with two chairs. His handcuffs were removed, and he was asked to sit on a chair. The constable stated, 'Bada Sahib is coming to see you. Do not misbehave; he has a bad temper.'

Phanindra said, 'Yes.'

A six-foot-tall police officer with many medals on his broad chest walked into the room. His piercing eyes took a disgusted look at Phanindra. He was clean-shaven. He walked around Phanindra's chair in an intimidating way and then sat in the front chair. He put one leg on another, stared at Phanindra for a minute, and then said in a hoarse voice, 'I am Khan Bahadur Abdul Aziz, special superintendent of police of the CID, Lahore. I am looking after the Lahore Conspiracy Case.' Khan offered Phanindra a glass of water.

Phanindra wiped the sweat off his forehead and took the glass.

Khan said, 'Look, Jai Gopal has told us everything. I know you are one of the members of the central committee of HSRA. You are involved in bomb-making, assembly bombing and probably in Saunders's murder also.'

'No, no, I am not involved in . . .' Phanindra paused for a minute and said, '. . . not in Saunders's murder.'

'Not many years have passed since Kakori. So you must know what is going to happen to all of you. You are responsible for conspiracy against the crown, the King himself. I am talking to you because you are the senior-most among these young lads. I am making you an offer. I will personally give you the crown's pardon. You will just have to provide me with some specific details.'

'What? Approver? No, I cannot become an approver.' Phanindra remembered the resolution of the party that approvers must be punished with the death penalty. The angry face of Azad holding his Mauser pistol appeared in his mind somehow.

Khan said, 'I understand your concern. By the time this case ends, all of your party members will be arrested and punished. You must understand this; your HSRA has gone to dust. A handful of members are on the run. They will be behind bars in a matter of weeks. Also, if you join us, your time behind bars will be reduced drastically.'

'No, I cannot.'

'What if I agree to absolve all charges against you?'

'It is not possible. After my statement, you will punish me like the others, and someone will murder me in prison.'

'The clause of absolution will be mentioned in the pardon. Also, you will be provided security as long as you need it.'

Phanindra remained quiet. Khan's eyes lit up. He stood up and said,' I understand that such decisions cannot be taken in haste. But, unfortunately, we don't have time. You will be taken back to your cell now. I will call you here after exactly one hour. Think about my offer. You are not going to get another one. Also, I have heard that you have been recently married. Decide the future of your family. Lahore Fort Jail is the best prison in Punjab. If you deny the offer, you will be taken to your comrades in Borstal Jail. Go now.'

Two constables took Phanindra back to his cell.

As Phanindra stood in the corner, his eyes wide with fear, the cold steel bars cast unsettling shadows across the poorly lit room. His thoughts were torn apart by a tornado of contradictory feelings as his heart pumped frantically like the beat of a drum. Having once been a revolutionary fighting for a cause he supported, Phanindra now stood on the verge of betrayal. The word 'Traitor' rang in his ears, sending his heart racing through his chest. He had once been a revolutionary who strongly believed that his efforts would result in change. But now he was perched on the edge of a dangerous path.

Phanindra's internal struggle intensified. The possibility of facing police torture loomed over him like a shadowy spectre, an unspoken threat that hovered on the periphery of his consciousness. He had heard the rumours, the stories of unspeakable acts inflicted upon revolutionaries by the CID to get information.

How could he decide between self-preservation and loyalty? Could he bear the shame that would always weigh heavily on his mind and cloud every waking moment?

Phanindra found himself at a crossroads. The weight of his decision threatened to consume him, tearing at the fabric of his being.

He understood, as he stood there, a lone figure in a sea of uncertainty, that any course he took would unavoidably affect his future. Would he make the ultimate sacrifice for his own survival by sacrificing his erstwhile allies? He would have to live out the rest of his days with the guilt of betrayal.

He remembered the face of his beautiful wife. He had promised her that he would return to her. What would she do without him? If he walked with Bhagat, he would be sentenced to life imprisonment at Cellular Jail. No, it was unacceptable. He had not been in favour of murdering Saunders. Nor was he involved in bombing the assembly. Why should he be punished for others' crimes? This was God's signal that he be saved. He would blindly follow the almighty crown and shut his ears and eyes towards people infected with the disease of patriotism. It was time to grab the opportunity and make the most of it.

Phanindra was taken back to the room where Khan was waiting for him.

Khan asked, 'So, Phani Babu, what do you say?'

'But what is in it for me?'

'I do not understand. You are not in a bargaining position, my friend. Absolving you of all the crimes is not enough for you?'

Phanindra gulped. He dared to look into the eyes of Khan and commented with bravado, 'No, not enough.'

'What do you want then? Speak up!'

'I want to know the status of Manmohan Bannerji.'

'He has also been arrested. My men will bring him in a few days.'

'I can turn him also into an approver. He will not disobey me. I was the one who initiated him into all this.'

'So the question is not whether you will help us. The question is your price.'

'And the price of Manmohan.'

'Say what you want. I do not have all day.'

'What can you give us?'

'A cash reward is the tradition so far.'

'Apart from cash?'

'Do you want a government job?'

'No.'

'Do you want to leave India? We have promised one of you the opportunity to study in London.'

'No, I won't leave.'

'Then, perhaps, land.'

'Yes.'

'Where?'

'In my home district, Bettiah.'

'Consider it done.'

'For both of us.'

'All right.'

'I need it in writing.'

'Before that happens, you must prove your loyalty to the crown.'

'How?'

'Tomorrow or the day after tomorrow, you will be taken to the identification parade. You will need to identify everyone accurately. Just to prove how deeply you were involved in this ruckus.'

Phanindra thought about facing Bhagat Singh. His hands trembled. Driven by terror, lines appeared on his face.

Khan put his giant palm on Phanindra's shoulder. It covered the entire shoulder. He said, 'Don't worry. Your safety is now my responsibility.'

'What else?'

'Tell us something we don't know. Prove your worth. '

Phanindra's tiny eyes shone. A hideous smile came to his lips. He suggested, 'I can give you Robin.'

'Are you talking about the mysterious Robin? The right hand of Sachindranath Sanyal? The legendary bomb-maker?' Khan nearly jumped off the chair.

'Yes, the great Robin.'

'I have worked in Calcutta. No one knows who he is. You had better not be bluffing. Also, he has been inactive for so long.'

'Inactive?' Phanindra chuckled. 'Who do you think taught us bomb-making? Robin is now the right hand of Bhagat Singh.'

Khan's eyebrows narrowed. He said, 'If your information is accurate and we get hold of Robin, then you will have whatever you want. Henceforth, you will be called as the King's witness.'

'Note down the address,' Phanindra said.

Khan wrote it down like an eager schoolboy and rushed out of the room.

Phanindra stretched his legs, put his arms behind his head and mumbled, 'King's witness.'

Chapter 4

June 1929

A young man was sitting on the porch of his hostel, drinking hot tea on a rainy morning in Calcutta. With a gust of wind, a police jeep stopped abruptly in front of the house. The young man took a sip of the tea, before looking at the police officer hurrying on to the porch.

The officer, followed by two constables with loaded rifles, came up to the porch. One of the constables muttered something in the officer's ear.

The young man asked, 'How can I help you?'

The officer replied, 'We are here to arrest you.'

'On what charges? I think you are unaware that I have been absolved of all the charges against me. There is some mistake on your part, I think.' And he continued to drink his tea calmly.

The officer, baffled by the young man's confidence, gave an angry look to the constable and took out the arrest warrant.

He read it aloud, 'For association with HSRA, Bhagat Singh, Sukhdev, etc. Code name Robin is hereby arrested . . .'

Although the name sent a chill down the young man's spine, he did not lose his composure. He finished the tea, stood up, and said, 'Officer, this is clearly a case of mistaken identity. I know no one by the name of Robin. Let me accompany you to the station, and I will convince your superiors properly.'

The officer said, 'Yes, that will be helpful.'

Meanwhile, the constable whispered in the officer's ear, 'Sahib, this is the man,' but the officer ignored him. The young man entered the house to change his attire before accompanying the police. The officer waited on the porch. After a minute, the officer heard a loud thud. He sent the constable inside to check it out.

The constable shouted, 'Sahib, he jumped out of the window and ran away.'

The officer cursed himself under his breath and chased the young man, jumping out of the same window. The young man ran like the wind on Hazara Road, leaving the officer far behind. But unfortunately, at the junction of Hazara Road and Lansdowne Road, a police vehicle came from the front and blocked his path. They arrested him. The young man laughed out loud for fooling the officer. The constable restrained him and put him in the police vehicle. While pushing him inside, many people gathered on the roadside to watch the drama. Nearest to him stood a milkman with his bicycle. He had tears in his eyes.

The officer, out of breath from running, felt insulted by the laughter, and punched the young man in the face and said, 'Jatindra Nath Das a.k.a. Robin a.k.a. Masterji, you are hereby arrested under the Lahore Conspiracy Case.'

Jatin Das winked at the milkman, before being pushed inside the police vehicle.

The milkman reminded him of one glorious morning. Back in December 1928, Jatin had been dining at Hazara Road mess. Around fifty students were having dinner, in a jovial mood. It was the night of fish rice, a special recipe of the mess cook. A tall man came in, sat on the opposite side, and said, 'Dada, my name is Bhagat Singh. I have come here from Lahore to meet you. I need your help with something.'

Jatin kept eating steamed rice and replied, 'Bhagat Singh of Punjab, I have heard your name. I know what you have done in Lahore. However, I do not associate with revolutionaries, and there is nothing that I can help you with. I believe in absolute non-violence.'

'I understand, Dada, what hardships you have gone through. You have a right to turn to the Gandhian way, but kindly understand this, you are our last hope. No one else of your expertise and calibre can help us attain our objective.'

The young man laughed, 'And what is your objective?'

'Complete freedom, political, economic and socialistic freedom. We will bring Inquilab to the masses of India.'

'Good for you. Look, Bhagat, I do not know what you have heard about me. I have been falsely arrested by the British earlier for association with revolutionaries. They failed to prove anything against me in court. Now I am gathering youth under Bengal Volunteers Forces to instil a patriotic feeling in them. I cannot lead my pupils on to the path of revolutionary terrorism. It is suicide. I am not interested in your project. You can have dinner here in my name, but there is nothing that I can help you with.'

Bhagat Singh smiled and said sarcastically, 'It is sad that the Royal Bengal Tiger has lost his sharp teeth or wants to hide them indefinitely.'

'Excuse me?'

'All that I heard about the great Robin seems like rumours after meeting you.'

Jatin Das was surprised and looked around to ensure that nobody had heard the name; he asked, in a hushed voice, 'Who told you about Robin?'

Bhagat Singh took out a letter and handed it over. It was signed by Jitendranath Sanyal.

The young man stood up and asked Bhagat Singh to follow him. They went to his room. Jatin Das closed the door behind them and said, 'Nobody knows my code name except Sachin Dada's family. What do you want from me?'

Bhagat said, 'Dada, you were the right hand of Sachindranath Sanyal; the name Robin is a legend in Bengal. There is no match for your skills in bomb-making. I want you to teach us.'

'No, Bhagat, it is too dangerous. Anushilan and Yugantar failed, Ghadar failed and HRA failed; what is the possibility that you will succeed? Your HSRA comrades killed a police officer now; what is the output? We are never going to get freedom through armed revolution. I have witnessed too many deaths. I know I cannot convince you of this, but I will not be part of this venture.'

'So you are afraid of death?'

'Not exactly. I am saying that it is not necessary to die. It is not a war.'

Bhagat stood up and asserted, 'I believe that a nation held down by foreign bayonets is in a perpetual state of war. Since open battle is rendered impossible to a disarmed race,

I attacked by surprise. Since guns were denied to me, I drew forth my pistol and fired. Poor in wealth and intellect, a son like myself has nothing else to offer to the mother but his own blood. And so I have sacrificed the same on her altar. The only lesson required in India at present is to learn how to die, and . . .'

Jatin Das completed the sentence, in a heavy voice, 'The only way to teach it is by dying ourselves. Vande Mataram. I have also memorized these last words of Shaheed Madanlal Dhingra. I worship him.'

Bhagat responded, 'This is the difference between you and me. You just worship Dhingra; I am walking in his footsteps.'

A heavy silence fell in the room. Jatin Das then smiled to himself, looked carefully at Bhagat, extended his hand, and finally said, 'You've won. Tell me, where should I come to die with you?'

Bhagat laughed and hugged him. They kept talking through the night about strategies and the technicalities of bomb-making. They came to their senses when birds began to chirp outside. It was almost morning.

Bhagat said, 'Dada, I will have to leave now. My friends must be worried.'

As they came outside in front of the hostel, a milkman was milking his buffalo in a tiny iron bucket. Bhagat Singh had an extraordinary liking for buffalo milk. He went straight ahead and without asking the milkman picked up the almost full bucket and gulped down the milk on the spot. The milkman kept staring but could not speak because Jatin Dada stood beside him.

When the bucket was empty, Bhagat Singh burped and handed over one rupee to the milkman, saying, 'I am sorry, but I could not control myself.' The milkman went away with a sour face. Jatin Dada and Bhagat laughed their hearts out.

On 21 December, Phanindra reached Calcutta with Manmohan and the Congress workers of Bettiah. There he met Kanwal Nath Tiwari, whose address he had given to Bhagat at a meeting in Delhi. Kanwal Nath greeted Phanindra and said, 'A tall man named Ranjit came looking for you.' Phanindra knew that Ranjit was a pseudonym of Bhagat.

The next day, Phanindra set up a meeting at an eatery and invited Bhagat and Jatin Das.

Phanindra introduced Jatin Das to Bhagat and whispered, 'Bhagat, this is the only man I know with the required skills. If only you can convince him, he will teach you.'

Bhagat replied, 'Phani Babu, I don't need to convince him.'

Phanindra, surprised, asked, 'Why? Do you know how difficult it is to find such a person?'

Jatin Dada said, 'Phani Babu, relax; we have already met and agreed to work together.'

Bhagat and Jatin continued discussing their plans. Phani Babu felt hurt because Bhagat Singh had bypassed him and met Jatin alone. But he chose not to say anything because he could not fulfil the task the party had given earlier.

In April 1929, when Bhagat and Batukeshwar Dutt threw bombs into the assembly, the following day, someone tapped on the door of Jatin Das; when it opened, it was the same milkman.

He handed one rupee to Jatin Dada and said, 'Dada, I cannot take this money. I feel honoured that he drank milk from my buffalo.' And then he showed the newspaper where photographs of Bhagat and Dutt were printed.

Further, the milkman said, 'Dada, if you meet him again, give this money back. Be assured, I will speak to no one. I feel lucky today. Vande Mataram.'

After producing him before the magistrate, the CID took Jatin Das straight to Lahore.

Khan Bahadur, superintendent, CID, went into Phanindra's cell. The king's witness was reading the newspaper.

Khan said, 'Phani Babu, your information was accurate. We got Robin. Thanks.'

Phani Babu stood up in a hurry and smiled shyly at the superintendent.

Khan said, 'Be ready; you will be taken to an identification parade today. I hope you identify all of them accurately. Then we will work on the next step.'

The mention of an identification parade sent shivers down his spine, awakening a whirlwind of conflicting emotions within him. Giving information to Khan was easy. But facing his comrades? How would they react?

His mind traced the memories of secrecy, camaraderie and shared dreams of freedom. The faces of his comrades haunted him, their unwavering determination etched deep within his soul. Each name carried a story—a story of sacrifice, resilience and unwavering belief. Phanindra felt the heavy burden of betrayal clawing at his spirit. How could he reconcile his past beliefs with the harsh reality of his present circumstances? But there was no turning back now. He composed himself.

Phanindra said, 'Don't worry, Sahib, I know all of them.'

'Also, Manmohan arrived here this morning. We have kept him in this building. At lunch, you must convince him to join you.'

'Sahib, he will not disobey me.'

'What do you know about the Maulania dacoity?'

'Sahib, the party had entrusted the task of collecting revenues by committing dacoities to the Bihar unit. A series of dacoities have been committed for almost a year, and thousands of rupees have been collected for the HSRA. This Maulania dacoity was meant to be one of the same kind, but it went wrong somehow.'

'How?'

'Our policy was not to harm anyone and just get the money without bloodshed. But sometimes, people tend to resist. So in Maulania, the landlord's family resisted, and someone got grievously wounded by a spear. Also, one of us, Kanwal Nath Tiwari, got hurt by the sword. Nevertheless, they escaped with the loot.'

'In how many dacoities, were you personally involved?'

Phanindra replied instantly, 'Not a single one, Sahib; I am not that type of a rebel. Even Bhagat Singh and Azad came to my place to insist on a dacoity, but I never participated in it.'

'But you were the head of Bihar.'

'Yes, all things happened in my name but were perpetrated by others. They were supervised by Manmohan and executed by a rebel named Yogendra Sukul.'

'Did you know that most of the perpetrators of Maulania have been arrested?'

'Yes, I have heard. What about Yogendra Sukul?'

'No, he is still at large.'

Phanindra made a bitter face. 'Sahib, you need to find him.'

'What can he do? Just a petty rebel.'

'No, Sahib, this man is more dangerous than my whole unit. He can make a lot of trouble.'

'All right, I will look into this Sukul. Phani Babu, do you have any idea or information about Azad?'

Phanindra replied, 'Sahib, if you try your best, you might find God someday, but you will never be able to find Azad. He is different.'

'We will see.'

With special protection, the police first took Phanindra to Borstal Jail. The superintendent lined up around twenty inmates on the ground, mixing revolutionaries with regular criminals. Phanindra walked up and identified eleven of them before anyone had even said their name out loud, and the superintendent noted it down. Next, the police took him to Lahore Central Jail. The superintendent made him walk in front of cells and identify the rebels. He walked on and stopped in front of one cell. The inmate was sitting on the ground, reading a book; his clothes were dirty and too short for his stature. A ray of sunlight came from the little window in the filthy dark cell. The inmate was engrossed in reading. The constable hit the baton on the cell railings and spoke, 'Get up and come forward.'

The unusually tall man stood up and walked towards the railings. His eyes gleamed in the dark cell. He had a jovial smile on his face, which disappeared when he saw Phanindra. After a moment, he said, 'How are you, Phani Babu? I heard they are treating you well.'

Phanindra did not expect this reaction. He was dumbfounded. The superintendent asked, 'Do you identify him?'

Phanindra looked at the ground in shame and muttered in a low voice, 'He is Bhagat Singh.'

Phanindra asked, 'Are you not angry, Bhagat?'

'Why should I be angry? It is not me that you have betrayed, Phani Babu.'

'What do you mean? I have turned approver against you.'

Bhagat Singh turned his head in denial and pointed his finger to the ground. 'Not me, not HSRA, you have betrayed her.' And he turned and walked inside to continue his reading.

Phanindra had expected a ferocious, angry reaction from Bhagat Singh, but his composure, calm smile and accusation of betraying Mother India felt more bitter than anything else. For a moment, he thought of taking his statement back and joining Bhagat Singh. It was the right thing to do. But then he saw the dirty clothes and the filthy cell. He loved himself more than he loved his country. Besides, the British would never keep Bhagat Singh alive to mock him. He knew there was no turning back from this path.

Phanindra then identified Batukeshwar Dutt in another cell.

Dutt asked, 'How are you, Phani Babu? I hear you are now promoted as king's witness.'

Phanindra replied, 'Dutt, you will not understand; I have a family to look after.'

'Ah, family! Yes. Do you know Bramhadutt Mishra?'

'Yes, he is from Cawnpore. I remember, he was your classmate from D.A.V. college. Now he is arrested.'

'Do you know what happened to Bramhadutt Mishra after the arrest?'

'Yes, he also became an approver.'

'Phani Babu, you trust the British too much. You don't know anything. Enquire around.' Dutt laughed mockingly and turned his back.

Phanindra returned to Fort Jail. He called the constable, Bankelal, who was from Bihar and known to him, and asked, 'What happened to Bramhadutt?'

The constable looked around and spoke in a hushed voice, 'You are not supposed to know this, but Bramhadutt has withdrawn his statement.'

'What? That is impossible. How did that happen?' Phanindra almost shouted.

The constable widened his eyes and spoke, 'Keep it down, Phani Babu. The case is not over yet. Bramhadutt agreed to become an approver after watching the interrogation techniques of CID. He also gave a detailed statement. But his wife sent a message through his mother. The message turned everything upside down.'

'What was the message?'

'The wife stated that she considers herself a widow, and the mother said she thinks her son died on the same day he betrayed Bhagat Singh and Azad. If a man cannot fulfil his promise to his comrades, why should a family rely on him?'

Phanindra asked, 'Then what happened?'

'Bramhadutt never expected such a response from his family. He withdrew his statement when he saw that his family was deserting him.'

'Damn, Bhagat Singh.'

'But don't worry, Phani Babu, you have your own team of approvers. Jai Gopal, Hans Raj Vohra, Manmohan, all these are following in your footsteps.'

'They are all insignificant. Nobody has the amount of information I do. Tell me, I heard a rumour about Sukhdev. Is he also turning into an approver?'

'Phani Babu, although I am a Bihari, I have lived my whole life in Lahore. Bhagat Singh and Sukhdev are like brothers. Everyone knows that. After being arrested along with Jai Gopal, he learned that Jai Gopal had become an approver. This infuriated Sukhdev so much. I don't know why.'

Phanindra said, 'Because he recruited Jai Gopal into the party. He trusted him blindly.'

'So, along with Jai Gopal, Sukhdev also started giving detailed information about the party and activities. After two or three sessions, he asked for some time with Jai Gopal to discuss something.'

'Then, what happened?'

'Sukhdev was giving information to earn the trust of the police officers to get some time with Jai Gopal, only to strangle him to death for betrayal. However, the officer got a hint of his plan and never let Jai Gopal close to Sukhdev. For that reason, you and Manmohan are being kept in separate buildings here.'

Phanindra remembered the cold stare of Sukhdev and felt an eerie feeling of a hand on his neck. He checked his neck. It was cold and sweaty.

The constable said, 'Relax, Phani Babu, nothing will happen to you.' Then he went away.

At lunch, Manmohan met Phanindra; they sat together in a corner, holding their plates. After ensuring that no one was listening to them, Phanindra asked, 'How did you get arrested?'

'Dada, as soon as I heard about your arrest, I went in to surrender myself.'

'You, fool, you could have stayed out and helped.'

'How, Dada? I am not good at these things without you. The police came looking for me after the Maulania dacoity. I was able to avoid them by hiding. But I heard about you the next day, and all my courage melted away.'

'Listen, I have also made a deal on your behalf with CID. If you become an approver, they will absolve us of all crimes. Also, we will get some land and money as a reward.'

'That is very good, Dada. Khan Sahib gave me a hint of it. He also expects me to become an approver in the Maulania dacoity case.'

'So what? Just do as Khan Sahib says. All these boys are going to die or rot in prison anyway. We have to think about our future.'

'Have you heard about Bramhadutt?'

'Yes, but don't have any second thoughts; we cannot go back now. Bramhadutt is nobody in the party. I am a member of the central committee, a provincial head. After what we are doing for the government, they will take care of us.'

'Whatever you say, Dada, you brought me into all this; now I will follow your word,'

'Trust me, it is good for you. Have you heard of any older revolutionaries?'

'No, Dada. Why?'

'Because they all die young.'

Chapter 5

June 1929

The jungle was dense and dark, with tall trees casting long shadows that stretched across the forest floor. The only sound was the rustle of leaves as a light breeze blew through the trees. Amid this silence, Yogendra Sukul waited at an ancient, ruined Shiva temple in the dense Udepur jungle for his fellow revolutionaries to arrive.

As he waited, Yogendra couldn't help but feel a sense of unease. His closest associates had been captured, and his once-secret hideout was now compromised. He knew that the police were on the hunt for him and the remaining rebels, and he could feel their presence in the air like a looming threat. Now the command of Bihar for HSRA had fallen on his shoulders. He heard the sound of footsteps approaching, and he tensed up. Did they belong to his fellow revolutionaries or the police? He held his breath, waiting to find out.

But as the figures emerged from the trees, Yogendra's fear turned to relief. His trusted comrades Rambinod Singh, Kapil Deo Rai, Nanku Singh, Gulali Sonar, Ramparikshan Sharma and others appeared at the ruined temple.

'Baba, what's going on?' asked Kapil Deo Rai, as he sat beside him.

'The police have arrested almost all our people,' Yogendra announced, his voice heavy with emotion. 'Manmohan and Phani Babu have betrayed us. They gave the police the names and addresses of all our revolutionaries, and now we're all in danger.'

No one spoke for a few minutes, then Yogendra asked, 'Rambinod, what is the news from Lahore?'

'Baba, the news is not good. Phani Babu and Manmohan have disgraced us in front of the nation.'

Kapil Deo asked, 'Baba, what should we do now? We have lost the people's trust.'

Nanku Singh said, 'I don't think any party members will trust us anymore.'

Yogendra said, 'I am leaving from here to meet Azad. I pray that he listens to what we loyal Bihari rebels have to say. Phani Babu and Manmohan have indeed committed the worst betrayal, but that does not mean everything is over. We are still alive and free.'

'But for how long, Baba?'

'As long as we stay focused and work for the nation, we are free.'

'What can we do now, Baba? More than 90 per cent of our comrades are in prison. The police are hunting us like hounds. We do not have any weapons or money.'

Yogendra looked in the distance, took a long breath and said, 'A few years ago, I met Azad on the banks of the Chambal River. The government had destroyed all the senior leadership of HRA in one blow. They hanged Bismil, Ashfaq, Roshan Singh and Rajendranath Lahiri. The rest of the leaders and members were imprisoned for life. Only Azad and Kundan Lal could escape. I used to work for the Diwan Sahib. I asked Azad the same question you are asking me now. What can we do now? When everything appears to be over?'

Rambinod eagerly asked, 'What did Panditji say?'

'Panditji smiled, put a hand on my shoulder and said, "We have a debt to pay Mother India. We cannot rest or lose hope. As long as blood flows in my veins, it is not over. Even if they kill me. I will be undefeated."'

'He is a legend!'

Yogendra said, 'He was alone back then. He strove hard and raised another batch of young men to die for the country. He started HSRA, which is bigger and better than HRA. He found gems like Bhagat Singh, Sukhdev, Rajguru and Jatin Das. If you think that HSRA is finished, you are wrong. The god of revolution is still breathing fire. It will take the whole of Europe to defeat a commander like Azad.'

Rambinod said, 'Baba, say the word; there is no turning back now.'

Yogendra said, 'Azad has entrusted us with the task of collecting revenue for the party and for defraying the expenses of the Lahore Conspiracy Case. We will keep doing our work as we used to before. Let me talk to our commander and assure him of our loyalty. The Bihari blood is not filled with betrayal. It is time to prove our worth. We will fight for Bhagat Singh and Azad until death.'

'What about Phani Babu?' Kapil Deo asked.

'I will shoot that bastard in the head any time with pleasure. He thinks he can walk away after betraying us. Where will he go? After the trial, he will either return to Bettiah or, if he is wise enough, go to London. Let us pledge something. Even if he goes to London, we will find and kill him. You cannot betray the Tiger and live in the jungle unscathed. There is no place for traitors in free India.'

Rambinod spoke. 'Baba, what are your orders?'

'Find new recruits for the party. Identify locations and landlords for dacoities. We need to keep the money flowing, even at the cost of our blood. Gentlemen, let us get back to work. It is our responsibility now to run the show.'

Yogendra then went straight to his village, Jalalpur. He was a respected figure in the area. After Maulania, he was being pursued by the police, so he had to sneak into the village at night. Two young men got the news from someone that Yogendra Baba was back at home. Around 4 a.m., the young men dared to knock on his door. It was still pitch-dark. They waited for a minute and tapped again. But there was no response.

They looked at each other in disappointment. Then ice-cold barrels of two pistols were placed on both their necks from behind. A firm voice came, 'Do not move if you want to live. State your name.'

The taller and fair one stuttered, 'Sinhasan Sukul' and the other one with a Gandhi cap said 'Baikunth Sukul.'

'Why did you come here at this time?'

Sinhasan answered, 'To meet you, Yogendra Baba. We wanted to see you.'

'For what?'

Baikunth exclaimed, 'Baba, we want to join your party to fight against the British Empire.'

Yogendra said, 'Baikunth, you are the elder son of Rambihari, am I right?'

'Yes, Baba.'

'I knew your father; he was a good man. After your father's death, your job is to care for your family. Do not think about joining the armed revolution.'

'But Baba, please listen to us,' Baikunth requested.

'All right, wait here for five minutes. Let me get my belongings. If you know I am here, then the police will also get to know the news soon. I have to leave.'

Both waited in silence. Yogendra came back with a worn-out khadi bag. He started to walk towards Aamrai, the forest of mango trees. For a while, no one spoke.

Sinhasan asked, 'Baba, we want to join your party.'

'Why?'

'To fight.'

'Do you know how to fight?'

'No. . .'

'Then learn and come back to me.'

Sinhasan remained silent. Baikunth said, 'Baba, I consider Bhagat Singh as my idol. I want to be like him.'

'Son, it is not easy to become Bhagat Singh. You will have to sacrifice everything dear to you.'

'I am ready.'

'Are you really?'

Sinhasan courageously said, 'You can test us if you want.'

By this time, they had reached the Narayani River. Yogendra turned to Sinhasan and said, 'All right, give me your hand.'

Sinhasan put his right palm in the firm hand of Yogendra. In the blink of an eye, Yogendra took out a knife from his bag and tried to make a cut in Sinhasan's hand. The latter withdrew his hand instantly.

Sinhasan then looked towards Yogendra and saw the utter disappointment in his eyes. Yogendra said, 'Pathetic. Don't dare to utter the name of Bhagat Singh.'

Then Yogendra ran and jumped straight into the Narayani River. The Himalayan river flowed in June with all its might, roaring like an industrial machine. It looked as though a stone thrown into the flow would break into pieces.

Around three kilometres south of Jalalpur, at Basanta Ghat, Yogendra quickly emerged from the river. He turned back and bowed to the river. At that instant, someone popped out of the water. It was Baikunth.

Yogendra smiled and gave him a hand. After catching his breath, he said, 'Baba, you did not test me.'

Yogendra said, 'Baikunth, your test is over; you passed.'

Baikunth stood, his eyes shining. 'Can I join you now?'

'Not now, son; the time is not right. You are too raw to enter this now. Just keep an eye on the events, and train yourself to fight. You have proved that you have the heart to do anything. Now train your body to sustain anything. Become a soldier worthy of fighting the mightiest empire in the history of humanity.'

'Baba, who will teach me to fight?'

'Don't worry, I will. Meet me here tomorrow at the same time.'

Baikunth bowed down to touch Yogendra's feet.

Yogendra stopped him midway and said, 'Son, in HSRA, everyone is equal. You should respect someone not for their age but for their work.'

'Baba, I want to ask you something. How is Bhagat doing in prison?'

'One who has found freedom in his heart, no one can bind him in chains. Bhagat is not an individual but an idea. This is a two-pronged strategy; we are fighting from outside, and he is fighting from the prison. Although his fight is tough and will result in only one thing—glorious death. He will bring Inquilab to the people in his own way. The rest of us must stand firm and do our duty towards the country. Mark my words, the coming generations of this nation will remember us only because we lived and worked shoulder to shoulder with legends like Azad and Bhagat Singh.

'Now, don't go back by swimming. And come tomorrow.'

Baikunth reached home after walking by the banks of the Narayani. The roaring of the water silenced all his thoughts. There was an elated smile on his face. He went home; his wife, Radhika Devi, was preparing lunch. She was worried about him. Baikunth and Radhika were married when they were very young children. She came to live with him ceremonially only after puberty. Baikunth, who was the same age as Bhagat Singh, completed his primary education at Jalalpur and, on that basis, got a job as a primary teacher at a nearby village called Mathurapur.

Although his education was basic, he was fond of reading anything he could find in the vernacular. Like all the men of his generation, he was obsessed with the charisma of a man called Mahatma Gandhi. Gandhi had launched the non-cooperation movement in 1920. Through the boycott of British organizations, products and laws as well as the promotion of indigenous goods and self-government, it sought to peacefully challenge British colonial power. As part of the movement, Baikunth adopted khadi for life. He worked passively for the Congress for a few years after the non-cooperation movement. But as an avid observer, he was exposed to revolutionary activities around him.

He was a fan of the *Pratap* newspaper, run by Ganesh Shankar Vidyarthi of Cawnpore. He used to wait for the newspaper and cherish especially the short biographies it published of revolutionaries from 1857 to the Kakori case. Later he learned that all these short bio sketches of legends were written by Bhagat Singh under a pseudonym.

Baikunth understood the psyche of the man who revered all the heroes who fought and died for the motherland. Almost every adult in the village knew about the involvement of Yogendra in the revolutionary circle. The village was populated mainly by Sukul families. They all addressed Yogendra as Baba out of the utmost respect. The previous year he learned that Bhagat Singh visited Jalalpur village to meet Yogendra Baba. Baikunth cursed his stars for not having been able to meet him.

In April 1929, he got hold of a newspaper with the photo of a man in a stylish felt hat printed on the front page. It was the day Baikunth saw the face of the god of revolution. He bought multiple copies of the newspaper and read every word a hundred times.

Radhika Devi saw the strange smile on Baikunth's face and asked, 'What happened?'

Baikunth opened his trunk, grabbed a newspaper with a photo of Bhagat Singh, sat before her, and said, 'Radhika, today I have found the purpose of my life.'

Radhika knew Baikunth's obsession with Bhagat Singh. That smile and the sight of the newspaper with the photo worried her. She asked, 'Just tell me what happened?'

Baikunth narrated the incident and told her that Yogendra Baba was ready to train him.

She asked, 'Are you going to join HSRA?'

'Not yet. Baba said, only when the time is right. After my training is complete.'

'Do you know what happens to armed rebels under this government?' Tears welled up in her eyes.

Baikunth understood her concern; he came closer to her, held her hand full of wheat flour, and said, 'Radha, don't worry; I am not going to do anything rash. I know you are my responsibility, but you and I still have a duty towards our country. Don't we?'

'Baikunth, I adore your patriotism but not at the cost of your life.'

'I understand.' At the same time, he looked away from her face.

She held his face towards her and voiced her concerns. 'Promise me you will not do anything without telling me.'

'Radha, this is not how it works. The revolutionary cannot put his family before the nation. I will not make false promises to you just to reassure you. I am sorry, I should have sought your permission before, but now I have pledged my life to Mother India.'

Tears rolling down her cheeks, she said, 'I understand your feelings very well. But along with Mother India, you also have a duty towards me. I am not saying that you should take my permission before any action. I trust you with my life and soul. I just want you to tell me what you are going to do. I promise I will never stand between you and your goal.'

'Then I promise to keep you informed of anything and everything, my love.' Baikunth embraced her and wiped her tears.

It rained heavily throughout the night. The Narayani River swelled to the brim and was almost threatening to enter the village. Yogendra reached Basanta ghat to find Baikunth, dressed in dhoti and kurta and drenched in water from head to toe, waiting for him.

Yogendra began immediately. 'Baikunth, there are three basic things you have to learn. Fighting with bare hands, fighting with weapons from the lathi to the sword and training in firearms from pistols to bombs.'

'Yes, I am ready.'

'I have found you a tutor at Muzaffarpur and arranged your stay with him until you are ready to fight. Now, I will teach you how to use my favourite weapon, the khukri.'

A broad smile appeared on Baikunth's face.

'Let us begin with how to draw the weapon first.' He picked out two humongous khukri knives from his bag. One had a wooden sheath, and the other had a leather scabbard.

Yogendra handed the wooden sheath to Baikunth and said, 'Tuck it into your waistline and draw the weapon.'

Baikunth tucked it into his waistline on the left side. Then he used his right hand and tried to pull out the machete, but it did not come out fully. The blade was stuck in the middle.

Yogendra said, 'You are dead if you cannot draw the weapon swiftly.'

Embarrassed, Baikunth pushed the blade inside, placed one hand on the sheath's lower side, and pulled once again with force. This time the blade did come out but with a scratching sound.

Yogendra said, 'Son, never hold the sheath from the lower side; it is where the blade is sharpened. If you hold and pull, the cutting edge might break, or it can come out, cutting the sheath altogether and making it useless. Give it to me.'

Then Yogendra showed him how to hold the blade from above and softly draw the machete like a feather. Yogendra gave it back and ordered, 'Practise.'

Baikunth practised a few times. He liked the feeling of the blade coming out swiftly, making a whistling sound. How the raindrops slid over the shiny steel blade. Then Yogendra handed him another khukri in a leather scabbard and asked, 'Place both khukris on either side and try to draw them at the same time.'

Baikunth did as instructed and mastered it in a few attempts. Yogendra was impressed. Then both of them walked towards a little patch of dense bamboo trees. Yogendra took a khukri and, in the blink of an eye, made an uppercut on the bamboo, and placed it back in the sheath. After a second, the bamboo broke into two. Baikunth's eyes widened at the feat. Everything had happened so quickly, he'd barely been able to see it.

Then Yogendra asked Baikunth to practise. But every time Baikunth tried, his knife got stuck in the bamboo or only cut through it partially.

Baikunth asked, 'Baba, it seems my knife has lost its sharpness. May I borrow yours to practise?'

Yogendra smiled and handed over his blade. Nevertheless, Baikunth failed. Yogendra said, 'Know your weapon like the palm of your hand. Consider it as an extension of your body. Breathe with the blade. Know every curve and imperfection of the steel. Move the dagger as smoothly as you move your hand to eat a meal. When you eat, your hand doesn't go to your nose, nor does it go to your eye. It stops right at your lips where you want it to. Exercise control over your weapon. Practise.'

Baikunth practised for an hour. Then he took out the lunch, cooked by Radhika that he had brought along, and offered it to his guru. Yogendra happily ate with him.

Baikunth asked, 'Baba, may I ask you something?'

'Yes, go on.'

'Swords and khukris are the weapons of the past. The British won our country with modern weapons like guns, rifles and cannons. So why do we train with such ancient arms or learn hand-to-hand combat? Why not focus on guns?'

'Baikunth, what you say is partially true. The technical superiority of weapons matters only in direct war. But we revolutionaries are fighting an indirect war where the number and power are skewed towards our enemy. We are short of resources, men and weapons. Still, we hope and fight to win. Training in hand-to-hand combat or with knives is necessary because it is the only proven method to make a man into a soldier.'

'How?'

'When you train with khukris, you practise strikes on the adversary. At the same time, your mind prepares subconsciously to get stabbed or cut in the fight. It makes your body ready for the injury. Even if you get hurt, your body does not go into shock in a fight. A steady mind is essential for revolution. You never know when or where the police dogs will attack you or when you will be arrested or shot.'

'Understood, but what about guns?'

'Guns and bullets are scarce in the party and only reserved for direct action. You will get an airgun with darts to practise and even a real one, if given a mission. Listen, how do you think the British won over India?'

'By modern weapons, guns, artillery and bombs.'

'No, you are wrong. Do you know how many actual British men are serving in India?'

'Yes, around one lakh.'

'And how much is the population of the country?'

'Around 30–35 crore.'

'Tell me again, how do they win, and how do they rule?'

Baikunth was dumbfounded. He did not say anything.

'All right, tell me, how did they win the Plassey?'

'The military general of Siraj ud-Daula, a man named Mir Jafar, betrayed the Nawab and helped the British to win the war.'

'Yes, but it is not that simple. Siraj thought he was going to win; you know why? Because Siraj had a well-trained army of 50,000 men, forty powerful cannons and ten dangerous war elephants. But the British army numbered only 3000. In addition, they had lost the fort. The battle was on the open ground. There was no chance that Siraj was going to lose.'

'Then, Baba, why did he lose?'

'Baikunth, if we want to achieve freedom in the near future, we must study the phenomenon of betrayal and the community of traitors very carefully. I have learned it the hard way. Mir Jafar, along with Jagat Seth, who was a wealthy merchant, formed a conspiracy with Robert Clive. Mir Jafar, who had a significant number of soldiers under his command, mixed them with the loyalists of Siraj. When the actual war began, the followers of the traitors did nothing. It led to great confusion and fear among the ranks of Siraj, and then a great massacre followed. The battle lasted for eleven hours, and only fifty-seven men of Clive's force were killed. But on Siraj's side, no one kept a count.'

'I understand, Baba. Just as Jaichand Rathod betrayed Prithviraj Chauhan, Mir Jafar was responsible for the onset of slavery under the British empire.'

'Not only Jaichand and Jafar but also the people who support such traitors or do nothing are responsible for the damage done to this country. British men are not our only enemy; the traitors among us are as well. It is time to identify them and take action.'

'Baba, why did Phani Babu betray the revolutionaries?'

'Baikunth, betrayal has become such a chronic disease in our blood; I hope I can find a solution to weed it out in this life. Nothing has harmed Indian revolutionaries more than approvers. The uprising of 1857 failed because of traitors like Gaekwad. The plan of Ghadar was leaked to the British just a day before the uprising. A rat in the fold gave away all the secrets about Kakori and now someone from our province has gathered the guts to betray Azad and Bhagat Singh.'

'Does it happen due to some inner conflict?'

'No, no, it is not like that. Two kinds of people become approvers after being arrested by the police. Some get scared after watching the inhuman physical torture of revolutionaries. They generally give information which is essential for their survival. They become approvers to save themselves. HSRA has an unspoken directive to forgive such weaklings.'

'And the other type?'

'The other kind is dangerous. Without bothering about the torture or taking time to become approver, they directly bargain with the government for rewards in cash and kind in return for information. For greed, they give away everything; they risk the lives of everyone involved in the revolution. Our own Phani Babu is the king of this category.'

'Understood. Is there anything we can do about it?'

'What will you do if you see a venomous snake in the middle of your house, ready to strike your loved ones?'

'Crush its head with one stroke of the lathi.'

'Exactly. There is little that can be done now. But we will be looking for the opportunity. It is high time that Indians recognize this; there will be no place for traitors in free India.'

After lunch, Yogendra parted ways with Baikunth, gave him his new tutor's address and promised to visit him regularly to check on his improvement.

The next day, Baikunth packed his bags, left a leave note for the school headmaster and went to Muzaffarpur. In the town, he went to the Tilak Maidan; it was around 6 p.m. Approximately fifty youngsters were gathered on the ground, each holding an oiled bamboo. They were standing in five neat rows, equidistant from one another. All of them were wearing white shirts, white trousers and Gandhi topees. Someone standing in front was teaching them lathi battle tactics. The leader wore a khaki shirt with two pockets, khaki shorts with knee-length socks and basic canvas shoes. On his command, all of them waved the lathi. Baikunth waited until the exercise was over. It was almost dark. It seemed as if it might rain at any time. Clouds had gathered in the sky.

Everyone hurried out of the ground, expecting rain as soon as the session ended. After making enquiries, Baikunth went to find the tutor. But the tutor had started walking away. He followed the khaki-clad formidable man, but it was hard to keep up with him. The man walked very briskly. During the exercise, he had not been able to see his face. The leader entered the narrow lanes of Muzaffarpur and soon vanished in a dark alley before he could meet him. Baikunth was disappointed. Now he had nowhere to stay in this town. Also, as per the instructions from Yogendra, he could not enquire about this man with the general public.

Dejected, Baikunth walked a little further. Suddenly, a whooshing sound came from behind, and a lathi swept him off his feet. He stumbled and fell to the ground; before he knew what was happening, the lathi had separated his bag from his shoulder and thrown it almost ten feet away.

When he tried to get up, the lathi came again and hit his legs, causing him to stay down. This time, he was hurt.

A hoarse voice came from the dark corner in front of him, 'Who are you?'

'Who are you to ask me? Why did you hit me?'

'Because you are following someone with a khukri in your bag.'

Then Baikunth understood; someone had seen the outline of his khukri in his cloth sling bag and reported it to the leader.

He raised his arms in defence and said, 'Listen, I did not mean any harm to anyone.'

'Tell me your name.'

'Baikunth Sukul.'

'Why are you here?'

'To meet someone.'

'Who?'

'I cannot tell you the name unless I know yours.'

'Who sent you?'

'No one. Why are you hitting me? Tell me your name.'

'Well, I will not say my name unless you make me say it.'

'What do you mean?'

'Pick up your bag, take out the khukri and fight.'

'But I do not want to fight.'

Another blow came and hit him on the chest, 'I will not ask again.'

Baikunth cried out in pain, picked up his bag, scrambled in the dark and took out the khukri. The blade almost shone in the darkness. Baikunth said, 'Look, this is dangerous; if the dagger hits you, it will do much harm. I repeat, I do not want to fight.'

The man in the darkness came forward; he was over six feet tall, in his late forties, with a trimmed full-grey beard, grey hair combed backwards and a pointed moustache, and powerful chestnut-coloured eyes. He took the fighting stance, holding his lathi in both hands, raised above his head, and asked, 'Are you ready?'

Baikunth bit his lip and said, 'I am.'

In the blink of an eye, the lathi came down. Baikunth ducked and slid his hand in the air by facing the blunt edge of the knife in front. The lathi came again and hit his wrist. The khukri fell down and Baikunth held the hurt wrist in pain.

The leader took the stand again and said mockingly, 'I thought you said you were ready.'

Baikunth picked up the khukri again and stepped back to take a stand. He took a deep breath and attacked the leader like a lightning bolt.

The lathi came again in a horizontal sweep. Baikunth stepped back. The lathi came up, targeting his chin. Once again, he jumped and waved it off. The khukri moved and caught the khaki shirt of the leader by its end.

Then the lathi rose and came down, aiming for his forearm. Instantly Baikunth switched hands, swept the khukri in an uppercut and before the lathi could strike a blow, he cut the bamboo into two pieces, slicing through it like cheese.

The leader smiled. He dropped the half of the lathi he was holding and said, 'My name is Ranendranath Roy Choudhary. Follow me, Baikunth; I was waiting for you.'

Baikunth smiled and followed. They went into a small two-room house. Ranendranath lit a kerosene lamp and offered Baikunth a glass of water.

The leader smiled warmly and said, 'You can call me Guruji. I run the Seva Dal camp around here and have received directions from Yogendra. He has very high hopes for you.'

'I pray that I can be worthy of his faith in me. I watched the exercise, and it was impressive. I have never seen anything like it. Forgive my ignorance; may I know what exactly Seva Dal is?'

'It is India's largest organized non-violent militia.'

'Non-violent but militia? I do not understand.'

'After the failure of non-cooperation, Congress did the flag Satyagraha in Nagpur, where many of the arrested activists tendered apologies to the British for fear of torture in prison. But some Congressmen, like our chief organizer Narayan Hardikar, did not yield. His idea was to establish a force of volunteers who would be trained in physical training, organizing capabilities and services to the Congress and the nation by being outside politics. To impart a sense of discipline and patriotism, we run Seva Dal across the country. We keep it non-violent as followers of Gandhiji, not to trouble the legalities.'

'Interesting, but if you are a Congressperson and follower of non-violence, why do you support revolutionaries?'

'Son, you have no idea who in Congress supports revolutionaries. We all have one aim but different paths, although I never suggest that anyone should join an armed revolution. For the brief period that you will be with me, I will try to convince you to leave Yogendra and join Congress every day.'

Baikunth laughed and said, 'Good luck with converting me. Let me ask you the most important thing: Will you teach me to fight like you?'

'Yes, you are here for that reason. You will live with me until your training is complete. Your guru has tested your perseverance; I have seen you have a heart to fight. But that is not enough to be a revolutionary.'

'What else is needed, Guruji?'

'An insane drive to die for this land. Do you want to die for this country?'

Chapter 6

July 1929

As soon as Yogendra got the much-awaited encrypted message, he travelled to Cawnpore by third class from Muzaffarpur. He was overtly conscious and looked all around him before taking any step. Right then, Yogendra was one of the most wanted men in Bihar. He moved around in the night to avoid any undue attention.

On the train, Yogendra rehearsed what to say when confronted by Azad about Phanindra's treachery. He felt as if a stone had been placed on his heart. For once in his life, he was embarrassed to look into Azad's eyes.

He reached the given address and waited in a nearby garden until dusk. Once the streets were deserted and he was sure that no one was around watching or patrolling, Yogendra moved like a cat towards the specified door on the first floor. After a rhythmic tap, he was welcomed inside. There were three men standing with their arms behind their backs in the room. Once his identity was verified, Yogendra was led to the inner chamber where commander-in-chief Azad was talking with Bhagwati Charan Vohra.

Before Yogendra could speak, Azad got up and embraced him. Bhagwati also welcomed him with a warm smile. Yogendra was dumbfounded by this treatment. He returned the smile but with some embarrassment. Eyes on the floor, Yogendra said, 'Panditji, I am here to apologize on behalf of Bihar. What Phani Babu and Manmohan did is unimaginable and detestable. We are still loyal to the cause and ready to sacrifice our lives at your command.'

Azad said, 'Yogendra, I did not ask for your apology. It is not supposed to come from you. Don't worry; the party does not hold a grudge against any of your comrades. The wretched traitors are solely responsible for their crimes and will be punished by the party in due time. Come sit with us.'

'Thank you, Panditji; your words have lifted the burden on my soul.'

'Don't worry. Until today it has been a record of sorts; no one recruited by me in HRA or HSRA has turned out to be an approver. Because I don't look for a man driven by ideology; I look for a man driven by action. I look for simpler men. Ideology can be melted away by the heat of police beatings, but blood and sweat cannot.'

Yogendra smiled and asked, 'Bhagwati Bhai, what is the news from Lahore?'

Bhagwati looked grave when he said, 'The news is not good. The Lahore Conspiracy Case trial has begun. The identification parades by approvers are over. But that was expected. The real worry is that Bhagat and Batukeshwar have started a protest by means of fast unto death.'

Yogendra stood up. 'What? Fast unto death? For what?'

Azad remarked, 'The treatment of revolutionaries in prison has always been pathetic. But they crossed the limit this time with our comrades. So, Bhagat demands that the revolutionaries must be treated as political prisoners. They must be given all facilities provided to a political or Anglo-Indian prisoner, like proper food, newspaper, access to books etc.'

Yogendra said, 'But the British will not change their minds. They will treat us like petty criminals. The fast will unnecessarily hamper his health.'

Bhagwati observed, 'Exactly. Bhagat knows this very well. But he is playing very strategically this time. First, he wants to show the country that the revolutionaries can also protest with non-violent means. As you must have seen, all these senior Congress leaders have termed us immature hot-headed young men with no sense of reality. Bhagat wants to break the belief that fasting for a cause is patented by the Congress.'

'What is the second cause?'

'Bhagat wants to underline the importance of armed revolutionaries and their contribution to the freedom struggle, which is often ignored by the masses. He wants the public to learn about the deplorable conditions in which a revolutionary is kept under the Raj; a revolutionary who is as dedicated to the cause as any Congressman but is treated worse than an animal.'

Yogendra exclaimed, 'I sometimes wonder how he can think of such complicated things at such a young age.'

Azad said, 'Still, there is a big problem with this type of protest. What if the British do not budge until . . .'

Bhagwati placed a hand on Azad's shoulder and assured him, 'Panditji, don't worry. Bhagat will manage.'

Azad stood up, walked around restlessly and then said, 'Bhagwati Bhai, it is a gamble. Not only the government but the public will test their patience. I do not want to lose Bhagat.'

Yogendra assured Azad, 'Panditji, we will not lose him. Let us trust him with his fight. You tell me, what are my orders?'

Azad said, 'Yogendra, now as the police are looking for you, your work will become more complex. But now more than ever, we need money to run the party and fund the case. We must keep the public informed and get the best help in the law for Bhagat.'

Yogendra answered, 'Panditji, I will handle it. Do not worry. The revenue for HSRA will not stop under any circumstances. However, if I may, can I ask you something?'

'Yes, go on.'

'What is the party's stand on traitors?'

Bhagwati answered, 'As per the party constitution, there is only one punishment for traitors, the death penalty.'

Azad explained, 'I understand that what Phani Babu has done is the worst betrayal. I have seen the same batch of traitors in the Kakori case. I had warned Bhagat earlier that if he surrendered, this would happen. But now, Phani Babu has become the king's witness. There is little we can do about him.'

Bhagwati said, 'Bhagat surrendered knowing very well that Saunders murder case would be reopened, but he also knew that the police have no proof against him. They cannot make a case against him without evidence.

Now the police are concocting a case by trying to prove that the pistol they found on Bhagat in the Assembly was the same pistol with which he killed Saunders in Lahore. But even that is not sufficient. Bhagat wants the case to run as long as possible to expose the true face of the British Empire. But the problem of traitors has made the situation infinitely more challenging.'

Yogendra asked, 'How? Phani Babu was not present when the assassination happened.'

'Yes, but Jai Gopal and Hans Raj were present. It had been Jai Gopal's duty to identify J.P. Scott; instead, that fool mistook Saunders for Scott and the rest, you know. Hans Raj also knew the detailed plan, and he, too, gave away everything to the police. Now they have an eyewitness and a weapon. Our side is getting weak.'

Yogendra asked, 'Bhagwati Bhai, what is the role of Phani Babu in all this?'

Bhagwati said, 'Phanindra Nath Ghosh is the main villain in this story, Yogendra. Try to understand. Jai Gopal and Hans Raj are nobodies, but Phanindra is a central committee member, a provincial head and the highest position holder of the party. He testifies to something worse than a murder.'

'But what could be worse than a murder?' Yogendra asked.

'A conspiracy against the king. His statement will prove that we have formed a full-fledged armed wing, a stand-alone functioning party aiming to dethrone the king from India. For that, we have done meticulous planning and taken several actions, trained our men, gathered and manufactured arms, and have a nationwide network and protocols with the sole aim of ending the British Raj. That, my friend, is a hundred times more damaging than the murder of a police officer.'

'What will happen next?'

'If Phani Babu goes on to give every minute detail about the party and gives them enough to establish a nationwide conspiracy by HSRA, then the government will hang our brothers. For that, only Phanindra Nath Ghosh will be responsible.'

Azad spat on the ground and said, 'Swine.'

Yogendra asked, 'What about the other traitors who are out? Can we send a message to Phani Babu to take back his statement?'

Bhagwati asked, 'How?'

Yogendra said, 'I remember at the Firoz Shah Kotla meeting, it was decided to punish the Kakori traitors. We could not do it due to other work. But I think if we take action against a Kakori traitor, Phani Babu will get the message and take the statement back.'

Azad smiled, slid the back of his hand over his moustache and said, 'All these years, I have wanted to strangle the traitors who betrayed my mentor, Bismil. I agree; this is the right time to kill some rats.'

Yogendra asked, 'Do you have anyone specific in mind?'

Azad, without hesitating, said, 'Banarsi Lal from Shahjahanpur and Sheo Charan Lal from Agra.'

Yogendra agreed. 'I hate Banarsi Lal.'

Bhagwati asked, 'Panditji, what did he do?'

Azad explained, 'There was a railway contractor at Shahjahanpur called Prem Kishan Khanna; he was a very good friend of Ramprasad Bismil. Khanna had a licensed Mauser pistol which he gave to Bismil for the revolutionary action, along with 150 cartridges. When the Kakori case ran in court, this bastard Banarsi Lal gave all the details of the plans related to the train loot, plus he gave away the identity of Khanna and the secret about the Mauser pistol.'

Yogendra said, 'The court was trying to give maximum punishment to Khanna when Ramprasad Bismil saved his friend and gave a statement that he forged Khanna's signature to purchase cartridges.'

Azad stated, 'Khanna is serving his five-year imprisonment, thanks to Banarsi Lal, and hence, in that region, no one dares to help or sympathize with revolutionaries.'

Yogendra asked, 'Please give me permission to execute that bastard.'

Azad shook his head. 'No, I won't risk my men for the rats. Let us try a new technique.'

Yogendra asked, 'What is the new technique?'

Azad said to Vishwanath Vaishampayan, 'Call Wireless.'

A short, young lad with sparkling eyes and a smirk entered the room. Azad said, 'Yogendra, meet Hansraj; his code name is Wireless. The boy is a scientist.'

Yogendra smiled, and the boy nodded.

Azad said, 'Wireless, suppose I want to kill someone without going into his vicinity . . .?'

'You can throw a grenade from a distance.'

'Not even by going to his town. How should I do it?'

'You can send him a bomb.'

Yogendra laughed. 'What do you mean by sending a bomb? Is he going to blast it himself?'

'No, the bomb will kill him automatically,' Hansraj said.

Azad asked, 'How?'

'I can design a box with a live bomb inside. You can send the box as a parcel by post or by hand. Once the lid is opened, the bomb will explode.'

'Will it not explode if it is not handled properly?'

'No. You can throw it on the ground or play cricket with it. Unless the lid is opened, it will not explode.'

'Are you sure it is possible?' Yogendra said, surprised.

'Yes, of course.'

Bhagwati asked, 'But how can we be sure that only the target will open the box?'

Yogendra said, 'We can send it by registered post, so the person has to sign to receive the parcel.'

Azad looked at Bhagwati and nodded. Then he said, 'Wireless, prepare two boxes. With the utmost care. I don't want any postman to get hurt.'

Wireless replied, 'Yes, Panditji, they will be ready in two days.'

Wireless went away. Yogendra said, 'Panditji, you are a genius; from where do you find such talent?'

Azad smiled. 'This country is full of gems. One just needs the vision to discover them. Now, it must be seen how the bombs work and whether Phani Babu will get the message.'

Wireless prepared the boxes, travelled to Fatehgarh, wrote on the parcel that it was from a cloth merchant, and sent it to Banarsi Lal by post.

The news spread like wildfire. In Fort Prison Lahore, the Bihari constable ran to Phanindra's cell. By now, a table, chair and a soft bed had been provided to him. A small temple in the corner of the cell had also been arranged.

Phanindra was just finishing his morning worship when the constable arrived.

He said, 'Phani Babu, there is bad news for you!'

Phanindra was doing the *arati* of the goddess Kali; he stopped and asked, 'What is it? Did Bhagat Singh escape from prison?'

'No, something worse than that.'

'What can be worse than that? Did the government approve of his stupid demands?'

'No, no, listen to me. There has been a lethal attack on one of the approvers of the Kakori case.'

'What?' The plate in Phanindra's hands almost fell.

'Yes, do you know Banarsi Lal?'

'Yes, he lives in Shahjahanpur. He gave a statement against Bismil. But I think the government has provided him with full security.'

'The security did not matter this time.'

'How did the attack happen? Who did it?'

'This is something no one can pull off. It is too absurd to believe. Banarsi Lal was having lunch when a postman arrived. The government had provided him with a full-time bodyguard. The constable was sitting outside the house under a tree. As the postman approached, the constable stopped him and checked his identification. Then Banarsi came out in surprise to receive the parcel. He signed the paper, and the postman went away. The parcel was from some cloth merchant, but Banarsi did not know any cloth merchants from Fatehgarh. Anyway, after washing his hands, he opened the hard-fitted box, and in an instant, the bomb exploded. The explosion burned more than half of Banarsi, and his palm was withered to the bone. He was grievously injured. Some shrapnel injured the constable as well.'

'Oh, God. Damn, you, Azad.' Phanindra's face went pale, and his hands and legs started trembling. He gathered some courage and asked, 'Is Banarsi alive?'

'I do not know; I guess he is admitted to the hospital; otherwise, we would have known.'

'What should I do now? There is no point in punishing the Kakori approver now, unless HSRA wants to send me a message.'

'That is exactly what I was thinking. Phani Babu, what will you do? Will you take back your statement?'

'No, no, I cannot. But then Azad will not let me live.'

'Phani Babu, you are safe here; do not worry. But after the case is over, what will happen? You chose the bad bargain. You should have asked for a post or home in London like Hans Raj Vohra.'

The constable left. Phanindra did not walk out of his cell that day. He had his lunch and dinner inside.

The next day, the constable returned and said, 'Phani Babu, Banarsi is alive. He is recovering. But there's been another attack.'

'On whom?'

'Sheo Charan Lal, in Agra.'

'Oh my God, what happened?'

'This time, the approver got lucky. After the Banarsi incident, all the officers taking care of approvers in the Kakori case were informed. When the second parcel reached Agra the next day, it was apprehended by the CID team before it was delivered to Sheo Charan Lal.'

Phanindra got up and smiled, his face brightened with hope; he said, 'I knew the government would protect us. There is no limit to the powers of the Raj. Long live the king.'

The constable mockingly replied, 'Yes, Phani Babu, as long as you are here and Azad breathes free air, long live the king.'

Chapter 7

July 1929

Two constables took Phanindra to the interrogation room, where around four police officers and a lawyer were sitting on one side of an extended bench. Khan Bahadur directed Phanindra to sit opposite them. Phanindra took a seat.

Khan Bahadur spoke, 'As per your statement, we are here convened to grant you pardon. Do you accept it?'

'Yes, Sahib.'

'Read and sign this document.'

Phanindra signed the document.

Khan Bahadur stated, 'Tomorrow, you will be taken in a special coach by the team of CID officers to the locations you described in your official statement. You will identify the exact spots where the HSRA worked, acted or stayed at every place. Am I clear?'

'Yes, Sahib.'

'Any questions?'

'About the security . . . I have heard about the attacks on other approvers.'

Khan Bahadur furiously reprimanded, 'What part of special railway coach and team of CID officers did you not understand?'

'Sorry, Sir.'

The following day, Phanindra was taken to Lahore railway station. He was surrounded by ten armed constables. There was a magistrate and a team of four officers accompanying him. They hurried to a particular coach generally reserved for high-ranking officials. The train took them to Delhi first.

They went in the police van to Firoz Shah Kotla Fort. Phanindra showed them the fort ruins in which the covert meeting had been held, and HSRA established. He also led them to a mango tree under which they had waited. The watchman of the fort was arrested by the police. He remembered the group of young men gathering and making speeches. Phanindra led the police to the Maharathi press, where he had rested for a day. The owner of the press was also arrested.

Then the company went to Calcutta. The magistrate asked, 'What happened in Calcutta?'

Phanindra said, 'After killing Saunders Sahib, Bhagat Singh and Rajguru escaped from Lahore by train and came to Calcutta to hide.'

One of the police officers asked, 'How is it possible? I was on duty at Lahore railway station for fifteen days after the murder. I barely slept. Not a rat passed from there without my permission.'

Phanindra said, 'Sahib, you do not know Bhagat Singh. Your people were looking for a shooter whom no one had seen. There are no eyewitnesses to the murder. So taking advantage, Bhagat was dressed as a high-ranking officer with a felt hat, polished cane and expensive overcoat, while Durga Bhabhi accompanied him as his wife; she even had her three-year-old son Shachi with them.'

'Who is Durga Bhabhi?'

'She is a revolutionary, wife of Bhagwati Charan Vohra. The couple have dedicated their family and wealth to the cause.'

'How did Rajguru escape?'

'He was with Bhagat and Durga Bhabhi all the time. He was dressed as their servant. All of them travelled by first class. At Lucknow, they disembarked the train and sent a telegram to Calcutta, before catching another train to Calcutta. Rajguru went south from here.'

'What did the telegram say?'

'Bhagwati Bhai was underground because of warrants against him in the Meerut Conspiracy Case, and also, he was in Calcutta for the Congress session. His wife, Durga Bhabhi, sent a message, saying she was bringing her brother along. In fact, she has no brother. But Bhagwati got the message and made the arrangements.'

'Where did they live? How can so many Punjabis hide in Calcutta?'

Phanindra said, 'There is another female revolutionary called Sushila Didi; she arranged a hideout for them.'

'Where?'

'At the mansion of Seth Sir Chajju Ram.'

An officer exclaimed, 'It is ridiculous; the government has awarded Chajju Ram the title of Sir because of his service to the crown. Why would he entertain rebels?'

Phanindra replied, 'Sahib, patriotism is a strange disease; if you catch it, the most rational man starts to behave like a fanatic. Chajju Ram was not interested in sending his daughter to a missionary school, so he requested a tutor from Kanya Vidyalaya, Jalandhar. The principal sent Sushila Didi. She was given a few rooms to herself in the mansion, and that is where she hid all of them.'

'How did no one suspect them? Bhagat Singh is hard to overlook.'

'He kept himself in a dark room throughout the day, pretending to be sick and lying on a bed. In case anyone enquired, he also had some fake medicine bottles beside the bed. However, he moved out after dark.'

'All right, what did you do here?'

'I introduced him to the bomb-maker, Jatin Das, a.k.a. Robin, on 25 December 1928. It seemed they had already met and were teasing me for no reason. It was planned that Jatin would teach us how to make bombs, and then we would mass-produce them for the action. For a start, he asked us to look for a suitable place in Agra for bomb-making and teaching. Calcutta is a hub for revolutionaries, so for safety reasons, Agra was chosen. We sent someone for the job. But a problem emerged.'

'What problem?'

'The first thing we needed was gun cotton. To make gun cotton we needed mounds of ice. But it was winter, and we knew that ice would not be available in Agra. However, even in winter, ice was available in Calcutta. So it was decided that we would make gun cotton in Calcutta, then carry it to Agra for the rest of the procedure.'

'Where in Calcutta did you make gun cotton?'

'I booked a room on the highest floor of the Arya Samaj Mandir where Kanwal Nath Tiwari, an accused in this case, was residing. Jatin gave us a list of things required, and Bhagat gave us the money.'

'Then?'

'Kanwal Nath and I went to College Square and purchased the items. We did not purchase all the items from one place to avoid suspicion. On the appointed day, Bhagat Singh arrived on time, and I went to Bango Basi College to bring Jatin Dada. He gave me two bombshells, and I handed them over to Bhagat. Kanwal Nath brought around 15–18 kg of ice. Jatin Dada showed us how to make gun cotton. Then by chance, the property owner came to visit us. There was some ice on a plate. He asked, "What are you doing with ice in such cold weather?" Kanwal Nath replied, "Our friend here has a high fever; we are using it on his head." Somehow, we saved the day by hiding the moist gun cotton in our pockets.'

The police later arrested the property owner and took his statement as well.

The officer asked, 'All right, what next? What happened to those two empty bombshells?'

'Next, the party headquarters was shifted to Agra with the sole aim of preparing bombs.'

The same evening, the CID team and Phanindra boarded a train to Agra. Phanindra took them to the Nuri Gate area in the city and pointed out a two-storey house. Phanindra said, 'This is Hing ki Mandi house, belonging to Bharosi Lal. The upper floor was rented by us for ten rupees per month. This house was used for manufacturing explosives from January to March 1929.'

Immediately the police sealed the property and arrested Bharosi Lal.

Next, Phanindra directed them towards another house a short walk away from Hing ki Mandi. 'This is Nai ki Mandi,' he said. 'We used it as our residence for a rent of thirteen rupees per month.'

The officer asked, 'Who rented this and how?'

'Gaya Prasad, who had a clinic and was in charge of headquarters at Ferozepur, sold all his medicine stock, came here and rented this house from the owner . . .'

The magistrate noted the information and asked, 'Describe your stay and work here in detail.'

Phanindra thought for a minute and then said, 'Sahib, I can keep talking about our stay here for the rest of the day. Since you asked, let me elaborate on everything I experienced here. I don't know exactly what will be helpful to you.'

'Go on.'

'I went back to Bettiah from Calcutta and arrived here in January when I received an encrypted message from the party. It was raining heavily on the night I reached Nai ki Mandi. Somehow in the dark, I was able to locate the address. In the unbearable cold, I was drenched in water. In a hurry, I forgot the tapping signal on the door. The door opened, and I was greeted by a revolver.

'It was the middle of the night, and Bhagat Singh was on sentry duty that night. He welcomed me inside and asked me why I did not tap the door using the code. I was shaking in the cold. He understood and lit some coal for warmth and gave me new clothes. There were three rooms; in each room, four or five men slept on the ground on dhotis or newspapers.

'I asked Bhagat, "Do you have anything to eat? I am hungry."

'Bhagat replied, "There is nothing left. You have to wait until morning."

'For the rest of the night, I had to sleep on a newspaper shivering in the cold on an empty stomach. Moreover, all of them were living in such unbearable, poor conditions. The clothes were dirty, and the food was terrible. It was so unappetizing that the mere sight of it made one's hunger vanish. There were no proper utensils to cook the food.

'Mind you, only Bhagat Singh and I came from affluent families. We were not used to such poverty. It was intolerable for me. One day, Bhagat showered all kinds of nawabi superlative adjectives on the food, as if he were dining with some nawab or king, to make everyone feel good. One day he gathered some money and bought proper utensils to cook and eat.'

A police officer asked, 'If they were such terrible conditions, then why did you stay?'

'Sahib, you will not understand the passion for Inquilab and the kind of men who lived here. Although I am an approver now, still, this was the best time of my life.'

'Best time living like stray dogs. Tell me, what else did you do here?'

'We discussed national topics, read serious books, debated, played cards for leisure or just sat in the moonlight enjoying the sight of the Taj Mahal. At times,

Bhagat Singh would get lost in his world of dreams for hours and say nothing.

'There was a joker amongst us, Bhagwan Das Mahore; you have not caught him yet. He has a massive build, and Bhagat always teased him as a great Hanumanji or a missing link in Darwin's theory of evolution. But despite his rough appearance, he has the voice of a trained singer. Bhagat would always tease him but then request him to sing; he used to sing a Marathi song, *Raja Kuthe Guntala*, a melody for the soul. I remember once, we were sitting near the Taj Mahal, and the sharpshooter Raghunath, alias M, once composed a couplet, and recited it before Bhagat Singh.

'Bhagat took out his revolver, handed it to Raghunath, and said, "Brother, shoot me in the head but never attempt poetry."

'I remember we laughed for hours after this.

'Sometimes Bhagat Singh used to sing in his raw voice; he was not a singer like Bhagwan, but his words pierced the heart; he sang 'Mera Rang De Basanti Chola'. Sometimes he sang lamentations from *Heer–Ranjha*.'

'What kind of music did Azad listen to?'

Phanindra said, 'Panditji was more interested in words than melodies. He often requested Bhagwan to sing some Bundelkhandi songs, which I did not understand. Once, I was assigned some task and returned to the banks of the Yamuna on a moonlit night, where Bhagat Singh was singing *Sarfaroshi ki tamanna ab hamare dil mein hai*, and Panditji was sitting in front of him with his eyes closed, tears rolling down his cheeks. The song belonged to his mentor, Ramprasad Bismil. There was no one else in sight. I did not dare to disturb them. I, too, sat there and listened to Bhagat. It was like sitting in a temple when God himself is singing.'

The magistrate said, 'Enough about the lifestyle; let us come to their activities.'

Phanindra's eyes were moist. He wiped them with his palm, exhaled a long breath, and said, 'As I said, Jatin Das, whose code names are Masterji and Robin, taught us how to make bombs here. After preparing the chemicals required for the bombs, Jatin Das arrived in Agra on 14 February. Then he began mixing the chemicals in the required proportion. It was decided that one of us must learn the process with all due attention to replicate it without bothering Jatin Das.

'Two empty bombshells were taken to Lahore by Sukhdev, who tried to replicate it there with some blacksmith. I guess the police caught Sukhdev through the link of the same blacksmith. Meanwhile, a plan was formed to rescue Yogesh Chatterji, a Kakori revolutionary, from police custody. He was stationed in Agra lock-up and would be transferred to Lucknow in two days. There was a meeting in which all of the central committee members were present. The plan was to rescue Yogesh by attacking the police vehicle in which he was being transported.'

'Then what happened?'

'After the preparation, Batukeshwar Dutt informed them that they had already taken Yogesh one day before schedule and kept him in Cawnpore lock-up. So, Azad, Bhagat Singh, some of the others and I took guns, pistols and a few bombs to Cawnpore. But the prison building was made of stone and was too formidable. Also, there were too many armed policemen. It was impossible to rescue him.

We dropped the plan at the last moment and came back. Bhagat Singh cried a lot that night owing to the failure.'

'What happened to the bomb-making then?'

'So Sukhdev returned after a few days with five bombshells forged at Lahore. Jatin Das filled the chemicals and fitted it with a striker. In total, five bombs of the first batch were ready.'

The magistrate asked, 'How do you know that they were ready? Did you test any bombs?'

'Yes, we had to—to check the efficiency. But it was impossible in Agra, as the noise would attract the attention of the police. Here, Panditji came to our rescue. The next day only three of us, Bhagat, Panditji and I, went to Jhansi by train, carrying revolvers and one bomb.'

The CID company then headed to Jhansi by train. After reaching Jhansi, at the request of Phanindra, a police van was borrowed, and they drove out of the city for half an hour. Phanindra asked them to stop at a spot and led the officers into the jungle. After reaching a hillock, he said, 'At Jhansi, we took a taxi and went around twenty miles out of Jhansi. Then we left the cab on the road and went into the jungle on foot for an hour. We stopped here on this hillock, and Bhagat took out the bomb. He asked me, "Phani Babu, will you throw the bomb? You are more experienced than I am."

'I was afraid; I thought it would explode in my hands. Such things happen if there is a slight mistake in bomb-making. I did not want to take the risk. So I said, "Bhagat, you do the honours; you were the one who convinced Jatin."

'While I hid behind a rock, Panditji and Bhagat laughed, and then Bhagat threw the bomb. The explosion was bigger than we had expected. The experiment was successful.'

The magistrate noted this down and asked, 'Now where?'

Phani Babu said, 'We wound up everything at the end of March because it was decided to throw bombs in the assembly to protest against the two laws.'

The magistrate asked, 'Who came up with the plan?'

Phanindra said, 'Sahib, make a guess; who do you think can devise such a plan?'

'I get it, your damn Bhagat Singh,' the officer said.

'Yes, he was disappointed after the outcome of Saunders's murder because it did not change the public's view of revolution. Our ideology was still distant from the masses. So he came up with a simple idea to catch the attention of the masses. By protesting in such a way and then surrendering himself to the cause. The intention was to open deaf ears without killing anyone.'

The officer remarked, 'Well, it seems he quite succeeded in it.'

'There was a central committee meeting on the proposal, and the plan was agreed upon, but Panditji did not want Bhagat to go in for the action. He did not want to lose Bhagat because whoever went in would not return. So as commander-in-chief, he ordered Bhagat to stay back, and the other two members were ready to go.'

'Then how come ultimately Bhagat Singh went to the assembly?'

'There was a quarrel between Sukhdev and Bhagat. When Sukhdev heard of the decision, he said some really harsh words to Bhagat Singh. Sukhdev hinted that Bhagat Singh considered himself too big to sacrifice his life for the cause. It hurt him a lot. Bhagat called the central committee meeting again and insisted on going into action.

Finally, Panditji yielded. But many others adored Bhagat so much that they still asked to go in his place.'

'Can you name some?'

'Lala Ram Sharan Das is a Ghadar veteran; he had spent years in prison since 1915. He asked Bhagat not to waste his life and let him go in his place as he was used to prison life. A Maharashtrian called M or Raghunath also went to Azad and protested. He wanted to go with Bhagat Singh. But Panditji said, "You need a good knowledge of English to argue in court."

'Raghunath replied, "If Bhagat gives me what to say in writing, I will memorize it completely. You can test me. If I miss even one word, then don't send me."

'But Panditji refused. There was a tussle between Raghunath and Bhagat for a long time. It was a bet; whoever gets arrested or dies for the country will win. They are insane.'

The officer said, 'All right, we know what happened in Delhi. Where did the party move after winding up the base in Agra?'

Phanindra answered, 'The headquarters shifted to Saharanpur.'

Then the company went to Saharanpur, UP. There Phanindra showed them a house in Chob Faroshan Mohalla. He said, 'This house was rented by Gaya Prasad, and I carried all the articles, chemicals and around fifty books from Agra.'

The officer intervened. 'Yes, the house was raided by us in May. We found all the books and articles.'

'This is it, Sahib; Saharanpur was our last headquarters. After the bombing in the assembly, you arrested most of the HSRA, and the rest you already know.'

The magistrate said, 'When you joined the party in Delhi, you said Bhagat and Azad came to your place in Bettiah to commit dacoities.'

'Yes, Sir.'

'Show us your place.'

Then Phanindra was taken to Muzaffarpur from Saharanpur and then to Bettiah via train. The news spread across town when the special coach stopped at Muzaffarpur to change trains.

Baikunth was practising lathi tactics with Ranendranath in Tilak Maidan. Someone came and whispered in Ranendranath's ear.

Baikunth asked, 'What is it, Guruji?'

'Nothing unexpected. Phani Babu is travelling to Bettiah with CID in a special railway coach to show them around.'

The eyes of Baikunth reddened; he clenched his fist and cursed, 'Bastard.'

In the evening, while Baikunth and Ranendranath were having dinner, Baikunth said, 'Guruji, I want to go to Bettiah to see what happens there.'

'What is the use of that?'

'I want to see the traitor.'

'What is going to happen if you see him?'

'I can look for a chance to kill him.'

Ranendranath's hand stopped between the plate and his mouth. He looked gravely at Baikunth and said, 'Do not get any silly ideas. What do you think of yourself? Are you the only one who wants to kill that traitor? What do you think Panditji or Yogendra Baba intend to do with him?'

'But they cannot do it now because the police are looking for them. Nobody knows me; I can do it.'

'But you are not a member of HSRA yet.'

'I don't need to be a member of HSRA to kill the rat.'

'I mean, the objective of the revolutionary party is that you cannot take any action or decision on your own. You have to follow the rules and discipline of the party, if you ever wish to be a member of HSRA. Individual heroism has no place in the revolution now. We are past that stage.'

'But Guruji, I want to see his treachery with my own eyes.'

'All right, you have my permission to go, but only if you promise not to do anything foolish. Listen, Panditji has already attacked two approvers. You cannot imagine Phani Babu's security. So just observe from a distance.'

Baikunth packed his bag and took along a khukri concealed adequately inside the bag. He caught the night train and reached Bettiah. In the morning, he asked around and located Phanindra's home in the Kali Baug area. At least fifty constables were roaming around.

After a while, the van took Phanindra to Sant Ghat garden, where he showed the CID where Bhagat and Azad stayed for two days. Baikunth quietly followed him, mixing in with the curious crowd at each location.

Next, the caravan went in the direction of Meena Bazaar. Baikunth travelled fast and entered the bazaar's narrow gully; he pretended to be looking for groceries in the shop just opposite Phanindra's shop.

Tens of constables entered the gully, securing it from both sides. Everyone had a loaded Enfield rifle on their shoulder. Phanindra entered with four British officers and one Indian magistrate. He talked joyfully to the neighbouring shopkeepers and assured them about his well-being. Then, he came in front of the shop where Baikunth was shopping and started chatting with the owner.

There was only a three- or four-feet distance between Phanindra and him. Just one constable with his back towards Baikunth. If only he could take out the khukri, take a single jump and thrust the blade into Phanindra's heart with his signature strike, all of it would be over. Of course, Baikunth would be killed on the spot, but the traitor would die, and it would end here. It seemed possible. This was his chance; this was the moment. Baikunth slid his hand into the bag and got hold of the handle. But just then, one of the officers called out, 'Phani Babu, we don't have time to waste on pleasantries. Let's get to work.'

And Phanindra turned around and joined them. The chance was gone.

Baikunth returned to Muzaffarpur with a sour face. He thought he had taken too much time to think. He remembered the words of Ranendranath. To become a revolutionary, you must be ready to die. Clearly, he wasn't.

Chapter 8

June–September 1929

The streets of Lahore had turned into a military cantonment. It was hard not to remember the massacre at Jallianwala Bagh, seeing the number of military personnel on the road.

Bhagat and Dutt were lying in a pungent-smelling cell. The previous night, they had been shifted to the same cell for this special occasion. A constable kept a close watch on them. Bhagat and Dutt were excited, but they had no energy left to move even a finger. They were lying almost unconscious on bamboo mats.

A constable came near the cell and shouted, 'Prisoners, stand up. It is time; you are being taken to court for the hearing.'

Bhagat replied, in a weak voice, 'I wish to stand, but sadly, I cannot.' His lips were parched and dry like paper.

The response was expected. It was almost a month since the madness had begun. In a few minutes, two Pathan constables arrived with makeshift stretchers made from bamboo. One of them opened the cell door and placed the stretchers near the feet of Bhagat and Dutt. A constable held one foot of each revolutionary and dragged them on to the stretchers like rag dolls. Their individual body weight was almost half of what it had been the previous month. The constables carried the stretchers out in the open. It had rained through the night, but the sky was now clear and a sudden bright ray of sunlight blinded Bhagat's eyes. Overcome by the heat and the effort of moving from the floor to the stretcher, their bodies ached all over. They drifted in and out of consciousness. In ten minutes, they were taken outside a small hall, inside Lahore Central Jail, where the magisterial court had been established, primarily to conduct the trial.

It was 10 July 1929. The fourteen revolutionaries, including Sukhdev, Shiv Verma, Bijoy Sinha and Mahabir Singh, had already been brought in a police vehicle. They were made to sit on a bench inside the court, still handcuffed.

Before they entered the courtroom, Bhagat signalled to the constable for water. At the same time, they heard someone announcing from inside that the court was about to commence. Rai Sahib Pandit Shri Krishan, special magistrate, had taken his place. Khan Bahadur arrived and scolded the policemen for being late. The constables rushed inside the room, without giving water to the men.

'Time is relative; its only worth depends upon what we do as it is passing'. Bhagat remembered the words of young scientist, Albert Einstein. He was lying amid a war. A war that he had initiated and meticulously planned. And today was the first face-off with the real enemy. He could not lose in the first battle.

Around one month back, in Delhi, on 12 June, the court had announced its decision. It awarded life imprisonment to Bhagat and Dutt. Also, it made sure that the convicts were placed on the Lahore train the same evening. Before leaving, Bhagat called a constable and asked to talk to the jailer.

The jailer arrived and asked, 'Tell me, what do you need?'

Bhagat said, 'Sir, I want you to give this letter to the press.'

The jailer took the neatly folded handwritten letter and asked, 'May I ask what is in it?'

Bhagat smiled. 'You are going to read it anyway, aren't you?'

The jailer opened the letter and read. It stated that Bhagat and Dutt were going on a hunger strike to protest against the treatment meted out to revolutionaries.

A frown appeared on the jailer's face. He said, 'But this is false. We are treating you the way we treat political prisoners. You and your friend are kept with European prisoners. What is the meaning of this?' He waved the letter.

Bhagat replied, 'Sir, this is not about you or this prison. You have taken the best care of us, and for that, I am grateful. However, this is for something that has haunted my past and is waiting for me in Lahore.'

'What do you mean by past? Have you been imprisoned before?'

'Yes, for a brief time, but this is not about me. This is about how the British government treats revolutionaries. This is about the inhuman torture and countless deaths my community has faced over the last fifty years.'

'I don't understand your motive.'

'You will. Very soon.'

'But you are a revolutionary, am I right? You threw bombs in the assembly, and now, within a month, you are talking about the Gandhian way of hunger strikes. Are you turning towards Gandhi?'

Bhagat laughed loudly and said, 'No, no, although fasting is synonymous with Gandhiji, my way will be different. It also proves our mettle that we are not hot-headed men and fasting is not bound to Gandhiji only.'

'All right, I will do as you have asked. Throwing bombs is easy; going on a hunger strike is difficult. I don't think you can manage it for more than a week. I will be watching you closely.'

Bhagat looked beyond the jailer and said, 'Thirty-five crore of my siblings will be watching.'

The jailer went away.

Phase One of Bhagat's game plan was over. Now was the time to start Phase Two. He wasn't going to waste a single day.

When Bhagat and Batukeshwar boarded the train from Delhi to Lahore, the police kept them in separate coaches. Bhagat requested the escorting officer that he be allowed to meet Batukeshwar. The officer brought a handcuffed Dutt to Bhagat's coach. They knew they would be kept separately at Lahore, hence they used this time to discuss their next course of action.

Bhagat was brought to Mianwali Jail on 17 June 1929. The city of Lahore was full of prisons. There was Lahore Central Jail, Borstal Jail, Fort Jail and Mianwali, among others. Immediately upon his arrival, he was shifted to a tiny cell. The room smelled of rotten, dead animals. The iron rods were completely rusted, and hay peeked from the crevices in brick walls. A tiny, square window, towards the west, was the only source of light. The ceiling was around six feet high. Bhagat could barely stand in the room. He felt claustrophobic.

In Delhi, he and Dutt had been treated a hundred times better. The cells were clean, the food was not tasty but looked hygienic, and the clothes provided were clean. Even when he was arrested for the Dusshera bomb blast in Lahore in October 1926, and had been put in Lahore police station for a few months, he had not witnessed such inhumane treatment.

A Mianwali constable provided clothes too short for the 5-foot-10 Bhagat. The shirt was torn and patched in places. It smelled of sweat and mould. Bhagat protested, but no one responded to him.

At lunch, Bhagat saw that there were two compartments, one for ordinary criminals and another for English and political prisoners. There were many Congress and European prisoners who were served in different queues. Their clothes were clean, and they were served adequately cooked food on clean plates.

The ordinary criminals were in a different queue and they were served different food, which looked like leftovers from the day before. The chapatis were thrown on to the plates as if they were beggars. The watery dal had no trace of actual dal. The sabji looked like a mixture of all vegetable leftovers cooked together in haste. The foul smell of the food around the table entered Bhagat's nostrils, and a feeling of nausea filled him. When he reached the counter, he saw vermin crawling on the floor among the waste food. Bhagat felt like vomiting and left the room in haste.

Panditji had given a detailed lecture about how revolutionaries were treated in prison, that they were tortured and punished to extract information from them, but he had never spoken about the food. Of course, he didn't have first-hand experience because he had never been arrested. But this was beyond tolerable. Although, at a subconscious level, he had been ready for such a thing to happen. The trajectory of action was already decided.

Bhagat returned from the food canteen and found a sentry; he asked, 'Please give me a pen and paper.'

The sentry smirked and replied, 'What do you need it for? This is a jail; you will not get any such things here. Get back to your cell if your lunch is over.'

Bhagat replied, 'Tell the jailer that the person who threw the bomb in Delhi's assembly wants to write a letter to the inspector general; let me know if he too refuses, along with both your full names.'

The sentry's face turned pale. He went to the office and returned with a writing pad, a fountain pen and an ink bottle. Bhagat smiled. He wrote a letter to the inspector general about starting a hunger strike to protest against the inhumane treatment meted out to revolutionaries.

Bhagat began to drink only water. The officials were watching cautiously. They thought of it as a desperate resort, undertaken by hot-headed Sikh boy. Everyone knew by now that he came from a wealthy family. A few sentries requested him to break the fast as the British were not going to budge. But he already knew that.

Bhagat's weight began to decrease drastically. In a week, he lost 3 kg.

On 25 June, the police shifted Bhagat to Lahore Central Jail, where they had kept Batukeshwar. He had also sent a similar letter to the inspector general and was on a fast like Bhagat.

Bhagat and Dutt were kept in adjoining cells. Bhagat called in a weak voice, 'Brother, how are you?'

Dutt replied, 'Still not hungry.'

Bhagat and Dutt laughed until their sunken stomachs hurt.

Meanwhile, Sukhdev, Jatin Das, Ajoy Ghosh, Bijoy Sinha, Shiv Verma and Dr Gaya Prasad were kept in Borstal jail. The news of Bhagat and Dutt's hunger strike reached them. Jatin Das and the others were worried. Sukhdev specifically didn't believe in fasting methods, but he understood the true motives of Bhagat behind this bold initiative.

On 10 July, the magisterial hearing of the case began in Lahore Central Jail. The government appointed Rai Sahib Pandit Sri Krishan as special magistrate. All roads leading to the jail were garrisoned, as they were during the times of Jallianwala Bagh.

The prisoners from Borstal Jail arrived in handcuffs.

In the sweltering heat of 10 July, the small makeshift courthouse created in Central Jail, especially for the Lahore Conspiracy Case, bustled with anticipation as the trial of Bhagat Singh and his comrades was set to begin. Among the prisoners, whispers of Bhagat Singh's ongoing hunger strike circulated, igniting a sense of camaraderie and determination.

Bhagat Singh and Dutt were carried in on stretchers. Bhagat's once-strong physique had been reduced to a mere shadow of itself. Shiv Verma's eyes welled up as he stared at his emaciated friend, a victim of the merciless ordeal of prison and hunger.

Despite his frailty, Bhagat Singh's spirit remained unbroken. As they gathered to discuss their defence strategy, his voice, though weakened, was filled with conviction.

'Bhagat, are you sure you can do this?' Shiv asked, concern etched on his face.

'I have never been more certain,' Bhagat replied in a feeble voice, a glimmer of determination in his eyes. 'We will fight.'

From 10 to 13 July, all the revolutionaries in Borstal Jail discussed the plan of joining the hunger strike with Bhagat. Jatin Dada was the only one among them who had previously experienced a hunger strike when he was in prison related to his activities in HRA. He warned his fellow comrades of the immense challenge ahead. He said, 'It was far more complex than any battle with pistols or revolvers. You will die every minute, and if any of you break down, it will be a collective defeat and insult. As far as I am concerned, I will not compromise until the government accepts our demands.' He continued, his voice firm, 'But I urge you all to test your limits before joining this hunger strike. You will still have my respect, regardless of your decision.'

Sukhdev was against the tactic of everyone joining the fast. However, he agreed when everyone else voted for it in consensus.

Jatin Dada said, 'Let us keep an undeclared fast for twenty-four hours. Test your will against the demon of hunger. If any of you wish to back out after it, it will be accepted. Only after twenty-four hours will I send a letter to the Home Member mentioning the names of participants.'

No one backed out. Jatin Das sent a letter to the Home Member, listing their demands as political prisoners similar to Bhagat.

Bhagat Singh persisted with his daily activities, reading, writing and attending court. Despite his deteriorating health, he never lost his sense of humour or his love for music.

On Sundays, Bhagat would visit his comrades at the nearby Borstal Jail, and they engaged in lively discussions about politics, economics and social issues. Each week, they would devour books on various topics, and then share their thoughts and opinions when they met.

One evening, as they sat under the dim light of a flickering lantern, Shiv noticed Bhagat's extensive collection of novels.

'You really do have a soft spot for literature, don't you?' he remarked, a hint of amusement in his voice.

Bhagat smiled. 'I find solace in the words of Dickens, Hugo and Gorky. Their stories help me envision a world beyond these prison walls.'

The first ten days of the hunger strike passed without much reaction from the authorities. Perhaps, they believed that the young revolutionaries would not endure the ordeal. To break their resolve, the jail officials left enticing food, milk and fruit in their cells, hoping to tempt the starving prisoners. However, the revolutionaries remained steadfast, either ignoring the temptation or throwing the food out.

They began leaving milk instead of water in the prisoners' pitchers. As their thirst intensified, the prisoners would approach the pitchers desperately seeking water, only to find milk, leaving them frustrated and parched.

One evening, as Ajoy Kumar Ghosh's thirst reached unbearable levels, he called for the guard and shouted, 'Water'.

The sentry replied, 'No orders for giving water.'

Enraged, Ajoy lifted the milk pitcher and smashed it on the floor. The splattered milk covered not only the floor but also the uniform of the sentry, who stared back at Ajoy, his face pale with fear.

On the eleventh day, the jail authorities commenced force-feeding the prisoners. A board of doctors was appointed to oversee the process. In cases where prisoners did not resist, a rubber pipe was inserted down their throats, and a measured amount of liquid food was poured in. However, the revolutionaries were determined not to allow food into their stomachs, making the force-feeding a harrowing ordeal.

For each prisoner, a team consisting of two doctors, one jail official and ten burly prison wardens was assigned. These strong men would pin down the prisoners, holding them in place while the doctor inserted the rubber pipe and poured the liquid diet. The revolutionaries, in turn, developed various methods of resistance. Some would cough at the right moment, causing the rubber pipe between their jaws and teeth to get dislodged, while others relied on brute force to resist the insertion of the tube.

Mahabir Singh, a wrestler, was one such prisoner who resisted the force-feeding with great determination. When the jail officials approached him, he first attempted to block their way. Only when they managed to subdue him would he be force-fed. One jail official was overheard remarking to a colleague about Mahabir's tenacity, saying that not even a single day during the sixty-three-day hunger strike had they been able to force-feed him in less than half an hour.

On the other hand, Bhagat Singh could not resist the force-feeding as effectively as some of his comrades. He could not put up much resistance due to the size of his nose, which made it easier for the doctors to insert the tube and feed him. Nonetheless, his spirit remained unbroken.

On 26 July 1929, Jatin Das found himself separated from his fellow prisoners, isolated by the police who intended to torture him at their leisure. The first round of wrestling and pinning him down had been a struggle, but the worst was yet to come. The doctor inserted a tube through Das's mouth, which he swallowed and clenched tightly between his teeth. Unrelenting, the doctor forced another pipe through the nostril. Desperate to breathe, Das tried to stop the tube from reaching his stomach, but it instead entered his lungs. In a rush and oblivious to Das's suffering, the doctor poured a *seer* of milk into his lungs and left him writhing in pain.

This horrifying incident unfolded in the prison hospital, where half a dozen of Das's comrades were also held, all confined to a single barrack block. Seeing Das in agony, they rushed to his side. His temperature rapidly rose, his breathing became laboured and punctuated by violent coughing fits. Concerned, his fellow prisoners raised a commotion, prompting the team of doctors to return after half an hour. The doctors, at a loss as to what to do, placed Das on a cot and attempted to administer medicine. Das, though barely conscious, found the strength to refuse, denying even the most heartfelt pleas of his comrades. He would not let the enemy force anything upon him.

In the following days, Das's condition deteriorated rapidly. He developed pneumonia, and his body became poisoned. Despite his worsening health, he continued to defy the doctors' attempts to treat him. His unwavering resolve inspired his fellow prisoners, who barricaded the doors to the barracks to protect him from being removed by the jail authorities. There was no improvement in his condition. Authorities offered bail to Jatin Das on health grounds. They did not want him to die inside the prison.

In the face of the stand-off, Das sent a message to the superintendent, refusing the bail offer. The jail authorities relented, and the barricades were removed only when the superintendent swore in the name of Jesus Christ that they would not try to remove Das against his will.

Das's condition worsened, and the doctor believed an enema needed to be administered to the patient. The doctors had tried everything, but Jatin Das would not agree to receive an enema. The pleas of the Congress leaders and members of the Defence Committee of the Lahore Conspiracy Case fell on deaf ears. Desperate for a solution, the superintendent went to ask Das's fellow revolutionaries in Borstal Jail for help. Sukhdev said, 'Perhaps Bhagat Singh could persuade Jatin Dada. He convinced him to join this madness in Calcutta in the first place.'

The authorities arranged for Bhagat Singh to be brought to Central Jail where Das was held. As Bhagat entered the room, Das's eyes lit up with admiration. Tears were rolling down Bhagat's face. He was also terribly weak, but he couldn't bear the sight of Jatin Dada like this.

Bhagat sat near him and took his hand; a tired smile appeared on Dada's parched black lips. Bhagat gently said, 'Dada, please let them do the procedure.' To everyone's surprise, Jatin Dada nodded in affirmation.

Bhagat smiled and replied, 'Thank you, Dada. I know you will recover very soon. The fight has just started. You can't leave my side. I need your guidance.'

Jatin Dada whispered, 'Bhagat, you cannot lie. This is my fight, and you will see, I will win.'

Bhagat left the room, sat on the floor, and cried like a child.

A superior officer, puzzled by Das's sudden change of heart, asked, 'Mr Das, can I ask you something?'

'Go ahead.'

'Why did you refuse everyone, including your fellow prisoners and Congress leaders, but just one word from Bhagat Singh and you acceded?

A tear rolled down Jatin Dada's cheek, 'Mister, you do not know who Bhagat Singh is. I cannot say no to him.'

The officer was dumbfounded. He had never heard or read of such acts by any revolutionaries in the history of revolutions.

A week later, Das gathered his fellow prisoners around him. His younger brother, Kiron Das, had been permitted to stay with him and had brought a packet of biscuits. Jatin Das distributed one biscuit to each of his comrades, saying, 'We are not breaking our hunger strike. This is our last common feast, a mere token of my love.' They all shared the biscuits, a symbol of their unwavering bond.

That night, Das conversed with his comrades until late, enquiring about those locked away in cells and listening to the song *Vande Mataram*. It was the last flicker of light from a rapidly dimming flame. His condition worsened; his hands and feet were swollen, and his eyes shut. Despite his deteriorating health, his mind remained sharp, and he communicated with simple nods.

On the sixty-third day of the hunger strike, the doctors tried to administer an injection as his condition worsened. They believed that unconscious and near death, Das would be unaware of their actions. Yet, as they held his arm and began to apply the spirit, he opened his eyes and, with a hoarse and frightening voice, uttered a single, defiant word: 'No.' Then he died.

Bhagat, Dutt and all other prisoners were inconsolable after the tragic passing. The nation acknowledged Jatin Dada's supreme sacrifice. Condolence messages kept pouring in. The most notable message came from Mary MacSwiney, the sister of legendary Irish revolutionary Terence MacSwiney, who had laid down his life after a record seventy-four days of hunger strike in 1920: 'Family of MacSwiney unites with India in grief and pride on the death of Jatindra Nath Das. Freedom will come.'

As the news of Jatin Das's tragic demise spread, a sombre atmosphere pervaded the town of Muzaffarpur where Baikunth had been training under the watchful guidance of Ranendranath. Baikunth was shattered; his grief knew no bounds. A special train had been arranged to carry the martyr's corpse from Lahore to Howrah, and thousands flocked there to pay their last respects. Baikunth could not bear to sit idly by while the train carrying his beloved Jatin Das passed through Gaya. He confided in his mentor, Ranendranath, who understood the depth of his anguish. 'I must go to Gaya, Guruji,' Baikunth pleaded. 'I must pay my respects.'

Ranendranath hesitated, fearing for Baikunth's safety amidst the emotionally charged crowds. But he saw the determination in the young man's eyes and finally relented. 'Very well, Baikunth. Go and pay your respects, but be careful. These are turbulent times.'

Baikunth nodded, his face a mixture of gratitude and sorrow. He boarded a train to Gaya, his heart heavy with grief. As he travelled, he heard stories of the tributes paid to Jatin Das at every station the special train passed through. Thousands bid farewell at Lahore cantonment, and at Delhi and Agra, masses flocked. In Cawnpore, a public meeting was held to express condolences for the loss of the brave martyr, and even Pandit Jawaharlal Nehru paid his tearful respects. Women led by the old widowed mother of Bijoy Kumar Sinha and the mother of Ajoy Ghosh created a heart-rending scene while crying loudly for the loss of one of their bravest sons. Despite the stifling police presence, people gathered in droves to pay their respects, showering the closed coffin with flowers and tears.

When the special train arrived at Gaya, Baikunth was amidst an enormous, emotional crowd. They were all there for the same reason—to honour the memory of Jatin Das, who had sacrificed his life for the cause of Indian independence. The air was thick with the scent of flowers and the hum of whispered prayers.

A hush fell over the crowd as the train carrying Jatin Das's body pulled into the station. The atmosphere was electric, charged with anticipation and grief. Baikunth strained his eyes to catch a glimpse of the coffin, his heart pounding in his chest.

The train stopped, and the masses surged forward to get closer to the martyred hero. Baikunth was swept up in the tide of humanity, feeling a strange sense of unity with the strangers around him. Together, they were mourning the loss of a man who had given everything for their freedom.

Pushing his way through hundreds of people, Baikunth finally reached the carriage carrying the coffin. He stood there, his eyes brimming with tears, staring at the closed casket. The sight of the black flag with Jatin Das's photo on the carriage door pierced his heart like a dagger. He wanted to scream, to cry out at the injustice of it all, but no sound came out.

Around him, people were offering flowers and silver coins, their hands shaking with emotion. Baikunth leaned down to pick up a handful of petals, his hands trembling. As he placed them on the coffin, a sob escaped his lips. 'Jatin Dada,' he whispered, 'you will never be forgotten. Your sacrifice will inspire generations to come.'

A man standing beside Baikunth, his eyes red from crying, turned to him and said, 'We will carry on his fight, brother. Jatin Das's spirit will live on in all of us. I pray to God, let my son become a revolutionary like Jatin Das.' Baikunth nodded, too choked to speak.

The train began to move again, continuing its journey towards Howrah. Baikunth watched it go, his heart aching with a pain that would never truly heal. Hundreds of people ran behind the train, the ones who couldn't catch a glimpse of the body.

As the train disappeared from view, the air was charged with the echoes of the slogans, 'Jatin Das Zindabad! Long live Jatin Das!'

For a fleeting moment, Baikunth saw a strange vision. The intensity of the atmosphere transported him to a different place in his mind, where he envisioned himself stepping into the shoes of Jatin Dada. He imagined himself in the glass box covered by ice and revered by thousands for the ultimate sacrifice. He thought of the weight of responsibility, the courage and the unwavering commitment required to make such a sacrifice for the motherland. A bittersweet smile appeared as he considered the honour of giving up his life for India's freedom.

Amid the swelling emotions, Baikunth remembered the words he had often heard: 'To be a revolutionary, one must be ready to die.' These words resonated deep within him, and he felt their truth reverberate through his very being.

As Baikunth stood there, enveloped by the sorrow and pride of the crowd, he experienced a profound internal turmoil. The idea of martyrdom both terrified and exhilarated him. He knew that the path of revolution was fraught with danger and sacrifice, yet he couldn't help but feel a sense of purpose and excitement at the prospect.

Slowly, the chaos around him began to fade as Baikunth's thoughts turned inward. He found himself grappling with the question of what it truly meant to be a revolutionary. Was it the willingness to die for one's country that defined a revolutionary? Or was it something deeper, something more personal and complex?

As he pondered these questions, Baikunth realized that the essence of being a revolutionary was not just martyrdom but also living for the cause. It was about standing up against oppression, fighting for justice and igniting the spirit of freedom in the hearts of his fellow countrymen. It was a lifelong commitment, and the sacrifices made along the way were merely a part of the journey. He knew what needed to be done.

Baikunth returned to Muzaffarpur. He knew that there was no turning back now. Ranendranath could see the fire in Baikunth's eyes. As they sat together in a dimly lit room, the air thick with the scent of incense and the low hum of conversation, Baikunth began to speak.

'Guruji,' he said, his voice steady and resolute. 'I have made a decision. I want to go to Lahore to see Bhagat Singh, Dutt and the others in court. I need to stand by them to learn from their courage and conviction. I must do this.'

Ranendranath looked at Baikunth, taking in the intensity of his gaze and the unwavering determination etched across his face. He could see that Baikunth had changed since the day he had left for Gaya; the young man before him now carried the weight of his purpose with pride and conviction.

With a measured voice, Ranendranath replied, 'Baikunth, I can see that your heart is set on this path. I understand your desire to be with our comrades in Lahore, but remember that the journey will be fraught with challenges and danger.'

Baikunth nodded, acknowledging the gravity of the situation. 'I know I am prepared to face whatever challenges lie ahead.'

Ranendranath, seeing the unyielding determination in Baikunth's eyes, sighed and put a hand on his shoulder. 'Very well, but you must promise me that you will be cautious and vigilant. Our cause needs brave souls like you, but we must also be strategic in our actions.'

Baikunth looked at his mentor with gratitude and nodded solemnly. As Baikunth prepared for the journey to Lahore, his resolve grew more assertive. He was finally going to see Bhagat Singh in person.

Chapter 9

October–November 1929

Baikunth managed to acquire for himself a journalist's backdated identity card from a Muzzaffarpur Hindi newspaper. He then asked permission from Radhika. She was apprehensive. No good news came from Lahore. But she could not hold him back. She understood that he had already crossed the threshold. There was no point refusing. She asked him repeatedly to be careful and come back soon. Baikunth boarded the third-class coach of the train from Gaya to Lahore.

His journey to Lahore was long and arduous; he absorbed the changing landscape from Bihar to UP, then to lush green fields of the land of five rivers, i.e., Punjab. Upon arriving in Lahore, Baikunth was struck by the city's charm: its narrow winding streets and towering minarets. Lahore was a bustling city filled with the sounds of horse-drawn carriages and the fragrance of fresh flowers.

The colonizers and the colonized lived side by side with visible tension in the air.

He felt awe while exploring the city, immersing himself in its rich culture and history. Baikunth stayed at a *dharamshala*, showing his identity card and purpose of reporting the trial. He applied for the pass to Pandit Shri Krishan's court. The police gave him dates from 21 October to 25 October. As the day of the trial drew closer, Baikunth felt a sense of anticipation and excitement building within him. He knew this would be a defining moment in his life and felt honoured to witness it. When the approved date finally arrived, Baikunth went to the courthouse, his heart pounding with excitement. As he entered the courthouse, he looked around at the sea of faces. A constable directed him to tables reserved for the press. The tension in the room was palpable, and Baikunth knew that he was witnessing history in the making.

A loud, coarse roar came from outside, 'Inquilab', the reply echoed by a group 'Zindabad'. Baikunth got goosebumps as he turned around. Bhagat Singh and Batukeshwar Dutt entered the court. Bhagat Singh was in a dusty, short cream kurta, which might have been white at some point, and shorts. He was a towering, slim figure with dishevelled hair but his face and eyes were radiating with determination. Another fifteen accused followed him, and the slogans continued. 'Samrajyavad!'—and the reply came, 'Murdabad!' Baikunth unconsciously stood in his place. Surprisingly he was the only one among the journalists to stand up.

For a second, Baikunth thought that Bhagat looked at him and smiled as if he recognized him.

The constables gathered all the revolutionaries in the dock. Still, the loud slogans continued sending waves of goosebumps around the room. The police, however, seemed unaffected.

The court staff was waiting to announce the arrival of the magistrate, but he couldn't because of the slogans of the revolutionaries. He stared at Bhagat helplessly, asking, with his eyes, for help. Bhagat nodded and raised his palms. The sloganeering stopped.

The court staff announced, 'All rise,' and special magistrate Pandit Shri Krishan came in and took a seat.

Jai Gopal, the approver, was called to the stand, and the audience watched with bated breath. This man's testimony held the power to change the lives of these young men who had dedicated themselves to the cause of India's freedom.

The room was tense, and the air seemed to crackle with energy. Jai Gopal began his statement, and it quickly became apparent that his intentions were far from noble. His words were laced with venom, designed to provoke the revolutionaries and break their resolve.

Jai Gopal had barely spoken for two or three minutes when he made a bold, taunting claim. He looked directly at the revolutionaries and said, '*Janab, ye aapke kiye huye hain, aur sachi hain* (You have committed these acts, and they are true).' The effect of his words was immediate and electrifying.

The revolutionaries' faces turned red with anger, and the spectators in the courtroom could feel the tension building like a powder keg ready to explode. The atmosphere was charged, the air thick with suspense. No one knew how the revolutionaries would react to this blatant provocation.

Suddenly, Prem Dutt, the youngest among the revolutionaries, could no longer contain his rage. His eyes flashed with fury, and he quickly took off his slipper, his hand trembling with anger and adrenaline. The room seemed to freeze for a moment as every eye turned to him, watching the scene unfold with a mix of shock and awe.

Prem Dutt hurled the slipper with all his strength in one swift, fluid motion, aiming directly at Jai Gopal. The projectile seemed to hang in the air for an eternity, the silent onlookers holding their breath as if time had slowed down.

The slipper missed its mark. However, Jai Gopal's face went pale. It was a symbolic slap against the betrayal and injustice the revolutionaries had faced. The room erupted into chaos as the tension that had been building finally reached its breaking point.

The revolutionaries leapt to their feet, their faces contorted with rage, while the spectators gasped and whispered among themselves. Sensing the potential danger in the situation, the prosecutor demanded that the court be adjourned, stating that the lives of the approvers were at risk.

Throughout the pandemonium, Bhagat Singh and the other revolutionaries maintained their composure, attempting to distance themselves from Prem Dutt's impulsive action. Bhagat said, 'Sir, we condemn the act by our comrade Prem Dutt and dissociate ourselves from it. I request the honourable court to let me make a statement.'

Rai Sahib Pandit Shri Krishan looked at Bhagat coldly and replied, 'Your request is denied.'

This left Bhagat no option but to submit a written statement to clarify on record that they were disassociating themselves from the slipper-throwing incident.

Prem Dutt, a juvenile and the youngest among the accused, realized his mistake; he said, 'Sir, I apologize for the act done by me, and I am ready for any punishment that you award. I wish to clarify that I alone am responsible for it and nobody else.'

The magistrate ordered, without even looking at Prem Dutt, 'I agree with the prosecutor that there is a threat to the lives of the approvers. Prem Dutt should be kept in solitary confinement for three months. Also, due to the unacceptable incident, I order that the accused be handcuffed throughout the proceedings. I ask the police to take the accused back to their respective jails. The court is adjourned for today.'

This decision angered Bhagat Singh and his comrades. Bhagat roared, 'Sir, we have already apologized for the incident. You have punished the individual for the act. You must consider that he is a juvenile and acted out of impulse. This is a court; no one should be handcuffed here. We refuse to come to court until you withdraw the order.'

The massive police forces forced the accused out of the courtroom, and Baikunth felt something horrible would happen.

The next day, on 22 October, Baikunth reached the court early. The assistant jailer of Borstal Jail came forward and said, 'Sir, all the accused refused to come to court handcuffed; we managed to bring five of the sixteen accused to the jail gate but could not make them enter the court.' The magistrate adjourned the court for the next day.

The next day, the police devised a sinister plan; the jailer promised that the accused would be taken to court in handcuffs but that they would be removed inside the courtroom. However, when the revolutionaries entered the court in handcuffs and asked the police to remove the handcuffs, their request was completely ignored. The proceedings of the court began. Something had changed inside the court. The polarization of opinions was extreme, with the judiciary and police on one end and the revolutionaries and the public on the other. The accused and the public felt humiliated and cheated. The court and police were in bed to execute the predetermined outcome of the trial. Baikunth was watching everything with a keen eye. He understood that soon a volcano was going to explode there.

The accused whispered to each other just before lunchtime. Everyone in the room could see the determination on the faces of Bhagat, Rajguru, Sukhdev, Shiv Verma and the others. Something was decided. During the lunch break, they asked for their handcuffs to be removed while they ate. Once the cuffs were off, the accused came back after lunch, and at the gate of the court, a constable was ready to put the handcuffs back.

Leading the line, Bhagat folded his arms across his chest and said firmly so that the magistrate could hear him, 'We refuse to be handcuffed in court.'

The constable said, 'How dare you refuse the order?'

Sukhdev replied, 'You will see now how we dare to stand against this unjust court.'

The tension exploded into a full-blown scuffle like a match igniting gasoline. Arms flailed, fists clenched, and shouts echoed through the courthouse as the police attempted to subdue the agitated revolutionaries. Bhagat Singh was a whirlwind of ferocity, his every move an assertion of his unyielding conviction.

Desperate to regain control, the police summoned the notorious Pathan policemen, infamous for their brutal and ruthless tactics. The hulking men stormed the courtroom, their massive, brawny frames casting ominous shadows on the walls. A chill swept through the crowd as the Pathans fixed their steely gazes upon the revolutionaries, their eyes glinting with malice.

A police officer, Roberts, pointed at Bhagat Singh, his voice dripping with venom. 'This is the man; give him more beatings.' It was an order that would unleash a torrent of violence upon the young freedom fighter. The eight merciless Pathans descended upon Bhagat Singh, their faces contorted in anger and cruelty.

The scene was a horrifying cacophony of cracking bones, anguished cries and guttural roars. With brutal force, lathis rained down upon Bhagat Singh, each blow landing with a sickening thud. His body crumpled under the assault, and the once-fiery revolutionary was now a battered, bloodied figure on the cold, unforgiving floor.

But the nightmare did not end there. The Pathans closed in, their heavy boots delivering vicious kicks to Bhagat Singh's ribs, head and legs. They deliberately kicked his testicles to inflict as much pain as humanly possible. The Pathans violated the helpless unarmed accused by inserting fingers into their rectums right before the magistrate. Each savage blow seemed to echo through the courtroom, a sinister symphony of pain and suffering.

The crowd watched in stunned silence, the weight of the unfolding horror pressing down upon them like a vice. In the gallery, Baikunth could no longer contain his emotions. Tears streamed down his cheeks as he bore witness to the brutalization of the revolutionaries, the image of their broken bodies forever seared into his memory.

The women in the courtroom gasped and sobbed, clutching their hands to their mouths in shock and despair. The air was thick with the coppery scent of blood, the gut-wrenching sound of bones shattering, and the choked cries of the battered revolutionaries.

But even in the face of such unimaginable cruelty, the spirit of the revolutionaries remained unbroken. Through swollen, bloodied lips, Bhagat Singh spat defiantly at his attackers, his eyes still ablaze with the fire of resistance.

The ordeal continued, each second stretching into eternity as the Pathans carried out their gruesome task. The courtroom walls bore silent witness to the savagery, stained with the blood and sweat of the brave men who dared to defy the iron grip of oppression.

Finally, the brutal beating subsided, leaving the revolutionaries battered, bruised and gasping for breath on the floor. The Pathans stood over their victims, their faces twisted in cruel satisfaction. The room was eerily silent, save for the ragged breathing of the fallen freedom fighters and the stifled sobs of the traumatized onlookers.

Through sheer will and determination, Bhagat Singh struggled to lift his head, his gaze meeting the eyes of his fellow revolutionaries. At that moment, an unspoken bond of solidarity was forged, a united front in the face of inhuman brutality.

The magistrate, his face a cold, emotionless mask, offered no solace to the battered revolutionaries. 'They themselves are responsible for it,' he said, dismissively, his words a chilling testament to the depths of his indifference.

Bhagat Singh, his body aching from the brutal assault, could no longer contain his outrage. He glared at the magistrate, his voice thick with contempt. 'I want to congratulate you for this,' he sneered. 'This thing is going on under your very nose.' The other revolutionaries seethed with anger, their eyes burning with indignation as they stared at the magistrate, who remained unmoved by their anguish.

Suddenly, Bhagat Singh's gaze fell upon his comrades, Shiv Verma and Ajoy Kumar Ghosh, who lay insensible and comatose on the courtroom floor. The sight of his fallen brothers ignited a fire within him, fuelling his fury. He turned to the magistrate, his voice quivering with rage. 'Shiv Verma is lying unconscious! If he dies, you are responsible for it!'

The courtroom teetered on the edge of chaos, the air thick with fear, horror and tension. The press, visitors and even the counsel for the accused were aware of the volatile situation unfolding before them. The police, desperate to maintain control and suppress the truth, clamped down on the press with an iron fist, enforcing strict censorship. In an act of blatant authoritarianism, Khan Bahadur took matters into his own hands, barking orders at the press representatives. 'Clear out! Now!' he demanded, his voice cold and unyielding. The visitors, too, were urged to leave, the danger in the air palpable and overwhelming.

As the courtroom door closed behind the last of the departing witnesses, the cries of the revolutionaries continued to ring out, a testament to their unbreakable spirit in the face of unimaginable violence and oppression. As they left, Baikunth could hear howls of 'Long Live the Revolution' and 'Long Live the Proletariat.' Baikunth's spirit had broken down. He literally had to drag himself out of the unholy premises.

But the ordeal didn't end there. After the court proceedings were adjourned for the day, the police launched another barbaric assault on Bhagat Singh and others within the jail premises. The ferocity of the attack left no doubt that the British authorities wanted to crush the revolutionary spirit of these young men and make an example of them for anyone daring to defy the empire. The news of the second attack leaked out and spread into Lahore. Baikunth heard it in his dharamshala; nothing could break him further, his pain fuelling his anger towards the British police, the judiciary and the approvers who had betrayed the cause. Baikunth said to himself, 'They think this will go unaccounted for. I will avenge the revolutionaries. With the last drop of my blood, I will make them pay for their sins. Bhagat Singh, this is my promise to you.'

On 24 October, the court adjourned for the same reason: the revolutionaries would not wear handcuffs in the court. Baikunth returned. On 25 October, the situation remained the same. The revolutionaries braced themselves for another harrowing trial of their fortitude. Without any warning or rationale, the judge commanded the police, 'I want all the accused in court with handcuffs on both hands.'

This was the only thing the police were waiting for. Officer Roberts and Hamilton Hardinge looked at each other and smiled viciously. Baikunth felt as if they were already prepared for the order from the magistrate.

The accused refused to yield. At first, they were permitted to return to their cells, but the situation soon turned sinister. All of them were summoned to the Central

Jail portico, where a menacing force of 300 armed policemen and jail wardens awaited them. As the revolutionaries faced this daunting challenge, the air hung heavy with trepidation and anxiety.

'We will not submit to this injustice!' Bhagat Singh proclaimed, his voice steady and resolute. His comrades echoed his defiance, standing united against the oppressive authorities. Even after inhuman beatings, Bhagat's voice did not falter. Baikunth, along with the public and the journalists, rushed out of the courtroom to witness the drama unfolding outside.

The resistance of the accused was met with a chilling ultimatum. Officer Hardinge commanded the policemen and inspectors, 'I want them handcuffed by any means necessary.' The police swarmed the revolutionaries like a pack of ravenous wolves, each fighter besieged by at least twenty to twenty-five officers. Alongside the brutal rain of batons and kicks, the police subjected the accused to even more vicious and invasive torment. Kicks were again aimed at their testicles in a cruel, methodical manner. Despite their suffering, the helpless revolutionaries clung steadfastly to their principles of non-violence, keenly aware of the insurmountable odds against them.

As the 300 armed policemen assaulted the fifteen defenceless prisoners, cries of pain intermingled with shouts of defiance. For every agonized scream, another voice would muster the strength to bellow, 'Inquilab!' To which the others, barely conscious, would respond, 'Zindabad!'

From outside the gates of Lahore Central Jail, Baikunth witnessed the nightmarish scene, his heart clenching with a maelstrom of emotions—anger, despair and shock. The horrifying spectacle of the revolutionaries being subjected to unspeakable cruelty unfolded before him. The anguished wails of the accused echoed through the jail portico, a chilling testament to the heartless might of the colonial regime.

It was more than Baikunth's soul could bear. He immediately returned to Bihar before he lost control.

Chapter 10

September 1929

A dilapidated building outside Gwalior city was the current office of HSRA. It was the middle of the night. One person, sitting on the roof, was feeling sleepy. Suddenly, he saw some movement in the nearby bushes. Someone wearing a dhoti hitched above his knees and a shawl over his head was approaching the building.

The lookout watched for a few seconds, ensuring no one was with him. Then he picked a heavy bamboo staff and tapped rhythmically on the roof. The same thing was done from below. They were also watching; everybody was alert now. Five revolutionaries were present on the premises, including the commander-in-chief of HSRA.

Sadashiv Malkapurkar went to the inner room. Panditji was fast asleep and snoring. Everyone else was awake and ready with their weapons to greet the stranger. Sadashiv shook Panditji and called slowly, 'Panditji, wake up.'

Azad woke up startled and said, 'Jatin, what happened to Jatin?'

Sadashiv said, 'Panditji, are you all right?'

Azad shook himself awake and replied, 'Yes, I had a bad dream. Tell me what happened?'

'There is a stranger at the door.'

'Only one?'

'Yes.'

'Bring him in.'

Due to the commotion, Bhagwati Charan Vohra also woke up.

At that exact moment, a rhythmic coded tap came on the door. Bhagwan asked without opening the door, 'Who is it?'

'It is me, Madhukar; I have a message.'

'What is the word?'

'Bagha.'

Bhagwan opened the door; the person outside had removed the shawl. Bhagwan took him inside and checked him for weapons. Two other revolutionaries were standing a foot away with hands ready on pistols. After he was searched, Bhagwan asked, 'Tell me, what is the message?'

Madhukar smiled and said, 'The message is for Panditji only.'

Bhagwan replied, 'But Panditji is not here.'

Madhukar replied, 'The person who sent me here said that Panditji would be waiting here.'

'Where are you coming from?'

'Akola in Berar Division of Central Province.'

Bhagwan signalled to Yashpal; he went inside and told Azad everything. Within a moment, Yashpal came back and took Madhukar inside. Azad offered a seat to Madhukar, and Yashpal gave him water.

Madhukar spoke. 'Panditji, Namaste. I am here at the request of M. He asked me to give you this and ask for an answer.' He took out a piece of paper rolled neatly inside a small steel tobacco box.

Panditji unrolled it, and read, 'Permission to felicitate FS, of Bombay, For Robin, for Ranjit. -M'. Robin was the code name of Jatin, Ranjit the code name of Bhagat and M the code name of Rajguru.

Azad handed the note to Bhagwati and asked, 'Bapubhai, read it.' Then he looked at Madhukar and said, 'Sleep here tonight. I will give you my answer in the morning.'

Madhukar left the room. Yashpal made his bedding on the roof.

Panditji was tense after reading the message. He said, 'Bhagwati Bhai, what do you think?'

Bhagwati replied, 'I think he is definitely doing his work in Berar region of Central Province. I say, yes. For the same reason.'

Azad thought briefly and ordered, 'Sadashiv, call Bhagwan, Yashpal and Vaishampayan.'

Everyone gathered in two minutes.

Bhagwati spoke, 'Friends, we have received a message from our beloved Rajguru, alias M. Panditji had sent him back to Bombay Province to work in the area. Now, he is watching the proceedings of the conspiracy case. He is also watching how Jatin Dada, Bhagat and others are fighting death every day. So now Rajguru is asking permission to felicitate the governor of Bombay, Frederick Sykes.'

Bhagwan asked, 'What, felicitate? What has he done for us? I say, he must shoot him down.'

Azad laughed. 'Hanumanji, Rajguru is asking for the same thing. It is his way of asking for permission.'

Bhagwan felt embarrassed.

Azad said, 'It has been decided that Rajguru will make a plan for the same. Sadashiv, you will take selected weapons and bombs to Rajguru; book the earliest ticket tomorrow. Who do you want to take with you?'

Bhagwan implored, 'Panditji, please send me this time.'

Azad put his hand on his shoulder and said, 'Take the necessary chemicals and bombshells to Akola. Assist Rajguru; I will come there when everything is ready.'

Madhukar left in the morning with the message.

On 10 September, Sadashiv and Bhagwan boarded the 198-Allahabad Express from Gwalior station. The next evening, the train reached Bhusawal junction. They had to change the train there for Akola. They had a big iron trunk with them. Bhagwan said, 'Sadashiv, you wait on the platform with the trunk; I will go and enquire about the Akola train.'

Sadashiv said, 'Brother, there are CID spies at every station. Moreover, this is a junction. We should not go around asking questions. It can be dangerous.'

Bhagwan realized Sadashiv was right. He said, 'Let us hire a coolie; he will directly take us to the train.'

'Good idea.'

Bhagwan called a coolie and asked him to get them to the required platform. The coolie picked up the trunk and started walking. Up ahead, there was a commotion. The coolie was walking towards it. Around 20–25 people were standing around. Bhagwan thought they were a group travelling together. Then two of them bent down and opened their trunks. In a moment, Bhagwan saw that two constables were checking the luggage. The ignorant coolie was walking right into the trap.

When the coolie reached the spot, the constable stopped the coolie with his baton and said, 'Hey, put that down and open it.'

The coolie said, 'Sahib, please let me go; there is nothing in this trunk. Please have mercy on this poor coolie. Otherwise, I won't get any money for my work.'

'Shut up; do as I say.'

Bhagwan and Sadashiv looked at each other. They realized it too late; it was an excise checkpoint. People coming down from the north had to be checked at Bhusawal for any suspicious belongings, including opium, ganja and charas. The coolie kept arguing with the constable. Bhagwan looked at Sadashiv and said, 'Let's run away while these two are fighting.'

Sadashiv asked, 'Fool, did you forget what is in that trunk?'

Suddenly Bhagwan remembered the fiery stare of Azad. Around a year ago, Azad had given Bhagwan a Mauser pistol to be kept safe in Jhansi. After a month, Azad arrived and asked for the gun. Sadashiv went into the kitchen and brought out an aluminium container. He opened it in front of Azad, but there was nothing there. It was enough to make the commander mad. He instantly remembered that he had shifted it to another place. Sadashiv ran inside and brought it back. He had hidden it under a heap of old newspapers.

Azad was fuming; he loved his Mauser as if it were an extension of his body. He said, 'I don't care if you and Bhagwan get captured by the police; the weapons are more important to me than you buffoons.'

There was no option other than to face the constable. Bhagwan had a slightly faulty pistol pinned to his waist and a few cartridges in the inner pocket. He managed to hold three cartridges in one hand, and with the other, he felt the pistol's firm handle and said something in Sadashiv's ear. If things went sour, there was only one thing they could pull off. There was a Mauser pistol, a few bottles of chemicals and cartridges in the trunk.

The constables were talking in Khandeshi Marathi. Sadashiv understood what they were saying and spoke up. 'Sahib, there are only medicines in my trunk; nothing is objectionable.'

The constable was irritated by the constant pleading of the coolie and now Sadashiv. He shouted, 'Open it now.'

Sadashiv sat down and opened the trunk; Azad's Mauser was on top of a dhoti. Sadashiv quickly folded it in the dhoti and lifted it up. He turned the trunk towards the constables and said, 'Look, nothing is in it. These glass bottles have Ayurvedic powder in them. You can taste it if you want. Should I take it out for you?'

The constable shook his head and said, 'Move the bottles; what is beneath it?'

'Nothing, Sahib, just clothes.' There was a paper bag beneath the bottles. Sadashiv explained the types of medicines it contained. A trickle of sweat ran down Bhagwan's forehead. He started chanting a random Sanskrit *shloka* to distract the constable.

Instead, the constable asked, 'What is inside?'

Bhagwan explained, 'Sahib, this medicine is described in Ayurveda as the next Sanjivani; it revitalizes the whole system. It can give strength to the organ which has gone limp. I hope you understand. I can make some portions for you if you need some.'

This was the last straw. The constable leaned over and picked up the paper bag. It had sixty cartridges for the Mauser pistol. The eyes of the constable widened as if he had seen a vile snake. The train on the next platform started moving.

Bhagwan placed his hand on Sadashiv's shoulder, pressed it and shouted, 'Go, go, go.'

Before the policeman could recover from the shock, Sadashiv closed the trunk, picked it up on his head and hastily ran towards the moving train. It was his last chance to escape.

One constable ran behind Sadashiv.

Bhagwan shouted, 'Hey, come here.' And he jumped onto the rails and ran in the opposite direction from Sadashiv. It was his plan to distract the police while Sadashiv escaped.

One constable ran behind Sadashiv while he pulled a string, and a whistle popped out of his pocket; with all his energy, he whistled. The other one jumped on the rails and followed Bhagwan.

A swarm of policemen arrived on the scene. Bhagwan took out his pistol and shouted, 'Turn back if you want to live.'

The constable ran as if he didn't hear it. Bhagwan pulled the trigger aiming at a spot near his leg. As the bullet passed a foot away from the constable, he fell back in fear, scratching his knees over hard-edged rocks between the rails.

Bhagwan came to the end of the rails and jumped over the signal wires only to find a horde of policemen coming towards him. He had been running towards a police station.

It was over for him. He turned around and looked at Sadashiv. He couldn't see him in the bunch of khaki-wearing bastards. For a moment, it felt as if Sadashiv had succeeded. The opposite platform was vacant. The train was gone. Amid the chaos, Bhagwan smiled for a second, but then he caught the glimpse of an iron trunk and Sadashiv lying on the platform with four constables pinning him down. Bhagwan's throat choked up, and the policemen grabbed him and dragged him away. His eyes were fixed on Sadashiv, and he muttered, 'Sorry, Panditji, we have failed you.'

At the end of the day, Sadashiv, Bhagwan and Panditji's Mauser ended up in Bhusawal's prison. They were not afraid of the police anymore; they were terrified of what Panditji would say, that he had given them a straightforward task and even then they had failed so stupidly. There was no point in hiding their identities. As the officer learned their names, he understood that they were the absconders in the Lahore Conspiracy Case. Immediately, a telegram went to Delhi and Lahore. Before the end of the day, a response arrived from both places.

Within two days, the police put them on a train, and they were taken to Lahore. It took three days to reach Lahore. When they arrived, the news broke. Jatin Dada had passed away after his legendary hunger strike of sixty-three days.

Sadashiv bemoaned, 'They have murdered Jatin Dada.'

Bhagwan replied, 'The time will come; we will hit back.'

Sadashiv nodded. 'We will.'

The identification parade started soon, and many approvers were feeling guilty about the death of Jatin Dada.

In Borstal Jail, one by one, approvers arrived to identify Bhagwan and Sadashiv.

Hans Raj Vohra, one of the main approvers in Saunders's murder, arrived with his head down. Bhagwan and Sadashiv were very well known to him. Hansraj was one of the youngest recruits of the party. He used to love listening to Bhagwan's songs and often requested him to sing some songs.

Bhagwan's eyes were aflame as Hans Raj approached. Sadashiv asked him to calm down. The police officer asked, 'Do you recognize who they are?'

Hans Raj raised his head as if a heavy burden was on his back and said, 'No, I have not seen them before.' He was ashamed of himself. Bhagwan felt hopeful. At last, Panditji's warning bombs had worked to inflict terror in the traitors' hearts, and Jatin Dada's sacrifice had shamed them.

Hans Raj went away. Other petty approvers also failed to recognize them.

The police officer was getting restless.

Then Phanindra Nath Ghosh walked in leisurely; it was his fifth identification parade, and he pronounced, loud and clear, 'Maharasthri alias Kailash. He is from Maharashtra or belongs to a Maharashtrian family from the Central Provinces.'

The police officer asked, 'Where have you seen him?'

'In Lahore, Agra, Jhansi and Delhi, he was recruited by Azad and is one of his favourites.'

Bhagwan angrily replied, 'Don't you dare to take the name of the commander-in-chief with that vile tongue! Do you realize who you are crossing?'

'Yes, I am perfectly aware of what I am doing. The revolution is over, lad. Face reality.'

'It is not over as long as the last one of us is alive. It is not over until all these white monkeys leave the land. It is not over until the commander-in-chief twirls his moustache with pride. And it is not over until Bhagat himself says it is over. Did you forget Phani Babu? The revolution will not be over until the exploitation of man by man is made impossible. I had such high regard for you. There's still time. Nothing is lost. You realize that you are standing in line with the most loathsome traitors in Indian history. Refrain from joining the ranks of Jai Chand and Mir Jafar. Turn back otherwise—'

Phanindra snapped, 'Otherwise, what will you do? Are you blind? The whole HSRA is behind bars. It is finished.'

'Are you forgetting who is still free?'

For a moment, a line of terror moved on the face of Phanindra. But he gathered himself and looked around. He was surrounded by khaki on all sides.

'I guess he failed to keep you out of prison; let us see how long he stays out.'

'He will stay out until you leave prison; count your days, Phani Babu. It is not easy to betray us.'

'I am being practical here. You can live and die in your utopia. I have a family to look after. I can see the naked truth. You cannot go to war with the mightiest empire in the world by assembling a bunch of passionate, imbecile and inexperienced idiots. I was there when Ghadar failed,

I saw what happened to the Kakori heroes, and I know what would happen to me if I stayed on your side.'

'Phani Babu, you don't know what will happen to you if you stay on the enemy's side.'

'I will see.'

'Count your days.'

Jai Gopal was intimidated by the conversation. He, too, identified Bhagwan and Sadashiv and went away.

Around fifteen revolutionaries were kept in Borstal Jail. They had been fasting since July. After the death of Jatin Dada, they had called a halt to the strike but were still weak and recovering.

On Sunday morning, the jailer arrived, and Bhagwan and Sadashiv were kept in the same cell. The jailer said, 'You will be returned to Bombay Province tonight.'

'Why?'

'Since most of the approvers couldn't identify you and your role in the Saunders murder is not yet proven, you will not be a part of the Lahore Conspiracy Case. They will run a separate case for you called the Bhusawal Bomb Case.'

'But—' Sadashiv began.

Bhagwan stopped him. Going out of Lahore meant there was still some scope for escape.

The jailer was about to leave when he said, 'Well, Bhagat Singh and Dutt will be brought here in some time.'

Bhagwan jumped up when the cells were opened and all the prisoners gathered in the open. Bhagwan and Sadashiv hugged every brave friend. When it came to Sukhdev, Bhagwan hesitated.

Bhagwan exclaimed, 'Sorry, we failed you.'

Sukhdev smiled and replied, 'Don't worry, you were caught by a silly mistake. Everything's not lost. At least now the British government knows the length and breadth of our operations. You have filled more terror into their hearts. Come here.'

Bhagwan hugged Sukhdev; he could make out each of Sukhdev's ribs.

At the same time, the little gate of the ground opened, and two frail young men walked in. It took a moment for Bhagwan to recognize Bhagat.

The firm, vibrant, beautiful Bhagat had been reduced to a mere shadow of his former self.

Bhagwan remembered their initial meetings in Mozang House. Bhagat used to tease Bhagwan a lot and, once, they had wrestled. Bhagat was taller, and Bhagwan was bulkier; Bhagwan thought he would win. But, within a minute, Bhagat's sharp moves and skill won over Bhagwan's brute strength, and he yielded. Then Bhagat teased him a lot about singing his favourite song.

Bhagwan and Sadashiv approached and hugged Bhagat and Dutt. Tears flowed from Bhagwan's eyes. He realized how they had failed Azad and Bhagat. He learned how much Bhagat and the others had suffered in the last five months.

Bhagat exclaimed, 'Hey, Bhagwan, good to see you. Stop crying like a baby. Let us wrestle like old times; what do you say?'

Bhagwan chuckled, while crying, and replied, 'Even now, I know you will win.'

Bhagat laughed aloud, patting Bhagwan, and said, 'Yes, I know and, ultimately, you will have to sing.'

'I will. But, Bhagat, they are taking us back to Bombay Province.'

'Why? I thought Phani Babu has already identified you.'

'He did, and I could not get close enough to strangle him,' Sadashiv said.

Bhagwan said, 'I don't know, Bhagat, these white monkeys are playing some kind of game.'

Sukhdev intervened. 'They will make an example out of both of you. By staging a trial in Deccan, they will portray to the people of south and west India how hazardous it is to stand up against the Raj.'

Bhagat said, 'Let them do what they can; we will show defiance. Bhagwan will sing a song of rebellion in the heartland of Chhatrapati Shivaji Maharaj. The people of that land have not forgotten the grand rebel king and his exploits.'

Bhagwan smiled and said, 'I will fight for you, I will fight for Jatin Dada, I will fight for Panditji.'

Chapter 11

September 1929

Khan Bahadur was reading the case file of Bhagwan and Sadashiv. Deputy superintendent Syed Shah was sitting across from him. He had already gone through the file.

Syed Shah asked, 'Sir, what do you think? Why were these two going to Akola?'

Khan Bahadur removed his cap, placed it on the table and ran his hand through his steel grey hair. His facial muscles were tense.

Khan Bahadur said, 'It is evident that Azad established another bomb factory at Gwalior. In Sadashiv's suitcase, they found chemicals, empty bombshells and ready bombs along with a Mauser and sixty cartridges.'

'Bhagwan also had a pistol on him, which he fired at the constable.'

Khan nodded and continued, 'No doubt these men are trusted by Azad, but their rank and status in the party are secondary. They were not going south for action—'

Syed completed the sentence, 'Azad was sending this lot to someone else. These two were only carriers.'

'Exactly.'

'Who could it be?'

'I have a name in my mind. Get Phani Babu here immediately.'

Syed rang the bell, and a constable appeared. Syed gave him his orders, and he went out running. Khan Bahadur kept reading every detail from the file. After ten minutes, two constables arrived with Phanindra. He was in a white kurta and dhoti. Being an approver, he wasn't bound to wear the jail uniform.

Phanindra came in and stood near the table. Khan Bahadur took the notepad and started scribbling something on it. In between, he would look at the file and then resume writing again. Syed waited patiently; the chair beside him was vacant, but nobody offered it to Phanindra. Syed didn't even glance at him. They behaved as if Phanindra was not even present in the room.

When the scribbling stopped, Khan Bahadur put down the pen and looked at Phanindra. A sheepish smile was on his face, like a beggar standing before a temple.

Khan Bahadur said, 'I hope you have met our new guests at Borstal.'

'Yes, Sahib, I have identified them.'

'While your friends refused to identify him. What kind of leader are you, Phanindra?' The voice of Khan Bahadur sharpened.

Phanindra's face turned pale. He answered, 'Jai Gopal also identified both when I prompted him, but Hans Raj and the others did not because . . .'

'Because what?'

'Because of the hunger strikes and the death of Jatin Dada,' Phani said, looking at his feet.

'This is not how things are going to work. I need unconditional loyalty from approvers.'

'You have mine, Sir,' Phanindra replied instantly.

'Then tell me, why were they going to Bombay Province?'

Phanindra stayed quiet momentarily and then said, 'How would I know, Sir? I have been here for five months.'

'Speak up, Phani Babu; there's no time to waste. I know more than you think I do.'

'There is only one possibility, Sahib. Based on what I have heard and the quantity of armoury they were carrying, Panditji is trying to move his base to Deccan.'

'Why?'

'Maybe because your actions in northern India have made it impossible for revolutionaries to breathe free.'

'That I know; what else? Why Deccan?'

'Sahib, they must be planning some action there, and someone might be preparing the ground for HSRA.'

'Who? All of your jokers, except Azad, are behind bars.'

'One of the most dangerous men whose nuisance value is next to Azad, our finest sharpshooter in the party, is still out.'

Khan Bahadur chuckled. 'Sharpshooter, my foot. You, idiots, shoot cardboard using a dart gun and call yourself sharpshooters. Do you even understand the meaning of sharpshooting?'

Phanindra replied sharply, 'Sahib, I am talking about a man whose first bullet pierced through the heart of John Saunders. His single bullet killed your deputy superintendent. Then he walked away. Bhagat fired four shots only to make sure that he was dead. I am talking about a man who has never missed his mark; he is famous for not wasting a single bullet.'

Syed Shah turned towards Phanindra, 'Who is he?'

Khan Bahadur stood from his chair and spoke, 'His code name is M.'

Syed Shah was shocked. Khan Bahadur knew more about it. He was teasing Phanindra to get more information.

Phanindra replied, 'Yes, they might be going to M.'

'What does M stand for?' Syed Shah asked.

'I don't know, maybe Maratha; he is from Maharashtra; that is all I know about his identity.'

'What else? When did you meet him?'

'I have seen him in Lahore in Mozang House; he was with us during the stay at Agra. I know that he was the first one to shoot Saunders. He was also involved in the rescue planning of Jogesh Chander Chatterji. I don't know who recruited him for the party.'

'What is his position in the party?'

'Well, he is not the intellectual type like Bhagat and Bhagwati Charan Vohra. M is more like Azad. A soldier. He doesn't participate in intellectual debates on poverty and socialism, but he comes from a destitute family and has seen all colours of poverty. His insight into discussions was instrumental. His relationship with Bhagat is the most curious one. They have some sort of bet or race or challenge going on between them.'

'About what?'

'About who will die first for the country.'

'Mad men, anarchists,' Syed Shah said.

Khan Bahadur said, 'Well, I think I know where your sharpshooter is.'

Now, both Phanindra and Syed were shocked. Syed Shah said, 'What?'

'Yes, I firmly believe that the man you are speaking about, the M, and the suspect that CID is closely watching in Pune, are one and the same person.'

Syed Shah said, 'Then tell me, Phani Babu, if we catch him, will he break?'

'No, Sahib, He will die but he will not break.'

'You said he comes from a poor family; what if I offer him money?'

'Sahib, if you catch him alive, you will understand what a peculiar creature M is. He is infected with a specific disease endemic to that area.'

'Which is?'

'Maratha pride.'

'Yes, I know, but Andaman has broken many a Maratha's pride like a twig. Shall I tell you names?'

A bitterness welled up in Phanindra's voice; he said, 'Sahib, I know who gave away the noble cause in recent times, but M is made from different stuff. Let me tell you about an incident; when we were in Agra, Panditji was explaining methods and tactics of police torture, and no person could bear the pain. At the time, Rajguru was making chapatis on a fire. He put the blazing red iron tong on his chest and he did not utter a sound as he got burnt.'

'Then what happened?' Syed Shah asked.

'Then, at night, when everyone was asleep, Azad heard a painful moaning coming from M and woke me up. We went to him. When I touched him, he was burning with an extremely high fever. When Azad woke him up, he showed us the ugly blister on his chest. I asked, why did you do it? M said that he was testing himself to endure the police torture.'

'Lunatic,' Khan Bahadur said, with disbelief and disgust.

'Sir, we have to catch him,' Syed Shah said.

'Yes, we will. That is the reason why the two newcomers will be tried in Bombay Province. The case will provide a background to uncover what conspiracy is being planned in Maratha land. But Phanindra, we need your help in this.'

'Anything for you, Sahib.'

'When I get confirmation from the Pune team, you will accompany my men there to identify him before we arrest him.'

Phanindra's eyes went wide. 'Sahib, don't put me as bait in front of the wounded lion. That Maratha is insane; he will kill me before I can identify him. I will accompany you to any corner of the world if you arrest him first. But not before.'

'Do you think you have any choice here?' Khan Bahadur asked, in a stern voice.

'Sahib, I turned on my comrades only to save my life. Now you are asking me to risk it. I know that there is no option for me. But you should also understand that without my statement in court, you cannot establish a conspiracy against the crown. You have one ace in this game. It is your choice where to use it.'

Khan Bahadur did not like the insubordination but understood the point Phanindra was making. He replied shortly, 'You can go now. I will think about it.'

The same evening, Khan Bahadur got a telegram from Mumbai.

'Our friend has successfully acquired the trust of M alias Shivram Rajguru. The plan seems to involve the assassination of the governor of Bombay, Frederick Sykes. The likely venue is Race Course, Governor's Cup, date 27 September; awaiting your instructions.'

The same telegram went to the deputy inspector general of CID, Holland. He orchestrated the strategic movement of his police officers and informers, meticulously planning to apprehend Rajguru. Around midnight, he called Khan Bahadur and gave him some instructions. Only four days were left until the Governor's planned visit to Pune. Syed Shah was called in early the following day, with luggage for two weeks. He was sitting in his chair, awaiting instructions.

Khan Bahadur ordered, 'Take Jai Gopal. Don't tell him anything until the last moment. That man has a chicken's heart. He will die of morbid fear. Change his appearance, get him to mingle with the crowd. Hide him, if possible. But make sure he sees M from a sufficient distance. Do not come back without that sharpshooter. I want him alive.'

'Yes, sir.'

Once Bhagwan and Sadashiv were arrested, Rajguru began to worry about the plan, and his restlessness kept growing day by day. He decided to act on his own. He left Akola and went to Pune, which was his native place. He stayed with a friend, Savargaonkar.

Rajguru had a revolver with him. Using his contacts in Pune, he tried to gather more weapons for the action. A man named Keskar met Rajguru; he was the relative of a renowned Congress leader. He promised to provide Rajguru with some pistols.

He met Rajguru frequently and gained his trust. On 27 September 1929, Keskar came to Rajguru and chatted about how the British police were not keeping their promises regarding the hunger strikes of revolutionaries. This enraged Rajguru. Further, talking casually, Keskar whispered, 'Bhau, did you know that the governor of Bombay is coming to Pune?'

A cold chill ran down Rajguru's spine. He tried to hide his excitement, kept a poker face and asked, 'When and why?'

'Oh, tomorrow, the racecourse has a Governor's Cup tournament. He will be there for the inauguration, I guess.'

Savargaonkar said, 'Let him come and go; it is none of our business. On 29 September, they are showing a documentary on Jatin Dada's funeral in a theatre.'

Rajguru said, 'We will watch the documentary for sure.'

After Keskar left, Rajguru opened his trunk and took out a tin box. It contained a revolver and cartridges of 0.45 mm. Rajguru picked up the gun and gripped the handle. His hand knew every ridge and groove on the black metal. He smiled and started putting bullets in the revolver. Savargaonkar stared at Rajguru but chose not to speak.

The next day, the racecourse was filled with thousands of people. Hundreds of policemen were roaming around, keeping everything in control. The governor's entourage arrived on time. Rajguru couldn't catch a glimpse of the man as two lines of policemen surrounded him as he walked from his car to the pavilion.

To the left of the VIP section, Syed Shah stood in civilian clothes in the crowd, looking at the group in the opposite pavilion. The VIP section was in the middle of two pavilions filled with the public. Syed saw someone in the crowd, then nodded to a person standing behind him. Three Pathan constables dressed in civilian clothes brought forward a short man with a long red cotton *gamcha* wrapped around his face. The Pathans served as walls on each side of Jai Gopal. Now, Jai Gopal stood exactly behind Syed Shah's wrestlers. Syed Shah asked him, 'Look in the crowd and tell me if you see a familiar face.'

Jai Gopal was terrified because of the mystery. He leaned out just enough to get a glimpse and said, 'No, Sahib, I don't recognize anyone.'

'Don't act smart. Do as I say. Look carefully.'

'Sahib, please tell me what is happening.'

'Just do as I say, and you will understand. There is no reason to panic.'

Jai Gopal leaned out again and started observing the faces closely. Suddenly, he saw someone, a thin, dark man, wearing a white shirt and a Gandhi cap. His features were sharp, as if chiselled in basalt rock. His dark eyes were fixed on the governor's movement. Both hands were folded behind him, below his kurta. Jai Gopal's legs gave way, and he almost fell down. Syed held him, and the Pathans surrounded him again. Jai Gopal's eyes widened, and his mouth remained open.

Syed Shah asked, 'What is it?'

Slowly Jai Gopal looked up, moved his tongue on his dry lips and said, 'It is him, the dark man in the Gandhi cap—M.'

'Are you 100 per cent sure?'

'Sahib, how can I forget him? Arrest him immediately, and please take me out of here. If he sees me, his bullet will come to my head before I blink.'

Rajguru was standing next to the pavilion in the crowd, waiting for the formalities to end and the race to begin. He slowly moved towards the boundary of the VIP section to get close enough to take aim. However, the hordes of security and the public discouraged Rajguru from taking action. It was not wise to put innocent people's lives in danger. Also, it would be tough to escape. Rajguru could see governor Frederick Sykes, and his hand tightly gripped the revolver while he calculated the outcome of his actions. His heartbeat increased. He could not get a clear shot as there were too many people standing around the governor. He took a deep breath. His lungs filled with cold air. He felt a tingle on his skin, as when he and Bhagat had killed John Saunders.

Jai Gopal's heart felt as if it was going to come out of his ribcage. He joined his hands, tears in his eyes, and said, 'Sahib, please take me out of here. I don't want to die. '

Syed Shah looked at Jai Gopal with disgust and said, 'Stay here; I want to see what he will do.'

Jai Gopal said, 'He will act before a thought comes to your mind. If you wish to live, please attack, arrest or shoot him down now.'

The governor stood up to make a speech. Rajguru saw the opportunity for a clear shot. Syed Shah's hand went to his Mauser.

Rajguru's thumb went to the oiled hammer of his pistol. His thumb pulled it back, and he heard a satisfactory click. Syed Shah held his breath. This gamble was going to prove costly.

Chapter 12

September–October 1929

Rajguru calculated the act in his mind. In the next second, he was going to take out the revolver and shoot at the governor's head. The bullet would enter the skull near the right ear, and it might leave from the left temple. If he missed the mark, there was no other chance. Anyway, he would be caught for sure, or worse, would be shot down. But it would not stop there in any case; there would be a stampede or, worse, police firing on the public.

In an instant, Bhagat's words rang in his ears, *We understand the value of human life . . .*

Rajguru cursed in Marathi under his breath and said, 'This is your lucky day. Frederick. Live for another day.' He turned and started making his way out of the crowd.

Jai Gopal spoke up again. 'Sahib, please arrest him; he is leaving.'

Syed said, 'Shut up, you spineless mongrel. I will arrest him, but on my terms.'

Syed, too, had calculated what would happen if he tried to grab Rajguru. He was armed and alert, and he was not going to surrender easily. Syed did not want any loss of life on his watch.

After the event, Syed Shah called Kavthalkar, the local CID officer at Dak Bungalow. Syed Shah told him that Jai Gopal had identified Rajguru, and that it was time to make the final move as planned. Kavthalkar came out of the bungalow with a broad smile.

The next day, on 29 September, Rajguru and Savargaonkar went to watch the documentary on Jatin Dada's funeral. It left everyone teary-eyed. Rajguru was inconsolable; Savargaonkar had to control him for fear of drawing undue attention. Anger and sorrow were bursting in Rajguru's heart. He returned to the room in the evening, talking about memories of Jatin Dada at Agra.

Around 8 p.m., Keskar arrived at the room with a khadi bag. Rajguru changed the topic. After greeting them, Keskar put his hand in the sling bag and took out an old pistol. He placed it in front of Rajguru. When he checked it, Rajguru found that the barrel of the gun was broken. He asked, 'What is this? The barrel is broken.'

'Yes, it is faulty, but if you can repair the barrel, it'll be as good as new.'

Savargaonkar almost scolded, 'You promised a working pistol; this is a piece of crap.'

Keskar looked down and replied, 'I am sorry, I only had this one. I promise to find you more.'

Rajguru put a hand on his shoulder. 'Don't worry; at least you tried. But Savargaonkar is right; this is crap; no one can repair this.'

Keskar asked, 'Can you please show me what a proper weapon looks like. I have never seen one.'

Savargaonkar looked at Rajguru and gave a stern look. Rajguru ignored him. He was already feeling depressed after watching the documentary on Jatin Dada's funeral. Rajguru smiled and took out the tin box from his bag. Inside was a pitch-black revolver with cartridges.

Keskar's eyes widened; he folded his hands in namaste and said, 'Brother, you are a true patriot and a great revolutionary. I feel fortunate to be in your presence. I will try hard to find you weapons.'

Keskar left and walked around for an hour to see whether he was being followed. After midnight, he went to CID officer Kavthalkar. He was fully dressed and ready in his office. Syed Shah was sleeping on a chair. When Keskar arrived, he discussed the weapon Rajguru possessed.

Kavthalkar and Syed Shah decided on a plan, and around twenty armed constables walked out of the police station in minutes. A jeep and a police van stopped near Rajguru's residence. It was about 1 a.m. Syed Shah nodded, and a dozen constables barged into the room in seconds. Rajguru and Savargaonkar were caught before they fully woke up from sleep. Police found the tin box with a revolver and fifteen cartridges and, from his coat pocket, another fully loaded automatic revolver was seized. It was over. Syed Shah left for Lahore the next day with his trophy, Shivram Hari Rajguru, alias M, alias Raghunath.

Azad learned the news the next day. He was shattered. His most trusted soldier was also behind bars now.

Vaishampayan was concerned about Azad. They contemplated the next step. At every step, they were losing a vital member of the party. Only a handful of them were out of jail. Vaishampayan asked, 'Panditji, what should we do now?'

Vaishampayan thought Azad was drowning in sorrow and there was nothing left to be done.

Azad said, 'Did you know what happened when Bhagwan Krishna was about to be born?'

'No.'

'Kansa had murdered seven of Devaki's children in prison and, of course, he was going to murder the eighth one.'

'Then what happened?'

'By God's grace, a terrible storm came to Mathura, like no one had ever seen or heard. Bhagwan Krishna was born in prison, and the prison doors opened.'

Vaishampayan said, 'That much I know already. Then Vasudev, his father, carried him out to Gokul.'

'No, it was not that easy; although God opened the prison gates, Vasudev still had to face the wrath of Yamuna. To save his only child, the only hope for humanity, Vasudev had to risk his own life and carry his only surviving newborn right into the ferocious river.'

Vaishampayan asked, 'What does this mean?'

'God will help you only when you have the guts to sacrifice everything.'

'Tell me, what should I do?'

Addressing Vaishampayan by his pet name, he said, 'Bacchan, it is time to rescue Krishna from Kansa's prison. Mind you, we are not going to get any divine help. We must break the prisons ourselves and rescue Krishna by risking it all.'

'Understood; what are my orders?'

'Bacchan, they have kept Bhagat and Dutt in Central Jail while others are in Borstal Jail; both prisons are approximately 200 metres from each other. They allow Bhagat and Dutt to visit our comrades in Borstal every Sunday. Initially, Bhagat used to walk from Central Jail, but now they use an armed van. So, you will leave for Lahore and observe the Sunday schedule minutely, then report back. Send a message to Bhagat telling him to be prepared for a rescue operation. Enough of the judicial drama; it is time to take swords in our hands.'

Vaishampayan left Cawnpore and arrived in Lahore; for three or four Sundays, he observed Bhagat and Dutt's schedule and noted every detail. He sent the message to Bhagat through visitors, but Bhagat refused to be rescued. After a month, Vaishampayan returned to Cawnpore, only to find that an urgent Central Committee meeting had been called. Vaishampayan went to see Azad; he was talking to Bhagwati Charan Vohra. Yogendra Sukul of Bihar was also present.

Azad saw Vaishampayan and embraced him.

Vaishampayan said, 'Panditji, I have completed the task. Can we discuss the plan in the meeting?'

Azad pondered over it and replied, 'Yes, you can, but something else is proposed by Bhagwati Bhai. We will put the issue to the vote.'

Vaishampayan agreed. In the evening, all the dignitaries gathered, and the meeting began. Bhagwati Bhai spoke first, 'The restlessness and anger within each of us is evident. Bhagat, along with fifteen of our comrades, is behind bars. Rajguru, Sadashiv and Bhagwan have been added to the list. The plan to assassinate the Bombay governor has failed. In fact, we were unable to assist Rajguru. The intent to terrorize approvers has also failed. We failed to save our dearest friend Jatin. We read every day about the torture inflicted upon our brothers by this farce they call a judicial system. Hence, I propose an action that will underline everything we stand for. An act which will make Britain realize that they are playing with fire.'

Yashpal asked, 'Bapubhai, what do you propose?'

Bhagwati stated, 'I propose to cut off the head of the snake.'

Yogendra asked, 'What does that mean?'

Azad replied gravely, 'It means that we will now assassinate the viceroy of India, Lord Irwin.'

Everybody held their breath for a second. Azad observed the reaction with his penetrating stare. Yogendra replied first, 'I am ready.'

Azad, twirling his moustache, smiled and nodded at Yogendra.

Yashpal said, 'But this is dangerous and unprecedented.'

Bhagwati replied, 'Yes, it is dangerous but not unprecedented; in 1872, a prisoner at Andaman killed Lord Mayo for personal reasons. In 1907, revolutionaries tried twice but failed. In December 1912, Basanta Kumar Biswas and the great Rash Behari Bose threw a bomb at Viceroy Hardinge, who was entering Delhi on an elephant.'

Azad continued, 'Hardinge suffered significant injuries but lived. However, if we proceed with this plan, we will ensure that Irwin does not live to see another sunrise.'

'How will we do it?'

'This time, we will do it remotely. Bacchan, go and call Wireless.'

Hansraj, alias Wireless, entered the room, Azad nodded at him, and he began to speak. 'I can build a bomb which can be detonated by an electric spark from a long distance. But I will need a few things, which are hard to find.'

Bhagwati said, 'Tell me how it will work. As far as I know, the bombs that Jatin Dada taught us to make, using picrates, cannot be triggered by electricity.'

'I am not going to use picrate. I will need a new chemical, TNT (Trinitrotoluene), a detonator of fulminate mercury, and a good battery that can hold at least six cells.'

Bhagwati said, 'But TNT is only used by the army. How will we get access to it?'

Azad replied, 'I will arrange for the TNT, detonator and battery; you don't worry about it. Just assure me that it will work.'

Wireless said, 'Panditji, it will work at least ten times better than the picrate bombs.'

Yashpal asked, 'But how will we get near the viceroy? After the Assembly bombing and Rajguru's plan to assassinate the Bombay governor, I know that security around Irwin has been beefed up to such an extent that it is impenetrable. His public appearances have also been curtailed. I say, it is impossible.'

Azad said, 'There was a proposal last year when our comrades had assembled in Delhi to form the HSRA.

Unfortunately, no one who was present at that meeting is here with us. But there was a proposal to bomb the Simon Commission. Of course, it was very much protected, but the plan was to bomb their train.'

'How?'

'The practical part did not materialize due to various reasons. But the picrate bombs were ready with us. Either we had to throw them from outside or from inside the train. However, I specifically asked Wireless to devise a mechanism to do it remotely.'

Yashpal was shocked. 'Do you plan to bomb the viceroy's train?'

'Yes.'

Bhagwati said, 'Panditji, if the viceroy is on the train, and we place the bomb on the railway lines, then the possibility of Irwin getting harmed is minimal.'

Azad said, 'Bhai, I understand the nature of the problem. The only solution is to make the bomb powerful enough to blow away at least two adjoining bogeys. What do you say, Wireless, is it possible?'

'Panditji, it is possible. In the great war of 1914, TNT was also used in landmines, powerful enough to blow up the train. Basically, I am going to build a landmine, which can be triggered by electricity.'

Bhagwati said, 'Irwin is scheduled to return to Delhi on 29 October from Bombay. I have a located a spot around 9 miles away from Delhi.'

Azad smiled; his eyes lit up. He rose and spoke, 'I am a man of few words; I have been fighting this war long enough. After Kakori, I saw my comrades and mentors go to the gallows or sent to Andaman. I stood my ground and built this party again from scratch and found gems like Bhagat, Sukhdev, Jatin Das and Rajguru. Today the most precious of HSRA are behind bars, and His Excellency Lord Irwin is trying his best to get them hanged. We come from families who cannot afford square meals; we cannot even afford the legal help required in the conspiracy case. His Excellency thinks that the Congress party has distanced itself from Bhagat Singh; no one is backing the revolutionaries. But they forget that Chandrashekhar Azad is still alive. They succeeded in murdering Jatin Dada most viciously and got away with it. The sham they are putting up in the name of the judicial process, they think no power above them can hold them accountable. My brothers, the time has come to give His Excellency a taste of his own medicine. Let us take fireworks to his doorstep. Inquilab Zindabad!'

All the revolutionaries stood up and echoed the call.

Azad had contacts in the armoury near Allahabad. He arranged the supplies required, and within a week, Wireless prepared the bomb.

Meanwhile, Azad went to Cawnpore and met Ganesh Shankar Vidyarthi. Yogendra Sukul was also there.

Vidyarthi was the most respectable member of the revolutionary family. His articles in *Pratap* played a crucial role in infusing revolutionary ideas into the masses. He wrote extensively on the Lahore Conspiracy Case. When the plan was discussed with Vidyarthi, he implored, 'Panditji, I request you to delay the bombing. In the last month (October 1929), Irwin promised dominion status to Gandhiji in the near future and a round table conference to discuss the Constitution of India. After receiving a backlash from England, Irwin took back his words in front of Gandhi and Jinnah. The demand for complete independence raised by Bhagat Singh in Lahore court is causing repercussions throughout the country. The nation wants complete freedom, not the mockery called dominion status. Subhash Bose and Nehru had rejected the offer altogether. Hence, due to the arguments of Bhagat in the court and the mood of the youth of India, the Congress party is finally planning to take a stand on complete independence in their Lahore session.'

Yogendra added, 'Panditji, the session will happen next month. If you permit, I want to visit the session and personally meet Gandhiji.'

Azad asked, 'Why? Have you forgotten that the CID dogs are looking for you?'

Yogendra answered, 'Yes, I know, and I will be careful. I want to ask Gandhiji's help regarding the Lahore Conspiracy Case. I will explain our stand to him and convince him to aid us in judicial proceedings to ensure the future of Bhagat Singh and others.'

Azad sternly said, 'Do you seriously think Gandhiji will help us?'

Yogendra said, 'I have known him since the Champaran Satyagraha; I hope he will listen to me patiently. I know he doesn't support our methods, but believe me, Gandhiji is the only *astra*, which can prevent the British from passing the death sentence. If he speaks for Bhagat from the dais of the Lahore session, England will listen.'

Azad folded his hands and went into deep thought.

Yogendra remarked, 'If we harm Irwin, Gandhiji will not help us.'

Azad replied, 'That part I understand.'

Vidyarthi added, 'Panditji, the aim of HSRA is complete independence, and it is against the demand of dominion status. The party's dream is coming to light due to the hard work of Bhagat. He forced Congress to change its twenty-year-old stance of dominion status from behind bars. Surely you don't want to discredit Bhagat's diplomacy?'

Azad let out a long sigh and said, 'All right, I will put this on hold until you meet Gandhiji or Congress's declaration on complete independence. But don't think that Irwin's crimes will go unpunished. He will face my justice sooner or later.'

After the meeting, Azad sent a revolutionary on a secret mission to Madras. It took three days to travel to that city. On the first platform, a specially decorated train was present. It was the official travel wagon of His Excellency Lord Irwin, called the Viceregal train. It was decorated with marigold flowers from the engine to the last coach.

W.H. Smalley, the special Viceregal train master, was standing on the platform, supervising the arrangements and decoration of the train.

The revolutionary went near the stationmaster and asked, 'Sahib, Bada Babu is in Madras?'

'Yes.'

'This train is specifically for him.'

'Yes.'

'I mean, only Babu travels in this train? No one else?'

'Are you a fool? This is a special train for His Excellency; his staff and servants also travel on it.'

'Can I see him? I mean, when will he be arriving at the station?'

'I don't know. Nobody knows except him.'

'Oh, I understand. Sorry for my ignorance. What coach does he travel in?'

'Third coach. Why are you asking?' The station master was irritated by now.

'Nothing, Sahib, I just asked out of curiosity; it is my first time seeing this beauty.'

'All right, get moving now.'

The revolutionary turned and muttered, 'The third coach it is.'

Chapter 13

November 1929

Kali Pado Bhattacharya and Pulin Behary Roy, two young men from Howrah, couldn't shake the deep sense of sadness and anger that had consumed them ever since they'd learnt about the death of the revolutionary Jatindra Nath Das. The fire of revolution burned within them, and they knew they had to do something.

Kali said, 'Jatin Dada's sacrifice is haunting me. Whenever I remember his last procession, my heart cries, and I feel helpless. The British just let him die. I can't get over it!'

Pulin said, 'Yes, Kali, It's heart-wrenching. I thought the Raj would be ashamed of the sacrifice and would act as per justice, but now they've beaten up Bhagat Singh and the others in court. Right in front of the magistrate. They were just brutally kicked by hundreds of constables until some of them lost consciousness.'

Kali, agitated, asked, 'How dare they treat our heroes like this?'

Pulin replied, 'I found it funny that Bengal is the birthplace of the Indian armed revolution. We gave hundreds of martyrs to the motherland. We have always been at the forefront of sacrificing our lives. A Bengali leads from the front and gives up his life fighting with Bhagat Singh, while another Bengali, Phani Babu, is leading the traitors to put a noose around the neck of Bhagat. Shame on him. Our people are betraying us, and the British are showing no mercy! It's high time we took matters into our own hands.'

Kali said, 'I also can't stand it any longer. The rage inside me is boiling over. We must clean the slate for Bengalis. It is a matter of honour now.'

Pulin said, 'We need to stand, just like Bhagat Singh, Azad and Jatindra Nath Das did.'

'You're right. It's time to take a stand, no matter the cost. We must ensure traitors like Phanindra Nath Ghosh receive the punishment they deserve.'

'Let's plan. We need to send a clear message that we will not tolerate betrayal and oppression. We must join the fight for our country's freedom and make our Bengali brothers proud. We'll make sure Ghosh pays for his betrayal. We'll make him regret siding with the enemy,' Pulin said, his voice filled with determination.

With their hearts set on avenging their fallen brother, Kali and Pulin planned their journey to Lahore.

Upon reaching Lahore on 19 November 1929, Kali and Pulin blended into the city, posing as watchmakers. They went to Moolchand's mandir in Naulakha Bazaar, where they were permitted to stay until 23 November. For four days, they assimilated into Lahore and gathered the necessary materials for the plan.

On 23 November, Kali and Pulin went to the dharamshala of Deviram Chetala in Ramgali, seeking accommodation. Deviram, a kind-hearted man, allowed them to sleep in the kitchen as no rooms were available.

The duo hired a tonga the following morning and went to Lahore Central Jail. As they approached the prison, Kali whispered, 'Remember, Pulin, we must remain vigilant. We can't afford to make any mistakes.'

Pulin nodded, his face a mask of determination.

At the jail, they conducted a reconnaissance of the area, noting the layout and security measures. As they were returning, they struck up a conversation with the tonga driver, discreetly gathering information on the whereabouts of the residences of CID special superintendent Khan Bahadur Abdul Aziz and special magistrate Rai Sahib Shri Krishan. Kali specifically asked and confirmed the location of Phanindra Nath Ghosh.

With the necessary information in hand, they finalized their plan. They were going to create coconut bombs, sneak them into the court, and assassinate Ghosh when he came to give his statement.

On the fateful evening of 24 November, Kali and Pulin returned to the dharamshala. After 7 p.m., they huddled together in the dharamshala kitchen. They laid a newspaper on the floor and started preparations.

'Remember what we learned by ourselves in Howrah, Pulin?' Kali asked as they mixed the chemicals. 'One wrong move, and it's all over.'

Pulin nodded, his hands steady as he filled the coconut shells with the volatile mixture.

They had successfully filled one coconut shell and worked on the second when disaster struck.

'Kali, be careful!' Pulin shouted as the coconut shell slipped from Kali's grasp.

In that instant, the bomb exploded, sending a shock wave throughout the dharamshala. The duo jumped away just in time, but the force of the explosion left them stunned and injured, and their eardrums likely ruptured. Debris flew through the air, and the kitchen roof was blown away.

As the dust settled, Kali and Pulin found themselves amidst the wreckage, their hearts pounding and their plan in shambles. The residents of the dharamshala, startled by the explosion, quickly gathered at the scene.

'What happened here?' a man shouted, as others gasped at the destruction before them.

Kali and Pulin exchanged worried glances, realizing that not only had their plan failed, their cover was blown too.

Within ten minutes, the police arrived, whistles screeching and lights flashing. They found Kali and Pulin amidst the rubble and chaos, still disoriented from the explosion. The police discovered the intact live bomb, newspaper cuttings with photos of Bhagat Singh and Batukeshwar Dutt tucked into their pockets close to their hearts, and a sharp, lethal knife.

As they were handcuffed and led away, Kali and Pulin shared a glance, their eyes filled with both defiance and regret.

In the following days, they were tortured, interrogated and eventually charged with possession of explosive materials and conspiracy to commit murder. Throughout the trial, Kali and Pulin's admiration for Bhagat Singh and their hatred for Phanindra Nath Ghosh was apparent. They refused to express remorse for their actions, instead reiterating their dedication to the revolutionary cause.

In his final statement, Kali declared, 'We sought to avenge our brother Jatindra Nath Das and bring justice to a Bengali traitor. We regret nothing, for we acted in the name of our country and the heroes who have come before us.'

Pulin echoed his sentiments, adding, 'Our only regret is that we failed to complete our mission. But know this: our cause will live on, and others will rise to finish what we started.'

The judge, unmoved by their passionate declarations, sentenced Kali and Pulin to seven years in prison for their crimes.

With their heads held high, Kali Pado Bhattacharya and Pulin Behary Roy stepped into the darkness of their prison cell, their spirits unbroken and their love for their country and its heroes undimmed.

Baikunth was exhausted from the rigorous khukri training in the bamboo forest the day before and overslept. Suddenly, a loud thud near his head startled him awake. He rubbed his eyes to see his mentor, Ranendranath, standing above him with a newspaper roll in his hand.

'Wake up, Bihari! The Bengalis are still leading the fight for our nation,' Ranendranath exclaimed proudly. He tossed the newspaper at Baikunth, which landed on his chest with a heavy thump. Ranendranath had never called him a Bihari. Ranendranath was himself born and brought up in Bihar. Baikunth found the nomenclature amusing.

He sat up and read the newspaper. His eyes widened with surprise as he saw the headline about two Bengali youths attempting to assassinate Phanindra Nath Ghosh, an approver in the Lahore Conspiracy Case. He couldn't believe it. How could two young men not associated with any revolutionary organization attempt such a dangerous mission?

Ranendranath smirked, seeing the shock on Baikunth's face. 'You'll keep practising on bamboo while someone else will do the work that is supposed to be done by you.'

Baikunth said, 'This is wonderful. This shows how much people love Bhagat Singh and other revolutionaries. I salute the courage of these boys. I wish I could live up to Bihar's aspirations and yours.'

Ranendranath's eyes glinted with pride, on hearing Baikunth's words. 'Listen carefully, Baikunth. You need to be smart in your approach. You can't afford to be reckless like these boys. You need a plan, a strategy and, most importantly, patience.'

Baikunth nodded, soaking up every word Ranendranath spoke. He knew he had much to learn but was willing to take on any challenge. He replied, 'We will strike only once, and it will be lethal.'

Chapter 14

November 1929

As the evening exercises at Tilak Maidan ended, Baikunth and Ranendranath walked back home. At the door, Baikunth had just taken out the keys to unlock the door when he saw that the lock was broken. He looked at Ranendranath, who nodded back. Baikunth just had a bamboo staff with him. He kicked the double-panelled door with all his might, and it parted in a cloud of dust. The interior was pitch-dark.

Ranendranath took the initiative and stepped forward. Baikunth stopped his teacher and entered the room with a defensive stance.

He entered cautiously, on high alert, aware that something dangerous lurked in the dark. Suddenly, someone struck out from the shadows, a stick whistled through the air. But Baikunth was quick and deftly dodged the attack, his own bar hitting back with precision and power.

The two fighters moved through the house in a blur of motion, their sticks clashing and clattering as they struck and parried. Baikunth's stick-fighting training was tested as the attacker's experience and skill pushed him to his limits.

Despite the difficult situation, Baikunth remained focused and determined. He anticipated the attacker's next move and countered it by landing a solid blow on his opponent's shoulder. The mysterious attacker stumbled and Baikunth saw his chance. He lunged forward, delivering a final strike to knock out the attacker, but somehow, the staff lost its weight in the middle of the air. The air moved out of the cavity of the bamboo with a sharp, whistling sound. Something shone in the dark like a silver flash. The attacker had cut the staff in half, right before it fell on him.

For a second, Baikunth took an offensive stand; half the staff had a pointy edge now. But then something moved inside him. He recollected the silver spark. The broken staff fell from his hand. He clasped his hands together, bowed and exclaimed, 'Yogender Baba, *pranaam*.'

Ranendranath was already inside the house and was waiting for this moment. He lit a kerosene lamp, and the room was lit up, in an orangish hue.

Yogendra smiled at Baikunth, looked at Ranendranath and said, 'Congratulations, you have trained this lad very well.'

Ranendranath replied, 'Not very well, I guess. First, he loses his weapon; next, he puts down the stick when he recognizes you.'

Yogendra said, 'About losing the weapon, the boy was ready to attack with half of the stick. And what's wrong with recognizing me?'

Ranendranath replied, 'Oh, seriously? One shouldn't trust anyone waiting in the dark with a machete.'

'But he knew me; he recognized me.'

'So Bhagat really knew Phanindra Nath Ghosh, who stabbed Bhagat Singh in the back in broad daylight.'

Yogendra's face darkened, and he said, 'Yes, I know how much it hurts that the head of Bihar is the face of betrayal. Phani Babu and Manmohan have blackened our faces at a national level. But, there's very little that we can do about it now.'

Ranendranath said, 'Exactly, my point. There is very little that can be done once you join HSRA. This boy is good. Let him work for the Seva Dal or Congress. Why do you need one more life to be spent behind bars?'

Yogendra said, 'Ranendranath, you were a revolutionary once. You left us and now work for Congress. It is your choice. Baikunth wishes to work with us; that is his choice. Let him decide.'

Ranendranath said, 'Fair enough. But ask your newbie, what has he done?'

Yogendra turned to him with a stern look.

Baikunth said, 'Baba, I went to see Phani Babu at Bettiah; I had a chance to kill him.'

Yogendra angrily asked, 'Who authorized you to go to Bettiah?'

Baikunth replied, 'I went there on my own.'

Yogendra reprimanded, 'Boy, you cannot be a part of a revolutionary party if you cannot follow orders. Remember, you are a soldier.'

Ranendranath intervened, 'And what does a soldier do?'

Baikunth replied in an embarrassed voice, 'Follows orders, but . . .'

'But?'

Baikunth replied, 'I am not just a mindless soldier; I aspire to become a revolutionary, like Bhagat Singh, to critically think and analyse the situation. Not just follow anything blindly but to follow my ideology, to choose a path of action which is good for my country.'

Ranendranath said, 'Baikunth, you are right. You are not just a cog in a machine. You will think and act. You should question everything, even your superior, when they order you. Or you can join Congress. Here everything is decided democratically.'

Baikunth said, 'The other day, Bhagat said that the sword of revolution is sharpened on the whetting stone of ideas. And I cannot get that thought out of my head now.'

Yogendra patted Baikunth's back and said, 'I guess, you are on the right path to becoming a revolutionary. Think about everything, but never question orders. We are an army, not some philosophical club. But first, tell me what happened at Bettiah.'

Baikunth replied, 'The CID had brought the traitor to show where and how Bhagat Singh and Panditji met him. I went to Meena Bazar and waited in the opposite shop. He was there in front of me for five minutes. I had a khukri with me; I could have easily taken him out . . .'

Yogendra said, 'But you didn't find the courage? Because there was no chance of you getting out of there alive.'

Baikunth bowed his head and said, 'Yes, I was afraid.'

Yogendra asked, 'What if the party asks you to do it now? Will you be able to do it now?'

Baikunth's face lightened up. 'Yes, definitely. I will do it.'

Yogendra said, 'Even at the cost of your life?'

For a second, Baikunth's eyelids fluttered, and he said, 'Yes, even at the cost of my life.'

Yogendra exhaled and said, 'In the fraction of a second after my question, you saw your wife's face. Am I right?'

'Yes.'

'Believe me, there's nothing wrong with your reaction. It's just that you are not ready yet.'

'But Baba, you saw what I can do with weapons; I am learning to shoot now. I will learn about bombs very soon.'

Yogendra shook his head and said, 'Do you realize what kind of courage it takes to manufacture harmless bombs and throw them in the Central Assembly, then surrender yourself, only to be one hundred percent sure that they are going to hang you, ultimately? Do you understand the gravity of the situation? Do you understand what kind of heart you need to go on a hunger strike for more than 100 days and watch your brothers die a slow, torturous painful death every day?'

'Yes, Baba, I understand. I cried for days after Jatin Dada died. I even went to see the train carrying him.'

'No, Baikunth, you are missing the point. Every soul felt bad for Jatin Dada, but a true revolutionary will envy his death. He has achieved something which will be unforgettable in human history.'

'What?'

'A warrior's death. Baikunth, you will be ready when you are—'

Ranendranath completed the sentence, 'Ready to sacrifice your life for the cause.'

'Yes.'

Baikunth remained silent.

Ranendranath asked, 'So, tell me, why are you here?'

Yogendra replied, 'I came here to check on Baikunth. I will stay for the night and leave in the morning.'

Baikunth and Ranendranath prepared dinner. After eating, Baikunth and Yogendra set out to walk on the banks of the Budhi Gandak River. It was a foggy and cold night.

Baikunth said, 'It is not suitable for you to travel. The CID is looking for you.'

Yogendra replied, 'There is no point in hiding; today or tomorrow, I am bound to get caught or shot. I have to do the work assigned to me.'

Baikunth said, 'Baba, if you don't mind, please tell me what went wrong at the Maulania dacoity?'

Yogendra replied, 'Baikunth, it was my job to plan the nitty-gritty of the action. I had done my job well. It is always our first priority not to shed the blood of our own countrymen. But the nature of action is always unpredictable. It was 7 June, and the monsoon had not yet started. The land was dry, and the weather was very hot. I sent Raghuni Chamar to take weapons from Phanindra as he was the committee member of HSRA, and as per the party rule, it was the responsibility of committee members to hold onto weapons. Raghuni learnt that Phanindra was not in Bettiah, and he went to Manmohan Bannerjee. Manmohan gave Raghuni three swords and one revolver. Manmohan had a chicken's heart. He always lived in the shadow of Phanindra. They never participated in any dacoity. I had asked Raghuni to call Manmohan to join the action, but he refused. Instead, he went to some wedding so he could have a solid alibi. However, I never counted on such buffoons for action.

'The moon was obscured by dark clouds, casting an eerie shadow over the house of Bauk Mahto, which was slightly isolated from the village of Maulania. We heard that it belonged to a wealthy landlord, and that most of his family members were going to some function in the adjacent town. We were armed with spears, swords and guns and had gathered outside the house. After observing the building for over four to five hours, we found at least four men in the house. It was risky to initiate action. But I took the call. Just after midnight, I signalled for my men to advance.

'Kanwal Nath Tiwari asked, "Baba, how will we do it?"

'I replied, "We need to be quick and efficient. Get inside, grab everything of value and leave no trace and no violence."

'The group advanced towards the house, and as we were about to enter, suddenly, the door opened, and a man emerged from inside the house.

'He was terrified on seeing our weapons, and he asked in a shaky voice, "Who are you, people? What do you want?"

'I spoke firmly. "We are revolutionaries, and we have come to take what rightfully belongs to the people. Do not resist; we promise no one will be harmed."

'However, the man turned and ran inside the house, shouting, "*Dakoo, dakoo*". As the house was on the periphery, it was unlikely that his cries would reach the village. Still, he left us no choice. We went inside, drawing our swords.

'In the narrow alley which joined the drawing room with the interior, three men attacked us with swords. A fight ensued. Suddenly, I saw that Kanwal Nath's wrist had been slashed. Blood started spurting out of the wound. This infuriated my fellow comrades, and someone thrust a spear into the homeowner's stomach, rupturing most of his internal organs. I learnt later that his name was Saral. He fell to the ground, and I could see that he would not survive. The landlord's family fell back. All of them were injured, but Saral was grievously hurt.

'We moved ahead and asked for the valuables. They guided us to a small room and showed us an iron safe. We took the valuables and quickly dispersed into the night, leaving behind a trail of blood and chaos.

'Manmohan returned to Beria on the evening of 8 June after the dacoity was completed. On his return, he met Raghuni, as per my directions. Raghuni gave Manmohan an account of the dacoity at Maulania and handed him the swords, revolver and ornaments taken during the dacoity. It was later realized that Kanwal Nath Tiwari had a gash on his arm when one of our fellow revolutionaries missed his intended target and struck Kanwal by mistake with his sword. Kanwal, after satisfying Manmohan's queries, went to a dharamshala at Bettiah. On the morning of 8 June, his injury was attended to by sub-assistant surgeon H.S. Lahiri. On 10 June, Manmohan Bannerji visited him there, taking with him some money which had been procured during the dacoity. He gave the money to Kanwal Nath Tiwari for his expenses.

'Meanwhile, the CID arrested Phani Babu in Calcutta on 8 June. The news reached Manmohan in two days, and he realized that his days were numbered. On 11 June, Inspector Baghchi visited the dharamshala and saw Kanwal Nath Tiwari with a bandaged arm. On 14 June, a police party visited the house of Manmohan Bannerji, but he hid from them. On 16 June, however, he gave himself up and was arrested. Raghuni was also detained and tortured to become an approver. On 20 June, he was taken to Lahore where Phanindra, who had already turned traitor, convinced Manmohan to join his league. This traitor never had his own opinions throughout his life. Hence, he always agreed with whatever Phani Babu said. Also, it is suspected that Phani got a pretty deal for Manmohan. Then Manmohan was brought back to Bettiah again, where he and Raghuni produced and handed over to the police the property in Manmohan Bannerjee's possession, which had been stolen in the Maulania dacoity, as well as the swords which had been used in that dacoity. Manmohan was taken back to Lahore on 14 July; on 23 July, he made a statement to a magistrate and accepted pardon.'

Baikunth asked, 'What will you do now, Baba?'

Yogendra said, 'Something big is being planned by Panditji. I cannot tell you the details, but I have some tasks. I will leave tomorrow for Lahore. The Congress session is going to be held there in a few days. I am planning to meet Gandhiji to discuss Bhagat Singh's case.'

Baikunth was shocked, 'But you cannot travel to Lahore. They are looking for you everywhere. You will be caught.'

'Baikunth, some day I am bound to get caught. I cannot let fear stop me.'

'But will Gandhiji listen to you?'

'We have known each other since the days of Champaran Satyagraha. I guess he will listen to me. Acharya Kriplani and Ganesh Shankar Vidyarthiji are going to arrange the meeting. This could be our chance to save Bhagat and stop what Panditji is planning to do. If this doesn't work and Panditji succeeds in his plan, there is no going back to non-violence. Baikunth, a storm is coming; it will either take away the alien rule of the British or it will sweep the revolutionary movement aside.'

Baikunth asked, 'Baba, what is the meaning of dominion status that Gandhiji is asking for?'

Yogendra smiled and said, 'Dominion status means India will be part of the British empire. But the British will allow Indians to run their country. India will be autonomous within the British Empire and will have an 'equal status' as Britain but will have an 'allegiance to the Crown'. What it means is that King George V will continue to reign as the Emperor of India.'

Baikunth asked, 'Where did this term come from?'

Yogendra said, 'Congress has been asking for dominion status since the times of Dadabhai Nauroji and Lokmanya Tilak. However, the nature of dominion status evolved over time, asking for more and more freedom. Even the Nehru report asked for the same with some more conditions. The Raj appointed the Simon Commission to draft constitutional reforms as a gradual move towards dominion status for India, but as there was no Indian on the panel, the Congress party denounced it. You know what happened to the Simon Commission, right?'

'Yes, I know. Then Congress established the All Parties Conference.'

'Exactly, this conference was tasked to draft a Constitution for India. It submitted the famous

Nehru Report. The report was prepared by a committee chaired by Motilal Nehru, with Jawaharlal Nehru acting as the secretary. Gandhiji gave Irwin one year to accede to the demands of the Nehru Report, failing which he would launch Civil Disobedience.'

Baikunth asked, 'Baba, forgive my ignorance, but why do our leaders not ask for complete independence? Why do these Congressmen keep quoting Bhagat Singh's name as a hindrance against dominion status?'

Yogendra laughed loudly. 'Bhagat Singh's ideas are like tornadoes sweeping across the minds of youth, clearing away the age-old meek demands of the rulers. He asks for nothing but complete independence. He says in dominion status, the Gora sahibs will be replaced by Brown sahibs, and the poor and downtrodden will suffer as before. No one spoke to India's main party with such determination. Now youth like you are speaking the language of Bhagat Singh. The people are pressuring Congress leadership to leave the demand of dominion and adopt the single goal of complete independence. If this happens, mark my words, Bhagat Singh has already won the war. He made the biggest party in the country adopt revolutionary thought to cope with the changing mindset of the nation.'

Baikunth said, 'Baba, Bhagat Singh is going to change this country; we need to save him somehow.'

Yogendra sighed and replied, 'Unfortunately, British and Congress leadership understand very well that if Bhagat Singh survives, they will both lose many things. But, yes, we will fight till death to save Bhagat; he is the future of free India.'

Yogendra left for Lahore the following day. Hundreds of people were flocking to Lahore for the Congress session. There was only one name on everyone's lips—Bhagat Singh. Some condemned him for being reckless, and some admired his courage. Everyone was eager to listen to what Gandhiji was thinking.

The Congress party had established a makeshift town called Congress Nagar for the session. The CID found it very difficult to track and identify revolutionaries in such places.

Yogendra met Vishwanath Vaishampayan, Acharya Kriplani and Ganesh Shankar Vidyarthi, and the aura and moral pressure created by Bhagat's statement in court proved fruitful. On 19 December 1929, Jawaharlal Nehru passed the historic 'Purna Swaraj' resolution. This was a landmark movement in the struggle for independence, and the revolutionary movement was implicitly responsible for it.

The language of Bhagat Singh crept into the Purna Swaraj resolution:

> We believe that it is the inalienable right of the Indian people, as of any other people, to have freedom and to enjoy the fruits of their toil and have the necessities of life so that they may have full opportunities for growth. We also believe that if any government deprives people of these rights and oppresses them, they have a further right to alter or abolish them. The British government in India has not only denied the Indian people their freedom but has based itself on exploiting the masses and ruined India economically, politically, culturally, and spiritually. Therefore, India must sever the British connection and attain Purna Swaraj or complete independence.

India has been ruined economically. The revenue derived from our people is out of all proportion to our income. Our average income is seven pence (less than two pence) per day, and of the heavy taxes we pay, twenty per cent are raised from the land revenue derived from the peasantry and three per cent from the salt tax, which falls most heavily on the poor.

Village industries, such as hand-spinning, have been destroyed, leaving the peasantry idle for at least four months and dulling their intellect for want of handicrafts. As in other countries, nothing has been substituted for the crafts thus destroyed.

Customs and currency have been manipulated to heap further burdens on the peasantry. The British manufactured goods constitute the bulk of our imports. Customs duties betray evident partiality for British manufacturers, and revenue from them is used not to lessen the burden on the masses but to sustain a highly extravagant administration. Still more arbitrary has been the manipulation of the exchange ratio, which has resulted in millions being drained away from the country.

Politically, India's status has never been so reduced under the British regime. No reforms have given real political power to the people. The tallest of us have to bend before foreign authorities. The rights of free expression of opinion and free association have been denied to us, and many of our countrymen are compelled to live in exile abroad and cannot return to their homes. All administrative talent is killed, and the masses must be satisfied with petty village offices and clerkships.

Culturally, the education system has torn us from our moorings, and our training has made us hug the chains that bind us.

Spiritually, compulsory disarmament has made us unmanly. The presence of an alien army of occupation, employed with deadly effect to crush in us the spirit of resistance, has made us think that we cannot look after ourselves or put up a defence against foreign aggression, or even defend our homes and families from the attacks of thieves, robbers and miscreants.

We hold it to be a crime against man and God to submit any longer to a rule that has caused this fourfold disaster to our country. We recognize, however, that the most effective way of gaining our freedom is not through violence. We will therefore prepare ourselves by withdrawing, so far as we can, all voluntary associations from the British Government and will prepare for civil disobedience, including nonpayment of taxes. We are convinced that if we can withdraw our voluntary help and stop payment of taxes without doing violence, even under provocation, the end of this brutal rule is assured. Therefore, we solemnly resolve to carry out the Congress instructions issued from time to time to establish Purna Swaraj.

The news reached Delhi on the morning of 20 December. For Azad, this was a tremendous victory for the revolutionary movement. Bhagwati was overjoyed.

Azad kept reading the newspaper and saw news that Irwin would return to Delhi on 23 December.

Azad called for an immediate meeting. Veerbhadra Tiwari, Yashpal, Bhagwati and others gathered together. Azad said, 'Irwin is coming back to Delhi on 23 December. I think we should go ahead with our action plan.'

Veerbhadra objected, 'But we have not received any message from Yogendra or Vidyarthiji about the meeting with Gandhiji. We agreed to wait until it is done.'

Azad smiled and said, 'I was waiting for the resolution of Purna Swaraj. Bhagat and HSRA have won. There's nothing left to discuss with Gandhiji. He cannot do anything in any matter which is under judicial proceedings of a murder. That much I know about Bapu. Also, whether Irwin lives or dies will not affect his decision.'

Bhagwati replied, 'I agree; let's go ahead.'

Azad asked, 'Wireless, is the device ready?'

Hansraj Wireless replied, 'Panditji, it is ready; I planned to detonate it via remote control, but that couldn't happen. So we must put a wire on the bomb for the trigger.'

Bhagwati ordered, 'Wireless, show us the device and brief us about it.'

Wireless walked into the room, holding a shining, yellow brass lota. The lota was sealed from above with only a wire going in. Wireless walked carefully and placed it like a feather in the middle of the gathering. Veerbhadra slid back a few feet, eyeing the shiny bomb.

Wireless said, 'This is a wired electric switch-operated bomb. The wire must be attached to the bomb, while the button will decide the explosion on the other end. I have put an Excelsior-type battery made in Czechoslovakia in 1929; it is of 4.8 voltage and contains nine cells arranged in three sets. The explosive that I have used is Trinitrotoluene, and the detonator is a fulminate of mercury. No picrates have been used this time. The casing is brass, so the shape resembles a common domestic lota. It is cast and not beaten out with a hammer. The uniform thickness of the casing is not meant to cause injury as a bomb but holds enough explosive to wreck a train. In other words, this is a proper mine.'

Azad said, 'Outstanding, Wireless. Now Bapubhai, tell me the plan.'

Bhagwati replied, 'Panditji, the plan is to do maximum damage to the train. Our source went to Madras and confirmed that the viceroy travels in the third coach. This special Viceregal train has a total of twelve coaches; nine coaches have six-wheeled bogies, and the others have four-wheeled bogies. The average speed of the train is 40–50 mph. So, we have to consider momentum too. The plan is to choose a spot to blow up the mine under the third coach. But considering the speed and momentum, it is hard to be accurate. Hence, the spot of the bomb assumes the utmost importance. The spot must be slightly higher than the ground so that after the mine blows up, even if we miss the coach, the train must derail, causing a great deal of damage. I have found the perfect spot, around 300 yards away from the walls of Old Delhi Fort, a single railway track going into Old Delhi. The exact spot is an embankment around 30 feet high. The objective is to blow up the third train coach and derail it on the slope to cause maximum damage.'

Azad nodded and said, 'Sounds good to me so far.'

'But there is a practical difficulty.'

'What is it?'

'Actually, the issue lies with the spot. The location is near the Old Delhi Fort and near Delhi in general. The gang man checks the track on that portion regularly; his shift runs from 4 a.m. to 4 p.m. The main issue is that we will have to hide the wire underground, or it will be visible to the naked eye. The wire can also be damaged by trespassers or domestic animals.'

Yashpal said, 'So we will go there at night and hide the wire.'

Azad raised his hand, and Yashpal stopped talking. Azad said, 'Wireless, tell me how much wire is required for this action.'

Wireless replied, 'At least 300 metres for the safety of our people.'

Azad nodded. 'Yashpal, the hiding of wire underground will take at least three hours; also, if you do it at night, you will have to use torches, which will easily attract attention.'

Yashpal said, 'Sorry, Panditji, I did not realize.'

'You are new to action. Every minor aspect has to be thought through,' Azad said.

Bhagwati said, 'Hence we need your wisdom and experience.'

Panditji thought momentarily and finally said, 'Bhagwati and Yashpal, you will go to the Old Fort after three. You will wait for the gang man (person responsible for taking care of railway tracks) to leave at 4 p.m. After that, you will move to the spot and without being noticed by anyone, you will start hiding the wire. At least three inches under the ground. Cover it with grass. If possible, tie grass on the top of the trap in open places. Arrange the wire as if the switch must come to a hiding place around a bush or something, without anyone seeing it. Cows and buffaloes graze there; ensure that their movement does not disturb the wire.'

Yashpal asked, 'Then what about the bomb?'

Azad said, 'The night before the action, one of you will go to the spot and verify that the hidden wire is intact.

And at the time of the act, one of us will go in the dark, put up the mine in the centre of the rail track and join the wire. The same person will be responsible for detonating the bomb. Remember, you will not use any light such as a torch to place the bomb on the track.'

That evening, Bhagwati and Yashpal went and hid in the Old Delhi fort. After 5 p.m., they came out and casually walked to the designated place. Bhagwati had a loop of wire hidden under his shirt, and Yashpal had brought small, handy digging tools.

The sun was going down and the light was dimming; no one was in sight. Yashpal started digging, and Bhagwati started putting wire in the little trench, burying it and covering it with dried grass. At places, he hid it by tying long grass over the wire. The switch was placed down the slope behind thick bushes. It was done.

On the evening of 22 December, Azad ordered Yashpal and Bhagram to execute the plan. After midnight, Yashpal wore khaki clothes and took a motorcycle to the Old Delhi Fort. Thick fog was lying on the landscape like a blanket. They checked the working of the wire using a battery and tester. Then at around 4 a.m., Yashpal took the heavy lota and fixed it in the middle of the rail track. Then he went to the other end and lay down and hid himself in the bushes. Bhagram had parked a motorcycle near the spot so they could escape later.

Around 8.30 a.m., as Yashpal and Bhagram were lying down, they could feel vibrations in the ground. Although the sun was up, they were still blinded by fog. But the increasing vibrations made it clear that the train was approaching. Yashpal was ready. Like a bullet shot out of a gun, the train appeared out of the mist. Both confirmed it was the Viceregal train. As the second bogey passed the spot, Yashpal shouted, 'This is from Bhagat Singh and Jatin Das.' He pressed the trigger, and instantly the mine detonated. The deafening sound was followed by thick smoke. Yashpal stared in disbelief. Smoke was emanating from the third and fourth coaches. However, the train continued on its journey as if nothing had happened. It did not derail due to its high speed. Bhagram dragged Yashpal to the bike. There was no time to lose. Yashpal and Bhagram rode away as per the escape plan.

Chapter 15

December 1929

Viceroy Irwin was in the sixth coach when the bomb exploded. He heard the thundering sound, and terror gripped his heart. He sat down immediately. His legs started shaking.

A few guards approached him in minutes, and someone said, 'Sir, it seems there has been a blast under the train.'

It took a moment for Irwin to understand what was happening. His tongue darted across his parched, dry lips. Then he understood the meaning of the words. Irwin asked in a shaky voice, 'What's the damage?'

The guard answered, 'Sir, two guards and one waiter are injured. It went off below the fourth coach. The bomb blew a big hole of around ten feet in the floor and the roof of the coach. Thankfully, due to the train's speed, we didn't derail.'

'Any casualties?'

'Not yet, sir.'

Irwin didn't say anything, but the photos of Bhagat and Dutt published in the newspaper appeared in front of his eyes, and a name kept ringing in his ears like a deafening blast—Azad.

As the train entered the station, Irwin was quickly taken outside. He immediately asked his security to take him to the church first. Irwin sat down on his knees and prayed for half an hour.

The news spread like wildfire. Gandhiji condemned the act of bombing and said, 'I thank God because the friend of India, Lord Irwin, escaped unhurt.'

Gandhiji went to meet Irwin on the same day and enquired about his well-being. Although Irwin escaped by luck, he realized the capability of the revolutionaries.

The next day, on 24 December 1929, Gandhiji arrived in Lahore for the Congress session. Yogendra and Ganesh Shankar Vidyarthi were waiting for Bapu. After two days, Acharya Kriplani, senior leader in the Congress and an old associate of Yogendra, led them to the tent one night when there were fewer people around Bapu.

Yogendra and Ganesh sat at the rear of the line of people waiting to meet Bapu. Gandhiji saw Yogendra and stopped talking to the person he had been speaking to. Yogendra bowed and said, 'Namaste, Bapu.'

Gandhiji smiled and continued with his meetings. He asked the assistant to refrain from bringing anyone else in. At last, only Yogendra, Ganesh, Kriplani and Gandhiji remained in the tent.

Pushing his round glasses to his eyes, Gandhiji looked closely at Yogendra and smiled but said nothing.

Yogendra said, 'Bapu, it seems you do not recognize me.'

Gandhiji laughed and said, 'Ganesh, tell Yogendraji that Mohandas does not forget his friends.'

Everyone laughed. Gandhiji continued. 'Ganesh, in the days of Champaran Satyagraha, I came to know Yogendra; we fought together shoulder to shoulder.'

Yogendra completed, 'And we won because of your leadership.'

Gandhiji replied, 'We won that battle because of your solid support.'

Yogendra said, 'But, Bapu, the war is still going on; it needs to be won. You are our general.'

Gandhiji asked gravely, 'Tell me, is the war to be won by bombs and pistols? How are we going to get independence by blowing up the viceroy's train? Please explain.'

'Bapu, I understand your difference of opinion with revolutionaries, but the unjust system of the Raj makes people like me take up arms.'

Gandhiji kept quiet, smiled again and said, 'Let us not go into the classical debate. All right, tell me, what can I do for you?'

Yogendra looked at Vidyarthi, who nodded. Yogendra said, 'Bapu, I am here on behalf of HSRA to discuss the case of Bhagat Singh and the other boys.'

Gandhiji replied with a poker face, 'The case is going on in the magistrate's court; what can I do about it?'

Yogendra said, 'Bapu, the government is conducting a farce in the name of a judicial trial. You are a learned barrister. You are aware of their hunger strike, the sacrifice of Jatin Das, and the recent inhuman beating and torture inside the court.'

Gandhiji replied, 'I respect the bravery of these boys. Jatin Das's sacrifice will never be forgotten. I am also aware of the mishaps in the judicial process; party newspapers have already written about it.'

Yogendra said, 'Bapu, I am thankful for your support. What I am asking you to do is to be more vocal about the demands of the revolutionaries. You are going to launch civil disobedience against the government. I ask you to include a sympathetic angle towards revolutionaries in the same.'

Gandhiji pondered over Yogendra's request for a few moments, and then said, 'I sympathize with Bhagat Singh and his cause, but I cannot support him openly, nor can I include the cause of armed revolution. Yogendra, violence begets violence and is not the way to attain freedom for India.'

Yogendra, disappointed, implored Gandhiji, 'But Bapu, Bhagat Singh is a hero to millions of Indians. He is ready to give up his life for the cause of our country's independence. Please, can't you do something to save him?'

Gandhiji sighed and shook his head. 'I understand your feelings, but I cannot change my position. If the boys give it in writing that they have made a grave mistake by choosing the path of violence, and now they want to do penance for their sins, if they publicize this position, I might fight for their lives openly. But I know Bhagat Singh will not do it. Bhagat Singh's hands as well as mine are tied to our own respective ideologies. We both understand the actions and outcomes of our work and are ready to face them. There's minimal scope for doing anything else.'

Yogendra and Vidyarthi left Gandhiji's tent, disheartened. Although Gandhiji had refused to help them in their cause, Yogendra was still determined to go to any length to save Bhagat Singh and his comrades.

Khan Bahadur was tasked with conducting a high-level inquiry into the Viceregal train bombing. The police were utterly clueless as to the identity of the perpetrators. It was the first time such powerful explosives and technology had been used. Frustrated by the lack of progress, Khan Bahadur turned to his favourite approver, Phanindra.

In a dimly lit room, Phanindra sat uncomfortably in a chair, beads of sweat trickling down his forehead. The atmosphere was tense, charged with an electric sense of anticipation. Khan Bahadur stood imposingly before him, his stern gaze boring into Phanindra's soul.

'Phani Babu, you know why you're here,' Khan Bahadur began, his voice cold and commanding. 'We need information, and you're going to provide it.'

Phanindra replied in a feeble voice, 'Sir, I have told you everything I know, which is on record. Please let me know how can I help you?'

'Are you aware of what happened in Delhi on 23 December?'

'No, Sahib, I have been in prison for the last six months. How would I know what is going on outside? '

'All right, let me break the news to you. Some lunatic tried to bomb the Viceregal train in Delhi.'

'What?' The colour drained out of Phani Babu's face. 'Is Lord Irwin safe?'

'His Excellency was saved by chance; he was in another bogey when the bomb went off.'

'Sahib, how can I help with it?' Phanindra's voice was shaking.

Khan roared, 'Don't you dare play games with me. This is serious. This is above Saunders's murder and your shitty conspiracy. Tell me, who in India has the guts to bomb the train of the viceroy?'

Phanindra looked at the ground and said, 'Sahib, there is only one who is afraid of nothing.'

Khan asked, 'Give me a name.'

Phanindra replied coldly, 'Sahib, you already know his name. I warned you earlier about him, but you paid no heed.'

'Azad?'

'Yes, commander-in-chief of Hindustan Socialist Republican Association, Chandrashekhar Azad.'

Khan banged his massive fist on the table and shouted, 'Now the man has crossed his limits. It is over for him. I will catch him and skin him alive.'

Phanindra replied, 'Please forgive me, Sahib, but it is almost impossible to catch him. I warned you earlier. You don't know what Azad is capable of. Even if you managed to kill every last revolutionary on this subcontinent and left only Azad alive, the British Raj would still be in danger. That man can conjure rebellion out of stones.'

'Enough of this nonsense; I will see that he is caught, dead or alive. You just give me the information I need.'

Phanindra squirmed in his seat, the weight of his treachery heavy upon his conscience. He hesitated before speaking, his voice trembling slightly. 'I . . . I remember hearing about a similar plan. It was orchestrated by Bhagat Singh and Chandrashekhar Azad for bombing the special train carrying the members of the Simon Commission in 1928. However, it didn't succeed.'

Khan Bahadur's eyes narrowed, his interest piqued. 'Go on. Tell me more about the materials they used.'

Phanindra swallowed hard. 'They were planning to obtain dynamite from the Jharia coal fields in Bihar. Azad's friend Santosh Kumar Mukherjee has connections there, and Batukeshwar Dutt's brother also resides in Jharia.'

Khan Bahadur leaned in closer, and said, his voice low and menacing, 'I will come back in five minutes.' Khan walked out and sent out a telegram for confirmation of what the material was. He received an immediate reply by wire, that prima facie, the material seemed to be TNT and not dynamite.

Khan returned to the interrogation cell and said, 'It is not dynamite; it is TNT.'

Phanindra nodded, his voice barely above a whisper. 'Then, Sahib, only one possibility remains, which you will not like.'

'Speak.'

'The armoury of the Raj.'

'How is it possible?'

'Sahib, Azad has many contacts and sympathizers in the army. Such explosives are used only in the army.'

It was Khan's turn to go pale now. His brain tried to make sense of how far this conspiracy went.

The interrogation was over. Khan was about to leave the room when Phanindra got up and said, 'Sahib, there is one request.'

'Speak.'

'Until you get Azad, don't release me from prison.'

Khan stared at Phanindra with blazing red eyes and walked away without replying.

Chapter 16

January 1930

Baikunth stood in the crowded marketplace of Muzaffarpur, the vibrant colours and sounds of the bazaar starkly contrasting with the turmoil brewing within him. Clutched in his hand was the latest edition of *Young India*, which he had picked up just moments ago. As he scanned the front page, his eyes caught the headline: 'The Cult of Bomb'. He felt his heartbeat quicken in anticipation, knowing that the article was Gandhiji's response to the recent bombing of the special Viceregal train by Azad, Bhagwati Charan and their fellow revolutionaries.

The paper trembled slightly in his hands as he began to read. He was enveloped in a whirlwind of emotions: anger, confusion and betrayal. It was as if Gandhiji's words were a dagger aimed straight at the hearts of all those fighting for India's independence through armed revolution. Baikunth couldn't believe that the great leader, who had once been a beacon of hope and inspiration, would now choose to condemn the people who had sacrificed everything for their motherland.

Baikunth's mind raced as he contemplated responding to Gandhiji's intellectual challenge. Who could match wits with the great leader and defend the revolutionaries' cause? The names of Bhagat Singh and Sachindranath Sanyal rose in his thoughts, but they were already in prison.

Later that day, Baikunth stood tall at Tilak Maidan, his lathi held firmly in his hand. Sweat glistened on his forehead as he swung the stick, striking an opponent. The sound of wood hitting wood echoed through the field. Around thirty young members of Seva Dal were standing in the queue and observing the fight keenly.

As he continued his routine battle exercises, a young man appeared at the edge of the field. Baikunth narrowed his eyes, watching the stranger approach. 'Who are you and what do you want?' he called out.

The young man stepped forward, his eyes scanning the area. 'I'm looking for Ranendranath,' he said.

Baikunth frowned. 'He's not here. What do you need him for?'

The young man hesitated for a moment before answering. 'I'll tell him myself.'

Baikunth shook his head, not liking the stranger's attitude. 'Fine, wait till the end of the exercises. I will take you to him,' he said, motioning for the young man to wait.

Together they made their way through the streets of Muzaffarpur until they reached Ranendranath's home.

The young man introduced himself as Chandrama and explained that he had been sent by Yogendra for training.

Chandrama's father, a former police officer, resigned after witnessing the non-cooperation movement's atrocities to become a dedicated Gandhian.

Ranendranath said, 'Yogendra thinks I have opened some kind of ashram for budding revolutionaries. Good God. You are welcome. Let me tell you something, I can teach you ways to fight, but I am a Gandhian myself. I would advise you not to jump into the armed struggle but as your mentor, and Baikunth's too, says: It's all your choice.'

Ranendranath would use Gandhi's article to prove his point. He started quoting lines from Bapu's article daily to Baikunth and Chandrama to change their minds before they jumped into an armed struggle.

Soon Baikunth and Chandrama became friends and the two were engaged in intense training. Baikunth was enjoying the challenge of sparring with someone new.

As they trained, they exchanged stories and laughter. Baikunth found himself drawn to Chandrama's easy-going nature and quick wit. They shared jokes and humorous anecdotes, lightening the mood of the otherwise serious training sessions.

As the days turned into weeks, Chandrama's skills improved. He and Baikunth became a formidable team, each supporting the other during training sessions. And although their time together was brief, the bond they formed was strong. At the end of another session, as the sun set on the Tilak Maidan, Baikunth and Chandrama stood side by side, their lathis at the ready. They shared a knowing smile, ready to take on whatever challenges came their way.

The room above Solomon Company in Aminabad, Lucknow, was cramped and dimly lit, a far cry from the opulence of the city's grand monuments. But for Azad, Vaishampayan and Bhagwati Charan Vohra, this humble space had become a refuge from the watchful eyes of the British authorities and a sanctuary for their revolutionary discussions.

As the three men sat huddled around a small wooden table, their expressions were a mix of frustration and determination. Angry messages from fellow revolutionaries lay scattered before them, each a response to the article by Gandhiji in *Young India*. The hurt and disappointment in their comrades' words were palpable, and it fuelled the fire that burned within them.

Azad and Bhagwati exchanged glances, their eyes conveying the weight of the decisions they were about to make. As the silence stretched, it was clear that the path ahead would be challenging. Finally, Azad broke the silence, his voice steady and resolute.

'Bapubhai,' he said, addressing Bhagwati, 'it is time to drop another bomb now.'

Bhagwati looked at Azad, and for a moment his gaze held a mixture of concern and resolve. He asked, 'What do you mean, Panditji?'

'It is time to show that we also have a voice and morals to do what we do. You will draft an article, based on our discussions, regarding the core philosophy of our armed revolution. It is time to fight with a pen. Let me know when your draft is ready.'

'Yes, Panditji.'

Bhagwati drafted an article after multiple discussions with Azad as a response to Gandhiji's article and titled it 'The Philosophy of the Bomb'.

Revolutionaries printed it and distributed it throughout the country. On 26 January, when the Congress declared Purna Swaraj and called for Indians to celebrate the day as Independence Day, revolutionaries distributed the pamphlet to thousands gathered at Congress functions in every major city.

Baikunth was going through the latest *Young India* when he found a loose pamphlet with the headline: 'The Philosophy of the Bomb'. His heart skipped a beat as he realized it was a response to Gandhiji's criticism. His hands trembling with anticipation and curiosity, he unfolded the pamphlet. He couldn't help but rush to the last page to see who had penned this bold rebuttal. To his amazement, the signature at the bottom read 'Kartar Singh, President of HSRA'. Baikunth's heart swelled with pride and hope, knowing that it was inspired by Kartar Singh Sarabha, the great martyr of the Ghadar revolt.

With goosebumps prickling his skin, he carefully read every word of the pamphlet, each sentence igniting a fire within him. The decisive arguments presented by the author refuted Gandhiji's claims and highlighted the importance of revolutionary action in the fight for India's independence. It was evident that the author's words were a rallying cry for all those who believed in the path of armed struggle.

As Baikunth read the pamphlet repeatedly, he committed each word to memory. He gave it to Chandrama. Both discussed every argument in a hushed tone.

Ranendranath broke into their discussion by saying, 'May I know what is being discussed?'

Baikunth replied, 'Guruji, HSRA has written a befitting response to Gandhiji's article. In fact, you should read it. It will clear your head.'

'I don't need that kind of nonsense. I have read enough revolutionary literature to join Yogendra. Somehow, with luck, I escaped unhurt. Now I don't need that kind of negativity, and I feel nothing is left to discuss after Bapu's article.'

'That is judging before knowing the other side. If you go through this, you will question Bapu's attitude.'

'Don't boast about things you don't understand, boys.'

Chandrama said, 'Guruji, we do understand what we are talking about.'

'All right, let us discuss first, then we will proceed.'

'Go ahead,' Baikunth said confidently.

Ranendranath asked, 'Tell me why the revolutionaries consider themselves above everything? Beyond criticism or public scrutiny?'

Baikunth replied quoting from *The Philosophy of the Bomb*, 'We are neither above public scrutiny nor dislike criticism. This article itself is the answer to the criticism. Our problem is about the crusade launched by Gandhiji against our community. Like all the articles and debates you have seen after the 23 December train blast.'

Ranendranath said, 'Why should there not be a crusade against you when your chosen path of violence jeopardizes the fight for freedom?'

Baikunth quoted from the article, 'Let us, first of all, take up the question of violence and non-violence. Violence is the physical force applied to commit injustice, and that is certainly not what the revolutionaries stand for. On the other hand, what generally goes by the name of non-violence is, in reality, the theory of soul force, as applied to attaining personal and national rights through courting suffering and hoping thus to finally convert your opponent to your point of view. When a revolutionary believes that a certain thing is his right, he asks for it, pleads for it, argues for it, is willing to attain it with all the soul force at his command, bears the greatest amount of suffering for it, is always prepared to make the highest sacrifice for its attainment, and also backs his efforts with all the physical force he is capable of. This is our Satyagraha.'

'Satyagraha is non-violent practice; there is no place for any physical force.'

Chandrama retorted, quoting from the article, 'This definition has been concocted by Gandhiji. Satyagraha literally means insistence upon truth. Why press for the acceptance of the fact by soul force alone? Why not add physical strength also to it? While the revolutionaries stand for winning independence by all the troops, physical and moral, at their command, the advocates of soul force would like to ban the use of physical force. Therefore, the question is not whether you will have violence, but whether you will have soul force and physical strength or soul force alone.'

Ranendranath asked, 'But why use force when we can only gain independence using soul force, Satyagraha? Why is there a need to shed blood?'

Baikunth replied, quoting from the article 'We believe that the deliverance of our country will come through revolution. This is not just about an armed conflict between the foreign government, its supporters and the people; it will also usher in a new social order. The revolution will ring the death knell of capitalism and class distinctions and privileges. It will bring joy and prosperity to the starving millions seething today under the terrible yoke of foreign and Indian exploitation. It will bring the nation into its own. It will give birth to a new state—a new social order. Does Satyagraha talk about these things?'

Ranendranath observed, 'Satyagraha is ushering in a new social order. We don't follow the diktats of Marx or the Soviet Union; the terms proletariat and bourgeoisie can't be exactly translated to Indian society. We need a domestic solution, not a foreign one. It is not about the objective; it is about the means. What is the necessity of using terror to achieve our ends?'

Baikunth answered, using the lines from the article, 'Guruji, you need to understand why terror is resorted to. The restlessness of youth, the more apparent realization of national bondage and a growing, intense, unquenchable thirst for freedom only breed terror for the oppressors in the country. It is a phase, a necessary and inevitable phase of the revolution. This thesis can be supported by an analysis of any and every revolution in history. It instils fear in the hearts of the oppressors. It brings hopes of revenge and redemption to the oppressed masses. It gives courage and self-confidence to the wavering. It shatters the spell of the superiority of the ruling class and raises the status of the subject race in the eyes of the world because it is the most convincing proof of a nation's hunger for freedom. Here in India, as in other countries in the past, the use of terror will develop into the revolution and the revolution into independence, social, political and economic.'

Ranendranath commented, 'But Congress has a more mature way of handling the freedom struggle, and masses have given the party a single hand to deal with the British. If the masses of India prefer Gandhiji and Congress, then why is there a need for armed struggle? Anyway, all of your efforts have failed; Anushilan, Ghadar, HRA—and now HSRA is on the brink of collapse. I can count the achievements of the Congress; what are your achievements?'

Baikunth said, 'Did you not see how the masses supported Bhagat, or how people rallied behind the train carrying Jatin Das's corpse, or did you forget how the masses cried when Bismil and Ashfaq were hanged? Your achievements, and ours, mean nothing until we achieve complete socio-politico-economic independence. Congress is striving only for political independence. Even there, let me point out, what was the need to change its creed from Swaraj to Complete Independence? Tell me?'

Ranendranath said, 'That is due to public awareness, and some credit goes to Bhagat Singh and the revolutionaries, I agree. But see what Congress is doing; it will launch a massive movement against the Raj.'

Chandrama retorted, quoting from the article, 'Guruji, as a logical sequence to this, one would expect Congress to declare war on the British government. Instead, we find it has declared war against the revolutionaries. The first offensive of the Congress came in the form of a resolution, denouncing the attempt made on 23 December 1929 to blow up the viceroy's special train. It was drafted by Gandhi, and he fought tooth and nail for it, with the result that it was passed by a trifling majority of eighty-one in a house of 1713. Was even this bare majority a result of honest political convictions? Even though the Congress is pledged to non-violence and has been actively engaged in carrying on propaganda in its favour for the last ten years, despite the fact also that the supporters of the resolution indulged in abuse, called the revolutionaries 'cowards' and described their actions as 'dastardly'—and one of them even threateningly remarked that if they wanted to be led by Gandhi, they should pass this resolution without any opposition—despite all this, the resolution could only be adopted by a dangerously narrow majority. That demonstrates, beyond the shadow of a doubt, how solidly the country is backing the revolutionaries.'

Ranendranath said, 'But Gandhiji has the majority; Bapu has toured this country multiple times from Kashmir to the Indian Ocean. He knows the true India. And it is a proven fact that the masses believe in non-violence.'

Baikunth replied, again quoting from the article, 'Bapu thinks that based on his experience during his latest tour in the country, he is right in believing that the large masses of Indian humanity are untouched by the spirit of violence and that non-violence has come to stay as a political weapon. Let him not delude himself on the experiences of his latest tour in the country. Though the average leader indeed confines his tours to places where only the mail train can conveniently land him while Gandhi has extended his tour limit to where a motor car can take him, the practice of staying only with the richest people in the places visited, of spending most of his time on being complimented by his devotees in private and public, and of granting *darshan* now and then to the illiterate masses who he claims to understand so well, disqualifies him from claiming to know the mind of the masses. No man can claim to know a people's mind by seeing them from the public platform and giving them darshan and *updesh*. He can, at the most, claim to have told the masses what he thinks about things. Has Gandhi, during recent years, involved himself in the social life of the masses? Has he sat around the evening fire with the peasant and tried to know his thoughts? Has he passed a single evening in the company of a factory labourer and shared with him his woes?'

'And you revolutionaries claim to know the masses?'

'Yes, see the background of the families of the accused in the Lahore Conspiracy Case. See the statement of Phanindra in which he remarks that they did not have enough money to buy a square meal. Still, they dreamt of freedom. This is true in India. We assure Gandhi that the average Indian, like the average human, understands little of the fine, theological niceties about Ahimsa and loving one's enemy. The way of the world is like this. You have a friend: you love him, sometimes so much that you even die for him. You have an enemy: shun him, fight against him and, if possible, kill him. The gospel of the revolutionaries is simple and straight. It is what has been since the days of the Ramayana and Mahabharata, and no man has any difficulty understanding it: we affirm that the masses of India stand strongly with us because we know it from personal experience. The day is not far off when they will flock in their thousands to work for the will of the revolution.'

Ranendranath said, 'But Gandhi's popularity today means that the efficacy of non-violence has increased. He hopes someday to convert the foreign rulers to his way of thinking.'

Chandrama laughed. He said, using the words of the article, 'Sorry, but tell me, how many enemies of India has he been able to turn into friends? How many O'Dwyers,

Readings and Irwins has he been able to convert into friends of India? If none, how can India be expected to share his "growing faith" that he will be able to persuade or compel England to agree to Indian independence through the practice of non-violence?'

Ranendranath was angry; he said, 'Well, what have you achieved by blowing up the Viceregal train?'

Baikunth answered, 'If the bomb that burst under the Viceroy's special had exploded properly, one of the two things suggested by Gandhi would have indeed happened. The viceroy would have either been badly injured or killed. Under such circumstances, there certainly would have been no meeting between the leaders of political parties and the viceroy. The uncalled-for and undignified attempt on the part of these individuals to lower the national prestige by knocking at the gates of the government house with the beggar's bowl in their hands and dominion status on their lips, despite the precise terms of the Calcutta Ultimatum, would have been checkmated. The nation would have been better off for that. If, fortunately, the explosion had been powerful enough to kill the viceroy, one more enemy of India would have met well-deserved doom. The author of the Meerut prosecutions and the Lahore and Bhusawal persecutions can appear to be a friend of India only to the enemies of her freedom.'

Ranendranath remarked, 'But such revolutionary activities hinder constitutional reforms, laying waste the labour of mass movements.'

Chandrama said, 'Why should Gandhi mix up the revolutionaries with the various constitutional reforms granted by the government? We never cared or worked for the Morley–Minto Reforms, Montague Reforms and the like. These the British government threw before the constitutionalist agitators to lure them away from the right path. This was the bribe they paid to support the government in its policy of crushing and uprooting the revolutionaries. We raised the standard of independence long ago. We have lived for it. We have ungrudgingly laid our lives down for the sake of this ideal. We claim that their sacrifices have produced a tremendous change in the mentality of the people.'

Ranendranath noted, 'Bapu says violence impedes the march of progress and thus directly postpones the day of freedom.'

Baikunth replied, 'Take contemporary instances where violence has led to the social progress and political freedom of the people who practised it. Take the case of Russia and Turkey, for example. The party for Progress took over the state organization in both countries through an armed revolution. Yet social progress and political freedom have not been impeded.'

Ranendranath asked, 'Did you forget why non-cooperation failed? Because the mob went out of control due to violence.'

Baikunth said, 'Bhagat and Azad left their schools for non-cooperation. Azad received lashes for shouting *Mahatma Gandhi ki Jai* slogans when he was fifteen years old. You should know all the revolutionaries are disillusioned Gandhians from the shock of non-cooperation. We will even go further and state that it was mainly the mania for non-violence and Gandhi's compromise mentality that disrupted the forces that had come together at the call of Mass Action.

It failed to achieve what were considered to be the just rights of Indians in South Africa. It failed to bring "Swaraj within a year" to the Indian masses.'

'What is your problem with Gandhi now? I remember in 1924, the HRA published what they called the Yellow Pamphlet. It was their manifesto written by Sachindranath Sanyal. You have been discussing the exact same things. What is new in your argument now?'

Baikunth said, 'Our problem now is to make Gandhi stop bullying the revolutionaries.'

Ranendranath laughed, saying, 'Gandhi can be anything you say but not a bully; please mind your language.'

Baikunth quoted from the article, 'Can't you see, Gandhiji has called upon all to withdraw their support from the revolutionaries? He is asking the public to condemn revolutionaries so they may get isolated and be forced to suspend their activities. It is a pity that Gandhi does not and will not understand revolutionary psychology despite his lifelong experience of public life. Life is a precious thing. It is dear to everyone. If a man becomes a revolutionary and goes about with his life in the hollow of his hand, ready to sacrifice it at any moment, he does not do so merely for the fun of it. He does not risk his life simply because sometimes, when the crowd is in a sympathetic mood, it cries 'Bravo' in appreciation. He does it because his reason forces him to take that course, because his conscience dictates it. A revolutionary believes in reason more than anything. It is to reason, and reason alone, that he bows. No amount of abuse and condemnation, even if these emanate from the highest of the high, can turn him from his set purpose. The highest folly is to think that a revolutionary will give up his ideas if public support and appreciation are withdrawn from him. Many a revolutionary has now stepped on the scaffold and laid down their life for the cause, regardless of the curses that the constitutionalist agitators rained plentifully upon them. If you will have the revolutionaries suspend their activities, reason with them squarely. That is the one and the only way. For the rest, let there be no doubt in anybody's mind. A revolutionary is the last person on earth to submit to bullying.'

Ranendranath acceded to Baikunth and Chandrama. 'All right, I see it now. From your point of view, Gandhi should not have tried to isolate you. I agree. What else is your problem, except the classic unsolvable non-violence debate?'

Baikunth said, quoting from the article, 'HSRA invites our countrymen to come forward and join us in carrying the banner of freedom aloft. Let us establish a new order of society in which political and economic exploitation will be impossible. Let nobody toy with the nation's independence, which is her very life, by carrying out psychological experiments in non-violence and other novelties. Our slavery is our shame. When shall we have courage and wisdom enough to shake ourselves free of it? There is no crime that Britain has not committed in India. As a race and a people, we stand dishonoured and outraged. Do people still expect us to forgive and to forget? We shall have our revenge—a people's righteous revenge on the tyrant. Let cowards fall back and cringe for compromise and peace. We ask not for mercy, and we give no quarter. Ours is a war to the end—to Victory or Death.'

Ranendranath listened to Baikunth and nodded. He announced, 'Children, your training is over. You are ready. There is nothing left that I can teach you now.'

Chapter 17

February 1930

In January 1930, Jalgaon Prison in Bombay Province held two revolutionaries far away from their comrades. The sun cast dark shadows across the weathered walls of the prison. Inside, revolutionaries Bhagwan Das Mahore and Sadashiv Malkapurkar were locked in a shared cell, feeling the weight of their situation.

Bhagwan and Sadashiv sat on the cold floor, their backs against the damp stone walls. The cell was dimly lit, with a beam of sunlight streaming through the small, barred window. The sound of distant cries and footsteps echoed through the corridor.

Sadashiv sighed. 'I can't believe we're here, Bhagwan. We've trained so hard alongside Bhagat Singh and Panditji, yet here we are. At least, they should have kept us in Lahore.'

Bhagwan nodded. 'It's a cruel twist of fate, Sadashiv. But we can't let this break our spirits. We must find a way out and continue our fight.'

Sadashiv teared up, 'Sometimes, I feel so hopeless. What if we never get out of here? What if our struggle is all for nothing? I have a gut feeling; the government will not let Bhagat Singh live. They will find a way to kill him like they murdered Jatin Dada.'

Bhagwan said, 'The possibility is there. Bhagat is not going to get out alive, but we will have to learn from him. He is wreaking havoc on the Raj even from behind bars. So will we. If we can't escape, we will fight from inside.'

Sadashiv asked, 'But how?'

At the same time, a constable came to the prison door. Bhagwan and Sadashiv looked at him without getting up.

The constable signalled that Bhagwan should come closer. As Bhagwan went near the bars, the constable whispered in his ears, 'Your hearing is fixed for 21 February in Jalgaon Sessions court. They are bringing someone from Lahore to testify against you. Be ready.'

It was expected. There was no one in Deccan to testify against them except the Excise Police, who had caught them with explosives. But their statements were not enough to establish that they were revolutionaries and associated with HSRA. They would need witnesses from Lahore.

Bhagwan turned around and said, 'Sadashiv, they are bringing approvers from Lahore.'

'Turncoat bastards! Phani Babu and Jai Gopal will come—only these two had identified us in Lahore.'

Sadashiv thought for a moment, staring at the dust-filled light beam from the window with a grave, determined expression. Then he looked at Bhagwan and smiled mischievously.

Bhagwan asked, 'Why are you smiling?'

Sadashiv said, 'I just asked, what can we do from prison? We can't argue like Bhagat or sustain hunger strikes like Jatin Dada. But there is something that we can do.'

'What?'

'Execute Jai Chand and Mir Jafar.'

Bhagwan replied, 'Are you insane? How is it possible? We will see them in court under the complete protection of CID and the police. They will not come near us, not even in the range of ten feet.'

'Yes, I know.'

'Then how?'

'It may sound silly but listen to me.'

Bhagwan replied, 'Go on, we are not short of time.'

Sadashiv said, 'When we are inside the court, they will have to unshackle our hands. Also, the Mauser, bullets and bombs will be placed in front of us as exhibits, and the approvers will be on the other side. Right?'

'Go on, I am listening.'

Sadashiv said, 'If somehow you can restrain the constable around us, I can jump and grab the Mauser, assemble and put a magazine in fifteen seconds, and before anyone can do anything, *bam*. I will shoot Phani Babu right in the middle of the head.'

'Huh, you are going insane. There's not even a one per cent chance that this could work.'

'I am ready to take a chance even if it's less than one per cent.'

Bhagwan shook his head and said, 'It is impossible. Not worth taking a risk. The police will shoot us in court.'

Sadashiv said, 'Did you say it's not worth taking a risk? Do you understand we can end all the menace right here by killing the approvers? The court hasn't passed the judgement, and the approvers have not been cross-examined yet. If we succeed, there's a high chance that Bhagat will live. They have nothing against him except these turncoat pigs. What if the police shoot us? Is our life worth more than Bhagat's and Jatin Dada's? Did you forget how Jatin Dada gave up his life? Did you forget how hundreds of constables tortured our brothers in October right before the judge? You are Panditji's best shooter. Can there be any better way to serve the motherland, as Panditji taught us?'

Bhagwan said, 'I know all of this, I didn't mean offence to our friends, but you need to understand this is impractical. The way we were caught at the station was enough humiliation for us. If we fail again, I fear we will become a laughing stock.'

'We have committed a cardinal sin by getting caught with one Mauser, one pistol, bombs and cartridges. They were more valuable than the Kohinoor for Panditji. I want to absolve myself. I don't want to rot in prison for the rest of my life.'

Bhagwan said, 'I agree. Let us take Panditji's approval first.'

Sadashiv smiled and shouted, 'Guard.'

A constable arrived with an irritated face and asked, 'What is it?'

'We want to write a letter to our lawyer. Can you please get us pen, ink and paper?'

'All right, I will ask Sahib first.'

'No problem, take your time.'

When the paper came, Sadashiv wrote a letter to Raghunath Vinayak Dhulekar, asking for an urgent meeting regarding the case in the sessions court. Dhulekar was a prominent lawyer and Congress leader from Jhansi. He had taken up the case of Bhagwan and Sadashiv without any cost. He sympathized with the armed revolution and helped Azad in every possible way.

Three days later, Dhulekar arrived at Jalgaon Prison. He was a Gandhian wearing a khadi kurta and dhoti and had a radiant smile. He could speak ten languages, including Marathi, Odia, Sanskrit and Arabic.

Bhagwan and Sadashiv got up when he arrived. A constable respectfully placed a chair outside the cell and stood around six feet from Dhulekar to supervise the conversation.

Bhagwan said, 'Sir, our hearing in the sessions court is fixed on 21 February.'

Dhulekar smiled and said, 'Yes, I know. Don't worry about the court; I will manage. Did you want anything else?'

Sadashiv subtly signalled towards the constable, and Dhulekar understood. He began to talk about the Lahore Congress, the resolution of Purna Swaraj, and how it would change the nature of the freedom struggle.

The constable soon got bored of Dhulekar's speech and walked away.

Sadashiv whispered, 'We want you to convey our message to Panditji; we plan to execute the approvers in the sessions court using our weapons displayed as exhibits. Please take his approval and views for the action.'

Dhulekar's smile widened, and he said, 'Consider it done. Whenever I think I have seen everything, Panditji's boys surprise me with something innovative. God knows where he found you.'

Bhagwan said, 'Sir, we were nothing when he found us. In fact, Panditji and Bhagat are sculptors of our personality and madness.'

Dhulekar rose and said, 'It is an honour to serve you. I will be back soon. Jai Hind.'

Within a week, Dhulekar came back with a broad, hopeful smile.

Bhagwan and Sadashiv were all ears to hear the message.

Dhulekar said, 'The commander-in-chief appreciates your valour and eagerness to prove your mettle. But given the circumstances that you were arrested in, it is difficult to rely on your judgement. So, he will send someone to finalize every last aspect of the proposed action.'

Bhagwan and Sadashiv nearly jumped. They could hear the message in the tone and language of Panditji. They were happy because the action was approved.

The sun had barely risen, casting a warm glow on the city. It was three days since Dhulekar had left. A constable came to the duo and said, 'Sadashiv, your elder brother Shankarrao Malkapurkar is here to see you, along with his lawyer.'

Sadashiv replied, 'Lawyer? But we already have Dhulekar.' Then he stopped speaking.

After a few moments, Shankarrao walked in with someone. The lawyer wore a sharp white shirt, trousers, a black blazer and a white tie. Donning his typical round glasses and clean-shaven look, the lawyer smiled at the prisoners.

Bhagwan nearly screamed, 'Bapubhai.'

It was Bhagwati Charan Vohra. He had dared to visit the comrades inside the prison, while he himself was absconding in the Lahore Conspiracy Case and Viceregal train bombing.

After seeing him after so many days, Bhagwan and Sadashiv wanted to hug him. But they could not afford to display affection.

Bhagwan said, 'Bapubhai, you shouldn't have taken such a risk for us.'

'Brothers, you have been entrusted with an extraordinary mission by the party. Also, I was missing you.'

Then Bhagwan and Sadashiv whispered at the same time, 'How's Panditji?'

'Panditji is as good as he can be, a living war machine. What about you? Are these monkeys treating you properly?'

'Yes, Bapubhai.'

Bhagwan asked, 'Tell me, is Panditji angry with us because of how we were caught.'

'No, it happened accidentally. It was not your fault. But it is a huge loss for the party. Very few can shoot like Bhagwan.'

Bhagwan asked, 'What is Panditji's message?'

Bhagwati smiled and started imitating Panditji, 'Picking up a Mauser pistol from the exhibit is out of the question, so it is my responsibility to provide you with a weapon before the hearing begins.'

'All right.' Bhagwan was eager to listen to everything.

'Both of you need not participate in the action. Bhagwan will take the lead, as he is a good shooter. Only if required, Sadashiv will help. Panditji leaves it up to the judgement of Sadashiv. Basically, he doesn't want both of you hanging on the gallows. One will remain in the back. Bhagwan, you will ensure that no innocent person gets hurt during the action.'

'Yes, Bapubhai. Anything else?'

'The most important thing, for which I have arrived here.'

'What is the message?'

'If you get the chance to kill one, then execute Phani Babu first. If you get a chance to kill both, very good. But focus on the priority. Phani Babu is out in the open to destroy armed revolution single-handedly by testifying against every revolutionary in India.'

'Understood.'

Sadashiv asked, 'But how will you send a weapon to us?'

Bhagwati smiled, 'Don't worry about that; we will use the technique which Chhatrapati Shivaji Maharaj used to escape from Agra.'

Sadashiv asked, 'What do you mean?'

Bhagwati replied, 'Remember, he sent boxes of food and sweets to temples and dharamshalas every day from where he was detained. And due to the routine and the repetition, the soldiers began to pass the boxes unchecked. And then one day, it is said that Shivaji Maharaj himself escaped inside the box or carrying the box.'

Sadashiv asked, 'I know the story, but how will you apply it here?'

Bhagwati answered. 'So instead of going out, the food will come in daily for you. From the day after tomorrow, you will have a severe stomach ache and vomiting due to prison food. Shankarrao will secure permission to arrange a home-cooked meal for you daily. And he will bring your tiffin daily.' Shankarrao was Sadashiv's elder brother.

Sadashiv said, 'Understood. Bapubhai, thank you.'

Bhagwati replied, 'Be prepared for the action and outcome, Bhagwan; I hope you have not forgotten how to assemble a gun.'

Bhagwan replied, 'Panditji has trained me to do it blindfolded.'

Bhagwati smiled and said, 'I hope to see you again soon. Under a free sky.'

Sadashiv and Bhagwan's eyes welled up. They knew that they were never going to meet again. Not under any circumstances.

As per the plan, Sadashiv ate flies and started vomiting. The doctor was called. Shankarrao used advocate Dhulekar's influence to get permission for a daily tiffin. On the night of 20 February, Shankarrao smuggled parts of an eight-shot Webley and Scott pistol and eight cartridges to Sadashiv, hidden under a pile of rice in a tiffin box. Bhagwan managed to hide it in the cell by digging out a portion of the floor. The pistol was assembled and ready to spew fire.

It was the dawn of 21 February 1930 and the morning air was filled with palpable tension. The police escorted the revolutionaries, Sadashiv and Bhagwan, from their prison cells to the Jalgaon Sessions Court for their hearing. The sessions court was around two miles from the prison. The revolutionaries were taken on foot to the court. Bhagwan had managed to strap the loaded pistol in his shirt, hidden from the watchful eyes of the guards. He had a plan ready; it was time to avenge the death of Jatin Das, to punish the snakes among them. He imagined the proud smile of Bhagat and Azad when they found out what Bhagwan had done for the country.

As news of the trial spread like wildfire, thousands of people from neighbouring villages and towns had flocked to the court premises to catch a glimpse of the two fearless revolutionaries, friends of Bhagat Singh, who had dared to challenge British rule. The atmosphere was charged with anticipation and excitement.

Inside the courtroom, Bhagwan and Sadashiv sat in the dock, their heads held high and their eyes blazing with determination. They had been through a lot together, fighting for their country's freedom, and now they were ready to make the ultimate sacrifice, if needed.

The judge's chair and witness box were ten feet away from the duo. Ten armed policemen were standing around the accused, besides a few around the witness box. Bhagwan saw that there was a high chance of missing the shot and killing some innocent policemen. Then he saw Khan Bahadur Abdul Aziz—the man thirsty for the blood of revolutionaries.

In front was a blue oil-painted wooden table with a shawl used as a table cover; on it, the Mauser pistol of Azad, sixty cartridges, bombs and chemicals were placed as exhibits. Bhagwan glanced at Sadashiv, who seemed to understand the unspoken question in his eyes. If the action happened in the court, Sadashiv would try to get the Mauser and assist Bhagwan in completing the mission. But there were too many people in the court.

The duo had discussed the wildest possibility. What if they managed to kill Phani Babu and Jai Gopal, take the Mauser and successfully escape the court premises, and then present the Mauser back to Azad? How happy he would be!

However, cruel reality faced them with the mask of violent death. They understood the importance of standing up for their beliefs, even when the odds were stacked against them. As the trial began, the two men listened intently to the proceedings, all the while scanning the room for the approvers. Bhagwan's finger rested discreetly on the pistol's trigger hidden beneath his shirt, waiting for the opportune moment to strike.

Jai Gopal arrived in the courtroom first, and his statement began. Bhagwan had a clear shot, but he did not proceed. The message from Azad was unambiguous. Phanindra Nath Ghosh needed to die first. He was the most crucial approver in the Lahore Conspiracy Case. It took around two hours to complete the statement of Jai Gopal. The court halted the proceedings temporarily for lunch.

Sadashiv and Bhagwan were led out of the courtroom, their hands tied together with a single pair of handcuffs. They were closely surrounded by ten policemen, ensuring that the duo would not escape. Behind the court, a couple of chairs were placed for the accused. The pair took a seat while Shankarrao, brother of Sadashiv, brought a tiffin. In front of them, a tent was set up where the approvers could rest and have lunch. They could see that the little khaki-clothed tent was heavily guarded by Punjab police, who had brought the approvers from Lahore. They were members of the CID. As the cloth door moved along with the wind, Bhagwan saw Jai Gopal and Phanindra sitting and chatting. The sight of these traitors, safe and sound and comfortable, fuelled Bhagwan's determination to complete his mission.

When the duo was seated for lunch, Bhagwan requested the guards to unshackle their handcuffs so they could eat properly. The guards, after some deliberation, agreed to his request, but they remained vigilant, watching the pair closely.

As soon as their hands were free, Bhagwan seized the opportunity. He looked at Sadashiv and whispered, 'For Jatin Dada, Bhagat, Rajguru, Sukhdev.

Sadashiv replied, 'For Panditji and the motherland.'

Bhagwan clenched his fists, and with a sudden burst of energy, he bolted towards the approver's tent, catching the guards off guard. A sub-inspector, Nanak Shah, realizing Bhagwan's intentions, tried to stop him and stood in the way, but Bhagwan was too quick. Without stopping, he shot the sub-inspector towards the leg, and the bullet went through his groin. The man crumpled to the ground in pain.

Bhagwan rushed inside the tent, his eyes fixed on the two traitors who would not have imagined the scene in their worst nightmares. As their eyes widened in shock, another bullet was fired from the pistol. The bullet pierced the left arm of Phanindra, and he fell back along with his chair. The second bullet whizzed past Jai Gopal's head, barely grazing his ear. As Bhagwan prepared to fire a third time, his heart sank as he realized that his pistol had jammed.

Before Bhagwan could try to fix the jammed weapon, the police officers swarmed into the tent, quickly subduing him. Bhagwan thought he had got Phanindra but saw that the bullet had missed its mark and only gone through the arm. The mission's failure weighed heavily on his heart as they restrained him. He had come so close to exacting vengeance on the traitors who had betrayed their cause, yet had failed in the end. The pistol might have jammed due to the moisture from the rice in the tiffin box.

Phanindra gasped as the bullet tore through his left arm, the pain shooting up his shoulder and down his fingers. He clutched the wound with his right hand, trying to stem the flow of blood. His eyes flicked to Jai Gopal, who was slumped against the wall, a trickle of blood running down his temple.

Sadashiv, who had remained outside the tent, watched the scene unfold in disbelief. As the police dragged Bhagwan away, their eyes met briefly, and they exchanged a look of camaraderie.

But Phanindra hardly noticed the developments (unbearable pain was searing in his arm). He tried to stand up, but his vision swam and he collapsed back onto the ground. He knew he needed medical attention, but he wasn't sure if anyone would come to his aid.

He looked over at Jai Gopal, who was still unconscious. Blood soaked the collar of his shirt, and his breathing was shallow. Phanindra knew that he needed to do something to help him, but he couldn't move his arm without experiencing a wave of agony.

Within seconds, the tent was swarming with armed guards. Tens of constables started kicking Bhagwan and hitting him with batons and lathis. In a moment, the crowd outside the courtroom erupted in shock, awe and admiration. The loud crackling sound of gunshots was heard by everyone. Khan Bahadur rushed to the spot. His face went pale after seeing the blood and injuries.

Sub-inspector Nanak Shah, who had now recovered, asked in a fearsome voice, 'Why did you shoot me?'

Bhagwan replied, 'Sorry, I didn't mean to hurt you. I was only trying to get the turncoat pigs. You just came in the way.'

Bhagwan and Sadashiv exchanged a regretful glance. Bhagwan felt that he had ruined the plan in haste and was responsible for losing another pistol belonging to the party. His teary eyes reflected his feelings of failure.

The news of Bhagwan's failed assassination attempt spread like wildfire among the thousands gathered outside the courthouse. Despite the mission's failure, the crowd's admiration and respect for the two revolutionaries grew. They began to chant, 'Inquilab Zindabad!' in unison, their voices swelling with pride and defiance.

As the cries of support filled the air, the crowd refused to let the injured approvers, Phanindra and Jai Gopal, be taken to the hospital. The people began to shout, *Let these dogs bleed to death here.* They were determined to prevent them from receiving any aid.

As time wore on, Phanindra's condition worsened. His arm had started to swell, and his head was pounding with a fever. He could feel himself slipping into unconsciousness, but he fought it off, not wanting to give up. Bhagat Singh's face appeared in front of his eyes. He was sure that this was his end.

The situation quickly escalated as the masses grew increasingly agitated. The police, already on edge from the earlier assassination attempt, were now faced with a full-scale revolt. They tried to maintain order, but the sheer number of protestors overwhelmed them. The police force was in shortage due to an ongoing railway workers' strike in Bhusawal.

The injured approvers, their faces pale and contorted with pain, began to realize the gravity of their situation.

Unable to safely transport the wounded men to the hospital, the police had no choice but to call the civil surgeon to the courthouse. As they awaited the doctor's arrival, the atmosphere grew even more tense. Angry protestors started pelting stones at the police officers, their fury only intensifying with each passing moment.

Inside the courthouse, Sadashiv and Bhagwan were being held in a makeshift holding cell, their hands still bound by the cuffs they had worn earlier. They could hear the crowd's roars outside and knew their actions had sparked a powerful movement. Despite the consequences they now faced, they couldn't help but feel a sense of pride for the fire they had ignited in people's hearts.

As the civil surgeon arrived, he was quickly escorted to the injured approvers, who were now lying on the ground. The doctor administered first aid, doing his best to stabilize their condition amid the chaos. The police, recognizing the volatility of the situation, began to strategize on how to safely evacuate the wounded traitors and restore order.

The situation outside the courthouse had spiralled out of control. What had started as a demonstration of support for the revolutionaries, Bhagwan and Sadashiv, quickly morphed into a full-scale riot. The city's Youth League leader, an ardent follower of Netaji Subhash Chandra Bose, who had always shown sympathy for the revolutionaries and their cause, led the furious crowd.

As the rioting intensified, the overwhelmed police officers struggled to maintain order. Desperate to quell the violence, they arrested one of the rioters, hoping it would send a message to the others. But this action only served to fan the flames of rebellion. Enraged by the arrest, the protestors began to attack police vehicles, their fury growing with each passing minute.

In a daring rescue attempt, a group of rioters managed to free the arrested individual from the grasp of the police. This bold move further emboldened the protestors, who saw themselves as champions of the revolution. Meanwhile, the Lahore police, fearing for the safety of the wounded approvers, whisked them away to the nearby Revenue office building. From there, they managed to escape towards Bhusawal, narrowly avoiding the wrath of the angry mob.

Simultaneously, Khan Bahadur and the district superintendent of police escorted Bhagwan and Sadashiv to the Dak Bungalow, hoping to keep them safe from the ongoing chaos. But peace was short-lived. To disperse the frenzied crowd, the police fired four gunshots into the air. While no one was injured, the tense atmosphere only grew thicker.

Despite the warning shots, the protestors refused to back down. Two hours later, they regrouped in front of the Dak Bungalow, their anger now fuelled by the perceived injustice against their comrades. One group of rioters stormed the sessions court, defacing the building and shattering the glass panes. They burned the tents and signboards, their rage manifesting in a whirlwind of destruction.

The situation remained volatile until midnight, when reinforcements arrived from Bhusawal. The extra force brought a semblance of order, and they finally managed to restore calm in the city. Later, in their absence, the court sentenced Bhagwan and Sadashiv to life imprisonment, and sent them to Cellular Jail, Andaman.

Chapter 18

April–June 1930

After the assassination attempt on Phanindra and Jai Gopal, the CID went berserk. They started catching and torturing suspects.

Meanwhile, Gandhiji was signalling an open disobedience movement against the Raj. In March 1930, Mahatma Gandhi called for the Dandi March, a non-violent act of civil disobedience against the British salt monopoly. It was known as the Salt Satyagraha. The entire nation was moved by this satyagraha, and people from all walks of life joined in the cause, determined to fight for India's independence through peaceful means.

Kishori Prasanna Sinha was a Congress leader from Hajipur, Bihar; he started travelling to nearby villages to spread the message of Gandhiji and the disobedience movement.

Kishori was a good acquaintance of Gandhiji, Subhash Chandra Bose and other revolutionaries. His wife, Suniti Devi, was also active in politics. Kishori knew Yogendra from the time of the Anushilan Samiti and had always supported the armed revolution. Also, he hailed from a village near Jalalpur, where Yogendra and Baikunth were from. He knew that Yogendra was wanted by the police in the Maulania dacoity and Lahore conspiracy cases. So, Kishori was surprised to see Yogendra Sukul during the Lahore session of the Congress in December 1929.

After formal greetings, Kishori said, 'Baba, you should not be roaming in daylight. They are looking for you.'

'I know, but I had to come here for urgent work.'

Observing his sorrowful face, Kishori stated, 'I guess the urgent work has failed.'

'Yes, Bapu is still reluctant to help revolutionaries.'

'You cannot blame him for his stand.'

'I agree, he is right in his place, but the nation demands that the life of Bhagat be saved.'

'Anyway, tell me if I can be of any service.'

'Now, since I've seen you, I have a favour to ask.'

'Please go ahead.'

'There's a boy, Baikunth, from my village. You need to take him under your wing for Congress activities. After the Viceregal train bombing, the British will not stop until every last one of us is caught, shot or hanged. This boy is new; he has not done anything; if you take him, there is a chance he will remain away from the dangers of police for revolutionary activities.'

Kishori said, 'It will be my pleasure. I will contact him.'

Taking Yogendra's request to heart, Kishori sought out Baikunth's address. The training with Ranendranath was complete and Baikunth was back to teaching at the primary school at Mathurapur. Kishori went to Baikunth's house. Baikunth came out and recognized Kishori. After formal greetings, Kishori said, 'Baikunth, I am asking you to join the Gandhi Ashram for congressional activities full-time.'

Baikunth said, 'Dada, I know about your work and Bapu's Dandi march. However, I am already part of Seva Dal and working under Ranendranath at Muzaffarpur. So it is difficult to join you full-time.'

Kishori smiled and said, 'Baikunth, I am here on the instructions of Yogendra Baba. I know what you do; I respect it. I have known Yogendra for ten years now. But it is the need of the hour that, for the time being, you should join Gandhi Ashram in Hajipur.'

'But I have not done anything yet; there is no apparent danger for me to operate under Seva Dal.'

'After the Viceregal train bomb and Jalgaon fiasco, a terrible crackdown has been ordered on your creed. If you want to help the party, you need this disguise. Understand this, you cannot do anything from behind bars.'

Radhika Devi, Baikunth's wife, had been listening to the conversation all along.

She intervened, 'I think it is an excellent choice to lie low for a while. If any order comes, you can always work as per the directions.'

Baikunth implored, 'Radha, you don't understand; it is not about working in Congress; it is about getting caught as a Congressman.'

Radhika asked, 'What do you mean?'

'As the Civil Disobedience will peak, mass arrests of Congress workers will follow nationwide. As per the mandate, I will have to surrender to the police. Then if I am behind bars, how can I be of any use to my party?'

Kishori replied, 'That is the exact point behind joining the Gandhi ashram.'

'How?'

'Yogendra Baba wants to get you behind bars as a Congressman so that the CID won't see you as a revolutionary; plus, at every huge Congress movement, those arrested are termed as political prisoners and are released as soon as the movement is over. You must remember what happened to the prisoners of the non-cooperation movement. They were released shortly, absolved of all charges.'

Radhika insisted, 'Please, listen to Kishori Babu; I am terribly afraid of the news going around.'

Kishori said, 'Listen, you have been trained by Yogendra and Ranendranath; they are ensuring that the party's ace is saved for now to be used at the proper movement.'

Baikunth replied dejectedly, 'Anyway, if it is Yogendra Baba's order, then I will follow.'

Kishori said, 'Also, along with you, I want Radhika Deviji to participate in the movement.'

Baikunth smiled and said, 'Yes, Kishori Babu, we all have heard how Suniti Devi handles Gandhi's ashram. It is the need of the hour that our ladies should come to the front to fight the battle for independence.'

Radhika Devi was embarrassed. 'But I have never been to any procession or protest. I can't join; let me handle my home.'

Baikunth stated, 'If you are not coming, I will also not go.'

Kishori said, 'Don't worry, I will ask Suniti to talk with you. I will take your leave now. Baikunth, you know where to find me.'

Baikunth smiled and nodded.

In another week, Suniti Devi picked up Radhika Devi from her house. Baikunth and Radhika started living at Gandhi Ashram, Hajipur. Suniti Devi formed a squad with Radhika Devi and two other women, Krushna and Sharada. They started picketing liquor shops and boycotting foreign clothes. Baikunth was grateful to Kishori and Suniti Devi. He was happy to see his wife finding purpose in her life and fighting for the country.

Kishori and Baikunth started the Anti-Chowkidari Tax movement at Purab Bidupur station, around seven miles from Hajipur. Bihar is landlocked, so there was no scope for the Anti Salt Tax movement. But there was a tradition of Chowkidari Tax in Bihar from 1907. The village would appoint a watchman, *chowkidar*, and pay tax to him, which would go to the government. As per directions from the central committee of Congress, in Bihar, the Anti Chowkidari Tax movement became a huge success. Baikunth and Kishori travelled to every possible village in the area and received a tremendous response from the people.

The police started retaliating against the protestors. Kishori was about to be arrested in Bidupur. Baikunth took him to Hajipur. The next day, the ashram was filled with thousands of protestors. The police arrived again to arrest Kishori. With the help of Baikunth, Kishori again escaped from the ashram just to confirm the charges under which the police sought him. In the evening, when he quietly returned, Suniti Devi verified that Kishori was wanted for Anti Chowkidari and not under the Maulania dacoity case. Although Kishori was not involved in the dacoity, he was still a well-known sympathizer of revolutionaries. He feared that the police might get him involved in the dacoity case.

Kishori then went to Baranti village, and Baikunth kept working in Hajipur ashram. Within a week, when Baikunth was leading a procession in Hajipur, the police arrested him along with all the protestors. Hundreds of prisoners were taken to Patna Camp Jail.

In 1930, the Patna Camp Jail was a vast area enclosed by barbed wire fencing. The prisoners lived in small brick blocks with tin roofs. Around 5000 inmates occupied the penitentiary, with nearly 100 people sharing a single block. Upon arrival, the police provided each prisoner with a kurta, shorts, a plate and an iron lota. Most prisoners were farmers, labourers, illiterate individuals and protestors of the civil disobedience movement. The police supplied the rations, but the inmates themselves prepared their meals.

Baikunth was imprisoned in the Patna Camp Jail, isolated from his fellow revolutionaries. The atmosphere was grim, with overcrowded living conditions and a sense of hopelessness among the prisoners. Baikunth struggled to adapt to the harsh environment, feeling the weight of the separation from his comrades.

His days were monotonous, filled with laborious tasks and a constant battle to maintain his physical and mental well-being. Baikunth longed for the camaraderie and purpose he had felt as part of the revolutionary movement.

The dreary and oppressive atmosphere of the camp left him feeling demoralized and disheartened.

As days turned into weeks and months, Baikunth's resolve began to waver. His once strong spirit gradually succumbed to the despair and desolation that permeated the prison. But even in his darkest moments, Baikunth never lost faith in the HSRA. In the depths of his heart, he held on to the belief that Bhagat Singh and other comrades would be freed one day by Azad.

In Punjab, Azad had hired a man and tasked him with forging coins due to acute shortage of funds to run the party. But the plan failed miserably.

By the end of March, the Lahore Conspiracy Case had turned out to be an absolute fiasco and was moving nowhere. Revolutionaries had been successful in unmasking all the unethical practices deployed by the court for convicting the accused. Inderpal, a member of HSRA, had rented a house in Lahore's Krishna Nagar Mohalla, with the help of Bhagwati. It was at this house that discussions about rescuing the comrades took place.

Wireless was pulled in to find some ingenious solution to rescue Bhagat Singh.

He came to Panditji and stated, 'Panditji, I have a plan to rescue all the comrades.'

'How?'

'If you provide me with some chemicals, I will make a stupefying gas called pimpta gas. I will create a mechanism to release the gas inside the court, making everyone around unconscious.'

'But then even Bhagat, Sukhdev and others will also become unconscious.'

'Yes, there you and others come in and carry them away.'

'Not bad; give me a list of what you need.'

Hansraj asked for lab equipment and a specific amount of cocaine.

Inderpal arranged for the cocaine from somewhere, but it was not pure. Hansraj needed laboratory-quality cocaine. However, it could not be acquired.

Hansraj then asked for licorice powder, which was provided immediately. He kept experimenting, but the result was not up to the mark.

One day Inderpal and Sukhdev Raj found Hansraj himself in an unconscious state in the lab. Panditji was aggrieved and ordered him to abandon the experiment. They had to come up with another plan because, using his extraordinary power, the viceroy had declared a new special tribunal to decide the fate of the revolutionaries in six months.

The same kind of tribunal had been constituted for Ghadar revolutionaries in 1915, under which more than fifty revolutionaries were hanged to death. It was famously called 'Na Vakeel, Na Daleel, Na Apeel'—Sans Counsel, Sans Pleas, Sans Appeal.' The court's decision was final; there could be no appeal to any higher court. The trial before the tribunal started on 5 May 1930.

This was a moral victory for Bhagat Singh and his comrades. They were successful in revealing the true, evil face of the British Raj. The viceroy was ready to murder the revolutionaries without putting them through the due process of law. Azad and Bhagwati decided that the time had come to rescue Bhagat, and the plans began to be expedited. Azad sent a message to Yogendra to continue the dacoities, for the operations needed funds.

On 26 May 1930, Yogendra Sukul and his team meticulously planned and executed a dacoity at Jhajra in the house of Mahant Ram Sundar Das. After thorough reconnaissance and strategizing, the group moved swiftly and discreetly, catching the wealthy establishment off guard. They successfully managed to loot a sum of Rs 4000. The operation was executed with precision, and the group left no traces behind, avoiding detection by the authorities.

A few days later, on 31 May 1930, Yogendra Sukul led another dacoity at Dheulana. It was in a mansion belonging to the erstwhile Jamadar of Bela Factory, Rajbali Thakur. The stakes were higher, as the target held an even more enormous fortune. With the experience of the Jhajra dacoity, the group was even more efficient and bold. The revolutionaries swiftly infiltrated the premises, overpowered the armed guards, and gained control of the situation. They managed to secure a staggering Rs 6500, once again evading capture and leaving no clues for the authorities to follow.

Yogendra arrived at the safehouse in Delhi, feeling proud and accomplished after successfully executing the dacoities. He was eager to share the news and hand the money to Panditji. Sukhdev Raj welcomed him inside as the door opened, but Yogendra immediately sensed something was amiss.

'What's going on?' Yogendra asked. 'Why does everyone look so down? I have some great news and a substantial amount for our cause.'

'Yogendra, we have some terrible news. Bhagwati Charan Vohra is no more. He died in a tragic accident while testing bombs.'

Yogendra, shocked by the news, struggled to find words. 'I . . . I don't understand. How did it happen?'

'It was three days ago. Bhagwati took some bombs to Zakhira, a forest near Lahore, for testing.'

Sukhdev Raj narrated what had happened. 'It was a cloudy afternoon; Bhagwati Charan Vohra and Yashpal were preparing to test the newly made bombs in Zakhira forest. As we reached the remote testing site, he carefully unloaded the bombs from his bag and inspected each one. The dense forest provided the perfect cover, and he was determined to test their effectiveness.

I took out one bomb; its pin felt loose. I showed it to Yashpal. He refused to test it. Bhagwati took the bomb from my hand and asked us to take cover. We asked him to let it go, but he said there was no time. As we took cover, Bhagwati took out the pin. In that instant, the bomb exploded before he could throw it. The explosion was intense and sent dirt and debris flying. As we rushed, he was lying on the ground, one hand had been ripped from the shoulder, there was a massive injury to his stomach, and the entrails were coming out.'

Sukhdev Raj stopped and broke down, crying profusely.

Azad said, 'Even then, he said, don't drop the plan to rescue Bhagat. He needs to be retrieved at any cost. By the time help reached him, Bhagwati was gone.'

Yogendra saw tears in Panditji's eyes for the first time. Yogendra's throat was choking. Bhagwati had taken Bhagat's place in the party. Azad was assured that he and Bhagwati would fight together.

In a heavy voice, Azad said, 'Sometimes, I feel cursed. First, my mentors, Bismil and Ashfaq, left. Then Bhagat, Rajguru, Sukhdev and Dutt. Everyone thought it was over. But I still had some fight left. I went on. Then Bhagwan and Sadashiv left. And now Bhagwati. Tell me, Yogendra, am I destined to fight alone? What will I do without all of them?'

Yogendra felt the weight; tears were rolling down his cheeks. He said: 'Panditji, I remember there was this favourite sher of Bapubhai. *Dare tadveer par sar fodna sheva raha apna, vasile hath hi na aaye kismat aajmai ke.* I heard it a few times but never understood it. Once I asked him to explain, he laughed and said that it is our habit to fight tooth and nail with destiny to achieve our goal, but alas, throughout our life, not even once are we able to get the means to achieve our goal. I told him it is so pessimistic that it says we cannot get what we want. And he said, no, we don't, but the first part of the couplet is important; we never stop trying.'

The room fell silent as the group paid their respects to Bhagwati Charan Vohra, their fallen comrade. His death proved once again that the path ahead was filled with danger and uncertainty.

Azad turned his head towards the window, his body shaking as the commander-in-chief of the Indian armed revolution cried his heart out. After a few minutes, Panditji gathered himself, wiped his eyes and said, 'That is the message, we never stop trying. My mentor, Shaheed Ramprasad Bismil, used to repeat this at every adversity: *Yuun khada maqtal mein qatil keh raha hai baar-baar, kya tamanna-e-shahadat bhi kisi ke dile mein hain?*' (Stands the enemy in the gallows thus, asking, does anyone have wish to be a martyr?)

Sukhdev Raj continued, '*Dil mein tuffanon ki toli, aur nason mein inquilab, hosh dushman ke uda denge hamein roko na aaj* (A storm of desires is in our hearts, and revolution flowing through our veins. The enemy's consciousness will be shattered, don't stop us today).'

Yashpal said, '*Dur reh paye humse dam kahan manzil mein hain* (The destination doesn't have courage to stay away from us? The destination is within reach).'

Yogendra finished, '*Sarfaroshi ki tamanna ab hamare dil mein hain* (The desire for revolution is in our hearts).'

Yogendra nodded, determination filling his eyes.

Yogendra: 'We will carry on. Panditji, what are my orders.'

Azad said, 'Lie low and wait for my instructions. What is the status of the boy you were training?'

Yogendra replied, 'Panditji, Baikunth is ready to join us. I have deliberately asked him to join the disobedience movement to remain out of the radar. He is in Patna Camp Jail but will be released soon as the movement ends.'

Azad stated, 'Good decision; our job is to protect the next generation of revolutionaries. Bring Baikunth to me once he is out.'

Yogendra exclaimed, 'Panditji, he would be overjoyed to know you're calling him.'

It was a dark and tense night on 11 June in Malkachak, Bihar. Yogendra was in Gandhi Kutir, trying to lie low on Azad's instructions. The police were searching for him relentlessly, but he had managed to evade them.

Unbeknown to Yogendra, the police had received a tip-off about his location. As the clock struck midnight, a team of officers stealthily approached Gandhi Kutir, ready to apprehend their target.

A watchful revolutionary kept an eye on the surroundings from a mango tree nearby. As the police closed in, he sensed their presence and shouted a warning relentlessly.

Startled by the sudden commotion outside his door, Yogendra awoke with a jolt. His instincts, honed by years of living on the razor's edge, spurred him to reach for his hidden weapon. But before his fingers could close around the cold metal, the door was flung open, revealing a swarm of uniformed officers, their faces a mixture of determination and fear.

'Don't move, Yogendra! You're under arrest!' barked the police chief, his voice shaking with the weight of his words.

Time seemed to slow as Yogendra, his heart pounding in his chest, assessed the situation. He knew that his capture would be a devastating blow to the revolution, and he would not go down without a fight. With a feral roar, he lunged at the two constables who dared to approach him, his powerful, rippling muscles propelling him forward with the force of a raging bull.

Yogendra's body was a masterpiece of strength and agility, each sinewy curve and bulging vein a testament to his relentless dedication to the cause. His broad shoulders and chiselled chest strained against the confines of his thin cotton shirt, while his corded arms and legs seemed to possess a life of their own, striking with the speed and precision of a viper.

The small room became an arena of chaos as dozens of policemen wrestled with Yogendra, their combined efforts barely enough to contain the force of his fury. The air was thick with the sounds of grunts, shouts and the clash of bodies, as Yogendra fought like a cornered tiger, his every move a desperate bid for freedom.

'Get him down!' the police chief roared, his face flushed with anger and frustration. 'We can't let him escape!'

Yogendra's eyes blazed with defiance as he fought on, his breath coming in ragged gasps. 'Keep trying, you slaves,' he spat, his words punctuated by the thud of fists against flesh.

For half an hour, the epic struggle raged on, the very walls of the room seeming to tremble under the onslaught. But eventually, even Yogendra's indomitable will could not withstand the sheer force of numbers, and he was finally restrained, his limbs bound by thick ropes.

As they led Yogendra out of the room, the police chief sneered, 'You thought you could hide from us forever, didn't you? Well, we've got you now.'

Despite his situation, Yogendra remained defiant. 'You may have caught me, but the game is not over yet.'

The police handcuffed him and waited till the first light. In the morning, they began searching the room and premises. They discovered a stash of weapons, including a loaded Welby revolver, twenty cartridges, khukris and maps of Jahjra and Dheulana. The police also found a handful of forged coins.

Yogendra awaited trial for the multiple charges against him in Chhapra jail. On 26 July 1930, arrangements were made for the hearing to begin inside the prison. However, Yogendra's fellow revolutionaries, led by Rambinod Singh, demanded that the judicial hearings be conducted in an open or proper court.

The day was hot and oppressive as the sun beat down mercilessly on Chhapra. The revolutionaries gathered, their faces resolute and determined. They shouted slogans, demanding justice and transparency for their comrade, Yogendra.

Rambinod Singh yelled, rallying his fellow protesters. 'We demand an open hearing!'

The crowd echoed his words, their voices growing louder and more insistent; they started shouting slogans of 'Inquilab Zindabad' and singing patriotic songs. The air was thick with tension and anticipation. Yogendra felt pride and anxiety inside his cell and listened to the chants and slogans.

As the protest continued, the local authorities found it increasingly difficult to start the proceedings. The noise and unrest outside the jail were beginning to attract the attention of the local press and public, putting pressure on the officials.

The authorities, determined to maintain control over Yogendra, sent in constables to put chains around his hands and feet. Yogendra's anger flared up as the constables approached him, and he cursed them.

'You'll never chain me down!' he shouted, his eyes blazing with defiance.

The constables, taken aback by his sudden aggression, hesitated momentarily. Seizing the opportunity, Yogendra launched himself at them, using his powerful limbs to fend them off. The first two constables crumpled under his fierce blows, unable to subdue him.

Seeing their comrades fall, the other constables retreated and returned with reinforcements. Seven more policemen entered Yogendra's cell, determined to restrain him. Yogendra, however, fought back with the ferocity of a lion. He roared as he threw punches and kicks, his body a whirlwind of movement.

The struggle echoed throughout the prison, drawing the attention of other inmates who pressed against the bars of their cells to witness the fierce battle. The constables, battered and bruised, began to retreat, their spirits broken by Yogendra's relentless fury.

Some constables abandoned their posts in the chaos, leaving Yogendra's cell door open. Spotting the chance to escape, he dashed toward the exit. His heart pounded as he sprinted down the dimly lit corridor, freedom within his grasp.

However, just as Yogendra was about to escape, he was cornered by a group of policemen alerted to the commotion. Despite his valiant efforts, he was finally captured and subdued, but not before leaving a lasting impression on those who had tried to restrain him.

The prison was filled with whispers of Yogendra's daring attempt to break free, and his indomitable spirit became an inspiration to the other inmates. However, the warden realized that Chhapra's jail could not handle a rebel like Yogendra. Colonel Marxus happened to be visiting the Chhapra prison. He saw the fighting first-hand and the kind of energy Yogendra possessed. He immediately recommended that Yogendra be transferred to the more secure Motihari Jail. On the same day, he was taken to Motihari.

After six months of investigation, the High Court of Patna ordered the start of the trial against the revolutionaries in Motihari for the dacoities at Jhajra and Deulana. The courtroom buzzed with anticipation as the Tirhut Conspiracy Case, also known as the Motihari Conspiracy Case, was set to begin on 5 January 1931. Yogendra Sukul and twelve of his fellow revolutionaries stood accused, facing an uncertain future. The atmosphere was tense as the court awaited the arrival of a critical witness.

To the dismay of Yogendra and his comrades, the CID had brought their favourite traitor, Phanindra Nath Ghosh, from Bettiah to testify against them. As Phanindra entered the courtroom, a wave of anger and hatred washed over Yogendra. He cursed under his breath, 'That snake! How low can he go!'

Due to his statement in the Lahore Conspiracy Case, the fate of Bhagat Singh, Rajguru and Sukhdev had been sealed on 7 October 1930. The special tribunal had awarded them the death penalty. Phanindra was also an approver in the Bhusawal bomb case. Now, shamelessly he had appeared to testify in the Motihari conspiracy.

During his testimony, Phanindra provided a detailed account of the events leading up to the dacoities and identified the two revolvers found at Gandhi Kutir Malkachak as belonging to Yogendra. He recounted seeing one of the revolvers in the Udaipur jungle when Yogendra trained with Bhagat Singh and the other at the Agra bomb factory.

Yogendra's face contorted with rage, struggling to control his anger, as Phanindra spoke. He clenched his chained hands into fists, longing to silence the traitor once and for all.

As Phanindra continued to recount the incriminating details, Yogendra couldn't help but shout, 'You coward! How much did they pay you to sell your soul?!'

The courtroom erupted in chaos, and the judge had to call for order. Phanindra, unfazed by Yogendra's outburst, maintained a smug expression as he finished his testimony.

Throughout the trial, Yogendra and his fellow revolutionaries remained defiant, refusing to bow down to their accusers. Despite the heavy chains that bound them, their spirits remained unbroken, fuelled by their unwavering dedication to the cause.

As the case continued, the tension in the courtroom only grew, with the revolutionaries determined to face their accusers with courage and honour. At the same time, the traitor, Phanindra Nath Ghosh, played his part in sealing their fate.

The court announced its verdict on 30 March 1931. Yogendra was sentenced to twenty years of rigorous imprisonment. Ishwar Dayal Singh was sentenced to seven years of rigorous imprisonment and Basawan Singh to five years. Rambinod Singh was released.

Chapter 19

April–October 1930

The scorching sun beat down on Patna Camp Jail, the hot, dry air finding its way through blazing tin roofs, stifling the prisoners as they did their daily chores. Baikunth found it challenging to adjust to the monotonous and arduous life in prison. Most inmates were illiterate labourers and peasants who had never been exposed to the world of literature or intellectual pursuits. Only a few, like Baikunth, knew how to read and write.

Among the prisoners was Bibhuti Bhushan Das Gupta, a reputed Congress leader and sympathizer with revolutionaries. He was in Patna Camp Jail even before the civil disobedience started. He was a spirited and resourceful person. Along with impeccable storytelling skills, Bibhuti possessed a treasure in the prison. The jailer had allowed him to keep two books by Gurudev Rabindranath Tagore; one was *Geetanjali*, and the other was *Chayanika*. His favourite pastime was singing the poems aloud to his fellow inmates in Bangla and then explaining their meaning in Hindi in simpler terms. The prisoners found solace and meaning in the beauty of Tagore's words, a brief escape from the harsh reality of their confinement.

One day, as the prisoners gathered under the shade of a large banyan tree to escape the merciless sun, Bibhuti pulled out his worn copy of *Chayanika*. He began to read a famous poem called 'Maran Milan', meaning 'death wedding'. It was written by Gurudev in 1902.

As Bibhuti's melodious voice carried through the air, Baikunth sat among the group, his eyes fixed on the man, eager to understand every word. He could sense the depth of emotion in the verses, and although he partially understood Bangla, he struggled to fully grasp the complex ideas and imagery.

> I shall go to where your boat is moored,
> Death, death, to the sea where the wind rolls
> Darkness towards me from infinity.
> I may see black clouds massing in the far
> North-east corner of the sky; fiery snakes
> Of lightning may rear up with their hoods raised,
> But I shall not flinch in unfounded fear—
> I shall pass silently, unswervingly
> Across that red storm sea, Death.

At this point, Baikunth hesitantly interrupted and asked, 'Dada, please explain the meaning of the last two lines.'

Bibhuti, sensing the young man's earnestness, paused his reading, smiled warmly and asked, 'What is your name, young man?'

Baikunth stood up in his place and replied, 'Baikunth Sukul, from Jalalpur, Muzaffarpur.'

'Oh, so you are from the place of Shaheed Khudiram Bose.'

'Yes, Dada.' A sense of pride reflected on Baikunth's face.

'Baikunth, have you understood the rest of the poem, and do you have a problem with the particular last line?'

Baikunth felt embarrassed, and his face began to redden, but still, he spoke, 'Dada, I am no good in Bangla, but I understood the literal meaning of each line. Of course, this is the work of Gurudev,' Baikunth clasped his hand together, touched his head as a matter of respect and continued, 'so there must be some implicit and hidden meaning. I want to ask you to explain it to us.'

Bibhuti smiled and looked at Baikunth for a moment. He felt that something was unique about the boy. He said, 'I will explain it as I understood and eventually will come to your question.'

'Thank you, Dada.'

'Gurudev is tackling here the deepest, cosmic, most universal theme: mysterious Death, whose edicts we cannot resist and can never fully understand. The poet roughly marks three ways how one should be wedded to death. The first is when death comes stealthily, taking the mortal by surprise, like dying in sleep. In the second way, the end may come like Mahadeva taking a terrible form and inflicting horror on the viewers. Still, if the mortal looked at the fearsome state of Shiva through the eyes of Gauri, then it would be a satisfactory consummation. Now comes the ultimate way to die, where mortals call death and run to it; they are not afraid of its darkness and gloom. In fact, the mortal has found a purpose to celebrate the wedding with death as the epitome of his life's achievement, like the legendary fighter Khudiram Bose. Young Khudiram rose to the gallows with a smile; he accepted and celebrated death as his ultimate victory. That, my friend, is the best way to wed death.

But I shall not flinch in unfounded fear
I shall pass silently, unswervingly
Across that red storm sea, Death,

This is a way to pass this storm sea to meet death with our heads held high.'

Baikunth was lost in a trance, listening to every word of Bibhuti. He saw Khudiram, Jatin Das and Bhagat Singh. Now their faces were merging into each other; they all looked alike. Death, death. The word kept ringing in his ears. Baikunth felt a lump in his throat, moved by the profound wisdom of the poem. He looked around and saw that his fellow inmates were equally moved, their eyes glistening with unshed tears.

'What do you say, Baikunth? Do you understand it now?'

He came to his senses by the call of his name. He replied, 'Dada, I get it now.' His voice was filled with gratitude.

Instantly, Bibhuti replied, 'So, can you swim across the red storm sea like Khudiram?'

Comparing his existence to Shaheed Khudiram, Baikunth felt goosebumps all over his body. His eyes welled up, and he mumbled, 'I will, Dada.'

Baikunth's eyes remained fixed on Bibhuti Dada, his heart filled with gratitude for the newfound understanding and the sense of transcendence that the poem had given him. He knew that the words of 'Maran Milan' would stay with him forever.

Baikunth sat in his cell, his heart heavy with worry as he waited for news about the trial of Bhagat Singh and his comrades. His eyes were glued to each newspaper that made its way into the prison, scanning the headlines for any updates on their fate. Finally, one day in May, he received a small piece of news that Viceroy Irwin had appointed a Special Tribunal, a move that would have far-reaching consequences. The tribunal was set to handle the trial of Bhagat Singh, Sukhdev, Rajguru and several other revolutionaries. However, from the beginning, it became clear that the tribunal was nothing but a sham.

The proceedings were conducted in the absence of the accused, blatantly violating every principle of natural justice. The revolutionaries were denied the opportunity to defend themselves or present their story. The entire process reeked of prejudice, with the tribunal showing no interest in a fair trial.

As the trial progressed, a sense of impending doom hung. The revolutionaries, despite their absence, remained defiant and determined, their spirits unbroken. Baikunth couldn't help but feel a mixture of anger and despair at the blatant injustice playing out before the eyes of his countrymen.

Baikunth wondered what this would mean. Would this new tribunal be any different than the magisterial trial? Would they finally receive a fair trial, or would they continue to be subjected to injustice?

Over the next few weeks, Baikunth heard rumours and gossip about the trial proceedings. He learned that the accused were absent from court until 23 June and that a judge named Agha Haider was sympathetic to the revolutionaries and bound to a fair trial. Soon the government realized that it would be impossible to get the desired verdict if Haider was kept on board.

Baikunth's heart leapt when he heard that a new tribunal, consisting of Justice G.C. Hilton, Justice Abdul Qadir and Justice J.K. Tapp, had been appointed. He wondered if this would end this farcical trial or if his comrades would be subjected to more injustice.

As the days wore on, he heard more details about the charges framed against the accused.

1. Possession of arms and ammunition and going about armed without a license,
2. Committing and attempting to commit murder,
3. Committing robbery and dacoity,
4. Manufacturing, possessing and having under control explosive substances,
5. Rescuing and attempting to rescue persons detained in lawful custody, and most importantly,
6. Waging and attempting to wage war against His Majesty the King Emperor of India.

More troubling news came on the day when he learned that Bhagat Singh and his comrades had gone on a hunger strike for the third time. Baikunth imagined the toll this would take on their bodies and wondered if this would be the end for them.

As the days turned into weeks, Baikunth felt the weight of uncertainty pressing down on him. He longed to get news about Bhagat Singh.

Finally, on 7 October, the verdict was announced. Baikunth held his breath as he waited to hear the outcome. Ajoy Kumar Ghosh, Jitendra Sanyal and Des Raj were acquitted. At the same time, Kishori Lal, Jai Dev, Shiv Verma, Gaya Prasad, Mahabir Singh, B.K. Sinha, Kundan Lal and K.N. Tiwari were awarded life imprisonment. Prem Dutt, a juvenile, was sentenced to five years in prison. And then, the news that Baikunth had been dreading: Bhagat Singh, Rajguru and Sukhdev were sentenced to death.

Baikunth felt as though his heart had been ripped out of his chest. How could this be happening? How could fate be so cruel? He was trained to fight and ready to lock horns with the Raj, but he was trapped in his cell, powerless to help.

The death warrant of Bhagat Singh, issued by the Tribunal on 7 October 1930 to the superintendent of Central Jail at Lahore, read: '. . . This is to authorize and require you . . . to carry the said (death) sentence into execution by causing the said Bhagat Singh to be hanged by the neck until he is dead at Lahore, on 27 October 1930, and to return the warrant to the High Court with an endorsement certifying that the sentence has been executed.'

As the days passed, Baikunth found himself consumed with grief and anger. He couldn't believe that his comrades, who had fought so hard for their country's freedom, were now facing death. He wondered if there was anything he could do to help, anything that would make a difference.

However, the date of the sentence was delayed.

One day Bibhuti came to Baikunth and said he had a piece of news about Bhagat Singh.

Baikunth replied, 'Dada, please tell me.'

'All of his comrades are separated from him. Bhagat, Rajguru and Sukhdev will be kept separate until hanged.'

'I know about this one.'

'No, there is more. Someone related to Jai Dev Kapoor came today to see me. He was in Lahore and met Jai Dev, where he conveyed this thing to him.'

'What is it?'

'A few days ago, those who were taken to life imprisonment were allowed to meet with Bhagat for one last time. There gathering his courage, Jai Dev asked Bhagat Singh, "Sardar, you are going to die; I would like to know if you are sorry for it?"

'On hearing the question, Bhagat laughed loudly first, then turned thoughtful and said, "When I set foot on the path of revolution, I thought if I could spread the slogan of 'Inquilab Zindabad' to every nook and corner of India by sacrificing my life, I would think that my life has been of worth. Today when I am behind the iron bars of this cell, I can hear the roaring sounds of that slogan rising from the throats of crores of my countrymen. This slogan will hit the imperialists hard as a driving force of the freedom struggle until the end." Then after pausing a while, he said with his inimitable smile, "What more one can achieve from such a short life?"

'On seeing Jai Dev weep, he said, "This is no time to become sentimental. I shall soon be free of all worries, but all of you will have to traverse a long journey despite the heavy weight of responsibilities on you. You will not cower and will not stop halfway accepting defeat."'

Baikunth was listening intently, holding his breath.

Bibhuti said, 'What a man; I wish I could have met him. At least, see him once.'

Baikunth said, 'Dada, I have seen him. There is more to him than is discussed anywhere. He is not just a man; he has become revolution itself.'

Chapter 20

October 1930

The sun was setting on 4 October 1930, casting long shadows along the canal bank on the outskirts of Lahore. Khan Bahadur Abdul Aziz was in his car, feeling a sense of unease as they drove on the desolate road.

As they continued, suddenly, a loud bang echoed through the air. The driver, startled, slammed on the brakes, thinking a tyre had burst. 'What the . . .?' he exclaimed, his heart racing.

Before they could fully comprehend what was happening, a barrage of bullets whizzed through the air, mercilessly targeting the car. The armed personal guard instinctively tried to shield Khan Bahadur, and the shot went through his chest. Blood splattered on Khan Bahadur's uniform. The driver, hit by a stray bullet, gritted his teeth in pain but managed to stay conscious.

Knowing they were under attack, Khan Bahadur swiftly pulled out his weapon and yelled to his remaining guard, 'Get down and take cover! We're under fire!'

The guard nodded, fear in his eyes, and ducked low in the car, pulling out his weapon. They returned fire, trying to glimpse the assailants in the fading light. The sound of gunshots and the smell of gunpowder filled the air.

The attackers, realizing their element of surprise was gone, quickly retreated, disappearing into the shadows before they could be identified. Khan Bahadur and his companion continued to scan the area, their guns ready, but it was evident that the assailants had escaped.

Panting heavily and covered in sweat, a terrified Khan Bahadur surveyed the scene, his mind racing. The driver, wincing in pain, managed to speak through gritted teeth, 'They . . . they must have been revolutionaries, Sir. We . . . we need to get out of here.'

Khan Bahadur nodded, his face grim with determination. 'You're right. We need to report this immediately and get you medical attention.' Then he looked at the guard who had died in the seat, taking a bullet for him. Khan Bahadur saw himself in the guard's place. The shock was too much even for him. The driver shouted again, 'Sir, get in; we should not wait here anymore.'

Khan Bahadur got in, and the unhurt guard took the wheel.

As the news of the Tribunal's verdict spread, people across the country were overcome with grief and outrage. Death by hanging for Bhagat Singh, Sukhdev and

Rajguru. Life imprisonment for a few others and various punishments for the remaining accused. The revolutionaries had become symbols of hope and courage, fighting valiantly against the oppressive British regime. Their sentences seemed to be a cruel reminder of the harsh reality of colonial rule.

The sun dipped below the horizon, casting a dusky hue over the bustling streets of Bombay. Amidst the crowded chaos, a group of revolutionaries huddled together in the shadows, their eyes fiery and their hearts ablaze. Durga Bhabhi, a woman of extraordinary courage, had been hardened by the merciless loss of her husband, Bhagwati Charan Vohra. Bhagat was like a brother to her. The verdict that decided to end Bhagat Singh's life had been the last straw; now she was ready to make the British Raj pay.

As the conspirators whispered fervently, their resolve crystallized. The Lamington Road Police Station, that symbol of British tyranny, would bear the brunt of their wrath. Durga Devi, Vaishampayan and their fellow revolutionaries would strike in cold blood, a blow that would reverberate through the very foundations of the empire.

The night of 9 October 1930 arrived with an uneasy stillness. As the clock inched towards midnight, the anticipation among the revolutionaries reached a fever pitch. Concealed within a nondescript car, Durga Devi and her comrades crouched low, scanning the road with bated breath. The moment they had waited for was at hand, and they would not falter.

A second car appeared, weaving its way through the dimly lit street toward the police station. Sergeant Taylor of the Bombay Police, his wife and two friends were returning from an evening out, blissfully unaware of the dark cloud that loomed over them. As the vehicle pulled up to the station, the revolutionaries tensed, their eyes narrowing with a lethal focus.

Vaishampayan, gripping his revolver, glanced at Durga Devi. Her face was a mask of steely determination, her eyes smouldering embers that seemed to pierce the darkness. He could sense the fire raging within her, a fire that threatened to consume everything in its path.

'Now,' she whispered, the single word slicing through the silence like a knife.

With that command, the night erupted in a cacophony of gunfire. Bullets rained down upon the unsuspecting targets, shattering glass and tearing through flesh. Sergeant Taylor and his wife were hit, their screams of pain and terror piercing the air as they crumpled to the ground.

The revolutionaries, their faces grim and resolute, continued to fire, their guns unrelenting. Their hearts pounded in their chests, fuelled by a potent mixture of fury and vengeance. The message was clear: the blood of revolutionaries would not be spilled in vain, and the British Raj would pay dearly for their crimes.

The pandemonium caught the attention of nearby officers, who scrambled in confusion, desperate to make sense of the chaos. The revolutionaries, having made their point, prepared to make their escape.

'Go, go, go!' Durga Devi urged, her voice hoarse from the adrenaline that coursed through her veins.

The car roared to life, its engine growling in defiance as it sped away from the scene of retribution. The night was shattered by the sounds of sirens and gunfire.

'We will be victorious,' Durga Devi murmured, her voice barely audible over the roar of the engine. 'For my dear Bhagwati, for every life that has been or is yet to be sacrificed. We will not rest until our people are free.'

With their message delivered, the attackers sped off into the darkness. The assailants' car was later found abandoned near Andheri, its engine still warm from the desperate flight. Upon further investigation, the driver of the vehicle was discovered and apprehended. Under questioning, he confessed that Swami and Vaishampayan, and members of a local revolutionary party, had fired the shots in retaliation for the sentencing of Bhagat Singh and his comrades.

Chapter 21

November–December 1930

In the bustling city of Lahore, a spark of rebellion had been ignited in the heart of a young boy named Yashpal. At merely ten years of age, his world was set ablaze by the ideals of freedom fighters like Bhagat Singh and Bhagwati Charan Vohra. Yashpal, son of Khusal Chand Khursand, the editor of the *Milap* newspaper, had found his purpose in life—to follow in the footsteps of his heroes and fight against the oppressive British Raj.

As the sun rose each day, Yashpal would step out onto the dusty streets of Lahore, feeling the weight of history upon his small shoulders. He was driven by an unquenchable thirst for justice and his love for Bhagat Singh, who had become a symbol of rebellion. With a fierce determination, the young boy joined the Bal Bharat Sabha, a children's wing of the Naujawan Bharat Sabha. Before long, Yashpal was appointed secretary for the city of Lahore.

Each day, Yashpal would gather children from across the city to speak of the injustices perpetrated by the British Raj. His voice, though small, carried the thunder of a thousand storms as he delivered seditious speeches that ignited the fire within his young listeners. They would gather in alleys, parks and courtyards, shouting slogans and passionately protesting against the colonists who had held their country captive for far too long.

One day, as Yashpal led a group of young boys through the streets of Lahore, shouting slogans of 'Inquilab Zindabad' and 'Down with imperialism', their burning anger manifested into action. Incensed by the sight of a procession, a constable approached and sternly commanded, 'Hey, boys go home. You cannot march here.'

Yashpal stood near the constable, determined, and continued the slogan, 'Long live revolution, down with imperialism.'

Most of the boys were around eight to ten years old. The constable couldn't beat them or arrest them. To terrify the children, he raised his lathi and took the position of attack. Instantly, the boys descended upon the symbol of oppression, attacking him with a ferocity that belied their youth. The constable had to run away to save his honour. It was only a matter of time before the long arm of the law would reach for Yashpal.

In July 1930, Yashpal was arrested for his role in the attack on the constable. His father managed to secure his release on a bail of 1000 rupees, but the boy's spirit remained unbroken. When the tribunal announced the sentence of hanging his hero, Bhagat Singh, in October, Yashpal's anger knew no bounds. He was a whirlwind of rage, and his frail frame trembled with each vehement protest he raised.

By 8 November 1930, the forces of the British Raj could no longer ignore the young revolutionary. Yashpal was arrested again, and the punishment was severe this time. The child was sentenced to three months of rigorous imprisonment, followed by three years at the reformatory in Delhi.

As Yashpal was led away from his home, his mother wept silently in the shadows, her heart aching for her young son. But Yashpal held his head high, his eyes glistening with the determination that had come to define him. He knew that the road ahead was fraught with suffering and hardship, but he was prepared to walk on for the love of his heroes and the future of his country.

The dark walls of the prison loomed over Yashpal as he arrived, a stark reminder of the harsh reality that awaited him. But within those walls, the young boy would continue to carry the torch of rebellion, igniting the spirits of those around him with his unwavering commitment to the cause.

The story of the ten-year-old revolutionary from Lahore would echo throughout the nation and cross the seas to London. A report was called from London on the absurdly severe treatment of a juvenile and to verify whether the news had any truth. The investigation provided the report that the information was accurate. By then, public opinion was turning against the Raj. Finally, Yashpal's father managed to secure his release again on an exorbitant bail of 10,000 rupees. It was a task to gather such an amount for Yashpal's father. But, he knew, it was not cheap to walk in the footsteps of Bhagat Singh, and the nation demanded as many Bhagats as it could get.

Meanwhile, CID got information of an active group of HSRA in Kanpur. On 1 December 1930, after careful planning, the police trapped Kanpur unit's head Shaligram Sukul. They asked him to surrender. Shaligram refused and opened fire. The CID cornered his from all sides and shot him dead.

As the news of Yashpal and Shaligram was going around, Hari Kishan Talwar, a young man from Mardan, Punjab, felt a fire burning within him. He considered himself a disciple of Bhagat Singh and the other brave revolutionaries involved in the Lahore Conspiracy Case. Yashpal worshipped Ram Prasad Bismil and Ashfaqullah Khan, who were part of the Kakori Conspiracy Case. He had attended the Lahore conspiracy trial a few times and witnessed the volcano of revolution first-hand. The powerful court statements of Bhagat Singh had left an indelible mark on Hari Kishan's heart and mind. He became convinced that only a rebellion led by self-sacrificing youth could wrest independence from the formidable British Empire. Hari Kishan knew he could not remain idle while his country's manhood was tested.

The Talwar family, consisting of Hari Kishan and his two elder and two younger brothers, were devoted followers of the Khudai Khidmatgar movement led by Badshah Khan, also known as Frontier Gandhi. Their dedication to the cause of India's freedom was unwavering. Hari Kishan, filled with an urge to find meaning in his life, soon found himself in the company of like-minded young men. They decided to assassinate the notorious Sir Geoffrey de Montmorency, the

Governor of Punjab. The CID, the police lobby, bureaucrats and the Punjab governor were the main villains in Bhagat Singh's story for this young man. They had been reading newspapers and knew about the determination of the administration to hang the revolutionaries without a proper trial.

After brief planning by Hari Kishan, the date was set for 23 December 1930. Montmorency was coming to the convocation ceremony of the University of Punjab. This was a golden opportunity for Hari Kishan to target the evil mastermind. Dressed in European attire, he sneaked into the hall and entered the visitors' gallery, without the necessary pass. He had bought the gun for Rs 95. His father was a known marksman and hunter in the area. Hari Kishan was trained, along with his brothers, in shooting.

Hari Kishan sat in the fourth row from the dais. It was easy to aim if the target was steady. He wanted to shoot when Montmorency took his seat. As the governor entered, everyone stood up. Hari Kishan's heartbeat quickened. He was ready. Being short, he was unable to view the dais. When everyone sat down, he saw Montmorency beside Dr Sarvepalli Radhakrishnan, a respected Indian leader. Hari Kishan could not risk shooting Montmorency now. There was a possibility that Dr Radhakrishnan might get injured. He waited patiently until the end of the function.

When the convocation ceremony ended, Sir Geoffrey Montmorency rose to his feet and began walking towards the exit, flanked by a procession of dignitaries. As Montmorency descended the aisle, Hari Kishan, heart pounding in his chest, waited. With Montmorency just a few paces away,

Hari Kishan's eyes narrowed, and his grip tightened around the revolver concealed beneath his jacket.

'Enough is enough,' he muttered under his breath, adrenaline coursing through his veins. 'It's now or never.'

In a swift, fluid motion, Hari Kishan leapt onto his chair, revolver in hand. He took aim and fired two shots in rapid succession. The sound of gunfire echoed through the hall, followed by screams of terror and confusion.

Montmorency stumbled, clutching his left arm where a bullet had grazed him. The other bullet narrowly missed his back, embedding itself in the wall behind him. Hari Kishan cursed inwardly, blaming the rickety chair for missing his shot.

The police officers on duty sprang into action, racing towards Hari Kishan. Sub-inspector Chanan Singh advanced, despite Hari Kishan's warning to stand back. With a fierce glare, Hari Kishan yelled, 'I said, stand back, or you'll regret it!'

But Chanan Singh paid no heed and continued to advance. Hari Kishan fired again with no other choice, hitting Chanan Singh in the chest. The sub-inspector crumpled to the ground, blood pooling around his lifeless form.

Sub-inspector Wardhawan, undeterred by his fallen comrade, charged at Hari Kishan. 'You'll pay for this, you traitor!' he screamed, only to be met with another bullet to the thigh.

In the confusion and panic, Dr Medermott, an Englishwoman, was caught in the crossfire, sustaining injuries.

With all six bullets spent, Hari Kishan desperately tried to reload his revolver. His hands shook with adrenaline as he fumbled with the bullets, but it was too late. The police officers swarmed over him, pinning him to the ground and wrenching the revolver from his grasp.

As they dragged him away, he was beaten mercilessly and later subjected to brutal torture in the dreaded cells of Lahore Fort Jail. For fourteen days, he endured the most inhuman treatment, yet when his father, Gurudas Mal, saw him for the first time after his arrest, and the old patriot saw the bloody, swollen face of his son, his first question was, 'How did you miss the target after so much training in shooting.'

Hari Kishan smiled and explained, 'That jerky chair let me down.'

Following a trial, Hari Kishan was sentenced to death on 26 January 1931 for the murder of sub-inspector Chanan Singh. The Divisional Bench of the Lahore High Court confirmed the sentence.

While in Lahore jail, Hari Kishan demanded to meet Bhagat Singh. The authorities knew Hari had tried to kill the governor for Bhagat. They refused the demand. Angered, Hari wrote a letter to the warden and went on a hunger strike with a single request to meet Bhagat Singh once. The warden ignored the threat and letter. Day after day passed, and Hari's vitals started becoming worse. The police had the practice to begin force-feeding after ten days. The warden took the approval of his superiors. Hari Kishan's body had grown weak during his nine-day hunger strike, but his spirit remained unbroken. He sat on the cold floor of his cell, his resolve unwavering. Finally realizing that he would not give up, the guards reluctantly granted him a brief meeting with Bhagat Singh.

The guards led Hari Kishan down the dimly lit corridor. Hari Kishan's heart raced with anticipation as they approached Bhagat Singh's cell, and his eyes welled up with emotion.

The cell door creaked open, and a beam of morning sunlight came into the small stuffy cell. A slim person was holding a thick book in one hand and writing in a notebook. The light reflected from the book's page to the worn-out, fierce and determined face of Bhagat Singh. He closed the book and got up. His eyes met with Hari Kishan, and time seemed to stand still for a moment.

'Hari Kishan,' Bhagat Singh said softly, his voice filled with admiration and concern. 'You should not have risked your health for this meeting.'

Hari Kishan swallowed hard, struggling to find his voice. 'I couldn't bear the thought of not seeing you, Bhagat Singhji. You've been my inspiration, my guiding light in this fight for freedom. You are Inquilab.'

Bhagat Singh's eyes softened. 'Your courage and commitment are commendable, my young friend. But remember, our fight is not just about individual acts of bravery. It's about igniting the flame of revolution in the hearts of our countrymen.'

Hari Kishan nodded, tears streaming down his face. 'I understand and am ready to face whatever consequences come my way. But tell me, how do I carry on without you? What will our country do without you?'

With a sad smile, Bhagat Singh replied, 'Our physical bodies may perish, but our spirit will live on in the hearts of those who continue the struggle. Remember, it is the idea of freedom that we fight for, not just our own lives.'

As the guards prepared to end their meeting, Bhagat Singh clasped Hari Kishan's hands in a firm grip. 'Stay strong, Hari. We may be imprisoned, but our spirit remains unbound. Our sacrifices will not be in vain.'

Hari cried profusely, his tears falling on Bhagat's hands. Hari tried to bend to touch Bhagat's feet, but Bhagat held him and shook his head. Bhagat's throat choked with emotion.

Hari said, 'Bhagat Singhji, now that I have met you, I am ready to die happily.'

Bhagat choked in tears. He could not utter a word.

The cell door closed, and the constables literally dragged Hari Kishan away. In a hoarse full-throated voice, Hari shouted, 'Inquilab—'

Everyone in the surrounding cell responded, 'Zindabad!' Bhagat mumbled the same, but now his tears were unstoppable.

Hari Kishan, with a renewed sense of purpose and determination, walked away. Though their meeting had been brief, Bhagat Singh's words echoed in his soul, inspiring him to continue the fight for freedom, no matter the cost.

A day before his execution, Hari Kishan expressed his last wish:

'I pray to God that I may be reborn in this holy land, India, so that I may continue to fight the foreign rulers and liberate my motherland.'

He also requested that if his body were released to his family, they should cremate it at the same spot where Bhagat Singh, Shivaram Rajguru and Sukhdev Thapar were to be cremated and that they should immerse the ashes in the Sutlej River, where the remains of these heroes would be immersed.

On 6 June 1931, Hari Kishan's brother was informed that the last interview with his condemned sibling would occur that day. In the midnight hour of 9 June 1931, with a defiant smile, Hari Kishan ascended the gallows in Mianwali Jail, Lahore, and was executed.

Even in death, the authorities would not relent. His body was not returned to his family; he was cremated near the jail under strict supervision. Thus, Hari Kishan became one of the youngest martyrs to die for India's freedom struggle.

Hari Kishan's father, Gurudas, was also arrested and put on trial in Lahore. The shock of his son's execution and the guilt of failing to kill Sir Geoffrey took a heavy toll on Gurudas, and he passed away just twenty-five days after his son was hanged.

Chapter 22

January 1931

In July 1930, Azad and his fellow revolutionaries committed a daring heist, looting the Gadodia Store, in Chandni Chowk, Delhi, owned by Seth Laxmi Narayan Gadodia, a rich businessman. However, their success was short-lived, as the CID aggressively pursued them. Realizing the danger, the group decided to seek refuge in Allahabad.

As January 1931 approached, the Hindu month of Magh was about to begin, when pilgrims from all over North India would converge upon Allahabad to partake in the annual festival of Magh Snan. The group saw an opportunity to blend in with the throngs of holy bathers and avoid the watchful eyes of the CID.

With the help of an old associate, Azad and his comrades could secure two blocks of housing in Katra, Allahabad. One block housed Azad, Vaishampayan, Bhavani Singh Rawat and Surendranath Pandey, while the other was occupied by Durga Bhabhi and Sushila Didi.

Azad was determined to reorganize the party with the resources available to them. He planned to send some members abroad for training and financial support, hoping to strengthen their cause.

One day an informant showed up at the hideout looking for Azad. After a thorough search, the man was granted access to meet Azad. Within five minutes, he was back out the door, and Azad called for a briefing with the rest of the group.

'Friends,' Azad announced, 'we have information that the traitor Phani Babu is in Allahabad. The police are protecting him at a house in Chowk Bazaar. This is our chance. If we can get him in range, I will shoot him myself. It is time that the turncoat faces justice.'

Vaishampayan asked, 'Panditji, what are your orders?'

'Bacchan,' Azad said, 'he knows me too well, so I can't go near the hot zone. Take Bhavani Singh with you and verify his presence. Do a recce of the security present at the place. See if you can rent a house next to it, which could be our base for action. Remember, you are here with your family for Magh Snan.'

'Yes, Panditji,' Vaishampayan replied, and immediately he and Bhavani Singh went to Chowk Bazaar, hiring a tonga to take them there.

They finally located the house after an hour; it was a two-storey building made of brownstone with a six-foot-high compound. It was situated 200 meters from the Kotwali in Chowk Bazaar, and four constables were stationed on the ground floor. One window opened on the first floor;

during their second round on the road, Vaishampayan saw someone walking on the first floor, wearing a white kurta and a Bengali-style dhoti.

Vaishampayan whispered to Bhavani, 'You go and talk with the police. I'll hide behind that tree over there.'

Bhavani went in front of the house and called out, 'Is anyone here?'

A constable opened a small rectangular window in the front gate and asked, 'What do you want?'

'Sorry, Sahib.' Bhavani gave an expression of shock and said, 'Is this some kind of a police station?'

'No, why are you asking?'

'Sahib, I have come from Gadhwal with my family for Magh Snan. We are staying at a dharamshala for now, but the crowd is pouring into the city, as you know. I am looking for a house to rent for a month. I thought this house was empty, so I called for the owner at the gate.'

'No problem,' the constable said, 'many houses are available for rent. Ask around.'

'Thank you, Sahib,' Bhavani said. 'May I ask what the police are doing in this house? I mean, is this area safe for a family?'

The constable laughed. 'Don't worry, this is a good area. We are here on orders from superiors to guard a Bengali gentleman.'

Bhavani's heart raced as he realized they had found their target. He managed to keep his cool and replied, 'Oh, I get it. Thank you for your guidance.'

Bhavani and Vaishampayan then managed to secure a house precisely opposite their target on rent. The distance was less than ten metres across the street. Bhavani even paid a token amount as an advance. Back at the hideout, the group discussed their plan of attack.

'We need to act fast,' Azad said. 'Phani Babu is under police protection, and we don't know how long he'll be there. Bhavani, take Durga Bhabhi and Sushila Didi with you and take possession of the house. This will convince the owner that you have arrived here for Magh Snan. Observe the activities of Phani Babu and find the time and spot for action. Report to me in two days.'

The next day, Bhavani Singh took Durga Bhabhi, Sushila Didi and little Sachi to the house. The ladies looked after the kitchen, and the place was set. Bhavani observed the house continuously. Winter had engulfed Allahabad and Phanindra would walk on the roof, basking in the morning sun wearing a woollen sweater, socks and gloves. Then often in the afternoon and evening after 8 p.m., he used to sit in the window on the first floor smoking a beedi. Coincidentally, the window of Bhavani's house was exactly in front of Phani.

Azad's eyes glinted with conviction as he twirled his moustache and spoke with determination, 'Bhavani, I will come to the house at night. As the bastard sits by the window this evening, I will shoot him from across the street. Finally, the traitor is now on my mark. This will exemplify to everyone in this nation that there will be no place for traitors in independent India. Bhagat, Sukhdev, Sadashiv and Bhagwan will be overjoyed to hear the news once we succeed. Go now; there is no time to lose.'

Bhavani rushed back to the safe house; he saw the worried expressions etched on the faces of Durga Bhabhi and Sushila Didi. He tried to put on a brave face, but his fear was palpable as he asked, 'What's wrong?'

Durga Bhabhi pointed towards Phanindra's house, and Bhavani's heart sank as he saw a big lock on the gate. 'A police van arrived; they took Phani Babu along with the constables,' she said.

Bhavani's mind raced, trying to cling to any shred of hope. 'No problem,' he said, trying to sound confident. 'They must have taken him for some work. He'll be back soon.'

But Sushila Didi's words shattered his optimism like fragile glass. 'I don't think so. We saw his luggage being taken along with him.'

As the agonizing wait dragged on, the sky turned a fiery orange, signalling the approach of evening. Suddenly, Azad arrived, moving like a shadow. But as he approached, his face twisted with anger as he saw the lock on the opposite house's gate. 'I guessed it from the lock,' he spat out. 'What a lucky bastard. Even after multiple attempts, we fail to kill a rat.'

Durga Bhabhi tried to reassure him, but her words only stoked the flames of Azad's rage. 'Bhaiya, don't worry. Where will he go? Even if he goes to London, he will face justice. There is no pardon for what he has done to the party and our comrades.'

Azad's eyes flashed with fury, his fists clenched tightly. 'I agree,' he growled. 'Today was his lucky day, but he will not live to enjoy the life of a traitor. This blot on the face of Mother India should be washed away as soon as possible.'

The tension in the room was suffocating as they all waited for Azad's next move. Bhavani could feel his heart beating faster and faster, like a drumbeat. He could see the fire in Azad's eyes, could feel the anger and frustration boiling within him like a volcano about to erupt.

Chapter 23

February–March 1931

On the last day of February 1931, Baikunth's footsteps echoed through the grim corridors of Patna Camp Jail. He had been summoned by Bibhuti, and as he made his way to the meeting point, his mind raced with questions. Baikunth had never seen Bibhuti so distraught, and he couldn't shake the feeling that something terrible had occurred. The air felt heavy as if the very walls were holding their breath.

Upon reaching the meeting point, Baikunth found Bibhuti hunched over, his face buried in his hands. The sight of the firm, fearless Bibhuti Dada reduced to tears sent a shiver down Baikunth's spine. A crumpled newspaper lay discarded beside him, and a small, rectangular paper was folded neatly in his hand. The atmosphere was thick with tension and unspoken sorrow.

Bibhuti looked up as Baikunth approached, his eyes red and swollen from crying. 'Baikunth, my brother,' he said, his voice cracking with emotion, 'there's something you need to know.'

Baikunth's heart hammered in his chest, a sense of dread washing over him. He reached out, taking the folded paper from Bibhuti's trembling hand. 'What is this, Dada?' he asked, his voice barely above a whisper.

Bibhuti hesitated, his eyes filling with tears once more. 'Just . . . just open it, Baikunth,' he choked out.

Baikunth carefully unfolded the paper, revealing a pinch of ashes. His brow furrowed in confusion. 'What is this, Dada? Is this holy ash from some temple?'

Bibhuti shook his head, his face contorted with pain. 'No, Baikunth,' he said, his voice strained. 'These ashes are holier than the ashes smeared on Mahadev's forehead; this . . . this is all that remains of our commander-in-chief, Chandrashekhar Azad.'

Baikunth's heart clenched in his chest, and for a moment, he felt like the world had stopped spinning. He stared at the ashes in disbelief, his mind struggling to comprehend the enormity of what he had just heard.

'How . . . how did this happen?' he stammered, his voice barely audible. The general of the Indian armed revolution was no more. He was not capable of digesting the news. Baikunth subconsciously held Azad on an equal level with the epic warriors like Karna and Arjuna. For a simple soldier of HSRA, Azad was the centre of his universe. But the universe had shattered. The loss of its commander left the revolution feeling like an orphan, bereft of its guiding force, devoid of any hope and grappling with an uncertain future.

Bibhuti closed his eyes, the memory of the tragic event causing him visible pain. 'It was a shoot-out, Baikunth.

At Alfred Park in Allahabad. Azad . . . was cornered by the British police. An old associate visited me and gave a detailed account and the pinch of ashes.'

Baikunth listened in horror as Bibhuti recounted the fateful events that had transpired.

It was the morning of 27 February when Azad and his trusted associate, Sukhdev Raj, found themselves walking through the cold, foggy pathways of Alfred Park in Allahabad. The winter air bit at their faces as they moved quietly, their breaths visible in the chilling mist. Unknown to them, their steps were being closely monitored by a former revolutionary-turned-traitor, Virbhadra. Once he had confirmed the presence of Azad, Virbhadra slipped away to alert the authorities. Within moments, Nott Bower, the superintendent of police on special duty, and Thakur Bishweshwar Singh, the deputy superintendent of police, CID, arrived at the scene with their forces. The fog hung heavy, muffling sounds and cloaking their approach as they closed in on Azad and Sukhdev Raj. The moment Bower caught sight of Azad, he fired his weapon, the bullet tearing through the silence and striking Azad's thigh. The impact caused him to stumble, but the determined revolutionary quickly steadied himself, realizing the battle had begun. A fierce shoot-out erupted, with bullets slicing through the fog, their echoes punctuating the cold air. Azad's instincts took over, and he returned fire, his aim true as a bullet struck Bower's left hand, causing the officer to drop his weapon in pain while attempting to reload. Bishweshwar Singh, enraged by the sight of his superior officer being wounded, cursed Azad and raised his gun to shoot. However, Azad was quicker, his bullet finding its mark in Bishweshwar's face. The officer collapsed to the ground in a pool of blood. Surrounding constables continued to swarm, their bullets peppering the air around Azad from three sides as he sought cover behind a sturdy jamun tree. The relentless hail of gunfire seemed to stretch for an eternity, each passing second teetering on the edge of life and death. As his ammunition dwindled, Azad knew that the end was near. With his final breaths, he weighed the choice between capture and death, ultimately deciding that the enemy would not take him alive. The police continued their barrage, fearing to approach the wounded but still-dangerous revolutionary. In the chaos, Azad was struck once more, a bullet piercing his right temple, followed by another that tore through his right shoulder and ruptured his lung. Life slowly drained from Azad's body, his spirit slipping away amidst the cacophony of gunfire and shouts. As the last flickers of consciousness faded, he knew that he had fought valiantly and had made the ultimate sacrifice for the cause he believed in. When the gunfire finally ceased and the fog began to lift, the police cautiously approached the fallen figure of Chandrashekhar Azad. His lifeless form lay there, a testament to the unyielding spirit of the revolutionaries who dared to stand against oppression.

Baikunth's eyes brimmed with tears as he listened to the harrowing tale, the weight of the loss pressing down on him like a heavy stone. Azad had been more than just a leader to him; he had been a guiding light in the darkness that had enveloped his country.

'Dada, how did your friend get these ashes?'

Bibhuti again broke into sobs and said, 'The police performed his cremation hastily, but the Congress leaders Purushottamdas Tandon, Kamla Nehru and other students' unions organized a procession, honouring the urn carrying Azad's ashes. The march started from Khadi Bhandar to the meeting at Purushottamdas Park. Thousands of people walked bareheaded and barefoot to pay their respects to the martyr. At the park, many esteemed leaders spoke in praise of the commander, but in the end, a lady was asked to come on the stage. Her name was Pratima Sachindranath Sanyal.'

'The wife of legendary Kakori hero, Sachindranath Sanyal.'

Bibhuti nodded and continued. 'She was introduced by a leader, and then she rose to the stage and spoke merely three to four sentences. She said, "I was there when Khudiram Bose went to the gallows. After his cremation, thousands of people flocked and took a pinch of ashes to their homes; they sanctified Bose's ashes, placing them in amulets for their children in the hope that they, too, would be inspired to embrace selfless patriotism.

'"History is repeating itself. I am not here to give a speech. I am here to collect a pinch of ashes. Let every son of India be like Azad. Hold this in your hand and remind yourself that he paid the price for your freedom."

'After her speech, the crowd repeated her actions so that almost nothing was left for the ritual immersion at Benaras. My friend was gracious enough to bring this to us.'

Baikunth's eyes were flowing. He commented, 'Dada, when you and I perish, our remains will go to the Ganga and then to the ocean. But Mother India loved Azad so much, she did not allow his ashes to get immersed in the Ganga. He became one with his Mother India. During his last moments, he must be singing,

> Tell me, is this the way you wed, Death,
> Death? Unceremoniously, with no
> Weight of sacrament or blessing or prayer?
> Will you come with your messy tawny hair
> Unkempt, unbound into a bright coil-crown?
> Will no one bear your victory-flag before
> Or after, will no torches glow like red
> Eyes along the river, Death, Death?
> Will the earth not quake in terror at your step?
> When fierce-eyed Siva came to take his bride,
> Remember all the pomp and trappings, Death,
> Death: the flapping tiger skins he wore;
> His roaring bull; the serpent's hissing round
> His hair; the bom-bom sound as he slapped his cheeks;
> The necklace of skulls swinging round his neck;
> The sudden raucous music as he blew
> His horn to announce his coming—was this not
> A better way of wedding, Death, Death?
> And as that deathly wedding party's din
> Grew nearer, Death, Death, tears of joy
> Filled Gauri's eyes, and the garments at her breast
> Quivered; her left eye fluttered, and her heart
> Pounded; her body quailed with thrilled delight
> And her mind ran away with itself, Death, Death.

No one spoke for the rest of the day. The inmates worked without wearing footwear and headgear to pay condolences to the martyr. Baikunth made an amulet from the ashes and wore it on his neck reverentially.

In February 1931, the news of Mahatma Gandhi and Lord Irwin's talks regarding the Civil Disobedience Movement reached even the confines of the jail, sparking hope and anticipation among the prisoners.

From Baikunth's perspective, these discussions could significantly change India's struggle for freedom. He had heard whispers among his fellow inmates that Gandhi and Irwin were attempting to negotiate a peaceful resolution to the conflict. The very thought of a truce between the British Raj and the Indian National Congress stirred a myriad of emotions within Baikunth.

In his heart, Baikunth hoped that these talks would lead to the release of political prisoners like himself and his comrades. He longed to end the oppressive British rule and restore dignity and freedom for his people.

Yet, despite his optimism, Baikunth couldn't help but feel a twinge of scepticism. He questioned whether the British authorities would genuinely ease their grip on India and wondered if the talks would result in any tangible progress. After all, he had witnessed first-hand the brutality of British rule and the tenacity of the revolutionaries fighting for independence.

At the Viceroy's house, Lord Irwin and Gandhiji signed the provisional settlement on 5 March 1931. Political prisoners were released batch by batch, their freedom a testament to the potential success of the negotiations. Among the liberated was Baikunth, who eagerly awaited the outcome of the talks. With the Karachi Congress scheduled for 26 March and Bhagat Singh's hanging slated for 24 March, the entire nation looked to Gandhi with bated breath, hoping that he would manage to stop the execution.

Baikunth's release from Patna Camp Jail on 19 March filled him with renewed hope and determination. Before leaving, he penned a heartfelt note for his wife, Radhika Devi, assuring her of his love and commitment to their shared cause. With no time to spare, Baikunth embarked on a gruelling journey from Patna to Lahore.

The train sped through the countryside, the sun-drenched fields and small villages passing by in a blur. Baikunth's thoughts were consumed by the fate of Bhagat Singh and his comrades, as well as the crucial role that the upcoming Karachi Congress would play in determining the future of the revolution.

Upon his arrival in Lahore in the evening on 22 March, Baikunth checked into the same dharamshala where he had stayed in October 1929. The familiar surroundings evoked memories of past struggles and victories, further fuelling his resolve.

The members of the Naujawan Bharat Sabha held daily meetings to discuss the revolution's future and their imprisoned comrades' fate. The air was thick with tension and anticipation as they awaited the outcome of the various petitions filed in the high court seeking a stay on Bhagat Singh's execution.

On 23 March, another petition was filed in the High Court, only to be dismissed later that same afternoon. Time was running out, and the nation's collective heart raced with anxiety. As the sun dipped below the horizon, casting Lahore in shadows, the news of the dismissal sent waves of despair through the community of revolutionaries.

Despite the setback, the fervour and passion of the Naujawan Bharat Sabha did not wane. They continued to rally support and plan for the future, their spirits ignited by the possibility of change brought forth by the Karachi Congress.

Baikunth, like the rest of the nation, clung to the hope that Gandhi's efforts might yet sway Irwin to commute the death sentence. Sleep eluded him as he lay on his cot in the dharamshala, the weight of the impending execution pressing heavily on his heart.

The evening of 23 March saw the movement of police forces around Lahore Central Jail, indicating that the dreaded execution might be carried out ahead of schedule. The city held its breath as the whispers of early execution spread like wildfire. Inside the jail, the loud, defiant voices of Bhagat Singh and his comrades rang out, 'Long Live Revolution' and 'Down With Imperialism', their unyielding spirit echoing through the night.

Baikunth left the dharamshala amid the commotion of hundreds of people. The night dragged on with confusion and horror on everyone's faces. Each tick of the clock was a sombre reminder of the rapidly approaching unknown horror. He joined the throngs of people who had gathered outside Lahore Central Jail, their faces etched with a mix of hope and despair. Someone from the inside broke the news. They had hanged Bhagat Singh, Rajguru and Sukhdev at 7.15 p.m. The crowd went insane. There was no official confirmation.

The air was heavy with grief and disbelief as people gathered in hushed clusters, exchanging the latest rumours and whispers.

Among the murmurs, a chilling tale emerged—that the authorities had broken a wall behind the jail and secretly taken the corpses out for cremation at a remote location.

The very thought sent shivers down the spines of those who heard it, their hearts aching for the dignity that had been denied to the fallen heroes.

As the night wore on, an air of restless anticipation settled over the city, and then, suddenly, a truck rumbled into view. The crowd, drawn to the vehicle by curiosity and dread, pressed closer, desperate for answers.

An elderly man emerged from the driver's seat, his face grim and worn. In a voice heavy with sorrow, he confirmed the unthinkable—the constables had indeed taken the bodies of the martyrs to a desolate spot near the Sutlej River on the way to Ferozepur. They had been in the process of burning the bodies when the villagers of Gandha Singh Wallah, drawn by the glow of the pyres, had intervened.

The police, caught off guard and fearful of the growing crowd, had fled the scene, leaving the half-burnt bodies behind. The driver had taken it upon himself to bring the remains back to Lahore, driven by a sense of duty and respect for the departed.

The crowd, barely able to comprehend the horror of what they were hearing, pressed closer to the truck, their eyes searching for proof. The driver hesitated momentarily before pulling back the tarp that covered the truck's cargo, revealing a sight that would haunt the onlookers for the rest of their lives.

Before them lay the three revolutionaries' dismembered, charred remains, their bodies mutilated beyond recognition. The police had cut the corpses, before the burning, to make them unrecognizable. A collective gasp rose from the crowd, followed by a heart-wrenching wail of grief and despair. At that moment, the enormity of their loss became all too real.

An old man stepped forward among the grieving onlookers, his eyes fixed on the gruesome scene before him. With trembling hands, he reached out and gently touched a long, burnt hand among the remains, his anguish palpable. The silence followed was pierced by a single, guttural cry: 'Bhagaaaat!'

It was Sardar Kishan Singh, Bhagat Singh's father, who, in that instant, had recognized his son's hand amidst the carnage. The crowd, their grief amplified by the father's agony, wept openly. Someone arrived at the scene. Despite the havoc, people engaged themselves in preparing the proper final rites of the martyrs. The dismembered bodies were now being sewn back together by an old cobbler. An elderly person put a hand on Baikunth's shoulder and said, 'Son, look after the cobbler's work and get the bodies a proper bath afterwards.'

Baikunth couldn't say anything. The cobbler had difficulty identifying which body part belonged to Bhagat, Rajguru and Sukhdev. He was never faced with such a challenge. His hands were shaking. The legendary friends had been united in death, unrecognizable from each other. The cobbler did his work. Baikunth helped in bathing the bodies with the help of volunteers; his hands, stained with blood, were shaking.

No one could sleep that night. Baikunth's soul was broken beyond repair. He wished to burn the whole world down, knowing well that doing so would not quench his thirst for revenge. For a moment, he felt the urge to jump on Bhagat's burning pyre as there was nothing left to live for. The next day a huge mourning procession started from Neelagombad, where Bhagat and Rajguru had shot Saunders.

Around 50,000 people walked barefoot and bareheaded with the three flower-laden coffins. The men wore black bands and the women black clothes. The procession ran for about three miles. From the sea of black flags rose slogans of 'Bhagat Singh Zindabad', 'Rajguru Zindabad', and 'Sukhdev Zindabad'. Baikunth now realized the true meaning of death's wedding (Maran Milan).

> Why must you always come like a thief, Death,
> Death, always silently, at night's end,
> Leaving only tears? Come to me festively,
> Make the whole night ring with your triumph, blow
> Your victory conch, dress me in blood-red robes,
> Grasp me by the hand and sweep me away!
> Pay no heed to what others may think, Death,
> Death, for I shall be of my own free will
> Resort to you if you but take me gloriously.
>
> I shall go to where your boat is moored,
> Death, Death, to the sea where the wind rolls
> Darkness towards me from infinity.
> I may see black clouds massing in the far
> North-east corner of the sky; fiery snakes
> Of lightning may rear up with their hoods raised,
> But I shall not flinch in unfounded fear—
> I shall pass silently, unswervingly
> Across that red storm sea, Death, Death.

Baikunth returned from Lahore to Bihar, heartbroken. Now with more determination, he started training to shoot and fight with the khukri.

Chapter 24

April 1931

After the special tribunal had declared its verdict on 7 October 1930, Phanindra and Manmohan were taken out of Lahore Fort prison and returned to Bettiah. However, under the special instructions of Khan Bahadur Abdul Aziz, both were provided with an attaché of four armed constables each for their security. At any point, they were accompanied by the police as bodyguards. Phanindra and Manmohan had been rolled in as approvers for the Patna conspiracy case, Maulania dacoity case and the Tirhut conspiracy case. Hence, both were taken around Bihar, to attend the trials for these cases.

After the hanging of Bhagat Singh, Rajguru and Sukhdev, a telegram arrived at Bettiah. Phanindra and Manmohan were asked to report immediately to the district collector's office. The next day, both visited the office with their bodyguards. The collector welcomed them and handed over the grant of 50 acres of land in Bettiah for Phanindra and 50 acres of land for Manmohan in Beria. Phanindra and Manmohan's happiness knew no bounds. They had become rich beyond their wildest dreams. They also received a cash grant from the government. The crown had kept its promise. They learned later that Hans Raj Vohra refused monetary rewards and instead opted for a sponsorship from the Punjab government to take up studies in the UK at the renowned London School of Economics. Jai Gopal was rewarded with Rs 20,000. Khan Bahadur, who had led the investigation in the infamous Lahore Conspiracy Case, had played his cards well. The British government rewarded him with 50 acres of land in Lyallpur, a promotion to a higher grade, and later, the highest rank attainable. His rise through the ranks was unprecedented, as he was the only person during the entirety of British rule in India to join as a head constable and eventually become a deputy inspector general. The Aziz family's loyalty to the British seemed to have paid off in more ways than one. Even Khan Bahadur's eldest son, Masood Aziz, was appointed deputy superintendent of police in the Punjab Police in November 1931.

Phanindra had his shop running successfully in Meena Bazaar of Bettiah; now, he placed poor peasants to farm his vast lands. There was nothing to worry about. The worst period in his life was over. People around Bettiah looked at him with fear and disgust. Phanindra would carry his Mauser with him all the time. After some time, he became used to the public's hostile attitude. It was a small price to pay for a fortune.

One day, Phanindra gazed upon the table on which a steaming plate of machher jhol awaited him. The aromatic scent of the spicy cutla fish curry intermingled with the fragrant rice, tempting him to dig in without further delay.

His wife had gone to great lengths to prepare the dish, and the results were evident in the beautiful presentation. Each element was perfectly placed, a visual symphony that heightened the anticipation of the flavours soon to be savoured.

Phanindra picked up a piece of finely cooked fish, deftly mixing the rice and curry, when a memory surfaced unbidden. The image of a spartan room in Agra, where he had once lived with Azad, Bhagat, Jatin, and others, learning the art of bomb-making. Rations and cooking utensils were scarce, and they often went hungry.

Their food back then was a far cry from the luxurious feast before him now. Despite the hunger gnawing at their bellies, they had been happy and hopeful, united in their fight for the country.

As the memory played out, Phanindra's appetite waned. Guilt threatened to consume him as vivid images of his comrades being force-fed flashed through his mind. He remembered the brutality, how they were restrained, their hands and legs tied, an ugly rubber pipe thrust down their noses, milk poured in to keep them alive. He recalled the slow, agonizing deterioration of Jatin Das, the life draining from him day by day.

For a moment, nausea gripped Phanindra, and he thought he might vomit. But then, as if a switch had been flipped, arrogance swelled within him, drowning the guilt.

He reminded himself that they had chosen their path while he had chosen his own.

'I had to survive for my family,' he whispered, his voice tinged with defiance and desperation.

He looked up to see his wife and daughter watching him, their eyes filled with love and concern. He started eating as if he were coming straight from Agra's impoverished days.

Chapter 25

June 1931

In the quiet village of Mathurapur, nestled along the banks of a gentle river, stood a modest schoolhouse built of mud and straw. It was here that Baikunth spent his days nurturing the minds and spirits of the village children. He believed that education was the most potent weapon in the fight against oppression, and he strove to instil in his pupils the values of courage, wisdom and patriotism.

The sun cast dappled shadows on the earthen floor as Baikunth paced before his students, his animated gestures bringing to life tales of India's glorious past. The children, ranging in age from six to ten, sat cross-legged on simple woven mats, their eyes wide with wonder as they hung on his every word.

'And so, children,' Baikunth explained, his voice filled with pride, 'our great heroes, like Rani Laxmibai and Chhatrapati Shivaji, fought bravely to protect our motherland. They showed us that the spirit of resistance lives within each of us, and that it is our duty to defend our country and its people.'

A murmur of assent rippled through the young audience, and a small girl with braids raised her hand. 'But, Masterji,' she asked, her voice quivering with curiosity, 'how can we, mere children, protect our country?'

Baikunth smiled at her, his eyes warm and understanding. 'Do you remember the story of Yashpal from Lahore.'

'Yes, Masterji,' The same girl replied.

'Tell me, what was his age and what did he do?'

'Masterji, he was ten years old and he organized an agitation for Shaheed Bhagat Singh, and the police arrested him.'

Baikunth asked, 'Tell me, what was the age of Shaheed Khudiram Bose when he was martyred?'

'Masterji, eighteen years.'

'My dear child, the seeds of change begin with the smallest of actions. Commander-in-chief Chandrashekhar Azad was only fifteen years old when he was arrested and flogged for showing patriotism. So, age is not a barrier to become a fighter.'

'Yes, Masterji.'

As Baikunth's words echoed through the humble classroom, a sudden commotion at the door caught his attention. A young boy, no older than ten, stood in the doorway, his breath ragged from running. He was from Jalalpur, a neighbouring village, and his sunburnt face glistened with sweat.

'Masterji,' the boy panted, 'I have a message for you.'

Baikunth's eyes narrowed with concern as the boy approached. He whispered something in his ear and Baikunth's expression grew serious.

'Children,' he announced, his voice firm, 'our struggle for freedom continues, and I must answer the call. But do not fear, for I will return, and our lessons will go on. Until then, remember what I have taught you, and let the spirit of patriotism guide your hearts.'

The sun had long set on the small town of Motihari, casting an eerie glow on the towering walls of the prison. Inside, Yogendra found himself trapped in the clutches of his own circumstances.

It had been a little over two months since the verdict was announced in March 1931, in the infamous Tirhut Conspiracy Case. Yogendra had stood before the judge, his heart pounding, as the weight of the court's decision descended upon him. Twenty years of rigorous imprisonment—a lifetime, a crushing blow that threatened to extinguish his spirit.

On that fateful day of 18 April 1931, Yogendra and his fellow comrade, Kedarmani Sukul, were abruptly transferred to Motihari Jail. The dimly lit cells, devoid of any glimmer of hope, served as a constant reminder of their confinement. The days stretched into an endless parade of monotony, and the nights whispered tales of regret and longing.

But deep within the recesses of Yogendra's heart, a burning determination smouldered. It was in the oppressive shadows of the prison walls that his plan took shape—an audacious attempt to break free from the clutches of fate. With every passing day, his resolve grew stronger, fuelled by the flickering embers of desperation.

On 4 June 1931, the supplementary trial for the Maulania dacoity commenced within the confines of Motihari Jail. As the proceedings unfolded, Yogendra's frustration grew, gnawing at him from within. The relentless weight of imprisonment had eroded his patience, and he knew that time was slipping through his fingers like grains of sand. Yogendra sat in his cell, his mind racing with thoughts of escape. He had been imprisoned in Motihari for months and knew he couldn't stay there any longer. The conditions were deplorable, and he knew that his comrades outside would be working tirelessly to rescue him. The death of Bhagat, Azad and other comrades had broken him from within.

Yogendra knew he needed to act fast. He sent his mother a cryptic letter, hoping that someone would understand the code followed by HSRA. Baikunth, one of the few literate people in Jalalpur and surrounding areas, had left instructions at Yogendra's house to inform him if any letter came to the address of Yogendra. When the postman delivered a letter from Motihari Jail to Yogendra's home, Baikunth was called to read it. Baikunth read out the literal words and told Yogendra's mother of his well-being. Then he took the letter with him and using the key he decoded it and discovered that it contained the words, 'Revolver, bomb, hacksaw, chloroform, rope, money and a specific date.'

One day before the mentioned day, Yogendra heard footsteps approaching his cell. The door creaked open, and a guard stepped inside, telling him he had a visitor. Yogendra followed the guard to the visitors' area, where Baikunth awaited him.

'We're going to get you out,' Baikunth whispered. 'Everything is arranged as per the plan.'

'How?' Yogendra asked.

'A constable works here; he is from Champaran. He will slip you a little hacksaw. Start cutting the bars. The rolled steel takes time.'

'I am listening.'

'The jailer is sympathetic to the cause, even more so when he received the packet of money. The south wall of the jail will be bombed around 3 a.m. The jailer will give you enough time to escape. Chloroform, ropes and a revolver will be kept outside with rescuers, in case they are needed.'

'Got it. Just one most important thing.'

'What?'

'You will not be part of this action.'

'Seriously? When am I going to be part of something?'

'I will decide that. Do you have a problem?'

'Yes, I do. I have prepared the plan. And if you don't want me to participate, why did you go to such lengths to train me?'

'You will understand when the time comes.'

'As you say, boss. Also, there is one thing that is bothering me.'

'Go ahead.'

'CID has read your letter.'

'I know, but they can't read our cypher.'

'Our friend Pravrat Chakravarti is arrested in Bengal. They have his diary. I suspect that—'

'They have the key to the cypher and can read our letters.'

'Yes.'

Yogendra became serious. He thought for a minute and then said, 'Alert everyone. Keep only one or two persons for the mission tomorrow. And Baikunth, I repeat, I don't want you to be involved in this mess.'

'Yes, Baba.'

Yogendra was able to cut through enough bars to slip out by the following evening. He waited for the signal. There was a system in the jail to ring a bell every hour. The bell rang at 3 a.m., but nothing happened. Yogendra waited for the signal. The bell rang at 4 a.m., but still, there was nothing. Yogendra was running out of patience. He decided to slip out of his cell and run to the south wall.

He had noticed that the guards would always come to his cell on their rounds each night. Yogendra decided this was the perfect opportunity to implement his plan. He waited as the guard approached his cell around 4 a.m. Yogendra sprang into action. He leapt forward, grabbing the guard by the throat and throwing him to the ground. The guard struggled, but Yogendra was too strong. He quickly subdued the guard, left him unconscious, and took his uniform.

Dressed as a guard, Yogendra made his way through the prison, avoiding detection. He knew he had to move quickly before anyone discovered his true identity.

As he approached the south gate, Yogendra could feel his heart pounding in his chest. This was it. He took a deep breath and stepped forward, hoping that he would make it through.

The guard at the gate looked at him suspiciously, but Yogendra remained calm. He flashed his badge and told the guard he was on a routine patrol. The guard nodded, and Yogendra passed through the gate outside only to find a horde of CID officers waiting for him. The CID had nabbed one person from a nearby temple with a revolver, chloroform and a bomb.

Yogendra mumbled, 'So Baikunth's guess was correct. They are reading our letters.'

Due to the troublesome nature of Yogendra, he was shifted to Bhagalpur Jail. The Bhagalpur jailer took a particular interest in torturing him, and he could feel his resolve weakening. But he refused to break.

One day as he lay on his cot, he looked up at the jailer and spoke with fierce determination. 'If any one of us walks away from this prison alive, we will make sure you will have a painful death.'

The jailer scoffed, thinking Yogendra was bluffing. But little did he know that Yogendra had aligned many warders to his side and had smuggled notes out to revolutionaries of Chhapra and Muzaffarpur. They were all coming to Bhagalpur.

As Yogendra's defiant words spread throughout the prison, the other prisoners began noticing his muscular build and unwavering spirit. They looked to him as their leader and followed his every move.

Baikunth coordinated from a safe distance, ensuring that everything was in place for the attack. The plan was simple: gather as many armed men as possible in Bhagalpur and attack the jail from outside at once. The prisoners would fight from inside, and during the chaos of the escape, they would make sure to kill the jailer.

As the night of the attack drew nearer, Yogendra could feel the tension rising in the prison. The warders aligned with him were nervous, but he reassured them that they were doing the right thing.

However, their plans were thwarted by the CID, who had gotten wind of the plot. They arrived at the prison with dozens of constables, ready to apprehend anyone who tried to escape. Yogendra was undaunted but knew that he would not be able to run this time.

The Sessions Trial for the Maulania dacoity case started on 11 September 1931. Phanindra and Manmohan promptly appeared as witnesses and gave detailed testimonies against Yogendra and other accused. On 5 October 1931, the court announced the verdict. Yogendra and Kedarmani Sukul were found guilty and sentenced to another ten years of rigorous imprisonment each. After the verdict, Yogendra and other convicts were transferred to the most secure prison in Bihar, i.e., Hazaribagh Jail.

Over the next year, there were multiple attempts to rescue Yogendra but no one could succeed.

Chapter 26

October 1932

There came a knock on the door. A servant opened the door and looked up to see a CID inspector standing before him. The inspector came in and waited until Phanindra had finished his lunch. As Phanindra came into the drawing room, the inspector placed a pamphlet on the table and said, 'Have a look.'

Phanindra's face went white momentarily as he saw the image of an older man and woman holding the severed heads of Bhagat Singh, Rajguru and Sukhdev. A message was printed on the bottom 'Will you carry the traitor's blot, or will you dare to wash it away?' He knew immediately that it was a message from the remaining revolutionaries in Punjab, directed towards Bihar.

But he quickly composed himself, placing his hand on his Mauser, and expressed calmly, 'I don't understand what this means.'

The inspector looked at him with empathy but then handed him the picture. 'It's a message, Mr Ghosh,' he said. 'A message from those who seek to avenge the death of Bhagat Singh and his comrades. And it seems you are at the wrong end of the message.'

Phanindra took the picture, studying it carefully. He knew it was a call to action, a challenge to the people of Bihar to carry the traitor's blot or dare to cleanse it. But he also knew that he could not show fear or weakness in front of the inspector.

'I know what you're talking about, Sir,' he said, his voice steady. 'I am a loyal servant of the British Empire, as you well know. And I am confident that you and your people can handle any unforeseen situation. My trust in you is not misplaced, right?'

The inspector looked at him sceptically for a moment, then nodded. 'Very well. We are here round the clock, but be alert, Mr Ghosh. Keep the Mauser close to you always.'

Phanindra nodded, watching as the inspector left the room. He knew he was in grave danger now that the revolutionaries were closing in on him. But he was not afraid. He knew that the British Empire would do whatever it took to protect him.

And so he sat there, holding the picture of Bhagat Singh's severed head, and he felt nothing but cold, calculating resolve. He would not let anyone stand in his way. He would not let anyone challenge his authority. And he would do whatever it took to keep his enemies at bay.

Baikunth strolled through the bustling market of Mathurapur, the morning sun casting long shadows on the cobblestone streets. The air was crisp and cool, carrying the scents of fresh vegetables and spices. As he navigated the stalls, he mentally reviewed his shopping list, eager to return home with his groceries.

Suddenly, the market's hum was shattered by the sound of running feet and anxious shouts. A horde of police officers descended upon the scene, their faces stern and determined. Baikunth's heart raced as he caught sight of a young boy sprinting through the crowd, a bundle of newspapers clutched tightly to his chest. The wind whipped at his heels, tugging at the papers, threatening to scatter them like leaves.

Baikunth's eyes widened as a constable lunged forward, grabbing the boy's arm and sending him tumbling to the ground. The newspapers burst from his grasp, each sheet carried away by the merciless wind. The police officers, as if following an unspoken command, frantically dashed about, snatching the flying papers from the air.

One of the newspapers spiralled toward Baikunth, coming to rest near his feet. Driven by curiosity and a sense of foreboding, he unfolded the paper, only to discover a pamphlet tucked between its pages. The faces of Bhagat, Sukhdev and Rajguru stared back at him, their expressions resolute and defiant.

Understanding dawned on Baikunth; this was the reason for the police's frenzied pursuit. He hastily tucked the pamphlet into his sleeve, concealing the dangerous material. As a constable approached, Baikunth feigned nonchalance, handing the newspaper back to the officer.

'Here you go,' he said, his voice barely betraying the anxiety that roiled within him. 'The wind carried it away.'

The constable eyed him suspiciously, but nodded in thanks before hurrying off to continue his search. Baikunth's heart hammered in his chest as he resumed his shopping, acutely aware of the pamphlet hidden in his sleeve. The atmosphere in the market had shifted, tension and fear now palpable in the air. He moved quickly, eager to return home, away from the watchful eyes of the police. As he walked, the pamphlet seemed to burn against his skin.

Despite the mass confiscation of pamphlets, some copies reached the hands of Yogendra in Hazaribagh Jail. Both Baikunth and Yogendra spent much time for the next few days staring at the severed heads and the message printed below.

Chapter 27

October 1932

In September 1932, a letter was written by the DIG of Intelligence to Judge A.C. Davis. The letter stated that there was an urgent necessity to transfer Yogendra and his gang to Andaman as it was tough to keep them in prison in Bihar. The proposal was considered by the court to mark Yogendra and his associates as part of a Criminal Tribe to banish them to Andaman forever. Yogendra understood that his days on the mainland were numbered.

One day, Yogendra instructed his trusted comrade Kapil Deo Rai to write a letter to Phanindra. Kapil Deo Rai had good handwriting and was a one-point contact in writing letters to any prisoner's loved ones. On 20 October 1932, Kapil Deo wrote a letter to Phanindra.

Dada,

I had posted a letter to you earlier, but this evil deputy commissioner held it to himself.

I don't understand why you are afraid of writing to me. I believe you are not going to live more if you stop writing to me, and from my perspective, what is the harm in writing to an old friend?

If you can meet me in person or write to me and try to justify your side with an open heart, then there is a possibility that I may advocate your side to our comrades. I might succeed in changing others' opinions about you.

I truly, genuinely want to understand, Phani Babu; why did you stoop to such a level? Why did you do it? And I want to hear the answer from you directly. I know you will make excuses, but still, I want to listen to your side of the story without any prejudice.

Do you remember when you came to Calcutta after your marriage, and I asked you all sorts of questions, and yet you were trying to avoid me? In the end, you said that I might get weak due to this (marriage) under challenging circumstances, and I understand your perspective to some extent. But tell me, Phani Babu, would you still be breathing if I had been out of prison?

Just tell me, what is the punishment for your disgusting sin, if not death? Can there be any salvation for you? I suggest to you, please be ready for the outcome of your deeds. If possible, ask for forgiveness. Otherwise, the punishment is going to strike you very soon.

All the accused in the Patna conspiracy are here in Hazaribagh Sadar Jail. Some are marked as B category, and some are C category. Surprisingly, they have labelled me as a B-category prisoner; I wonder what I did to deserve such an honour. I will be writing an article on this topic for Dainik Pratap *regarding this injustice.*

Everything here is good; waiting to hear from you.
Worshipper of your feet,

Kapil Deo Rai
Maulania Case, Hazaribagh Sadar Jail.

Phanindra sat at his desk in Bettiah, a smug smirk playing on his lips as he re-read the threatening letter from Kapil Deo Rai. He had known that something like this would come, but he was confident in his security detail provided by the British government. The constables were highly trained and armed with automatic rifles, and they rotated shifts so that there was always someone with him. Phanindra was convinced that he was safe. Plus, he had his own automatic, loaded Mauser and his impeccable aim.

But as he sat there, a nagging voice began questioning his arrogance. What if the revolutionaries had a mole in the constabulary? What if they had already infiltrated his security detail? He tried to dismiss these thoughts, telling himself that he was being paranoid, that the revolutionaries were a spent force and that he had nothing to fear. But the doubts lingered, and he stared blankly at the letter.

'There's nothing to be worried about,' he muttered, trying to reassure himself. 'There's no one left to do the bidding of the revolutionaries. They're either in prison or dead like Bhagat. Kapil Deo Rai is just bluffing.'

But even as he spoke these words, a part of him knew that they were somehow hollow. The revolutionaries had been relentlessly pursuing him, and he couldn't shake the feeling that they were still out there, waiting for the right moment to strike.

Phanindra sighed and leaned back in his chair, staring out the window at the bustling street below. He wondered what it would be like to be free from the constant fear of assassination, to walk the streets without a care in the world. But Phanindra knew that he would never experience that kind of freedom. His loyalty to the British government had made him a target, and he would always have to be on guard.

As the day wore on, Phanindra became more and more restless. He tried to distract himself with work, but his mind kept reverting to the letter. He began to pace around the room, his thoughts racing.

Finally, he made a decision. He would not report the threat to the CID. He would handle it himself. He would show the revolutionaries that he was not to be trifled with.

With a new-found sense of purpose, Phanindra sat at his desk and began drafting a response to Kapil Deo Rai. He would show the revolutionaries that he was not afraid of them and willing to stand up to their threats.

At that moment, his three-year-old daughter stumbled towards him. She wore an oversized round hat on her head, which covered most of her face. Her tiny hands clutched imaginary guns, and she fumbled as she tried to approach her father.

She giggled as she reached her father and said, 'Baba, I want *bishoom bishoom*.'

Her father looked at her quizzically, not entirely understanding what she meant. But the little girl was determined to get her point across. She mimed a gun with her fingers and said, 'I want to *bishoom bishoom*.'

Phanindra's heart sank as he realized what his daughter was asking for. He didn't want her to be exposed to violence at such a young age. He asked her, 'Why do you want *bishoom?*'

The little girl's face lit up excitedly as she explained, 'Me and my friends were playing a game. Now they are playing as Gora Sahib, and I have become Bhagat Singh. I will *bishoom bishoom* Gora Sahib.'

Phanindra fell silent as he listened to his daughter's innocent words. He didn't know how to respond to her request. But the little girl wasn't about to give up. She pointed towards the pistol strapped to Phanindra's holster hanging on the wall and said, 'Baba, I want to be Bhagat Singh, Baba.'

The father looked down at his daughter and saw the determination in her eyes. He remembered the eyes of Bhagat Singh, his old friend that he had betrayed and led to death. He remembered his words, 'It is not me that you have crossed Dada; it is your own motherland.' He realized that Bhagat Singh had become immortal; what would happen when his own daughter learnt that her father was the person who betrayed Bhagat and was responsible for his death. Phanindra felt claustrophobic; he couldn't breathe. His daughter was saying the same thing again and again. His wife came out of the kitchen after hearing the name of Bhagat and carried the girl away. Now the toddler was crying. Phani's face looked like a dam full of floodwater about to burst. He remembered the sight of the banks of the Yamuna under the moonlit night and the Taj Mahal shining like a pearl, where Bhagat Singh sang 'Sarfaroshi Ki Tamanna', and the only listeners were Azad and himself.

Phanindra looked at his hands. There was a blot of ink on his finger. He put down his pen. There was nothing he could write. The time for remorse and repentance had gone.

Baikunth was teaching at his school in Mathurapur when someone arrived and handed over a small note. It read, 'See me at Hazaribagh. Baba.'

Baikunth knew it was urgent. He immediately went to Jalalpur to the house of Yogendra. He convinced Yogendra's aged mother and his two aunts that Yogendra wished to see them urgently. Hence, taking three elderly ladies with him, Baikunth travelled to Hazaribagh. His heartbeat increased as he stood outside the gates of Hazaribagh prison. As he waited for the guards to let him in, he couldn't help but think of what lay ahead.

Finally, the gates creaked open, and Baikunth stepped inside. Three elderly ladies now walked beside him. Baikunth knew this was the only way he could talk to his mentor.

They walked through the corridors, their footsteps echoing through the empty halls. Finally, they reached Yogendra's cell. Baikunth's heart skipped a beat as he saw his mentor for the first time in months.

Yogendra talked to his mother and aunts briefly and asked them to chat between themselves loudly. Then Yogendra looked at Baikunth and said, 'I'm glad you came.' his voice barely above a whisper.

Baikunth nodded, trying to hide the fear in his eyes. He knew what Yogendra would ask of him, but he wasn't sure if he was ready.

'Do you know why I called you here?' Yogendra asked, his voice growing stronger. 'Have you seen the pamphlet from Lahore?'

'Yes, Baba, it is embarrassing for Bihar. They ask us whether we will carry the blot or dare to wash it.'

Yogendra asserted, 'Baikunth, you are going to wash the blot from the face of Bihar. The party has made its decision. It's time for your mission.'

Baikunth nodded again, steeling himself for what was to come.

'Phanindra Nath Ghosh,' Yogendra said, his eyes burning with intensity. 'He needs to be eliminated.'

Baikunth nodded once more, his heart racing with fear and anticipation. He knew that this was the moment he had been preparing for, the moment that would define his life.

'But how?' Baikunth asked, his voice barely audible.

'If you can get a gun, shoot him until you are out of bullets; if you cannot get a pistol or revolver, get a khukri and stab him until every drop of blood in his vile body is drained. If you cannot get a knife, grab the traitor and strangle him with your bare hands until the life is choked out of him. And even if you can't get your hands on his neck, I say, use your teeth to rip his life out. This is your mission,' Yogendra said, his eyes never leaving Baikunth's. 'Go now and do not miss. You will not get another chance.'

Baikunth nodded, his mind racing with ideas. He knew that he had to act fast. The constable announced that the meeting was over. Baikunth escorted the ladies out of prison and back to Jalalpur.

Baikunth knew that he needed a weapon to make their plan work. He contacted Yogendra's friend and fellow revolutionary, Rambinod Singh, who possessed a revolver. He had been acquitted in the Tirhut conspiracy for want of evidence. However, Rambinod was hesitant to part with the revolver. He knew the risks involved and did not want to endanger himself.

Baikunth pleaded with Rambinod Singh, explaining the importance of the weapon in their plan. Eventually, he gave in to Baikunth's persuasive arguments.

It was a risky move, as Rambinod Singh could have been caught with the weapon, but Baikunth was desperate. He knew that the success of their plan hinged on having a gun at their disposal. Baikunth left the meeting with Rambinod Singh with a sense of relief but also a sense of unease. Baikunth's heart raced as he approached his home in Jalalpur. It had been months since he had last gone home, and he knew it might be his last chance to see his ailing stepmother. He pedalled harder on his bicycle, feeling the wind rush past him and the sweat bead on his forehead. As he arrived near his home, Baikunth could feel his pulse quicken.

It was a simple structure made of mud and thatch. One could see the walls made of mud and straw, which gave the house a natural, rustic appearance. The thatched roof was slightly sloped to allow rainwater to run off, and small streams of water could be seen trickling down the roof's edges during the monsoon season. Small windows allowed light to filter in during the day.

The entrance to the house was a small doorway with a thatched roof above it, which provided shade from the hot sun. The opening led into a dimly lit room with a low ceiling, where a few pieces of simple furniture could be seen. A charpoy stood in one corner of the room, with a low stool next to it. A few pots and pans were stacked against the wall, and a mud stove was in the corner of the room.

Through another doorway, there was a separate area where the family's livestock were kept. A few cows were tied to a post. The animals' presence gave the house a faint smell of manure.

He dismounted his bicycle and breathed deeply before walking towards the open door.

As Baikunth entered, he saw his brother, Hardwar, sitting in a corner. 'Hardwar!' he exclaimed, his voice cracking with emotion. 'How are you?'

Hardwar's eyes widened in surprise. 'Baikunth! What are you doing here?'

Baikunth walked towards his brother and embraced him tightly. 'I had to come. I needed to see Ma.'

Hardwar's expression softened. 'She's not doing well, Baikunth. You should prepare yourself.'

Baikunth nodded, his eyes filling with tears. 'I know. I just need to see her one last time.'

He placed his baggage in the corner and approached the back of the house. 'I'm going to take a bath in the well,' he called out. 'I'll be back in a few minutes.'

Hardwar watched as Baikunth disappeared out the back door. He couldn't help feeling relieved that his brother was finally home. He knew that Baikunth maintained his public image as a Congress worker but secretly worked with Yogendra and other revolutionaries. For a few years, Baikunth had lived in Mathurapur with his wife, Radhika. He had shifted to Hajipur Gandhi Ashram briefly but came back to run the school after being released from prison in 1931.

Around three years ago, when Baikunth decided to work fully for the HSRA, after meeting Yogendra, he called

Hardwar to Lalganj Tehsil and asked him to sign a document. Hardwar asked, 'What is it?'

Baikunth said, 'I am transferring my land to you.'

Hardwar was shocked; he said, 'What are you talking about? Baba has already made an equal division of our land. I don't want your share.'

Baikunth said, 'Look, brother, I have gone ahead on a dangerous path; there is no coming back. If I get caught or worse, the government will seize the land. I don't want it. So naturally, I would like you to keep it.'

Hardwar said, 'Does Bhabhi know about this arrangement?'

Baikunth smiled and said, 'Yes, and she agreed.'

Hardwar was moved and said, 'Bhaiya, the community will curse me. They will say that I have cheated you for the land. You are the reason for pride for the family and our village. Please don't do this.'

Baikunth put his hand on Hardwar's shoulder and assured, 'Brother, don't worry about the people; when the time comes, I will announce it personally.'

Hardwar signed the document reluctantly.

As Baikunth made his way towards the well, he felt a sense of calm wash over him. The sun beat down on his skin, and he could feel the cool breeze ruffling his hair. He undressed and jumped into the well, the cold water enveloping him.

He swam around for a few minutes, feeling the tension in his body melt away. He closed his eyes and let himself float, his mind wandering back to his childhood memories in this very place.

Suddenly, he heard screeching brakes coming from the direction of his home. He quickly got out of the water and wrapped a towel around his waist, feeling a sense of dread.

As Baikunth hid behind a tree, he saw a police car parked outside and a group of people standing in front of the house. Baikunth's heart pounded with fear and confusion as he tried to figure out what was happening.

The police officers were led by a stern-looking sub-inspector Mohammad Abdul Jabbar of Lalganj Thana, accompanied by a doctor and a schoolmaster. The Inspector of Lalganj, a senior police officer, and two constables were also present. Baikunth's brother Hardwar was visibly nervous and scared as the police entered the house and asked, 'Where is Baikunth? We need to speak with him immediately,' the inspector said.

Hardwar stuttered and replied, 'He doesn't live here; he has lived in Mathurapur for many years.'

The inspector held Hardwar's collar, pulled him closer, looked sternly, and asked, 'Don't act smart, kid; my men have seen him coming in this direction on a bicycle. Answer now, or you will regret this decision.'

Hardwar was shaking in terror; he stammered and replied, 'He . . . he's gone to the well for a bath. He should be back soon.' The police officers searched the house, turning over furniture and ransacking drawers for clues or evidence. The Daroga found the belongings of Baikunth, which matched the description of the information, a package tied in grey cloth on the bicycle's carrier. Daroga lifted it carefully and placed it on the floor. Then he sat cross-legged and undid the knot and began to look through it. In a minute, he found a revolver wrapped in a dhoti and a leather packet containing ten cartridges. The revolver was old-style and had six chambers to be rotated by hand.

The police officers waited for Baikunth to return, hoping to catch him red-handed. Chasing him in the fields was difficult, and they had no warrant. But Baikunth knew his only chance was to escape before the police could catch him. He slipped away from the well and ran as fast as he could, ducking behind bushes and trees to avoid being seen. After waiting ten minutes, the police called for more men and searched for him for hours, but he was nowhere to be found. The loss of the revolver was hurtful. His plan had just received a significant setback.

Chapter 28

October 1932

The air in the dimly lit room at Gandhi Ashram was thick with anticipation as six shadows huddled around a small table. Baikunth had brought them all here, by calling for a secret meeting. He had specially asked his old friend Chandrama to be there for the meeting. The atmosphere was charged with a sense of purpose as they prepared to discuss the mission that had been entrusted to them by Yogendra Baba.

As the conversation began, Baikunth spread out the neatly folded paper he had placed in the centre of the table. The others leaned in to examine the image, their eyes widening at the sight of the old Sikh man and woman holding the severed heads of the martyred revolutionaries. The message printed below was both a challenge and a call to arms: 'Will you carry the traitor's blot, or will you dare to wash it away?'

Kishori, a seasoned Congress leader and a sympathizer of the revolutionaries, said, 'I have heard about this pamphlet. The CID got hold of it before I could see it in person. But Baikunth, what is the meaning of this now?'

Baikunth looked around the room, meeting the determined gaze of each of his comrades. 'This,' he exclaimed, his voice filled with passion, 'is the objective of our meeting. Yogendra Baba has assigned me a mission, and I need your help to see it through.'

Kishori Prasanna Sinha asked, 'To do what exactly?'

Baikunth turned over the pamphlet; on the other side, there was a hand-drawn sketch of a man whose head was in a noose. He took a deep breath before replying. 'To execute the traitor, Phanindra Nath Ghosh.'

Hearing this, a wave of excitement and determination rippled through the room. The time had come to avenge the fallen heroes and show the British their spirit of resistance was alive and well.

Baikunth recounted how the police had gotten wind of his involvement with the HSRA and how they had managed to seize his revolver. How his mentor Ranendranath was arrested arbitrarily and taken to Bengal. Therefore, he had called this secret meeting to discuss and formulate a plan to carry out the mission.

The group listened intently, their hearts swelling with patriotism and a fierce desire for justice. They knew the path ahead would be fraught with danger, but they were willing to risk everything for the cause.

Chandrama remarked, 'Before we discuss who will participate in the action, let us finalize how we plan to do it.'

Baikunth repeated Yogendra's exact message: 'If you can get a gun, shoot him until you are out of bullets; if you cannot get a pistol or revolver, get a khukri and stab him until every drop of blood in his vile body is drained. If you cannot get a knife, grab the traitor and strangle him with your bare hands until the life is choked out of him. And even if you can't get your hands to his neck, I say, use your teeth to rip his life out.'

Kishori replied, 'I understand Yogendra's anger, but a proper plan needs to be formulated.'

Baikunth stated, 'I have been to Bettiah before; I have seen Phani Babu's house in the Kali Bagh neighbourhood. I have also seen his shops in Meena Bazaar. The action can be done at these points or somewhere on the way. But there is one problem.'

'What?'

'An attaché of four armed constables is assigned to Phani Babu, each holding an automatic rifle. At any point in time, at least one of them is guarding him.'

Kishori added, 'Plus, Phani Babu himself is an excellent shooter. I have heard that he always carries a Mauser with him.'

Suniti Devi intervened, 'He is married and has a little daughter. You must consider this if you choose to act at his home.'

Baikunth said, 'Also, there are a few significant constraints; one is of weapons and another of money and time.'

Kishori requested, 'Please elaborate.'

'As of now, we don't have any revolver or pistol. Most of my contacts in HSRA are either arrested or on strict watch.

Second, we need more money to buy a new gun. Plus, we have no time. Another approver of the Lahore Conspiracy Case, Hans Raj Vohra, is going to London. The government is going to look after him. If Phani Babu senses any danger and decides to leave the country, then our mission is finished. Also, the police regularly take Phani Babu to various cities and states as a witness in different conspiracy cases. There is no way to know that he will be there in Bettiah waiting to be executed. The police are also watching me. They grabbed the only revolver I could get my hands on.'

'I can make bombs, at least the coconut shell type,' Chandrama said.

Baikunth replied, 'I know, I can do that too, but they are untrustworthy, and there is no guarantee that it will eliminate the target. Remember, we will not get a second chance.'

Suniti Devi looked at her husband and said assertively, 'I will lead the action. I will try to find a gun using my contacts. Give me at least a month. I am trained in firearms but will need some practice. As a lady, I can easily walk into his shop in Meena Bazaar or even into his home without raising suspicion. Pritilata Waddedar sacrificed her life for the country just last month. Let me walk in her footsteps.'

Kishori held her hand in pride.

Baikunth said, 'Bhabhi, you are more than capable of completing this mission, but you are the only woman in our extended family of Hajipur Ashram. It will be challenging to run this family after you. Also, we don't have a month for the mission. Yogendra Baba has assigned this mission to me. I urge all of you to play a helping hand. Let me lead the way this time.'

Kishori said, 'I am also ready to lead the action. But I find it challenging to execute it without firearms. The security is too much.'

Akshaywat Rai and Chandrama simultaneously said, 'We are in for the action.'

Suniti Devi said, 'All right, now that everyone at the table is eager to participate, we should decide the name, based on a lucky draw.'

The others nodded their assent.

Baikunth looked nervous, but he did not intervene.

Suniti Devi wrote everyone's names on six chits of paper. Then she folded each chit and started putting them in a bowl. Kishori, however, stopped her hand midway, before she could fold the chit with her own name on it.

Kishori said, 'Everyone here agrees that you will not be part of the draw.' He removed her chit from the table.

Suniti Devi then looked at Baikunth. His facial expressions and eyes spoke with eagerness, conveying only one thing to her. She understood what Baikunth meant. She folded the chit with his name on it in a unique way. The five chits were placed in the bowl, and the bowl shaken.

Baikunth said, 'Bhabhi, please take out one name.'

She looked at the folded paper chits and picked one. She gave the folded chit to Kishori.

He opened it and exclaimed, 'Baikunth, it looks like God has picked you for this mission.'

Baikunth smiled, closed his eyes and said, 'Thank you, Bhabhi. I am indebted to you.'

Everyone around the table knew what had transpired in the draw, but nobody dared to question the dedication of Baikunth to the cause.

Kishori said, 'All right, Baikunth, tell us how you want to proceed and what is needed from us.'

Baikunth said, 'Let us clear some things first. I do not want to kill him at home in front of his wife and child. The traitor has betrayed the nation in the public eye. So justice should strike him in public only. Hence, the action point should be at Meena Bazaar or somewhere between his home and his shop.'

Everyone nodded.

'Further, there is no time to get a firearm. Chhat Puja is going to start two days from now, on 4 November. There is a high possibility that Phani Babu will be at home for the celebration. Also, to look for a gun at this stage means risking the operation. So I prefer to do this using the traditional weapon, the khukri. I trust the blade with my life.'

Akshaywat Rai protested. 'You cannot travel with a khukri to Bettiah. Even if you managed to get there with weapons, getting close to him in the presence of an armed bodyguard would be a challenge.'

Baikunth said, 'I will not travel by bus or train. I prefer to go there on foot or by bicycle. There will be hundreds of people travelling on the road for Chhat Puja. So, travelling will be easy. Getting close to him is the real challenge; I will have to wait for the right opportunity.'

Chandrama said, 'Baikunth, I have seen you train with Ranendranath; you can do this task, but take me with you. I will help, at least, to create a distraction on the scene or in some other way.'

Kishori, Akshaywat and Suniti Devi agreed, and finally Baikunth was convinced.

Baikunth said, 'All right. I also need someone to help me in this mammoth task. Chandrama, I am going home to my wife. Let us start our journey by tomorrow evening. Say your goodbyes.'

Baikunth stood at the doorstep of his modest home, knowing that this could be the last time he would lay eyes on it. The sun rose, casting a golden hue upon the humble clay walls and the thatched roof. He hesitated momentarily, mustering the courage to face his wife, Radhika, and share the news of his perilous mission. The weight of this secret bore heavily upon him. He had made a promise to his wife that he would inform her no matter what he was going to do, but now for the first time, he was going to break the promise.

As he pushed the door open, the familiar scent of home washed over him. He found Radhika busy with morning chores, sitting near an earthen stove, her silhouette framed by the rising sun's golden rays. She turned to him, her eyes lighting up with joy at the sight of her beloved husband.

'You're back,' she exclaimed, rushing towards him and embracing him warmly. 'I was so worried about you. Thank God you are here before the puja. I am almost done with the preparations. Until all the rituals of Chhat Puja are complete don't even think about anything else.'

Baikunth held her tightly, knowing he had to gently break the news. 'Radha,' he whispered, 'I need to talk to you about something important.'

Concern washed over her face as she stepped back, studying her husband's expression. 'What is it? Is something wrong?'

Baikunth led her to a woven cot in the drawing room and motioned for her to sit down. He sighed deeply, gathering his thoughts before beginning. 'Radhika, you know how dedicated I am to the cause.'

'Yes,' she replied, her voice filled with a mixture of pride and worry.

Baikunth continued, 'I have been assigned a mission.'

'A mission? What is it?'

'I cannot tell you for your own safety.'

'But is it . . .'

'Yes, it is dangerous.'

Radhika's eyes filled with tears as she struggled to comprehend what Baikunth had just revealed. 'But, why you? Can't someone else go in your place?'

He shook his head. 'No, my love. This is my duty, my responsibility. I cannot ask anyone else to risk their life for something I believe in so deeply.'

'Is it related to Shaheed Bhagat Singh?'

Baikunth's expression changed, and he said, 'Yes, it is.'

She reached for his hand, gripping it tightly. 'Baikunth, I understand your love for Bhagat, but there are other ways to serve the country. And, what came out of Bhagat's actions— we have lost Bhagat forever. No matter what you do, we can't bring Bhagat back.'

Baikunth looked down at his hand held by Radhika; for a moment, he saw blood on his hands, smeared when he was washing the corpses of Bhagat, Rajguru and Sukhdev. Baikunth replied, 'No, Radha. Bhagat is not lost. He lives in me. He lives in everyone who is free. We will celebrate Chhath, but the way would be different this year. I can see you have cleaned our house for the puja. Let me clean the country. There is a blot on Bihar, which needs to be cleaned. Your husband is going to do it.'

Radhika said, 'I can't bear the thought of losing you.'

He brought her hand to his lips, kissing it gently. 'I know. I love you more than words can express, and the thought of leaving you behind breaks my heart. But I cannot stand idly now. It is time to take a stand. '

Tears streamed down Radhika's face as she looked into Baikunth's eyes, searching for any sign of doubt or fear. She knew, however, that she would find none. She knew he would not back down from this mission. Baikunth stayed for the day. Radhika prepared his favourite meal. She did not allow him to leave her sight even for a second. When the sun went down and it was dark enough outside, Baikunth readied himself to leave. He stood in front of her.

'Promise me,' she whispered, her voice barely audible, 'promise me that you'll do everything in your power to come back to me.'

Baikunth held her gaze, his heart aching at the pain he saw in her eyes. 'I promise, Radhika. I will fight with every fibre of my being to return to you.'

The couple held each other tightly, savouring their final moments together. As the moon rose above the horizon, casting the room in a soft, dim light, Baikunth knew it was time for him to leave. He gently disentangled himself from Radhika's embrace and cupped her tear-streaked face in his hands.

'I love you, Radha,' he whispered, his voice thick with emotion. 'Remember that, always.'

'I love you too, Baikunth,' Radhika replied, her voice wavering as she tried to hold back a fresh wave of tears. 'Remember, if the time comes, don't look back or worry about me. I am always with you.'

Baikunth nodded and pressed a tender kiss to her forehead. He then turned and walked towards the door, pausing for one last look at his wife. She stood there, her eyes brimming with tears, a mixture of love and fear etched upon her face. Baikunth's heart ached, knowing the pain he was causing her, but he also knew that he had no choice, because the blood of martyrs was at stake.

Chapter 29

November 1932

The night was dark, and the air was chilly as Baikunth and Chandrama rode on their bicycles through the quiet streets of Hajipur, their minds racing with anticipation. As they reached Muzaffarpur by morning, they found Ranendranath's place locked. Baikunth knew that the police had taken their mentor to Calcutta. Baikunth had hidden his best khukris inside the house, and the duo had to enter through a window to retrieve them. They found the knives safe and took some much-needed rest inside the locked house.

In the afternoon, Baikunth discussed his plan with Chandrama.

Baikunth said, 'We need to erase any traces of our identities.'

'Like what?'

'We should change the way we look and clothes so that, in the worst case, nothing should be tracked back to our real identities.'

'Understood. Let's start with the bicycles first.'

Chandrama climbed through the window and went out to buy two small cans of oil paint. Any serial number or company logo was scratched off and painted over. He painted one bicycle a dirty green and the other one black.

'Why did you use green paint?' Baikunth asked, frowning at the unappealing colour.

Chandrama shrugged. 'It was the only colour they had. Better than nothing, right?'

Baikunth sighed. 'I guess you're right. As long as it helps us blend in and avoid detection.'

Chandrama said, 'The green one needs a carrier now that we have to carry the weapons.'

Baikunth replied, 'We don't have money for the carrier. We will manage it somehow.'

Chandrama suggested, 'We should travel to Bettiah from a different route. We should not go directly from Muzaffarpur. People know us here. If our journey is traced back to this place, it will be a problem.'

Baikunth thought about it and suggested, 'Let us go to Darbhanga. I have a friend from Jalalpur there. He will help us. We will take a different route from there to our destination.'

'What does your friend do there?'

'He is studying to become a doctor; he is in his second year at the medical school.'

Chandrama asked, 'But it is Chhat Puja season now. Will your friend be available there? He must have left for Jalalpur.'

'No, he failed one year due to poor attendance. I am one hundred per cent sure that he will be there. I was there in

August this year. His father has stopped him from coming home for Chhat and Diwali until he clears the exam.'

'Good.'

Around 10 p.m., they started their journey towards Darbhanga. The road was full of travellers travelling on bullock carts and on foot, visiting their native places for the Chhat Puja. On the morning of 4 November, Baikunth and Chandrama reached the hostel of Darbhanga Medical School. After parking their bicycles, they went to room number 41. Baikunth knocked on the door, but there was no response. He tapped again, harder. It was opened by a boy around the same age as Baikunth. It was clear he had been woken up. His hair was messy, and his eyes were swollen from deep sleep. It was Baikunth's childhood friend, Gopal Narayan Sukul.

Baikunth asked, 'Good morning, Gopal. Shouldn't you be studying at this time of the day?'

Gopal smiled sheepishly and said, 'Baikunth, come in. To hell with the studies, I am dying under the pile of books.'

Baikunth said, 'There is someone with me.'

'Please call him in.'

Baikunth signalled, and Chandrama walked in.

After a brief introduction, Gopal worriedly asked, 'Baikuth, don't mind me asking, but are you in trouble? I mean, are the police looking out for you?'

'Why do you ask?'

'I heard that the police found a revolver in your house. I have to complete my studies. If you get into trouble and they find you in my room, I will be rusticated from the college.'

Baikunth smiled. 'Don't worry, Gopal, we are here to stay for a night only. Believe me, you will not get in any trouble.'

Gopal smiled and nodded. He made arrangements for their breakfast and lunch by telling the cook at the hostel mess.

After resting for a few hours, Baikunth and Chandrama went out, taking their bicycles to a desolate spot on the Bhagmati River. The place was surrounded by bushes eight to ten feet high.

Baikunth was clad in a simple dhoti and khadi kurta. He exuded an air of humble elegance. He removed the Gandhi cap, sitting firmly atop his head, neatly folded it and kept it in his pocket.

Baikunth's smooth, clean-shaven face was accentuated by a thin, neatly trimmed moustache that seemed to dance upon his lips, adding a touch of refined charm to his otherwise austere appearance. His deep, piercing eyes held the fire of determination, a silent promise that he would never yield in the face of adversity.

Baikunth and Chandrama circled each other, their khukris glinting in the light. It was the last mock fight for the ultimate mission. They had been honing their skills and mastering the art of combat for years.

As they clashed, the sound of metal against metal echoed through the empty space. Baikunth felt a seething anger building up inside him; without warning, he charged towards Chandrama with a fierce battle cry, his khukri flashing in the sunlight.

Chandrama reacted quickly, dodging Baikunth's initial attack and retaliating with a swift counter strike. The two friends clashed in a flurry of steel, their khukris ringing out in a deadly symphony.

Baikunth attacked with all his strength. His movements were fluid and precise. Chandrama struggled to keep up, his khukri barely holding off Baikunth's onslaught. The two men fought fiercely, their eyes locked.

For a moment, Baikunth forgot that he was fighting his friend. All he could see was the face of Phanindra, the traitor who had sold out their comrades to the authorities. He channelled his rage into his attacks.

Chandrama sensed the change in Baikunth's demeanour and knew something was wrong. He tried to retreat, but Baikunth was too quick. Chandrama struggled to keep up with Baikunth's ferocity, his defences slowly faltering. In a moment of distraction, Baikunth landed a devastating blow. Chandrama tried to dodge it, but his thumb got in the way of the blade.

The sight of the blood brought Baikunth back to his senses. He stopped in his tracks, horrified by what he had done. He dropped his khukri and rushed to Chandrama's side, apologizing profusely.

'I'm sorry, my friend. I don't know what came over me. I thought I was fighting—'

Chandrama gritted his teeth, wincing in pain. 'Phani Babu, I know. It's all right, Baikunth. Now I am sure Phani Babu will not survive this time.' Baikunth ripped a corner of his dhoti and wrapped it neatly around Chandrama's thumb.

As they entered the hostel, Gopal noticed the reddened cloth on Chandrama's finger. Without a second thought, he sprang into action, opening his trunk and taking out the first aid box. 'Sit here,' Gopal said, gesturing to a nearby chair.

He carefully washed the wound with spirit and expertly applied a clean bandage.

But Gopal wasn't done yet. He knew what else Chandrama needed. He borrowed a bottle of Hazeline Snow cream from his friend, returning to hand it to Chandrama with a stern but caring look. 'Apply this regularly, and keep it clean until the wound dries. You will be all right.'

Chandrama's gratitude was palpable as he thanked Gopal, but Baikunth was waiting in the wings with a request. 'Tell me, what do you need from me?' Gopal asked, always willing to help.

Baikunth had a long list, including a pair of dhotis, money, torches, safety razors, a railway timetable, and even a carrier for his bike. But Gopal was undaunted. 'I will arrange all of these things for you by tonight,' he promised, determined to be of service.

True to his word, Gopal returned later that night with all of the items. But Gopal was still worried about his friend. 'Baikunth, tell me, what are you going to do?' he asked, concern etched on his face.

Baikunth's response was enigmatic and tinged with a sense of danger. 'You don't need to know,' he expressed.

But Gopal wasn't about to let him off the hook that easily. 'I am going to be a doctor,' he declared, 'and I know the cut of a khukri when I see one. Tell me that you are not going to do anything dangerous.'

Baikunth's eyes glittered with unspoken plans as he replied, 'What is not dangerous in this country? Living in slavery is dangerous enough.' He waved away Gopal's concerns. 'Leave it. What I am going to do, you will read about it in the newspaper.' Then, Baikunth asked, 'Tell me which way goes to Sitamarhi.'

Gopal drew him a rough map of Darbhanga and the way to Sitamarhi.

Before leaving, Baikunth turned to Gopal and spoke from his heart. 'Focus on your studies, be a great doctor and serve our people,' he said, his voice heavy with emotion. 'I am proud of you.' With that, he and Chandrama disappeared into the night, leaving Gopal with a sense of unease and a knot formed in his stomach.

The duo travelled to Sitamarhi, then to Motihari and ultimately towards Bettiah. They travelled only at night using torchlight, avoiding any checkpoints.

The road was rough and treacherous, with potholes and rocks strewn about. They had to be careful not to lose their balance and fall. Chandrama's heart was pounding in his chest, and he felt cold sweat on his palms. But he kept his eyes fixed on Baikunth, who seemed to be in control and to know exactly what he was doing.

On the early morning of 9 November, as they approached Bettiah, they saw the outline of a small house in the distance. Baikunth signalled to Chandrama that the destination had arrived.

They stopped at a lake before sunrise and finished their morning ablutions. While bathing in the lake, Baikunth worshipped the blades and initiated them by making a cut on his index finger to offer it his own blood. Chandrama followed.

Baikunth suggested, 'Let us go to his home and confirm his presence.'

Chandrama replied, 'And we will hit him when we get the chance, right?'

Baikunth observed, 'Yes, of course, we will have to improvise the plan as per the circumstances.'

They rode into the Kali Bagh area. Baikunth's sharp memory took him precisely to the house. It was the only house where an armed constable was sitting outside. They made rounds of the road, to confirm Phanindra's presence. At around 9 a.m., he came out on the porch and offered water to the sun as a daily routine in his worship. Baikunth saw his wife and little daughter. The night-duty constable was dozing and waiting for his replacement, as his shift had ended.

Chandrama asked, 'Baikunth, what do you say? I will take care of the sleepy constable; you can go to Phani Babu.'

Baikunth replied, 'No, the wife and child do not have to witness this. This is not the right place.'

After a while, the constable's replacement arrived. Then they rode to Meena Bazaar, which was bustling with crowds. Baikunth knew the location of Phani Babu's original family shop, near the western gate of Meena Bazaar, where he used to sell groceries. Earlier, he had owned only shop number 70, but now Baikunth found out that Phani has bought another shop just next to it. He had procured a license to sell alcohol. Hence, the new shop next to the grocery was a wine shop. Servants were operating the shop.

After marking the shops, the duo went to have lunch at the labourer's mess.

There, Chandrama said pensively, 'Our mission may be in jeopardy.'

'Why do you say so?'

'Look,' and he directed his hand towards a massive stone building. The King Edward VII Memorial Hospital was standing in all its might not far from the bazaar.

Chandrama said, 'Do you understand the meaning of this? No matter what we do, people will bring him to this hospital in just two minutes, and he will survive.'

Baikunth replied, 'No, he cannot survive. We only get one chance.'

'How? Trust me, let's switch weapons. Only a gun can do this job. Let us go back and come with a firearm.'

'No, I will make sure he dies. You do not understand. These British dogs can smell a gun from a hundred kilometres away. There is no going back from here. I trust my weapon.'

'Understand this, Baikunth; we must be extremely sure.'

'Indeed, I understand.'

Around 7 p.m., Phanindra arrived at the market with his bodyguard. His friend Ganesh Prasad Gupt was accompanying him. The shop owners of Meena Bazaar came out or stood in their place to greet Phanindra as he arrived. The man didn't even heed a few of the greetings. He was walking like a drunken, blind elephant. The local people knew that Phanindra was the favourite, blue-eyed boy of the government; they could get his help to expedite any work pending in government offices, hence he received a salute from every corner of Meena Bazaar. The armed constable provided an authoritarian aura to his personality.

As he approached the shop, his servants came out, bowed and greeted the owner with folded hands. Phanindra asked, 'How is it going?'

The servant replied, 'Good.'

Phani asked, 'What is the collection?'

The servant reported the day's collection of each shop.

Phanindra waved his hand, and the servants returned to the respective shops. One of them came back with a wooden bench. It was five feet long and one foot wide. He placed it in the middle of the street and wiped its surface clean with the cloth on his shoulder.

Phanindra and Ganesh Prasad Gupt sat on the bench while continuing their conversation.

Baikunth and Chandrama were standing in front of a tea and paan–beedi shop. A Petromax lamp was hanging up at around 8 feet high. The bright yellow light illuminated the alley leading to Phanindra's bench. Ganesh and Phanindra were laughing; Ganesh was narrating something to Phanindra with funny expressions, trying hard to make him laugh. His antics were working.

Anger was piling up inside Baikunth. Every crackle of laughter reminded him of the loud shriek by Sardar Kishan Singh when he saw his son's body disfigured. The thick shining gold chain, polished black chappals, starched white dhoti and pristine cleanliness reminded him of the soiled, dirty, short, tattered jail clothes of Bhagat, where he was beaten to a pulp in front of the magistrate. Baikunth saw how Phani's round belly moved in rhythm when he laughed. It reminded him of the brutal kicks delivered by the Pathan constables on the sunken stomach of Bhagat. The oiled black Mauser holstered to Phanindra's waist reminded Baikunth of the bullet wounds on the body of his commander-in-chief, Chandrashekhar Azad.

He remembered the ferociousness of the ten-year-old boy, Yashpal, the bravery of Kali Pado Bhattacharya and Pulin Behary Roy trying to bomb Phanindra, the daring act of Bhagwan Das Mahore at Jalgaon, the selfless sacrifice of Jatin Das, Bhagwati Charan, Hari Kishan and Shaligram Sukul. He could visualize the face of every martyr who had died for the cause. There was one common link: Bhagat Singh.

Unknowingly, Baikunth was grinding his teeth and clenching his fists. Clutching the amulet around his neck which held the ashes of Azad, he sensed a comforting warmth.

Chandrama observed that the constable came near Phanindra, told him something and then walked in the direction of the North gate, in the opposite direction. He was either leaving his shift or going to use the washroom. It was time.

Baikunth and Chandrama walked to the electric pole where their bicycles stood. They pulled out the khukris and removed the scabbards; they looked at each other. Baikunth whispered, 'For Bhagat Singh, Rajguru and Sukhdev.'

Chandrama said, 'For Chandrashekhar Azad and Bhagwati Bhai.'

They covered their heads with the shawls on their shoulders and walked towards the bench, holding the knives behind their backs.

Baikunth's heart was about to leap out of his ribcage. His breathing speeded up. The blood rush to the head made him deaf for a second. He walked with purpose, his hand resting casually on the hilt of his khukri. He inhaled a lot of air and stopped in front of Phanindra.

Baikunth spoke in a deep voice, 'Phani Babu.'

Without looking up, Phani arrogantly asked, 'What is it?'

'I have a message for you.'

'From whom?'

Baikunth replied, 'From Bhagat Singh.'

'What?'

Phanindra stared at Baikunth wide-eyed. The shawl flew off Baikunth's face as he roared. A long, sharp khukri rose in the air. In the wide open eyes of Phanindra, Baikunth saw the reflection of shiny, vicious steel coming down like a lightning bolt. Before Phani Babu could blink, the blade penetrated the top of his skull, slicing his brain and coming out in his mouth, cracking the soft palate. Phani's right hand went towards his Mauser pistol but went limp as the knife dug into his head. Baikunth then held Phani's face in his left hand, and, using all his power, he ripped back the machete. Phanindra gave out a loud, guttural cry, gargling blood. Baikunth, without wasting a second, thrust the blade again, this time into the back of Phanindra's head, just above the left ear. The sound of a cracking bone echoed through the marketplace. The cry stopped abruptly and turned to whining sounds as Baikunth pulled the khukri out, and Phanindra's body slumped and fell off the bench. People from every shop came out, heard the loud shriek, and witnessed the action.

Meanwhile, Ganesh Prasad Gupt rose from his place; he couldn't believe his eyes. After the first stab into the skull of Phanindra, Ganesh rushed towards Baikunth to stop him. Chandrama intervened and pushed Ganesh back, shouting, 'Stay back; this is none of your business.'

Ganesh still approached with hands to the chest, ready to strike. Ganesh jumped and punched Chandrama hard in the face. Chandrama now angrily raised his khukri and swiftly stabbed him in the chest. Ganesh still managed to hold Chandrama by the neck, trying to strangle him. Chandrama pulled back the knife and thrust it into his skull. Ganesh's grip loosened. Chandrama pushed him off, and both he and Baikunth ran towards the gate.

Baikunth and Chandrama were trying to mount their bicycles when a shop owner, Nand Prasad, ran towards them. The bikes were suddenly knocked flat onto the road, causing them both to tumble to the ground. Nand tried to hold the hand of Baikunth when Chandrama assaulted him by stabbing him right in the face. The knife went in from his left cheek and came out from the right.

Hundreds of people were gathering on the road. An escape on bicycles looked impossible. Baikunth looked at Chandrama and barked, 'Leave the bikes and follow me.'

Baikunth and Chandrama jumped off the road and vanished into the darkness. No one dared to chase them.

Chapter 30

Epilogue

When the constable came back, the world had turned upside down. People around the shops rushed to the spot. Someone brought a charpoy, and people helped to lay the wounded on the cot. Immediately the crowd picked up the cot, and they were rushed to the hospital's emergency section. Within five minutes of the incident, Phanindra and Ganesh were put on the doctor's table.

Both patients were alive and half-conscious. The on-duty doctor saw the wounds and mumbled, 'No one is going to survive.'

The police arrived with force. The bodyguard was suspended. The superintendent took Phanindra's statement.

The superintendent asked, 'Who attacked you?'

Phani struggled to speak; his face was punctured from above. 'I don't know.'

'Do you know the person who attacked you?'

'No.'

'What is the reason for the attack?'

Tears started flowing from the eyes of Phanindra, his face contorted in pain and agony.

The superintendent asked again, 'What could be the reason for the attack?'

Phanindra mumbled, 'He warned me not to . . . betray her.'

'Betray who?'

Phani's eyes pointed to the ground.

The superintendent asked, 'Who warned you? Give me their name.'

'Singh . . . Bhagat Singh.'

On 17 November, Phanindra passed away in the hospital. Two days later, Ganesh Prasad Gupt succumbed to his injuries.

A banner was seen throughout Bihar for the next few days.

Long Live Revolution

The murders of Bhagat Singh, Rajguru and Sukhdev are avenged.

On the direction of the party, I have punished the traitor.

All India Republican Association, Bihar Branch.

The road to freedom is dangerous. Revolution is the only true path to the nation's salvation. Accept it peacefully with an open heart.

By
A young man
14 November 1932

The police seized the abandoned bicycles and the luggage. They interviewed every eyewitness and asked them to describe the killers. Nothing in the luggage could provide the identity of the killers.

The CID inspector checked the luggage again and found a clue. There was a number '640' printed on a dhoti in blue. The kind which a dhobi puts on clothes to remember who it belongs to.

CID started its work by circulating the number, trying to find clues. By the end of the month, someone found out that a dhobi named Bengali in Darbhanga used this kind of stamp to number clothes. Bengali gave away the name of Gopal Narayan Sukul.

On 3 December 1932, police encircled the hostel of Darbhanga Medical School and raided room number 41, where Gopal was studying. He was arrested. On the same day, Gopal broke down and revealed the identity of Baikunth and Chandrama. He also agreed to become an approver in the case.

R.J. Hearst, DGP of Bihar and Orissa, announced rewards of Rs 500 on Chandrama Singh and Rs 250 on Baikunth Sukul as the CID believed that Chandrama was the person who killed Phanindra.

In January 1933, CID Cawnpore got a whiff that someone from Bihar was hiding in that city. It was the country's revolutionary capital; sub-inspector Shambhunath was notoriously thirsty for the blood of revolutionaries. He checked the communication from Bihar CID and learned about two absconding individuals, wanted in the murder of Phanindra Ghosh. Shambhunath knew Phanindra very well; he had used his help in cornering Azad to his final encounter. As Shambhunath enquired, he discovered that the Chauhan family had given refuge to Chandrama Singh. Shambhunath surrounded the house on 5 January 1933. Chandrama realized what was happening, and not wanting to risk the lives of the Chauhans, he ran out and tried to escape down an alley. However, the passage was blocked on both ends by the police.

Shambhunath shouted and asked him to surrender. Chandrama angrily shot at Shambhunath. However, he missed. There were no cartridges left with him. Chandrama surrendered. Shambhunath arrested him and sent him to Bihar.

In July 1933, an informer gave information about Baikunth to the CID. Immediately, a CID inspector Ramkedar Singh was sent to Hajipur. A railway bridge on the Gandak River joins Hajipur and Sonepur. Baikunth was coming home to meet his wife, Radhika. Radhika had been living in Hajipur Gandhi Ashram for the last six months. The police were lying in wait for him. Baikunth arrived from Sonepur. He descended the stairs. There was a bicycle. He picked it up and ascended another bridge on the side of Hajipur when four constables grabbed him. Baikunth left the bike and started fighting. In a scuffle, all of them fell down the stairs. Somehow, the police apprehended Baikunth. He was shouting slogans, 'Inquilab Zindabad', 'Bhagat Singh Zindabad', and 'Yogendra Sukul Zindabad'. When Ramkedar Singh searched Baikunth, he found a live bomb made from dried coconut shells sewn into the pocket of his kurta. To the good fortune of the police, Baikunth did not get a chance to use it. The police transferred Baikunth to Chhapra Jail. Radhika kept waiting for Baikunth, but he never returned.

On 1 December 1933, in Muzaffarpur Sessions court under sessions judge T. Leubi at Motihari Camp Jail, the trial was titled King-Emperor vs Baikunth Sukul and others.

Initially, Baikunth and Chandrama stated that they had neither assigned their defence to any lawyer nor wished the court to do so for them. However, later Baikunth gave his defence to Babu J.N. Banerjee. As the case proceeded, Baikunth gave a list of fifty persons he wished to bring in as a witness in his defence. The court refused it by saying that the accused should pay the charges first for transporting the witnesses as many were already locked in jails across the country, such as Patna, Hajipur, Benaras, Lahore, Cawnpore, Andaman etc.

As the trial neared its conclusion, the honourable judge asked the opinion of four assessors appointed.

On 20 February 1934, out of four assessors, only one, Prabhu Ojha, stated, 'I found Baikunth Sukul guilty in the murder of Phanindra Nath Ghosh and involved in a conspiracy against the King Emperor. There is nothing conclusive to prove Chandrama's role in this case.'

The remaining three assessors, Ramji Sukul, Avadh Prasad and Bishun Mahto, unequivocally stated, 'We do not find Baikunth and Chandrama to be guilty in the murder of Phanindra or part of any conspiracy.'

On 23 February 1934, refuting the majority of assessors, Sessions Judge T. Leubi sentenced Baikunth Sukul, aged twenty-six, to be hanged until death in the murder of Phanindra Nath Ghosh and conspiracy against the

King Emperor. However, without evidence, he acquitted Chandrama of all charges against him. The sentence of hanging till death was subjected to the approval of the Patna High Court. The judge asked Baikunth if he wished to say anything.

Baikunth looked at Leubi, smiled and answered, 'I am ready.'

Then he raised slogans, 'Inquilab Zindabad!'

On 18 April 1934, Patna High Court accepted the judgement of T. Leubi and the date of hanging was decided as 14 May 1934.

Baikunth was transferred to Gaya Jail. His old friend Bibhuti Bhushan Das Gupta was already there to welcome him.

The inmates sentenced to hanging were kept in ward 7. While political prisoners like Bibhuti were kept in ward 15. To create deterrence in political prisoners, it was a practice to bring the inmate to ward 15, cell number one, for the last night before hanging him to death. Usually, the prisoner would go insane the night before his death. He would shout, cry, laugh and beg for mercy, among many other things.

Bibhuti knew that Baikunth was in ward 7, but it was impossible to see him.

The sun was setting behind the ancient walls of Gaya Jail on the eve of 13 May 1934. Baikunth stood tall in his damp cell, awaiting his fate.

Radhika had journeyed from the Hajipur Gandhi Ashram, where she had taken refuge after her husband's arrest. She was alone, with no family to rely on, and the ashram had become her sanctuary. The night before Baikunth's execution, she arrived at the jail, determined to see her husband one last time.

The warder and a constable escorted Radhika to Baikunth's cell, and their eyes met as the heavy iron door creaked open. It was a fleeting moment, but it held the weight of a lifetime. The cell was dimly lit, casting a sombre hue upon their reunion.

'I am here,' Radhika whispered, her voice trembling with emotion.

'Radha,' he replied, his voice laden with love and sorrow.

They embraced each other tightly as if their bodies were one, connected by the invisible threads of their shared past. Tears streamed down Radhika's cheeks, and Baikunth gently wiped them away with his rough, shackled hands.

'Do not cry, my love,' he said softly, 'I am sorry.'

'Please don't say that.'

'I am sorry, Radha, I could not give you a good life; I could not give you a child. I failed you.'

'Please, don't; you have not failed me. I am proud of you and whatever you have done for the nation.'

'But what about you? I promised you a life with me; I am leaving you like this.'

'Baikunth, how can I exist without you?' Radhika sobbed, her chest heaving with anguish. 'You are my life, my world. I am not worried about survival. The question is, how will I live without you? What is the meaning of life without you? Can you do me a favour?'

'What?'

'Ask the Gora Sahib to hang me with you.'

'No, Radha, you are strong,' Baikunth replied, his eyes burning with conviction. 'You will find the strength to carry on. You will have to live for the day our country achieves freedom. I want you to live under the free sky. Also, please understand even if I am going to the gallows, your sacrifice is no less than mine. You were always my support, my power, the light of my life.'

As the minutes ticked away, Baikunth and Radhika reminisced about their shared life, dreams and unwavering love for each other. They spoke of the days spent under the sprawling banyan tree in their village, where they had been married as children, how they had fallen in love and the quiet nights under the starry skies, their hearts entwined as one.

'Promise me, Radha,' Baikunth implored, his eyes glistening with unshed tears, 'that you will keep our love alive in your heart. Let it be the flame that guides you through the darkest nights.'

'I promise, Baikunth,' Radhika replied, her voice resolute.

They held each other close, their breaths mingling in the humid air, and shared a final, passionate kiss. It was a bittersweet reminder of the love they had forged through the years, a love that would endure, even in the face of death.

The jailer appeared in the doorway, signalling that their time had ended. Baikunth and Radhika looked into each other's eyes, knowing these final moments would be etched into their souls forever.

'Goodbye, my love, take care of yourself for me,' Baikunth whispered, his voice barely audible above the sound of Radhika's quiet sobs. Radhika clung to him as if letting go would break her. Their fingers brushed against one another as they separated, the lingering touch a testament to the love that would outlive them both. With heavy hearts, they stepped away from each other, the distance between them growing wider as the jailer closed the cell door with a resounding clang.

As Radhika was led away, she glanced back at Baikunth, her vision blurred by tears. He stood tall, his shoulders squared, the epitome of courage and sacrifice. And at that moment, she knew she would carry his love and memory with her wherever life took her.

The oiled gates of ward 15 opened; the constable walked in and asked all prisoners to go to their respective cells. After locking every cell, Bibhuti heard a voice, 'Bibhuti Dada, I am here.'

Bibhuti knew it was Baikunth; he went near the iron railings and shouted, 'Vande Mataram, Bandhu.'

'Vande Mataram, Dada.'

Warders locked Baikunth in Cell number 1. Generally, the authorities would allow the inmates of ward 15 to meet the dying prisoner, but they decided not to do so for Baikunth. The warders would also remove any shackles on the prisoners, but Baikunth remained shackled. At night, dinner was served to everyone inside their cell. When the warders pushed the plate inside Bibhuti's cell number ten, Bibhuti saw two white periwinkle flowers. The warder said, 'They are from Sukul Babu.'

After dinner, a constable named Usman arrived for counting and sat near Bibhuti's cell. He asked, 'Dada, can I ask you something?'

'Go ahead?'

'Can the hanging of Baikunth Sukul Babu be stopped?'

'No.'

'If we appeal to the King in London?'

'No. Why are you asking?'

'Dada, I have never seen such a brave man. I am not lying. I have fought in the great war. They sent me to Jordan and Mesopotamia. I saw death from close range. I killed many and saw people getting killed in the hundreds. But never have I seen determination and pleasure in the eyes of a man waiting for death.'

Bibhuti remembered, 'Maran-Milan'. He smiled and said, 'Baikunth is made of different stuff. He is a revolutionary. Dying for his country is his ultimate dream.'

'I have been observing him since the day he entered Gaya Jail. His face glows like a rose. Never in the last twenty days have I seen him depressed or sad. There is always this enigmatic smile on his face. Surprisingly, when I checked his weight this morning, he had gained a few pounds since he was arrested. How can someone be defiant in the face of imminent death?'

'Haven't you heard about Bhagat Singh?'

'Dada, I was not fortunate enough to see Bhagat Singh; I feel lucky to meet Sukul Babu. You are the most knowledgeable man here. Please tell me if there is any way to save Sukul Babu.'

Bibhuti Dada saw that the constable was asking genuinely, so he decided to try something, 'Usman, there is a way if you are ready to take the risk.'

'Dada, I am ready to risk my life for Sukul Babu.'

'If you take Baikunth and me out of ward 15, I can get him to climb past the high western wall; once he crosses the road, there are only hills after it.'

Usman chuckled and said, 'Dada, this is impossible. You are not aware of what is happening outside your ward. Since Sukulji came here, armed constables have been posted round-the-clock outside the prison walls. Even as we speak, twenty armed constables are patrolling outside ward 15. The key to Ward 15 is with the superintendent. It is impossible.'

Bibhuti remained silent.

Usman went away; while going out, he stopped before Baikunth, and bowed namaste before him.

When the gates closed, Bibhuti asked, 'Baikunth, can you hear me?'

Baikunth replied, 'Yes, Dada.'

'How are you feeling?'

'Dada, I am ready. I was never as happy in my life as I am now. A handful of people get to die as per their dream. Bhagat worshipped Kartar Singh Sarabha all his life; he got to die like his idol. Azad admired the life and adventures of Bagha Jatin; he, too, got to die like Bagha. I have idolized Bhagat Singh as if he were a revolution personified. I am lucky enough to see him speak against the Raj. I am fortunate to work in HSRA and to avenge his death by killing a traitor who betrayed the nation. Dada, see, I got to die like Bhagat Singh. What else should I ask from life?'

Bibhuti was awestruck by the change in Baikunth's personality and attitude; he said, 'You truly lived Maran Milan.'

'Dada, the credit goes to you.'

'No, Baikunth, it seems that Gurudev Tagore has written the poem for you. Tell me, do you have any regrets?'

'There is one. I am leaving my wife here, alone, helpless. I didn't give her any child or any property. I worry about how she will live. Dada, we got married when we were children and found love as we grew up. She understood my ambitions and sacrificed her family and dreams for me. I had decided to dedicate my life to the country. There was no point in giving birth to children when I would not be around to raise them. She has never expressed any regrets to date. But I worry for her. I have a request for you.'

'Please speak.'

'When you are released, please work on stopping child marriages in Bihar. And ensure that my Radha has a respectable livelihood.'

Bibhuti Dada was crying; he said, 'Yes, Baikunth, go without any worries. This nation is indebted to you and Radhika Devi. We will take care of her.'

Baikunth requested, 'Dada, please sing the song of Khudiram Bose, "Hasi Hasi Parab Phansi".'

Throughout the night, Bibhuti Dada sang all the patriotic songs he knew. He stopped crying his heart out and sang again. Baikunth asked him to sing 'Maran Milan', and then he asked him to sing 'Sarfaroshi Ki Tamanna'. Baikunth would join in between to sing the songs.

When Bibhuti came to the last couplet of the song,

'Ab na agle valvale hain, na armanoo ki bheed,

Sirf mar-mitne ki hasrat ab dile Bismil mein hain.'

Baikunth repeated the last line repeatedly, *'Ab dile Sukul mein hain, ab dile Sukul mein hain, ab dile Sukul mein hain.'*

The bell rang at 5 a.m. The gate opened, and armed constables walked in. They bathed him in the adjoining washroom and gave Baikunth new clothes. Then they were ready to escort him to his death. Baikunth stopped before cell 10. Bibhuti was crying his heart out, holding his hands out to touch Baikunth. The constables did not allow it.

Baikunth smiled and announced, 'Dada, I am ready. I will go now. Don't worry, I will come back. The nation is not free yet. Inquilab Zindabad.'

They took him to the gallows. Baikunth refused to wear the black cloth around his head. He smiled as they fitted the noose around his neck. As the superintendent gave the signal, the lever was pulled, and the man who avenged Bhagat Singh died a hero's death.

The police did not give his corpse to the family. They did the final rites, leaving the family with ashes to do the rest of the rituals.

On 24 November 1932, the court declared Yogendra Sukul and forty members of his party as a Criminal Tribe and ordered the authorities to transport Yogendra and others to Cellular Jail, Andaman. He was tortured there in a peculiar and planned way so that he lost his vision completely. Radhika Devi lived her life in seclusion. She never remarried.

The government started a monthly pension for the widow of Phanindra Nath Ghosh. When Phanindra's daughter was married off in a few years, the government gave her Rs 1000 as a dowry.

Bhagwan Das Mahore and Sadashiv Malkapurkar were sentenced to life imprisonment at Cellular Jail, Andaman. They survived and came back to live in free India. Bhagwan wrote profusely about his comrades and got his doctorate in Hindi Literature. On 12 March 1979, Bhagwan was invited to a park in Lucknow to inaugurate a life-size statue of Chandrashekhar Azad. As he unveiled the statue, he was struck by the similarities. For a moment, he forgot that he was facing the figure. The schoolkids gathered for the function started singing 'Sarfaroshi ki Tamanna'. Bhagwan was lost in a trance. He went back to the days when he was arrested at Bhusawal and how he failed to execute Phanindra and Jai Gopal. Later in prison, he learned that someone from the party named Baikunth Sukul did his job perfectly, but still, the guilt remained in his heart. The sharp blazing eyes of Azad, his fingers twirling his sharp moustache. Bhagwan mumbled, 'Panditji, forgive me; I failed in my mission. I wish I had been there with you in Alfred Park.'

As if he heard Panditji's voice, 'Kailash, you lived your life like I dreamt of. Don't have any regrets. I am proud of you.'

Due to a sudden cardiac arrest, Bhagwan passed away in front of Azad's statue.

Acknowledgements

I would like to begin by expressing my heartfelt gratitude to Suhail Mathur, my literary agent from The Book Bakers, who initially planted the idea of this book in my mind. Over the past decade, I had dedicated myself to researching this armed revolution. As the idea developed, I discovered an untold story filled with suspense and action. It is due to Suhail's unwavering determination that this book is now coming to fruition.

Special thanks are due to Malwindersingh Waraich, affectionately known as Munshi, the legendary record keeper of the Indian armed revolution. Sir provided invaluable guidance and most of the reference material for this project. He is truly an inspiration. I am grateful to Prof. Chaman Lal and Sudhir Vidyarthi for their invaluable insights during the research and writing of this book. I am deeply grateful to Prof. S. Irfan Habib, Sanjeev Sanyal, Chaman Lal, Hindol Sengupta and Satvinder S. Juss for endorsing this book with their generous words. These eminent scholars have not only inspired me through their works but have also lent great credibility to this book. I would like to extend my heartfelt thanks to the legendary lyricist Sameer Ranjan for graciously supporting this story.

I must express my gratitude to Arun Shuklaji, a member of Shaheed Baikunth Shukul's family, and Yadavinder Singh Sandhu, a member of Shaheed Bhagat Singh's family, who shared many stories that now form an integral part of this book. I would also like to thank Amanul Haq, a journalist from Bettiah, who helped me locate the exact spot in Meena Bazar where the traitor Phanindra Ghosh was executed.

My publisher, Penguin Random House India, and my editor Deepthi Talwar deserve a special mention for ensuring that this book reaches my readers quickly and efficiently. Their efforts are truly appreciated.

Furthermore, I feel compelled to acknowledge certain individuals who have made invaluable contributions to my work. Many friends have formed a rock-solid support system for my creative pursuits. Abhijit Bramhanathkar went above and beyond to obtain the trial records of Baikunth Shukul from the Parliament library, enabling me to conduct thorough research for this book. Suraj Chakor, Babasaheb Khandare, Prasad Chaudhari, Harish Kale, Vishal Badve, Vinit Onkar, Pruthivraj Kakade, Vivek Thakare, Pravin Bhandekar, Nilesh Patil, Suryakant Surve, Rushikesh Deshmukh, Paresh More, Amol Jadhav, Ratnadeep Barkul, Gaurav Jadhav, Girish Khete, Sujit Wanjari, Dr Lokesh, Dr Pradip, Vasu Bagade, Yadav Amrute, Deepali, Anil Kadam, Sachin Vilegaonkar, Vivek Singh, Vivek Todkar, Pritam Kokane and Prakash Mohite, all generously contributed in their own unique ways.

Thanks to my colleagues and superiors from my office who encouraged me.

I am profoundly grateful to my brother, Aniket, who is always there as a solution to any problem. I am indebted to my cousin, Dr Aditya, the only family member who truly understands the craft, and has meticulously read and edited every single word I have written. I wish to acknowledge the memory of my late grandfather, Prof. Uttamrao Suryawanshi. He introduced me to the world of literature and dreamt of seeing my name alongside the logo of the little penguin.

Above all, I am eternally grateful to my father, who ignited my passion for stories of freedom fighters, my mother and my grandmother, who nurtured my love for words. Most importantly, I am deeply indebted to my wife, Sandhya, and our daughter, Mokshada, who selflessly sacrificed their time with me, enabling me to bring this book to life. Without their unwavering love and support, this book would not have come to fruition. Their belief in me made it all possible, and for that I am forever grateful.

Scan QR code to access the
Penguin Random House India website